ANGEL MEADOW

Also by Audrey Howard

The Skylark's Song
The Morning Tide
Ambitions
The Juniper Bush
Between Friends
The Mallow Years
Shining Threads
A Day Will Come
All the Dear Faces
There Is No Parting
The Woman from Browhead
Echo of Another Time
The Silence of Strangers
A World of Difference
Promises Lost
The Shadowed Hills
Strand of Dreams
Tomorrow's Memories
Not a Bird Will Sing
When Morning Comes
Beyond the Shining Water

ANGEL MEADOW

Audrey Howard

Hodder & Stoughton

First published in Great Britain in 1999 by
Hodder and Stoughton
A division of Hodder Headline PLC

10 9 8 7 6 5 4 3 2 1

British Library Cataloguing in Publication Data
A CIP catalogue record for this title is available from the British Library.

ISBN 0 340 71809 9 Hardback
ISBN 0 340 76656 5 Paperback

Typeset by Palimpsest Book Production Limited,
Polmont, Stirlingshire
Printed and bound in Great Britain by
Mackays of Chatham, PLC, Chatham, Kent.

Hodder and Stoughton
A division of Hodder Headline PLC
338 Euston Road
London NW1 3BH

There is no town in the world where the distance between the rich and the poor is so great or the barrier between them so difficult to be crossed.

Rev Richard Parkinson, 1841,
speaking of Manchester

1

The three little girls crouched in the shadows at the top of the narrow stairs, watching impassively as the brawny man their mother had brought home pulled down his trousers and climbed on top of her. His white buttocks turned to rippling amber in the light from the good fire that he had heaped up carelessly with coal, since he was unconcerned with anyone's circumstances but his own, before setting about the woman beneath him. Their mother had made no objection to his lavish use of what had taken her so long to earn, obligingly lying down on the rotting wooden floor before the hearth, pulling up her skirt and opening her legs.

For a moment or two he jerked convulsively then, with an exclamation of annoyance, he rose to his knees, looking about him at the bare and comfortless room.

"Ain't yer got somewhere more comfortable than this, missis?" he asked her. "This floor's playin' bloody 'ell wi' me knees. What's upstairs? Ain't yer got no bed?"

He stared up into the darkness of the staircase and the three children shrank back, for some of the men their mother brought home, on seeing them, had lost interest in Mam, stating a preference for a bit of young flesh and, on one occasion, at their mother's shriek, they had been forced to flee, eluding the man's grasp by the skin of their teeth as they raced along Church Court and round the corner into Style Street. With their hearts banging in their chests, for they knew exactly what the man had in mind for them, which was what was done to their mother, they had reached the safety of St Michael's Church where they had hidden for an hour before creeping back to Church Court. Both the man and their mother had gone by then, probably back to the beer house on the corner, the man, it seemed, having made do with Mam since he had no other choice. Mam sported a black eye, a split lip and a swollen cheek when she returned, but she had the few bob she had earned and the girls ate well for the rest of the week.

Mam heaved and wriggled under the man in an effort to please and his attention was caught once more. "It's warmer 'ere, chuck," she told him, making a show of great affection, throwing her arms about his neck and drawing him closer to her, at the same time obscenely heaving up her hips and grinding them against his. "An' we don't need a bed. See, look what I got fer yer. A lovely little 'ole fer that big cock o' yours. That's right, in yer go . . . Eeh, lovely. In't that lovely?"

The man appeared to agree that indeed that was lovely, for he heaved and grunted for the best part of five minutes before collapsing in a groaning heap on top of their mam. Mam groaned and heaved along with him, though her daughters could see her eyes gleaming in the firelight as they sent their message of comfort and reassurance to them over the man's shoulder. Whatever she might be their mam always did her best to protect them. She never brought her customers upstairs where, before she had learned better, she had been forced to defend them physically, earning, instead of the few pence she charged for her services, a face that for many days looked like a rainbow pattern of blues and purples and blacks, gradually fading away to green and yellow. Not that it interrupted her trade, for the men she picked up in the streets, the gin-shops and beer houses of Angel Meadow were not concerned with that part of her anatomy! There were men, and there were bad men, she had warned them: men who were content with the bit of comfort and pleasure she could give them; and then there were the others who had funny ways which included a fancy for children. Those sort must be avoided at all costs, though her daughters often wondered how you could tell one from the other until it was too late.

The little girls, huddling together for warmth, waiting for their turn by the fire, were exceedingly thin and indescribably dirty. Their hair was a thick, matted mass of tight curls which, it seemed, had never known the services of a brush; rich brown streaked with a paler brown, and alive with lice which hopped merrily from one strand of hair to another, even from one head to another. Their hands and faces, their necks, their ankles and feet, which were all that could be seen beneath their thin cotton shifts, were a uniform grey, with a thick film of black on the soles of their feet and between each toe. In their ears and the soft, childish creases of their necks was a layer of dirt that had seemingly not been disturbed since the day they were born. In addition to what appeared to be a permanent layer of general filth their fine skin was blotched here and there with what looked like mud.

Downstairs there was a stirring of movement as Mam and her customer groped for their clothing and began to pull themselves together after the enjoyment of their exertions. Mam sat up and fiddled with her tangled hair, giving an arch smile to the man, who did not return it.

"Owt ter drink in this 'ere place?" he asked, throwing himself down into the one chair the room sported, an ancient armchair from which the stuffing leaked and the springs poked. It creaked with his weight, then moaned most piteously as their mam tried to sit on his knee, since she believed in giving value for money and some men liked a bit of a cuddle afterwards.

"Gerrof, yer daft bitch," he roared, finding her attentions offensive now that his appetites had been satisfied. "D'yer want ter rupture me? Big fat cow like you. Any road, did yer 'ear what I said? Got any gin 'andy? I'll pay yer for it," he added and as Mam turned obligingly to the cupboard the child on the stairs saw the crafty look on the man's face and wanted to cry out to her mother to take care.

The bottle of gin her mother kept for "emergencies", which could mean anything from the fire going out, the loss of a farthing, or just a cold wet day, all of which depressed her, was produced from its place in the sagging cupboard and within five minutes it was empty, the man taking the last swig. Mam sat on the low stool, her shapeless body slumped over her knees in tiredness, staring vacantly into the fire, and when the man stood up abruptly she jumped, almost falling off the stool.

"Well, I'm off," he said heartily, reaching for his cap which he had thrown carelessly on to the dilapidated table when he entered the house.

"Right, chuck," Mam said, her eagerness to be rid of him and huddled up with her daughters on the palliasse upstairs so apparent her daughter wanted to shout to her to be careful. This chap looked as though he might be an awkward bugger and if he was and decided to give her mam a good hiding, which some of her customers did, there was nothing anyone could do about it. Her mam's trade was frowned upon, even by the hopelessly poor women who lived in Angel Meadow and she'd get no sympathy nor assistance from them next door nor indeed anyone, even if she screamed the place down. There was always someone screaming or giving what for to somebody else in Angel Meadow and no one took much notice. Not even the police constables from the station on St George's Road.

The man was at the door before Mam knew what he was up to.

"'Ere, don't forget me money, lad," she smirked, straightening up from the stool and putting out her hand to steady herself against the chimney breast. She had had a few at the beer house round the corner in Angel Street beside the bottle of gin she had just shared with her customer – whom she had never seen before and whose name she did not know – and was a bit inclined to wobble about, but she recognised a bilker when she saw one. He was trying to edge out of the door without paying her and her with three children to support. There wasn't a farthing in the house, her last "wages" having gone in the purchase of the bottle of gin, and unless she could get a few bob from somewhere, from this bloke, in fact, who owed her, the kids would have nothing to eat tomorrow.

"What money?"

Mam's jaw dropped, for though she had been cheated before she had not expected it of this one. Big, rough, his face mottled with drink, he had seemed good-natured enough when she had picked him up in the beer house. He'd treated her to a gin before accepting her offer of a "good time" and had even held her arm as though she were a lady on the short walk home from the beer house.

"Yer know what money, lad. The money what yer owe me. A bob, I said, an' yer agreed so I want what's comin' ter me or I'll run ter't police station on St George's Road an' fetch a copper."

"Yer'll get what's comin' ter yer, yer soft bitch, an' it won't be no bob. An' don't you threaten me wi't coppers, neither. I'm a respectable bloke, I am, an' don't need ter pay fer the likes o' you. Now get out o' me way or I'll land yer one."

"A respectable bloke!" Mam shrieked. "Then what the bloody 'ell are yer doin' round 'ere? Now, give me me money or I'll scream soddin' place down."

"Scream then, yer daft cow. 'Oo the 'ell's going ter take any notice of a whore like you. Now, are yer goin' ter get out o' me way or am I gonner make yer."

Mam stood before the door that led into the street, her arms outstretched dramatically across the frame. Her hair, so like her daughters', and the only pretty thing left of which thirty-one-year-old Kitty Brody could be proud, sprang about her head in a tangle of curls, lively with vermin but snapping with life and colour. True, it was filthy but its former glory was still evident. She was shapeless now after bearing fourteen children in as many years, her breasts barely discernible in the midst of her sagging flesh, her waist non-existent. She was bloated, which was extraordinary really, for she was half starved. After her girls were fed she spent every spare penny on gin, the only bit of comfort she was blessed with in her miserable existence. She was a familiar figure in Angel Meadow but the constable looked the other way, for she was harmless and when all was said and done she had to feed her children somehow. Most mothers sent their children to the cotton mills, of which there were hundreds in Manchester, the moment they were big enough to be taken on, but not Kitty. She had a strain of decency in her that had not been eroded by the life she had led nor the poverty and deprivation she had suffered. The loss of eleven children, each of which had devastated her at the time, though she had not wanted any of them, had slowly sucked the life out of her. She had no idea where the fathers of any of them were, nor did she care. Paddy Brody had buggered off at the birth of the eighth and the reason these three had survived was due only to the fact that for the first formative years of their lives she had taken in a lodger, a nice chap in decent work and kind to her in bed and who had given some stability to their lives. When he died in an accident in the mill it had left an enormous gap in her life but at least she had her three girls who, because of him, were made of stronger stuff than the rest. But she could not get work. She was turned away from every factory and workshop she applied to in Angel Meadow because of her growing addiction to gin, which made her unreliable, dangerous even when you considered the menace of the machines she would be in charge of and so she had taken to the only profession a woman like her could, that of prostitution, and they had survived.

The man lifted his arm and gave her a savage back-hander across her face and she screamed in agony as the force of it flung her head sideways, crashing her cheek against the wood. Still her hands clung to the door frame and with an oath he prised them loose, flinging her across the room until she finished up at the bottom of the stairs. Her eyes squinted dazedly up at her children, one already beginning to close and, as though their childish frightened faces, their reliance on her to put a bit of food into their mouths had stiffened her spine, she sprang up, mouthing a few obscenities of her own.

"Mam . . ." the eldest girl whispered imploringly, beginning to inch her way down the stairs on her thin buttocks, her sisters behind her, wanting to tell her mother to leave it but she had an Irish temper on her, did Kitty Brody, and no bugger was going to gyp her out of what was owed her.

The "bugger" was out of the door by now, turning for a moment to grin in triumph at Kitty, then he was off down the street in the direction of Style Street, Ashley Road and the bridge that crossed the River Irk.

"Come 'ere, yer bastard," Kitty shrieked, her hair standing like a dandelion clock about her furiously red face. "Yer owe me a shillin' an' if I 'ave ter chase yer ter whatever 'ole yer crawled out of, I'm havin' it. I don't work fer nowt, yer know. I've bairns ter feed an' me rent ter pay just like all't rest in't street."

"Oh, sod off, yer old tart," he shouted at her over his shoulder as he disappeared round the corner.

She began to run after him. Her legs pumped and her arms flailed, her hands forming fists as though, the minute she had hold of him, she would knock him senseless, but it was a long time since Kitty Brody had run anywhere and he was getting away from her. He was younger than she was and when she reached the corner he was just turning into Angel Street, the sound of his great enjoyment at having cheated her floating back between the narrow row of mean houses.

Breathing raggedly, she continued to follow him.

The three little girls stood on the doorstep in their thin shifts, watching as their mother tore round the corner into Style Street, even then not moving as she vanished from their sight. For several more minutes they remained there, expecting to see her come grumbling back round the corner, swearing she'd get her money *before* next time, telling them not to worry, she'd think of something, wondering if Nancy, her eldest, were to slip up to Ma Siddons at the gin-shop Ma'd give her a jug of gin on tick. She'd need it to settle her nerves, they all three knew that, for it didn't take much to unsettle them, and this encounter with the brawny man which had robbed her of a whole shilling she would look on as a disaster. What were they to eat tomorrow? she'd beg them to tell her and they would reassure her, as they had done a hundred times before, that something would turn up. She'd drink her gin – if she could get some – then fall into a drunken stupor, four of them in the bed which, now that the man had gone, they would drag downstairs in front of the fire. It was November and cold and the upstairs room, unlike downstairs, had no heating so during the winter they didn't use it. Except to hide in when Mam brought a man home! As soon as they heard a man's voice at the door mingling with their Mam's, they were up the stairs like three little rabbits at the sight of the fox.

"Well, I dunno where she's got to," Nancy said at last, not unduly worried, for her mother was known to be unpredictable. "'Appen she's found another customer." She was nine years old but already wise in the ways of the world: at least her world which was encompassed in the square mile of Angel Meadow.

"She'll bring 'im back 'ere, then," Mary, the second eldest said practically. "We'd best not bring bed down just yet. Let's sit by't fire, then if she fetches someone we can run upstairs."

"Aye, 'appen yer right. She'll not be long. See, Mary, put kettle on't coals an' when she comes in we'll all 'ave a cup o' tea."

The kettle was filled with an old tin cup kept for the purpose from the bucket which Nancy had filled at the communal tap at the corner of Church Court earlier in the day and with a sigh of pure enjoyment, for it was not often they had a fire of such decent proportions, the three children crouched over it. Nancy took Rose, still called the baby though she was seven years old, on her knee while Mary squatted on the stool recently vacated by her mother.

"She'll not be long," Nancy repeated, holding her little sister close to her, seemingly unaware of the squalid condition of the room that had been her home since the day she was born. Though the place stank, the child, having lived in it for so long, did not notice it. The floorboards were moist and rotting and the unpainted walls were streaked with grime which had been there for years. The window frames were spongy and rotten, ready to blow in at the first stiff breeze and the door to the street hung quite precariously to its frame. There were cracks in the plaster of both ceiling and walls from which little things scurried, forming and re-forming in patterns, and from the skirting board a mouse wandered, sat up, cleaned its whiskers, then, sensing the lack of anything edible in this place, skittered back down its hole. At the window, miraculously unbroken considering the urchins who played in the street all day and threw anything they could lay their hands on, was a scrap of fluttering fabric, thin, torn, but at least affording some privacy from prying eyes.

A cat yowled from somewhere in the street and another answered. A dog barked hoarsely and footsteps, clogs by the sound of it, rattled on the cobblestones. For a moment Nancy's eyes flew open, thinking her mother had returned, then, as the footsteps continued past their door, they drooped again and with Rose warm against her thin chest and Mary leaning against her, her head comfortably on Nancy's lap, the three little girls fell asleep.

It was broad daylight when they awoke, which meant it was late, for this was November when days were short, especially in the dark, deep caverns of the streets of Angel Meadow. Church Court was no more than five feet across with a gutter running down its centre, the windows of the back-to-back houses staring into the windows of the houses opposite or at the bare blank walls of mills, the towering forest of mill chimneys. Angel Meadow was a warren of narrow, packed streets, courts and alleys, which bred vice and disease, running out in each direction from St Michael's Church. The church and the paupers' burial ground about it was the only open space in that square mile of deprivation and destitution and it was here a horde of children, those not yet forced into the mills, played and shrieked, the Brody girls among them. Those who wanted to could find work in the dye works, the print shops, the foundries, the factories and workshops that abounded in Manchester but most families were employed in the cotton mills as spinners and weavers, as scavengers and piecers and all the other jobs that were a part of the trade on which the great city had founded its equally great wealth.

The fire still had a flicker in it, and with great patience and skill, Nancy coaxed it back to life, adding little slivers of wood bit by bit, then when it was drawing properly adding small pieces of the precious coal that stood in a cardboard box beside the grate. The water was still warm in the kettle they had put on the fire for their mam's cup of tea so, bringing it back to the boil and taking down the tea caddy, she spooned a mere half-teaspoon into the chipped brown teapot, pouring enough boiling water on to it to make one cup of tea apiece. With their hands round their cups, the little girls stared mesmerised into the fire, the warmth that they seldom enjoyed giving them an unusual sense of ease. With their feet tucked up under their shifts, they sipped the hot tea. There was nothing to eat.

"What we gonner do, our Nancy?" Mary said at last, tipping her head back to get the last drop of pleasure from her cup of tea. "Where d'yer think our mam's got to?"

"She'll be back soon, chuck. 'Appen that chap she ran after wanted another go."

"He never paid fer't first, our Nancy. She'd not be likely ter give 'im another." Mary's voice was scathing.

"I 'ope she brings summat back to eat. I'm bloody hungry." Rose sighed and huddled up closer to her sister. "Is there nowt?"

"There's nowt, our Rosie, so give over about it."

"I were only askin'." Rose's voice was aggrieved. For several minutes the sisters sat in silence. Usually their mother would be snoring her head off on the mattress on the floor, or upstairs sleeping off the worst excesses of the night before. They would get their own breakfast, whatever it happened to be. Thin porridge on bad days with stale bread and lard, or perhaps, if their mam had had a few customers, paying ones, a bit of bacon or even an egg apiece. Mam like them to drink milk, which she insisted a friend of hers who had worked as a skivvy at a big house and was privy to kitchen gossip swore was good for your teeth and certainly theirs were all sound. She sent them to the market last thing on a Saturday night to buy vegetables that had not been sold, and bits of meat or fish or poultry, anything that would not last until Monday, again on the advice of her friend whose employer had been a doctor. They were thin as lathes, the three of them, but they didn't seem to ail like many of the children in Angel Meadow, nor were they stunted or deformed. But then they had never worked in a cotton mill.

"Well, I suppose we'd best get dressed," Nancy said practically. "Now, promise yer won't tell Mam when she gets back but I've a penny or two put by . . . no, don't ask me," as both her sisters clamoured to be told where she had hidden it, and, more to the point, how she had managed it. "Whenever I could," meaning when her mam had been too drunk to notice, "I . . .

I pinched a farthing an' put it away, hid it so's Mam wouldn't know or else she'd have 'ad it fer gin."

Mary and Rose nodded their heads in perfect understanding, their identical golden brown eyes wide and gleaming in admiration of their sister's cleverness.

"Now, I'm not sayin' yer'd do it on purpose but just in case . . . well, by mistake like, yer let it out, I'm goin' ter go an' get it. It's upstairs an' yer not to come with me. All right?"

They nodded again, watching her as she climbed the steep narrow stairs that led to the empty room at the top. It was not entirely empty, for it was here that Nancy and her sisters, guided by Nancy, stored any old bit of what their mam called "junk" that they found or could pinch, but which Nancy thought might come in useful. They had nothing in the way of furniture, the Brody family, except the mattress and the frame on which it stood, the old armchair, the stool and the deal table. The rest was clutter, odds and ends of old pots and pans, the bucket that Mick O'Rourke had mended for them since it had had a hole in it, several eating utensils and a few dribs and drabs of bedding. Whatever was not in immediate use was kept upstairs in the one room with the tiny window that looked out over Church Court and directly into the window of the house opposite where, Nancy noticed vaguely, Mr Murphy was giving Mrs Murphy a good hiding.

She went directly to the far wall and with a bit of picking and pulling loosened a brick, putting it carefully down on the floor. Reaching inside the hole it left, she brought out a scrap of material in which something clinked. Unwrapping it as though it contained diamonds, she quickly removed eight farthings, then hurriedly wrapped the rest up again, looking over her shoulder as though suspecting her mam, her mam who did her best for them but who would drink it all up in an hour, was watching her. Thrusting the small package back in the hole, she replaced the brick then stood back to see if it was noticeable. Satisfied, she crept downstairs again. Triumphantly she opened her dirty hand to reveal to her sisters the eight farthings which added up to two whole pence.

"We can get us a bite ter eat now, d'yer see, an' when Mam comes 'ome she'll be 'ungry so there'll be a bit o' summat fer 'er an' all."

"Eeh, our Nancy, yer that clever," Rose murmured, sighing in deep satisfaction at the thought that they were soon to have something to eat. Probably only bread and lard, or, if there was enough money, perhaps bread and dripping which was much more tasty. Mrs O'Leary at the corner shop made her own from scraps of meat, which came from God knows where, and they didn't ask, but it was a good standby when you were famished.

It was dry out so they didn't bother with their clogs. The less they were worn the less they needed mending. Besides, the soles of their feet were protected by a thick layer of horn which had grown up over the years of going barefoot. They wore woollen skirts and tops, no undergarments, naturally, since they did not, and never had done, possess such things but, with the ragged shawls that Nancy had bought on the second- or even third-hand stall on the market which they draped across their heads and wrapped securely about their narrow shoulders, they were warm enough.

Bearing in mind that Mam might have been unsuccessful in getting her money off the brawny chap, or earned any more, for it had been late when she ran out, Nancy bought the least she could for a decent meal. Decent to them, that is. They didn't go to Mrs O'Leary's but to the market on Miller Street where food was cheaper and there was more to choose from. She spent a long time in choosing. Well, you had to when there was not much to go round.

A piece of scrag end, fatty and gristly and just about on the turn and therefore cheap, a bag of vegetables way past their best but still edible and five pounds of potatoes, rotten but again still edible. It would make a decent meal, in fact two if they were careful, and it would give Mam something to stick to her insides when she got home. She'd gone without her shawl and was bound to be perished.

The battered old stewpan simmered gently over the fire and though they all hung over it, mouths watering, they waited and waited for Mam; and when she hadn't turned up by early afternoon they could wait no longer.

Bloody hell, it was good, they kept telling one another as they shovelled it into their mouths, keeping some back for Mam, even though they could have eaten hers as well as their own. They were children with children's healthy appetites and they'd had nothing since yesterday, but that was Mam's and must be saved for her. She had not returned by the time night fell.

The next day was a repeat of the one before. A fumble in the secret hoard, a trip to the market, a plate of tripe and onions this time, which Mam always said was good for them, and the wait, anxiously watching out of the filthy window for the sight of her familiar shapeless figure.

At the end of a week they began to face the harrowing fact that their mam, whom they had loved without reservation, was not coming back.

2

The sergeant looked over the top of his desk at the three little girls who stood before it, a surprised expression on his florid face. It was not often the police station was visited by children, unless they were street urchins caught thieving who had not been fast enough to evade the arm of the law, which didn't happen often, he might add. Like bloody eels they were, real slippery customers, darting and diving with their catch in their hands, probably no more than a loaf of bread or a tanner out of a customer's change pinched from the counter of the beer house when the customer's back was turned, escaping up the warren of alleyways that cobwebbed Angel Meadow.

But these three had come in to the station of their own accord, scared stiff, poor little buggers, you could see that, creeping over the threshold clinging to one another, peeping round them as though they expected a copper to grab them and stuff them in a cell. They had sidled over to the desk, their eyes on the floor, then the tallest one had screwed up the courage to look up at him and he'd been quite stunned by the beauty of her eyes. He was not a fanciful man, ask his wife, and he'd seven children of his own but this one, beneath the layers of filth that coated her skin, was going to be a real looker. Aye, dirty she was, like most who lived round about but dirt couldn't hide the soft, golden brown depths of her eyes, nor the long silken lashes that surrounded them. It was like looking into a glass of whisky, which he didn't do very often since he couldn't afford it, but that was the colour of this kid's eyes; and when the other two peeped warily from beneath their long curling lashes he could see theirs were exactly the same.

He leaned on the desk and without realising it softened his voice.

"Yes, chuck, what can we do for yer? Lost yer pussy cat, 'ave yer?" He turned to wink at the constable who sat at a desk behind him and the constable was considerably startled, for the sergeant was not known for his joviality.

"No," the girl said gravely. "Me mam."

They had debated for hours, days, on what they should do. Every morning as soon as it was light they had draped themselves in their shawls and searched the alleys and courts around Church Court until dark fell, asking every woman they met had she seen their mam.

"'Oo's yer mam, chuck?" they were asked sympathetically but it was very evident that when they spoke her name, Kitty Brody was reckoned nowt a pound in these quarters and if she'd disappeared, well, good riddance to bad rubbish was their opinion.

After Mam had turned the corner out of Church Court they had no idea in which direction she had gone, running off after the cheating customer. She could have turned right along Ashley Lane under the railway bridge towards Newtown, which like Angel Meadow was a teeming refuge for the Irish; left towards the bridge over the River Irk or sharp left into Angel Street and St George's Rd and the centre of the city. It could have been any of them and so, patiently, day after day they walked the streets, searching any bit of spare ground they came across, going further from Angel Meadow than they had ever been in their entire life but with no success. They had even gone along the banks of the river, precariously clinging to the edge, for the water was foul with sewage, dead animals, the waste from the mills along its bank, its surface a floating, stinking slick of oil. They wandered round Strangeways Park brick field, climbing piles of broken bricks and debris, turning over heaps of rubbish until some chap shouted to them to get off out of it, chasing them off the site.

"It's no good, we've got ter go ter't police." Nancy's voice did its best to be positive, as though it were nothing out of the ordinary for a resident of Angel Meadow to hobnob with the law. It wasn't, in fact, but on the wrong side of it. For one of them to go voluntarily into a police station was unheard of and a measure of the desperation of their situation.

"Oh, our Nancy," Mary quavered and on Rose's pointed little face came a look of dread.

"I know . . . I know, but what else can we do? Mam's been gone fer a week now and . . . and God knows what's happened to 'er." Her voice broke, obviously fearing the worst. If she'd caught up with that chap he might have done anything in his fury. Beaten her senseless and left her for dead in an alley. Chucked her in the river or . . . or, well, whatever it was, they had a right to know and that was what the bloody police were for, after all, wasn't it, to keep the peace, to uphold the law and if anything had happened to their mam and that bugger was the cause of it then he should be found and put in prison. Surely, where they had failed, the bobbies could find him, and Mam.

"Mam didn't like the police, our Nancy," Mary persisted fearfully. "She used ter say they were for important folk, not the likes of us."

"I know she did but . . . well, what else can we do? There's only a tanner left in . . . upstairs, and us'll have ter find work soon. Unless yer fancy the workhouse, our Mary?"

The workhouse! It was the place that even the worst afflicted did their best to keep out of and though the Brody girls were not sure why, for they had seen no more of it than the big wrought-iron gates that guarded it, Mam said she'd rather spend the rest of her life on her back than go in there. They'd be separated for a start which was enough to frighten the wits out of the three little girls, for they had never been separated in their lives, from each other or from their mam. Now and again Mam did not come home for twenty-four hours which was why they hadn't worried unduly at first, staying out overnight with God knows who and God knows where – she never said – but she *always* came home. Until now.

"Yer mam?" the sergeant asked now. "Yer've lost yer mam?" He scratched his head and the constable at the table turned round to stare, for never in all the years he had been a policeman had anyone ever reported a missing mam. The station on St George's Road was the largest in Manchester, since it was needed to keep order in Angel Meadow where vice was prolific and even now the cells were full of drunks and layabouts who had been fighting, men and women caught thieving or fornicating in the gutters, wrong 'uns of all sorts and all waiting to be taken to the assizes. But this was a real poser and no mistake. Even the sergeant didn't seem to know how to proceed.

"Well, where did yer last see 'er, lass?"

"Last week. Seven days an' nights she's bin gone an' we'd like yer ter find her, please."

"Would yer now? Well, 'appen she don't want ter be found, 'ave yer thought o' that, chuck? 'As yer pa bin batterin' 'er about or owt like that?"

"We 'aven't got no pa."

"I see." He scratched his head again, for the effect of those three pairs of incredible eyes looking at him with every faith that he would find their mam for them was quite doing him in.

He turned to the constable. "What d'yer think, Constable Perkins?"

"Well, we could keep an eye out for 'er, Sarge, but a week's a long time to—"

"Yer mean yer think she's dead?" the tall one said flatly, her face expressionless. "An' if she is then it's 'im what did it."

"'Im? 'Oo?"

"Chap she ran after. He never paid her so she . . ."

The sergeant's face became visibly less concerned.

"Never paid 'er? What for?"

Nancy knew she had made a mistake and really, had she expected anything else. Mam was a whore and as soon as the bobby realised it he had turned scornful. A mam who was missing, a mam who stayed at home and looked after her children, or went out and did a decent day's work, was worth at least a bit of interest, but once the bobbies understood what Mam did to earn her living they had washed their hands of her. A whore who got herself into trouble was nothing to do with them. In fact she probably deserved whatever fate had befallen her and they certainly weren't going to waste their time looking for her. There was no use in relating the story to this man who was already turning away, for in his mind this was the old story of a whore being diddled out of her money and there was nothing they could do about it. She'd probably gone off with the very fellow who had diddled her!

"I should get yerself 'ome, lass. Yer mam'll turn up, you see. Now, off yer go. We're busy 'ere so get off 'ome."

"But . . ."

"Now then, there's a good lass, get off 'ome an' I bet yer mam's there wonderin' where the 'ell you've got to."

He turned away, as much to remove those disconcerting eyes from boring into his, as to get back to what he had been doing when the three little girls had come in.

"Come on, our Mary, our Rose. I can see we're gonner get no 'elp 'ere," Nancy Brody said, lifting her lice-infested head as though she were a duchess who was dismissing an impertinent footman. She turned on her heel, her thin back straight, her narrow shoulders squared and her sisters followed her, not quite so haughty since they hadn't the nerve of their Nancy.

When they got outside it all fell away and they were just three little girls who had lost the only person in the whole world who had given a damn about them. She wouldn't come back, they knew that. They had nobody, only each other and that would have to suffice.

"Where we goin', our Nancy?" they asked her anxiously as she took their hands in hers and began to walk up St George's Road towards Angel Street.

"Home fer a cuppa tea then ter't market ter get some grub. Then, when we've 'ad us a bite ter eat an' a good night's sleep, tomorrer we're goin' ter find us a job."

It was a fine day, for which Nancy thanked whoever was looking out for them, mild for November with a bit of sunshine easing its way between the tall chimneys of the mill. The chimneys cast long thin shadows across the busy mill yard and beyond the gate, but Nancy made sure she and her sisters were not standing in one since she wanted to be noticed. They were as close to the mill gates as they could get, for it was rumoured that they were taking operatives on this morning.

They were standing among dozens of others outside the splendid entrance to the Monarch Cotton Manufacturing Mill in Victoria Parade. She knew that for every job going in the mill there were more than enough folk to fill them. Women who could spin the yarn and men who could weave the cloth and children who worked as piecers and scavengers and it was one of these latter jobs that she hoped to get for herself and her sisters. She had never worked in a mill and had no knowledge of the system that was usual in such a place. The spinning-rooms in the Monarch Mill were divided into many identical cells, each one consisting of three people who were concerned solely with the operation of one particular pair of mules. The spinner was the senior member, who had absolute authority over her two assistants, one a piecer, the other a scavenger. She had no idea even of what they earned. So all she hoped for was that she and Mary might get put on as piecers and Rosie as a scavenger. Just a few shillings would see them through and would be riches to them after living for the past week on the scraps a tanner had bought. They must stay together, of course, for Mam would have insisted upon it. At least in the same mill. Monarch was a large mill belonging to Edmund Hayes who had started up in business with his father many years ago. There were departments for all the processes from cleaning the raw cotton to spinning and weaving, and, surely, she had said to her sisters as they folded themselves in their shawls and set off to make their way in the world, there would be something in that huge place for them.

Last night, for the first time any of them could remember, they had removed all the tattered rags that were their clothing and stood naked before each other. Three scrawny little girls who were frightened and hungry, for though they had been to the market and bought scraps of what was really nothing more than rotting meat and vegetables, it had not been enough to satisfy their appetites. They must eke it out, Nancy had told them gravely, for it might be a day or two before they got work and then they had to wait until the end of the week to be paid.

Careful not to spill any of it, Nancy had tipped hot water from the kettle into the bucket. When the kettle was empty she filled it again from the stewpot which contained cold water, setting the kettle in the bosom of the fire.

Rosie shivered, her bony frame cringing from the coming ordeal, but bravely she allowed her sister to begin the process that she had decided upon.

"We've got to be clean an' I mean all over."

"All over? Why? Nobody can see under our clothes. Can't we just do our faces an' hands? The rest's hidden."

"It doesn't matter, our Mary. We're starting summat new tomorrow: a new life without . . . without Mam and I've decided we must begin as we mean ter go on. Besides, there's bound ter be others after jobs and we've gotter be different, look different, ter get noticed. Ter be picked."

"I don't know what yer mean, our Nancy." Mary was plainly perplexed and Rosie just wanted to get it all over and done with and get her clothes back on. It was strange wearing nothing at all, seeing her sisters' bodies which were exactly like her own, grey and peculiar-looking with the bones all sticking out, and when Nancy began to rub vigorously at her chest with a cloth wrung out in the water she was absolutely astonished at what it revealed. From some hidey-hole of her mam's who, she supposed, to please her customers had now and again washed her face, Nancy had found a sliver of soap. It smelled quite horrible but when it was applied to the cloth and then to her body something quite lovely began to appear. They were all mesmerised as the smooth white skin gleamed through the muck, the firelight warming it to a rich cream. Their enthusiasm intensified and so did their vigour, for by now both Nancy and Mary were polishing Rosie as though she were made of a precious metal and she began to squeal.

"'Ere, 'old on. Watch where yer rubbin', our Mary. That 'urts," but she was as delighted as they were not only by the wonder of her lovely skin but by the magical feeling of lightness, of freshness, of stepping out of something nasty and letting it fall away. She stood on a bit of rag in front of the fire and tried to peer over her shoulder at her own back, running her hand over her chest and stomach as though she expected to feel different under her own hands. She smiled and smiled and so did her sisters, for they'd no idea that skin could be like this. They had trouble with her feet, though, for the layer of horn on the soles was thick and the filth was deeply encrusted and, short of shaving it off with one of those razors they'd heard men used, it had to remain.

"Now yer hair," Nancy ordered, picking off a couple of lice that had had the effrontery to fall out of Rosie's curls on to her immaculate little body.

"Oh, bloody 'ell," Rosie began to groan as, tipping her up, they put her head in the bucket of water. When it was thoroughly wet they stood her on her feet and began to rub at the mass with the soap.

"Be careful with it," Nancy warned Mary. "We want ter save a bit for you an' me."

It is doubtful that if they'd knocked on their neighbour's door they would have been recognised. Their hair was quite glorious, standing out in an abundant rippling mass of rich curls, a soft brown but with paler streaks in it. In fact, Nancy said worriedly, it had created another problem, for what were they to do with it all? She had no idea that hair could be so thick, and so much of it. It hung, since it had never been cut, to their buttocks, a springing cloak that would have to be tied back with something or they'd never get taken on at the mill with all that machinery about. She'd heard that if you weren't careful it could whirl at you like a demon, catching your hair or your hands and indeed Bridie Murphy's mam's little brother had had such a thing happen to him and had died of it. Perhaps they could bind it up with a bit of cloth from the scraps they had hoarded upstairs and which she'd known would come in useful one day.

Suddenly her face cleared and her two young sisters watched in astonishment as she leaped up the stairs. She came down a moment later with a triumphant look on her face. She waved a piece of what looked like greasy newspaper under their noses.

"I knew I'd kept this. I liked 't pictures in it. It were wrapped round them pies Mam brought 'ome a while back. Look. Look at this. I don't know what it's called 'cos I can't read the words but can yer see what's bein' done ter that hair?"

They could indeed. The picture showed a lady with long hair and a pair of disembodied hands were doing something quite intricate with it. First it was divided into three strands, then the right strand was placed over the middle one and the left strand over that until all the hair was in one long, tidy rope which the hands tied a lovely ribbon on. They hadn't got a ribbon, of course, but they could tear strips from Mam's old skirt, the one she wore to lounge about the house in and which, sadly, she would no longer need. They were made up with each other, practising again and again until each of them had a long plait – though they didn't know the name of it – as thick as a man's wrist, hanging neatly down their backs. Of course there were still curly bits round their foreheads and ears and on their necks, bits that were too short to go in the plait but they felt, and looked, wonderful, they told one another.

The only disappointment was having to put on again the filthy rags they had removed so reluctantly an hour since. They were stiff and unyielding, at once setting up a scratching against their newly discovered and tender flesh, but they'd just have to put up with it, Nancy said firmly. As soon as they'd got a few bob together, confident and making them feel it too, they'd go to the market and get some new things and then this lot could be washed. They were going to do a lot of things now, she told them. They were strong and straight and they would be good workers and whoever took them on would be so pleased with them it wouldn't be long before . . .

It was here that she ran out of dreams to pass on to them, for they were barely formed in her own nine-year-old mind. She had known nothing but this hovel, this place called Angel Meadow, this life her mam had forced on them. Not that she blamed Mam; she didn't. You had to do the best with what you'd got and sometimes that wasn't much, but Mam had done her best and you couldn't ask more of a body, could you?

A burly man came to the gate and peered between the bars. He was the "gaffer", the spinning-room overlooker and it was he who decided who was to be taken on out of the crowd of patient, be-shawled women who waited outside the mill gate. He was an important man, at least to them, and there was a small surge as they pressed closer in order to catch his eye.

They might have saved themselves the trouble, for at once it fell on the three young girls who were pressed almost in his face and the look of amazement that came over it was very evident. The other women had been muttering to one another on the strange appearance of the three girls, wondering who they were, and now, so did he. His eyes narrowed as they roamed over the taller girl. Thin, she was, but then weren't they all, but she was straight and bonny, her limbs, as far as he could see, with none of the stunting or deformities found in many of the children who came begging for jobs at his gate.

"Stand back," he ordered the women and obediently they did so, allowing him to open the gate. "You . . ." He beckoned to Nancy and at once she and Mary and Rose stepped forward through the opening. He blinked, for like the sergeant at the police station – and he had only seen them in their muck – he was fascinated, not only by their comeliness but by the fact that there were three of them, each an almost exact replica of the other.

"No, lass, I only want you," he said, indicating that Rose and Mary were to rejoin the others outside the gate.

Nancy lifted her head autocratically and the man gaped. "We work as a team, sir." Unknowingly she had spoken the correct words. "Was it a spinner yer wanted?" willing to be anything he asked for, spinner or piecer, which would give them employment.

"Aye, but . . ."

"I'm a spinner," she lied, "and this 'ere's me sister who's a piecer. Little 'un could scavenge fer me if yer took me on. One wage fer't two of us and p'raps a few bob for't little 'un."

"Nay, lass, it don't work like that. I'd pay you and out o' that you'd pay them. I couldn't—"

"That's all right. We're good workers, sir. Reliable an' good time-keepers."

"Where've yer worked?"

"'Ere an' there."

"Oh aye, an' how old are yer?"

"Thirteen, sir."

The gaffer looked her up and down. She was tall enough to be thirteen, or perhaps twelve but even thirteen was young to be in charge of a spinning mule; really you had to admire her spirit. She was looking at him, not with that piteous and humble yearning most of them did when they were after a job, but with her head up, her eyes steady as though to say she knew her own worth and he'd be a fool not to take her on.

He chewed his lip, hesitating while the women beyond the gate watched raptly. There had been an accident in the mill the day before, a careless spinner who had looked away from her machine for a moment and it had reached out and grabbed her loose hair, almost dragging her into its whirl of straps and gears and had it not been for the spinner next to her she might have died. As it was her hands were badly injured. Now this lass, with her hair fastened neatly back from her face, her look of bright intelligence, her belief in her ability to do the job exactly as it should be done, as he demanded it be done, was just the sort of lass that Mr Hayes liked to see at his machines.

"Can yer start now?" he asked them and three pairs of glowing golden eyes looked at him as though he were a god and three heads nodded vigorously.

"Right, come wi' me. Yer'll be next ter Annie Wilson so if yer've any questions yer can ask 'er. Yer'll 'ave two machines ter see to but then yer'll know that if yer've worked 'em before. I'll 'ave ter leave yer ter find yer own way about as I've not checked the yarn from each mule yet so . . . Well, follow me an' watch yer step, there's oil about."

The room to which the gaffer led them was fearfully hot, despite the open windows. Dozens of women and older children attended to the mules while others, younger and smaller, ran from machine to machine piecing any yarn that broke, or sweeping up the cotton waste; the smallest, who were surely not over the legal age, slithered on the oil-soaked floor beneath menacing straps and pulleys, chains and wheels to retrieve the oil-coated waste that collected there. There were young lads carrying empty roving bobbins, taking them to the machines and fetching away the full bobbins of spun yarn which were placed in an enormous basket on wheels which was taken away by an older lad. The three girls looked about them, stunned by the noise and the never-ceasing movement of the machines and those who "minded" them. The air was thick with "fly", the specks of mixed, clinging, cotton fibre and dust that hung in a haze above the machines.

At once Rose began to cough and Nancy turned to her in concern but the gaffer merely shouted over his shoulder, for the noise was deafening, that the lass would have to get used to it or she'd not last long.

They were led between a long row of machines, each pair looked after by a woman in the briefest of skirts and a scanty sleeveless bodice and Nancy silently went over in her head the accumulated rubbish that was upstairs in the house in Church Court. What they had on now, thin and worn as it was, would be too warm for this stifling heat. The lads wore fine cotton drawers and a sleeveless shirt and not one of the "hands" wore shoes. Their feet and ankles were a solid black to halfway up their legs. They all had a tallow-yellow hue to their skins and their hair, or what showed beneath their caps or scarves, was uniformly greasy. It was no wonder that they had been stared at outside the gate and it was the same here, the women watching them go by with their mouths open; had it not been for the gaffer's shout of annoyance which turned them back to their machines, damage might have been done, to them and the yarn they spun.

"Now then, lass, 'ere's yer machine so switch it on and let's see what yer can do. See, there, that's the switch."

A small child edged his way up to the gaffer's elbow, touching his arm timidly and the man turned to him, not pleased to be interrupted.

"What?" he snarled so that the child cowered away and at

Nancy's side both Mary and Rose looked as though they were going to take fright and bolt.

"Maister wants ter see yer, sir," the boy shouted, ready to dart away as soon as his message was delivered.

"Bugger it, what does 'e want?" he muttered, then turned to Nancy who was standing in front of the mules which had both sprung to life at the push of the switch, doing her best to appear calm and totally in control of what she was about to do.

"Yer'll 'ave ter get on wi' it, lass. I'll be back ter see 'ow yer gettin' on but I'm warnin' yer, if I don't like it there's plenty at gates ter take yer place so think on."

Nancy stepped up to her machine watched not only by her apprehensive sisters but by the woman who was working next to her, presumably Annie Wilson. She turned helplessly, terrified to put her hands near the pulsating machinery and the woman smiled.

"I like a lass wi' a bit o' gumption," she yelled, switching off her own machine. "An' it tekks gumption ter mind a spinnin' mule when yer've never set eyes on one afore. Yer 'aven't, 'ave yer? No, I thought not. Well, watch me. I'll tell yer only once then yer on yer own. I can't afford ter lose me wages."

"I'll make it up," Nancy told her breathlessly.

"Aye, lass, yer will. Now then, let's 'ope yer a quick learner. Us'll start wi' creelin' . . ."

3

The Brody girls! They were a constant source of wonder, envy and derision to the inhabitants of Angel Meadow: the wonder deriving from the way in which the three girls had "got on"; the envy over the way they had "got above themselves"; and the derision because they were, after all, three girls born and brought up in Angel Meadow and who were they to queen it over those who had not done so well?

The fact that the girls had picked themselves up – and been successful at it – after their mam disappeared, found work and got on with their lives, spending twelve hard hours each day at the mill and keeping themselves out of trouble, counted for nothing with the likes of Kate Murphy, with Teresa O'Connell and Eileen O'Rourke, all who lived in Church Court and liked to sit on their front step and watch the world go by rather than get involved with it. Stuck-up little madams, the Brody girls were considered to be, especially that Nancy with her nose in the air and what appeared to them to be a fanatical determination to avoid any contact with her neighbours, who would have been glad to air their views not only on the whereabouts of Kitty Brody, but on how the girls should further conduct their lives. They would have liked to see them carted off to the workhouse, where destitute orphans usually found themselves, and when it became obvious that this was not going to happen their pretence at concern turned to incredulity.

"We've jobs at Monarch, thanks, Mrs O'Rourke," Nancy told her neighbour on that first day, squaring her aching shoulders when Mrs O'Rourke, her eyes narrowed suspiciously as though she suspected the three girls to be following the same profession as their mother, her brawny arms akimbo across her chest, challenged her from her doorstep as the three children padded tiredly towards their own front door.

"Yer what?" Mrs O'Rourke's jaw dropped. She was clearly amazed. She had never worked since she and her Liam had wed, her Liam being a fairly decent provider when he wasn't sozzled. All her children still living, five of them, had jobs so she was free to sit about all day, on her doorstep when it was fine, and gossip with her neighbours. Her childbearing days were over. Her Liam, thanks be to the Holy Mother, had lost interest in the fumblings he had once demanded nightly beneath their grubby bed covers and besides, she'd "seen" nothing for five years now.

She had not approved of Kitty Brody but now she was gone she was perfectly willing to interfere in the lives of Kitty's daughters, and was affronted that her "help" was apparently neither needed nor asked for.

"Yes, we were took on this mornin', me an' our Rose an' Mary."

"Doin' what, fer Christ sake?" Eileen shrieked, for as far as she was aware, and nothing much got past Eileen O'Rourke, these girls didn't know one end of a spinning mule from the other. She did, though, for her mam had taken her to Jenkinsons, a cotton mill in Bromley Street, when she was seven and she'd worked there, first as a piecer, then as a spinner until she wed her Liam.

"I'm in charge of a pair of me own, Mrs O'Rourke," Nancy confided, referring casually to the two spinning mules that had so terrified her this morning, "an' I'm quite at 'ome in the jennygate." She lifted her head even higher, "An' Mary's piecin' fer me. Our Rose is clearin' waste or fetchin' bobbins. We're all quick learners and already know what creelin' an' doffin' means an 'ow ter do it. We even cleaned our mules before we left, didn't we, Mary?" glancing down at her sister who was almost asleep on her feet.

"But you can't mind a pair o' spinnin' mules, Nancy Brody. Yer only – what? – ten? eleven?" The sisters' ages were not something she had taken a great deal of interest in since it had no bearing on her life but she was pretty certain Nancy Brody wasn't old enough to be in charge of a pair of spinning mules.

"I'm thirteen, Mrs O' Rourke." Nancy's voice was cool as though daring Mrs O'Rourke to call her a liar, her expression plainly asking what the hell had any of it to do with this fat old cow? As far as she was aware there was no one who could poke their noses into the lives of the Brody girls. They never had before, and as long as they kept out of trouble, paid their rent on time and bothered no one they were free to get on with their lives. Which was what she intended.

She couldn't have done it without Annie Wilson, she knew that, and she often wondered at her own naïveté, or was it bravado, in imagining that she could simply walk into a spinning-room and take over the running of a pair of spinning mules.

Annie spent half an hour with her while her own machine stood idle and when the under-gaffer came over to see what the hold-up was she told him to bugger off, which he did, for Annie was the best and most hardworking spinner they had and if she wanted to stop and give a hand to the new girl then that was her business. She'd make it up, she told him, and she did.

It took no longer than the half-hour for the new girl to get the hang of it and though she was slow at first, watching intently every movement Annie made and faithfully copying it, when the gaffer came to measure with his wrap reel and balance the count of yarn spun at each mule he seemed satisfied with what she had done. Her sisters kept their traps shut and obeyed every order Annie or Nancy shouted at them, quick and lively as squirrels, darting from mule to mule, doffing the full bobbins from the spindles and replacing them with empty ones. The littlest one crept beneath the swiftly moving carriage and backstop, piecing together any broken threads – and there were five or six every minute – while the older girl swept the floor and helped her sister with the weft-carrying. And you could see that Nancy, as she had told Annie she was called, was not going to be satisfied until she could keep up with the best. By the end of the week, in Annie's opinion, Nancy would be, if not as swift and proficient as herself, then better than many who had been spinners for years and would not tolerate the least falling-off in performance of her machines. Annie, and one or two of the other minders, were convinced that even the most carefully set up self-actor fell short of perfection, despite the gaffer's ministrations, and few could resist, when the gaffer was not looking, the temptation to make small overriding adjustments to the strapping and nosing motions of their machines. This girl would be one of these, Annie could tell and it was not often Annie was wrong. She'd seen many a lass come and go but Nancy Brody was a stayer, Annie was certain of that.

They got through their first week at the mill, the Brody girls, earning eleven shillings, though it would not be long before Mary, catching the gaffer's eye as having the makings of a good spinner when she was big enough, would be clearing another half-crown. They began their working day at six o'clock. The operatives were up and stirring half an hour before and in a very short time the streets in the neighbourhood were thronged with men, women and children flocking to the factories, warehouses and mills in the area. The factory and mill bells began to ring at five to six, then, to the very minute, the engines were started and the day's work began. Those who were not on time, be it only for a moment, were fined twopence and though a short period of grace was given, it was not long before the gates were locked and those shut out were not only fined but lost a morning's work. The Brody girls were never among this number.

At eight thirty it was breakfast time. The engine stopped and the streets again became crowded with those hands who lived close to the mills. The Brody girls, conscious now, through Nancy, of course, of a good diet, since you needed stoking up in their line of work, and the need to watch every penny, brought their breakfast with them, eating the thick slices of bread and dripping, or perhaps a slice of bacon, washed down with hot, sweet tea they made from the water supplied by the mill owner. Five to nine and the bell sounded again and at nine the engine resumed its clamorous roar. There was very little talking during the break or at the machines where it was calculated that the minders walked approximately seven miles a day tending their machines. The machinery did all the work but the spinner superintended that work every moment of the day with vigilant attention, and with a greater or lesser degree of dexterity which was reflected in the wages paid. Annie, and soon catching up with her, Nancy, were the two highest paid minders in the mill, which employed almost two thousand workers. The mill itself was enormous, several groups of buildings separated from each other by streets but connected by subterranean tunnels in which iron tramways were laid for the speedy and easy conveyance of raw cotton, of spun yarn and of made-up cloth from ware-room to ware-room. Rose and Mary, who from the first were sent running on many an errand, for they were bright and intelligent and could be trusted with a message, were at first terrified by the tunnels, by the trams, by the thin, spare men who laughed and called out good-naturedly to them, by the unfamiliarity of this new life of theirs, when they had roamed free for the first seven or eight years of it, but very soon they became used to it and even smiled back at the men, Rosie, who was pert as well as pretty, answering them back with a bit of cheek of her own.

At one o'clock it was dinner time for everyone, master or man, for every workshop and office, every cotton mill, silk mill, print works, warehouse and dye works in Manchester ate at the same time. The hungry crowd swarmed out into the smoky brown streets, the smoky brown sky lowering above them and streets and lanes which before had been echoing and empty rang with the tramp of clogged feet. Long piles of warehouses lined each thoroughfare, many of them pillared and with stately fronts, alongside great grimy mills with their chimneys belching smoke into the already smoke-laden air, but the men and women of Manchester were used to it and philosophically ate their "butties" in its putrid atmosphere. Potato pie for the Brody girls, made by Nancy, who was good with pastry, sometimes with a bit of meat in it – this, of course when they had got on their feet financially – eaten by the side of the jennygate, and then it was back to work until the whistle blew at the end of the day. The thread spun at Monarch Mill was coarse yarn, used in the manufacture of cotton for shirts and trousers, hard-wearing and serviceable, much of it sent abroad.

They became accustomed to the thick, sunless air, the heat, the throb and boom of the steam engines and the clattering whirl of hundreds and thousands of revolving pirns and bobbins, the white flakes of cotton wool which specked their hair and clothing. The Factory Acts of 1833 and 1847 limited the working hours of children under the age of thirteen to forty-eight a week and forbade the employment of children under the age of nine in the mills, but what did it matter, the mill owners argued, for the majority of them crowding at the gates for work had no idea how old they were and neither had their mothers who sent them there in the first place. If they said they were ten or eleven or twelve, who were the factory owners to dispute it?

Mind you, Nancy Brody knew exactly how old she was, having questioned Mam when she herself was scarcely more than a toddler and her mam still able to function at a certain level. Sharp as two tin tacks was Nancy Brody, even at the age of four, five, six; her mam often said so. She knew the ages of their Rose and Mary as well, since they had been born so close to her. The rest of her family were no more than a faint recollection to her, little scraps of humanity who had been fed on a mixture of gin and "Godfreys" or "Mother's Quietness" as it was called, a cordial made up by the carelessly indifferent druggist and whose main ingredient was laudanum, which was given to them to keep them quiet while their mothers laboured in the mills and factories.

At the end of the first week at Monarch, a week that Nancy was often to wonder how they got through, since they had little to eat but scraps, they gloated all the way home over the eleven shillings she held in her hand, afraid to let go of it even to put in her pocket. They stopped on the way and bought a loaf of bread and a pot of dripping, a small packet of tea, a jug of milk and a hunk of coarse cheese from Mrs O'Leary and for the first time since Mam vanished they went to their verminous bed replete.

Nancy wouldn't, as yet, let them spend any money on anything except food, despite their Rosie's complaints that though they were clean underneath, since Nancy insisted they kept up the daily washes, their clothing was stiff with dirt. It was weeks before Nancy allowed herself to believe that this incredible wealth was not going to be snatched away from them, hoarding their few shillings behind the loose brick upstairs, still not revealed to her sisters. Just after Christmas, which meant very little to them, of course, since they had no cash to spare for frivolities, they made their way to the market at Smithfield, heading for the old clothes stalls.

The streets that led to the market were a solid mass of waggons and drays, enormous horses pulling them, goods being unloaded, and among the cheerful racket were men and women, some come straight from their looms or mules, and in great danger of being run down if not by the waggons then by the porters who were everywhere, dodging and laughing and chattering, for despite their poverty they were a durable lot.

A hurrying multitude all going in the same direction towards the market where the bargains lay. But not just bargains, for there were stalls on which gingerbread men were sold, and lemonade, baked potatoes, onion pies, muffins and all sorts of delicacies way beyond the pocket of the ordinary working man. They pushed and jostled, stopping to stare at corn plasters and painted buckets, at bootlaces and delicate china figurines and the three girls were enchanted, for though they had been here before they had never had a few bob rattling in their pocket. Or rather their Nancy's pocket!

It was at the market that many of the Irish found employment. One-quarter of the stall holders were Catholic and so were a large number of porters and labourers, and the hordes of street sellers and hawkers trading on the market's margins. It was to one of these that the Brody girls went.

It was Saturday afternoon and it seemed the whole of Angel Meadow, Strangeways and New Town were intent on making the most of the bargains to be had as the day drew on. The "Begorra"s and "to be sure"s were thick on the air and one might have been forgiven for thinking that the market stood in the middle of Dublin or Belfast. The crowds, the women in shawls, aprons and clogs, the men in velveteen jackets, homespun waistcoats and fustian trousers, were on the whole good-natured, turning over the goods for sale with a keen hand and eye, for every penny had to be made to count. The second-hand clothing stall was busy and the girls, Nancy towing the other two behind her, elbowed their way to the front. She would not, naturally, buy the first garment on offer. She meant to have a good look round first, for this was not the only second-hand clothing stall, glorying in the wonder of having money in her pocket to buy what she thought was good value. She had never done it before. Her mam had brought stuff home, carelessly telling them to "get yerself inter this or that", the remarks mostly directed at Nancy, for Mary wore what Nancy cast off and Rose wore what Mary cast off!

The stall holder was beginning to get irritable, for the tall bonny girl had fingered every garment on her stall, holding them up and then casting them down with a contemptuous air as though she were used to better than this.

"Holy Mother o' God, why didn't yer say it was high fashion yer were wantin', mavourneen?" she shouted in high dudgeon.

"'Cos if it is yer'd best get yerself down ter Deansgate. I've nowt in from Paris just now," winking at the rest of her customers and getting a round of laughter.

"I'm lookin' fer quality an' value," Nancy said in that high-falutin' tone she was beginning to adopt, or so their Rosie said. Ever since Mam went Nancy had taken to her role as protector of the family with great seriousness and in some ways it had gone to her head. She was proud of what they had achieved in such a short time and her imperiously held head and disdainful glances at those who couldn't get off their bums and do the same were getting her talked about.

At last she settled on three serviceable grey skirts, hardly worn, the stall holder told her, three bodices and three warm shawls. Their clogs would have to do this winter, though she did go mad and buy three pairs of warm woollen stockings which, she warned them, must be taken off the minute they got to their mules or the oil would ruin them.

They bought tripe and onions, a whole rabbit, unskinned, carrots and potatoes, all going cheap as the day drew to a close, and a ham bone with a fair amount of ham still on it which, when boiled with the vegetables, would make a nourishing pan of soup.

They idled their way through the crowds, stopping at every stall to pick over the goods on sale and it was then that Nancy's sensible practicality deserted her for several minutes and she reverted to the child she really was. There was a stall that sold ribbons and hairbrushes, combs and fans and stockings, pretty if soiled parasols, cheap soap and cheaper perfumes and, as though they were fastened together by an invisible thread, which in a way they were, the three little girls stopped.

"Come along, step up an' 'ave a look. Three pretty girls like youse'll be wantin' a ribbon in yer 'air, ter be sure," the old woman behind the stall cackled. "An' would yer look at me soap. Rose or jasmine, whatever yer fancy an' fresh made by me own 'ands this very day. Now tell me that don't smell lovely," and they could not argue with her. It did indeed smell lovely and the thought of warming the water by the fire and lathering themselves from head to toe with this magical aroma was too much for Nancy who couldn't get enough of being clean. Of smelling as she had now begun to notice her workmates did not, of knowing that comforting and comfortable feeling of freshness when she had washed herself. Mary and Rose, left to themselves, would have slipped back into their old ways if she'd let them but she, now that she had a few pennies to spare, so to speak, meant never to be dirty or stinking again.

She bought a bar of what the old woman called incongruously "Rosebud soap" and a hairbrush. She was tempted by the ribbons. Such lovely colours of scarlet and emerald and bright blue and though Rose and Mary both begged for one, Rose turning sullen when she was refused, she would not give in. And to regain her sense of purpose and practicality, she purchased a big bar of washing soap for their clothes which she meant to put in to soak, as Annie had advised her, this very night and hang to dry in the upstairs room.

The rent of the low, two-roomed, back-to-back cottage was two and sixpence, and thanks to Nancy, learning to be a good manager and already a sensible girl, they not only eked out a living, but began to put a farthing here, a halfpenny there, to one side. Nobody thought to question what three young girls were doing living alone, certainly not the landlord who came to collect his rent each week. So long as his money was in his hand he didn't care who put it there. He did notice that the eldest was growing into a real bonny lass with a cloud of tight brown curls and the loveliest golden eyes he'd only ever seen on a cat, but when he tried to put a hand on her she acted like a bloody cat an' all, clawing his hand away and spitting, threatening to tell her Sunday school teacher if he touched her again.

As the year ran on and became two, then three, he also noticed that the appearance not only of the three girls but of their home was considerably improved. Strips of matting were laid on the uneven floor and a chair arrived to match the one already in place by the fireside. A battered settle big enough only for one person, and then a cupboard, the open door revealing a shining assortment of plates and dishes, while beneath it were suspended on hooks a set of skillets, stewpans and assorted cooking and household utensils. A highly glazed teatray which reflected the firelight and even a couple of tiny prints on the freshly whitewashed walls. A clock, a little Dutch machine with a busy pendulum swinging openly and candidly to the right of the fireplace. There was a small mirror, a barrel or two containing meal and flour, a row of smoke-browned little earthenware ornaments and a muslin window-screen to replace the torn rags that had been good enough for Kitty Brody, and in the window bottom a row of cheerful geraniums in cracked pots. It was so attractive, cheerful and warm he began to wonder if it was time he put his rent up.

When he mentioned this carefully to the eldest girl she turned on him like a tiger.

"You do an' we're off," she told him fiercely. "Yer not the only landlord in Angel Meadow and this in't the only cottage. We could get decent lodgin's in Angel Street fer less than we give you, so think on. It's only our stuff what makes it look nice an' it'd go wi' us. Just because we're not as bloody feckless as the rest and have done the place up a bit don't mean yer can charge us more than the rest o' Church Court. Me an' me sisters've worked hard fer this so stick that on't wall an' dance round it. We're not payin' another penny. Now, here's yer money an' good-day to yer."

The reference to her Sunday school teacher was the absolute truth. That's where they went every Sunday, the Brody girls. To Sunday school. Not from any particular desire to learn about religion, prayers or a thirst for any other high moral knowledge but because Nancy insisted upon it.

"Why can't we go to Peel Park like the others?" Rosie would demand. "There's a band there on Sundays, Marie Finnigan told me. She's goin' wi' their Niall an' Gregory—"

"Can Marie Finnigan read?" Nancy interrupted curtly. She was busy at the task of whitewashing the ceiling – since she was the tallest – in her fierce determination to rid the cottage of the swarming creatures that had decorated its walls for as long as she could remember and when she'd done she meant to start on the upstairs. Mary was busy on the other side of the room, her tongue between her teeth, her eyes narrowed, as she did a tricky bit round the window frame. They had moved all their bits and pieces to the wall at the back of the room and when they had finished this side would move it all again and paint the rest.

"Well then!"

"Well then, what?" Rosie Brody was more aggressive than Mary, who would always docilely do as Nancy bid her. Their Rosie had a lot of her father in her, Irish and truculent with it, inclined to be volatile now that she had enough to eat, and ready to argue about everything, from whose turn it was to do the cooking to her reluctance to spend every waking hour when they weren't at the mill cleaning the sodding cottage, as she put it. Was it really necessary to scrub the floor so often, she would whine, and the windows already shone like diamonds. Not that she'd ever seen a diamond nor expected to but it would have been nice to have just one day a week when they weren't either at their looms or on their knees in the cottage.

"How many times do I have to tell yer that unless we can read an' write we'll end up like Mam. D'yer want that? D'yer want ter wed some chap like we see at Monarch an' have a bairn every year. Do yer? Mam was wed at sixteen, she told me once, and had eleven children. She was only in her early thirties, I suppose when she . . . when she left. If she was with us now in the end we'd have had her ter support and supply her with her gin but she's not so I mean ter get on somehow an' I'm takin' you two wi' me whether you like it or not, so shut yer gob, our Rose. An' that's why we're goin' ter Sunday school each week an' not ter Peel Park." Her voice softened, for she knew she drove her sisters hard, but what else could she do? She had this horror hanging over her, a picture of her mam lying on the kitchen floor with a man's bum pumping away at her and the nightmare of it happening to her or their Rose and Mary drove her on and on and she knew she would not escape it until she had . . . Well, she didn't really know, for Nancy Brody had no conception of what was beyond Angel Meadow but whatever it was it must be better than her mam had had. And she meant to find it.

"I know we have ter sit through a lot of old rubbish about God an' Jesus, our Rosie, and how he said ter bring all the little children to him, if yer can believe such a thing, but if that's the price we have ter pay then we'll pay it. Now get on with that wall. There's upstairs to do yet."

4

Mick O'Rourke was seventeen years old, a tall, powerfully built lad, light on his feet, which he had learned in the prize-fighting ring. He was a great favourite with the opposite sex and a porter at Smithfield Market. He was second-generation Irish, as were fifteen per cent of the population of Manchester, with a great deal of cheek and charm. From the day he first noticed Nancy Brody when she was fourteen years old, as a *female* and not just a kid who lived in the same street as himself, he wanted her. You got "nowt for nowt" in this world, though this did not always apply to handsome Mick, so he began to put himself out to be helpful to her.

He had forgotten that years ago, before her mam disappeared, he had found and mended a bucket for the Brody family, an old thing with a hole in it, rusty and seemingly beyond redemption but with a bit of metal cut from a pipe, a smear of glue and some ingenuity, of which he was not short, he had put it right.

It was the day of the Whit Walks. She was passing his mam's house, she and her sisters, for it seemed they went nowhere without one another, or so his mam said, with that sneer in her voice that appeared when she spoke of "Lady Muck" as she had christened Nancy Brody.

He saw her hat first, a pretty thing made of straw with flowers on it – he didn't know what sort – bobbing along just above the level of the windowsill, and was immediately intrigued. Who, in Church Court, owned a straw hat with flowers on it? he asked himself, and when he went to the door to investigate he was in time to see three straight backs, three gracefully swinging skirts, with three pairs of immaculately polished boots twinkling beneath them, walking away from him towards Angel Street. She was in the middle, her sisters one on either side of her and it was a measure of the fascination with which the street's occupants regarded them that every last one of them fell silent.

As she felt their eyes on her Nancy Brody lifted her bonnet even higher. She had made it herself; well, most of it, having found it, a simple, unadorned and somewhat battered pancake at the bottom of a pile of old rags on Mrs Beasley's stall one Saturday afternoon. Nancy and Mrs Beasley, she of the caustic wit that she had sharpened on Nancy on that first day, were old friends now, old combatants since Nancy had learned to bargain for what she wanted, often bringing the old woman down a farthing or two, which satisfied her enormously. Mrs Beasley admired that. She admired spunk and Nancy Brody had plenty of spunk. In the last five years she and Nancy had formed a sort of mutual respect born of their recognition in one another of a spirited refusal to allow the world to get the better of them. Mrs Beasley, who had kept her stall there ever since Smithfield was amalgamated with other markets in the 1820s, had stood at the same spot in all weathers, sometimes frozen to the marrow, or pelted with icy rain and sleet, sometimes hardly able to keep to her feet in the sweltering, sultry heat which was trapped beneath a pall of smoke in the deep canyons of Manchester during the summer, and she had a feeling the lass would have shaped the same!

She had taken a fancy to the bright-eyed young girl who had a strong vein of common sense and self-preservation in her that Mrs Beasley respected, seeing herself as she had been forty years ago. She began to put to one side bits and pieces she thought the lass might find to her liking, garments that were redeemable or with a bit of decent fabric in them that could be retrieved. Stockings and undergarments, which the sisters now wore without question, boots and bonnets and, with a great deal of ingenuity and a sense of style come from only God knew where, the Brody girls were so well dressed they caused a sensation every Sunday when they set off on their weekly visit to Ashley Road Sunday school.

And that was another thing. They could all three read and write and do sums, even in their head, and, since the opening of the Manchester Free Library in Castlefield, it was not uncommon to see the Brody girls stepping out along

Church Court with books borrowed from the library under their arms. Why in the name of the Holy Mother they still continued to live in Church Court, Mrs O'Rourke said to Mrs Murphy, who sported her usual Saturday night "shiner", she couldn't think, for with their hoity-toity, "we're better than the rest of you" attitude, it was a bloody wonder to her why they hadn't moved over to Higher Broughton by now.

They only wore their best frocks and boots on a Sunday, for on six days a week they laboured at Monarch Mill and on those days, except for their exceptional good looks, their well-fed appearance of health and cleanliness, they were no different to their fellow workers. Plain, short cotton skirts and sleeveless bodices, well-mended clogs, with woollen stockings and a warm shawl for winter. Their hair was neatly plaited, their only claim to singularity being the bright knot of ribbons each wore at the end of her plait.

They all three had a pair of mules of their own now and they were bringing home between them sometimes as much as two pounds a week. Though Annie still worked beside them she had aged and slowed down and all three had far outstripped her, spinning more yarn between them than any five other girls put together. They were quick, nimble-fingered, fleet of foot, clear-headed, their improved health giving them a head start on their contemporaries. They never stopped except when the engine did, walking the miles up and down the length of their machines, each with a piecer but sharing a scavenger to keep the spinning frames singing, if not exactly sweetly, then in a steady, rhythmic melody of outpouring yarn.

Mick O'Rourke leaned his broad shoulder against the door frame and watched her retreating back, quite pole-axed, it seemed, which was totally unlike his usual brash confidence when faced with a pretty girl. He had the wit, the cheek, the charm, the fluent tongue of his Irish forebears, and was never lost for a word. Put him beside a likely girl and within minutes she would be peeping up shyly, or boldly, whatever her nature, into his laughing face, convinced, as he meant her to be, that she was the very girl for him. Indeed that he had been swept off his feet by her loveliness and if she did not return his feelings he would be mortally wounded. He'd kissed the blarney stone, right enough, his mam was fond of saying, though he had been born right here in Angel Meadow and had never cast eyes on the green of Ireland nor indeed the stretch of water that had brought his grandparents to Liverpool many years ago.

Nancy turned her head to speak to her sister and in a shaft of sunlight which somehow found its way over the end cottage, he saw her long eyelashes fall and rise in a lovely slow, sensual movement, though if questioned he could not have admitted to knowing the word, or its meaning. Her profile moved in a smile, her lips curved and the skin of her clear jaw and throat were like the petals on a flower he had seen once in Philips Park when he was sparking a lass from over Holt Town way. They had a sort of house made from glass at the park, hot and moist and the girl – he couldn't even remember her name – had been led inside quite unable to resist him and had even allowed him to put his hand up her skirt to the equally hot and moist centre of her before she took fright. The creamy blossom he had noticed there, despite his teeth gritting in frustration, had been exactly the colour and texture of Nancy Brody's skin.

He came out of his trance and began to function, leaping to snatch his jacket and cap from a hook at the back of the door, shouting to his mam that he was off.

"Where yer goin', darlin'?" she shrieked from the dark back regions of the cottage.

"I dunno. There'll be plenty ter see in town, so there will, an' I might 'ave a look at Whit Walks."

"But it's not until Friday, our Micky."

"Them's Catholic walks on Friday, Mam. I've a fancy ter 'ave a look at Proddys'."

"Eeh, Mick O'Rourke, yer never!" As she came towards him she crossed herself apprehensively as though he had told her he was off to defile the sacred cross at St Luke's Church in St George's Road. She went to the door, following his progress down the narrow street, as did every man lolling against the wall having a peaceful smoke, every woman leaning in her doorway having an enjoyable gossip with next door and every child screaming and shrieking and throwing clumps of some unidentified filth at a cornered cat. They all stopped whatever they were doing to stare and the cat thankfully made its escape.

Eileen O'Rourke's mouth thinned vengefully when she saw who it was her son was chasing after, then she turned away, shrugging, beginning to smile, for if her Mick, who was as randy as once his father had been, thought he'd a chance of getting into that one's drawers he was sadly mistaken. His cock'd fall off before Nancy Brody gave in!

"Nancy . . . aay, Nancy, 'old on, will yer?" Mick shouted, throwing his cap to the back of his thick, chocolate-coloured curls and shrugging into his jacket. He straightened his red, spotted neckerchief against his brown throat and his lips curled up in a devastatingly white smile.

The three girls stopped and turned and when she saw who it was Nancy smiled too, which she wouldn't have done for any other lad, for if he had forgotten the bucket, she hadn't. Mick had only been ten or eleven at the time and she a skinny girl three years younger but his careless kindness to her mam had impressed her immeasurably. She had often wondered what they would have done in the early days without that bucket. It was all very well having a tap at the corner of Church Court with the good water the Manchester Municipal Council provided pouring from it, but if you'd got nothing to put it in what was the use of it? It had been a life-saver that bucket and was still in daily use despite their improved situation in life.

"Mornin', Mick," she said politely. "Lovely day."

"I dunno about the day bein' lovely, Nancy Brody, but to be sure I never saw a lovelier sight than the three o' yer. I've lived in this 'ere street all me life an' there's many a bonny Irish lass workin' on the market, but I swear by the Holy Mother I've never seen such a bevy o' beauties as the Brody girls."

He beamed at them with great good humour, at his best beneath their admiring gaze. He'd no idea how old they were, but they were pretty and smiling, all three of them and that was enough for Mick. She, the one he had his eye on, was tall with a fine slender figure but with a pair of full tits on her, high and round and perky, just as he liked them, and the sooner he charmed their owner the sooner they'd be in his hands. He meant to begin at once.

"Get away wi' you, Mick," Nancy said, but as easy and friendly as anything, just as though they had been talking together only the day before, which Mick took to be a good sign. The other two said nothing, both shy, he thought, which was not how he liked his women. Nancy wasn't, thank the Holy Mother. She regarded him steadily, candidly and his heart leap-frogged in his chest. She really was a looker. Her saucy hat clung to her mass of hair which rioted in lovely profusion about her head. She'd fastened the tight curls back with a knot of scarlet ribbon and from the nape of her neck it hung, or rather cascaded, down her back to her waist. He had an urgent desire to put his hands in it, for it was a warm, shining brown with streaks of gold and honey threaded through it, a colour that matched her eyes. He'd never seen anything like it before, so accustomed was he to the lank and often verminous locks of the girls with whom he consorted.

He swallowed convulsively, for in that fraction of a moment he was overcome by the strange emotion she had so suddenly aroused in him. There was trust in her eyes and a soft liking, with none of the coquettish posturing he had found in other lasses and for an incredible moment he felt the need to be gentle with her, to treat her as he would a decent Catholic girl towards whom he had honourable intentions, then he shook himself and grinned impudently.

"An' where are the three o' yer off to, then, an' lookin' so smart about it? To be sure I swear the good Queen up in London isn't half so fine as the Brody sisters."

Both Mary and Rosie preened and smiled at him, their eyes wide and wondering, then glanced at each other, smoothing down the fullness of their grey cotton skirts, but Nancy continued to regard him steadily, her eyes clear and without guile.

"We're off ter see the Whit Walks, Mick." She stretched her neck to look up at the patch of blue sky above, blue today because it was Whit Monday and the mills were closed. Smoke did not pour from the chimneys and the sunlight seemed the more golden for it, and the sky a more serene blue, like forget-me-nots. "It starts from St Ann's Square so me an' our Mary an' Rose thought we'd walk over, it bein' such a lovely day. They say there'll be over five thousand children taking part. Then there's teachers an' all the bigwigs in their top hats an' finery, an' their wives. We want to have a look at the fashions, don't we?" turning to smile at her sisters, speaking in the careful way she was cultivating and which so incensed Eileen O'Rourke.

"I were wonderin' why yer not walking yerselves. Me mam tells me the three of yer go ter Sunday school in Ashley Road. Is that right?" Not that he'd taken any notice of his mam's ramblings. Went in one ear and out the other but this bit of information seemed to have lodged in his brain and the words came out of it.

"Yes, we went for five years. We can all read an' write." Her pride in their achievement was immense and so it should be, for they were the only people in Church Court, indeed probably in Angel Meadow, who could. "Mrs Edwards – she was our teacher – wanted us ter become Sunday school teachers ourselves but . . . well, we didn't go fer . . . well, *God* or anything like that. He's not done much fer us nor me mam so why should we do anything for Him? What we've got we've got fer ourselves so we've stopped going now."

She made no bones of the fact that they had attended Sunday school for one reason only and now that that was achieved and the school was of no further use to her she was finished with it. She had better things to do with her life than waste it on other folk.

"She was always sayin' – Mrs Edwards – we'd to broaden our horizons and I reckon we've broadened them enough. Time to move on now," she ended briskly.

"An' what might that mean, Nancy Brody, broaden yer 'orizons?" Mick grinned amiably, for what did he care? His come day-go day life suited him down to the ground and his lack of education mattered to him not at all. He did a bit of bare-knuckle prize fighting, earning a purse or two, since he was young, strong and healthy and there were more than enough young women in the world who were delighted with his smooth tongue and rough lovemaking. He liked nothing better than a night drinking and betting on the cock fights that took place in the area. The life of a man, a *real* man and that was Mick O'Rourke and he saw no reason to change it, or, as Nancy had, to better himself. In his opinion he was good enough!

For a moment Nancy looked downcast. That this handsome young man who was studying her with a warmth she found somewhat disconcerting should be so poorly educated – could he not read? she wondered, saddened by the thought – that he did not know the meaning of broadening your horizons, quite horrified her. Education was more and more readily available to everyone now, through Sunday schools and the Mechanics Institute, one of which had opened in Miles Platting quite recently, just off Oldham Road, no more than a brisk walk from Angel Meadow. And mill owners were now compelled to supply two hours' education each day to all children employed in their mills, but it seemed Mick O'Rourke could see no advantage in it. She tried to explain.

"Well, it means to make use of everything that comes your way. Not to waste it. To notice things, to read about things and to learn from them. That's what we mean to do, isn't it, girls? You must see what's beyond the boundaries of your life, of what yer mam an' dad did," she went on seriously, quite spellbound by the incredible blue of his merry, twinkling eyes. "Perhaps yer didn't know but there's ter be an Arts Treasures Exhibition opened in Old Trafford this month an' we mean ter go and see it. I read that there'll be paintings by all the famous painters. Constable and Turner and Millais, which I've seen in books at the library, are going to be displayed there so this is our chance ter see them. That's broadening your horizons." Her eyes shone and her face had become pink with excitement and Mick O'Rourke was mesmerised by her.

"Yer don't say! Well I never, but what about fun, Nancy Brody? Where does that come in?"

"Fun?" Nancy looked mystified.

"Aye, a good laugh."

"A good laugh?"

"Aw, come on, lass, yer know what a good laugh is, though it don't seem ter me you do much of it." He'd plainly had enough of this stuff about paintings and such, his manner said, and if they stuck with him he'd show them what a good time was. "What yer gonner do when yer've seen the walks, eeh?" His grin was infectious and Mary and Rose turned to look at their Nancy in hopeful anticipation. By the standards of the day, though they were unaware of it, all three were relatively well educated. They had learned well, since they were bright and intelligent. A plain education, to be sure, with no French or music or art but for the past four years, ever since they had understood the written word, they had been reading whatever the gentleman at the free library recommended to them. Some of the books were dull, hard to get through, educational instead of entertaining, but enlightening to the three girls, revealing another world beyond Angel Meadow. Others were light, hugely enjoyable like *David Copperfield* and *Martin Chuzzlewit*, making their labours over the past five years worth every struggle.

But it was their Nancy who kept them at it. They did not join the other children in street games. They did not move across their own doorstep when they got home from the mill at night, so fun was a mystery to them. They were well nourished, warmly clad, well shod, and upstairs, hidden behind the loose brick, was a growing hoard of farthings, halfpennies, pennies, sixpences, even whole shillings, and when the time was right they knew their sister had plans for it. They did not know what. They, and she, were satisfied with what they had at the moment. It was enough for now. Nancy had only to say, "We don't want to end up like Mam, do we?" at the first hint of rebellion and it was suppressed before it had hardly begun.

"What about Belle Vue?" he asked them seductively.

"What about it?" Nancy looked wary.

"There's a zoo and pleasure gardens, they do say an' I've a fancy ter see 'em. What about you?" He raised his eyebrows questioningly and his smile deepened.

Nancy's vanished. She would dearly love to go, for who hadn't heard of the wonders of Belle Vue but it would mean spending money on something that would not be of value to them. She was so set on her course and the part her sisters were to play in it she could not afford to fritter away good money on pleasure gardens and zoos. The three of them, in the eyes of the folk who lolled in the sunshine on the doorsteps and against the damp and crumbling walls of Church Court and indeed all the alleys and streets that cobwebbed Angel Meadow, were as well dressed as they were sure the "quality" in Higher Broughton and beyond were. But Nancy knew better. She had studied the newspapers and periodicals displayed in the reading-room at the library that had advertisements for the latest fashions in ladies' clothing, and she was aware that she and her sisters were, in comparison to the very quality she so admired, meanly, drably dressed. They looked what they were: working girls. Worse: slum girls who worked in a cotton mill, but she intended to remedy that which meant every bloody farthing the Brody girls earned was spoken for and certainly not to be chucked away on the likes of roundabouts and sideshows and hurdy-gurdies.

Her sisters watched her avidly, their eyes bright with longing and she felt herself weaken. They were so much better off than their neighbours. In fact they were rich in comparison but, as Mick said, there was not much fun in their lives. They ate well but there was little laughter in their diet. They knew so much more than their neighbours but they were ignorant of games. They were warm and secure, thanks to her thrifty direction and their own hard work, but they got little pleasure, enjoyment, simple childish amusement out of the hard life they led. Still, it could not be helped. She must stick to her plan and so must they if the Brody girls were to amount to anything.

She was beginning to shake her head. Mary looked as though she were about to cry and Rosie's bottom lip stuck out mutinously. They had been elated earlier in the day at the thought of walking, with the rest of the sightseers, over to St Ann's Square to watch the procession set out from there to Collegiate Church. A day off in the sunshine. A chance to cast off their mill-girl image and wear the plain but decent dresses they and their Nancy had contrived for them, to tie on their bright ribbons – for only Nancy had a bonnet – and go and enjoy the day with the rest of Manchester; but now, with a few silky words, Mick O'Rourke had spoiled it for them by presenting them with something better that they could not have.

"It's free ter get in," he offered casually. His eyes twinkled impishly, innocently, giving the impression that he was a hell of a decent fellow who wanted nothing more than to offer them an enjoyable outing.

"Oh, Nancy, please, can us go? It'll cost nowt." Rose reverted to the speech of her early childhood in her breathless excitement and for a moment Nancy felt a spurt of irritation. She tried so hard to make her sister speak grammatically in readiness for their future and now here was this cheeky Irish Paddy undoing all her work, turning their heads and leading them to God knows what with his blandishments – and she knew what that word meant an' all, for she'd looked it up in the dictionary at the library!

"Please, Nancy, we promise not ter ask fer owt. Just let's go an' see th'animals. I've never clapped eyes on an elephant, not in't flesh, nor a giraffe, nor a tiger nor a—"

"Yes, yes, I 'eard yer, our Mary." Nancy also lost her grip on the English language in her confusion and, leaning indolently with one shoulder against the cottage wall end, his hands in his pockets, his eyes dancing with mischief, Mick O'Rourke watched the first crack appear in Nancy Brody's solid façade of the respectability she craved. The first small deviation from the fierce ambition that burned in her, the flames consuming her since the night she had realised that her mam would never return. That whatever was to happen in the lives of the Brody girls was to be achieved only by *her* efforts.

"I'll treat yer to a ride on summat, acushla," Mick said lazily. "Ter be sure 'tis a sorry day when Mick O'Rourke can't put 'is 'and in 'is pocket ter treat a pretty lass like yerselves. *Three* pretty lasses like yerselves." He jingled the coins in his pocket, come from the purse he had won only last night in a local prize fight.

Nancy turned on him like a vixen defending her cubs. Her eyes flashed great gold-shot lights and her face flooded with the red of her indignation. Laughingly he stepped away from her, his hands held up in a pretence of terror as she thrust her face into his.

"Yer'll do no such thing, Mick O'Rourke," she hissed. "The Brodys take charity from no one, d'yer 'ear? If there's any rides ter be 'ad then we'll pay for 'em usselves. Is that clear?"

She did not at that moment realise that without meaning to and against her will she had committed herself to Mick's plans for them, nor did she see the gleam of satisfaction in his blue Irish eyes.

"Whatever yer say, Miss Brody." His voice was mocking. "Now then, let's go an' see if the Proddy walks are as good as t' Catholic ones. But I'll not argue wi' yer over it, acushla, or I might get me 'ead bit off. See, will yer not tekk me arm? No . . . Then 'ow about you – Rosie, is it?"

And Nancy had no choice but to trail at the back of Mick O'Rourke who set off along Angel Street in the direction of St George's Road and St Ann's Square with one of her sisters, flushed and giddy with joy, on each arm. He was the most exasperating man she had ever met and in her job she came across a few who had been unwise enough to take on Nancy Brody. Though she was only fourteen – she could stand up to the best, or worst of them, with a reputation for having a tongue on her like a rattlesnake. She'd a way with words, words they'd never heard before, which tied them up in knots and up to now she'd not met one who could get the better of her.

On the walk from Angel Meadow to St Ann's Square Mick

kept turning back to look over his shoulder at her, beaming in great good humour, raising his eyebrows and winking as though to enquire of her that surely she could only agree that this was great fun.

And it was. At the end of it when, after he had seen them gallantly to their front door – not attempting to come in, for Mick knew how to play this game – they all agreed, sighing, that it had been perfect. The sun shone from a cloudless blue sky. They were jostled cheerfully by the milling crowds who were all going in the same direction, down Shude Hill and cutting through the packed and narrow streets to St Ann's Square. There were eight statutory holidays in England, and Whit Monday was one of them and the whole working population of Manchester meant to make the most of it. Whit week was the greatest jubilee of all, enjoyed by them all, and though the great majority of them could afford no other means of transport than their own two feet, they were determined to see as much of it as they could. There were fairs and plays and concerts, cock fights and prize fights. Businesses came to a standstill and pleasure reigned; in fact it got out of hand at times which was why the churches had tried to reclaim the masses with the organised processions of Whit week.

But the street entertainers were not to be outdone. Bands marched and blew and banged, ballad singers set up on street corners and street sellers screeched their wares, their voices drowned by the cacophony. Men and women, and even children, shouted and laughed and vanished into taverns together, tottering out later on unstable legs to sample the next enjoyment. From byways and alleys and back streets the crowds erupted so that cabs were forced to drive at a snail's pace through the throng, the cab drivers shouting and swearing at them to get out from under the horses' lethal hooves.

But the greatest wonder of all began when they had struggled back along Market Street and London Road after watching the procession. They strode out to the outskirts of the city to Hyde Road and the long country walk to Belle Vue Gardens. The fields on either side of the road were as much a marvel to the Brody girls, at least Nancy thought so, as anything they had seen, or were about to see that day, for they had never before walked beyond the urban sprawl of Manchester. It was May and the hawthorn hedges exploded with blossom, the meadows were vivid with the emerald of new grass and the yellow of cowslips. There were marsh marigolds and lady's-smock hanging over the small stream that ran in a ditch beneath the hedge bordering the road, though of course the sisters did not know the names of the plants just then but Nancy meant to learn them, just as she learned about everything that interested her. There were rows of books about plants on the library shelves. They heard the call of the cuckoo for the first time and watched as a pair of white-throated birds chased each other through the branches of a tree and were enchanted when a rabbit scampered across the road. Their continual halts to see this or that, to listen to the birds or inspect a hedgehog curled up in the grass, began to annoy Mick who had no interest in such things, but at last they reached the great raucous blast of the thirty-six acres that made up Belle Vue Gardens and Zoo.

They got lost in the maze, shrieking with pretended fear, for they knew Mick would find them, watched him on the bowling green and the firing range, applauding his prowess while he strutted and preened like a peacock. They strolled across the deer park, Mary and Rose confiding that they hoped they met no deer, for might they not be dangerous beasts with those fierce horns? Antlers, Nancy told them primly, for she liked to have things right. Really, they said, without interest.

There was a brass band and a licensed dancing saloon but though Nancy had been overruled on her stand against allowing Mick to pay for things, she put her foot down on this, though Mick did his best to persuade her, for he did so want to get her into his arms! They went to the tearooms instead and had tea and sticky buns which she insisted on paying for though the cost horrified her. They saw the elephants, the giraffes and monkeys and Rosie was taken up before Mick on a handsome horse on the merry-go-round, much to her delight.

It was dark as they walked the last weary mile home. They were all quiet, even the irrepressible Irishman and Nancy allowed it when he took her hand and put it in the crook of his arm. He felt he had made good progress today in the seduction of Nancy Brody.

5

Nobody was more surprised than Annie Wilson when Nancy confided to her that she and her sisters were to leave Monarch at the end of May.

"Leavin'? What for?" Annie's pallid, good-natured face registered her amazement. Her jaw dropped and her dismay was so strong she allowed her machine to falter and a thread to break.

"Oh, bloody 'ell," she cried, "see what yer made me do now, yer daft beggar. 'Ere, Elsie," to her little piecer, "see ter that thread, will yer, an' give over natterin' ter everyone what passes by," her consternation driving her to blame the child unfairly for her own mistake.

"I'll tell you later, Annie, at breakfast."

They sat in a corner of the yard on a pile of sacking, the end of May sunshine which had continued all the month falling on their white-speckled heads and shoulders, sipping their tea and eating their bread and cold bacon side by side. A few yards away Mary and Rose were gossiping with some other younger girls and Annie, who said nothing, of course, since it was her belief that it was best to keep your trap shut over what didn't concern you, believed that it was because of the way Nancy behaved that they converged towards girls younger than themselves. Nancy had got into the way of treating them as though they were still children, which, Annie supposed, in an ideal world they would be, and so, the more childish or light-minded their co-workers tended to be the more Nancy's sisters were attracted to them. They giggled and whispered, as young girls will, casting slant-eyed looks at the lads and young men with no thought for the future, which was Nancy's consideration, gathering for themselves a great deal of male attention, for they were, along with Nancy, the bonniest lasses in the mill. Apart from their feet and ankles they were as clean and neat as a newly wound bobbin of yarn. Their plaited hair was much copied now by the young girls who pleaded to be shown how to do theirs the same way, but though they did their best their lank and greasy locks looked nothing like the shining, curling glory of the Brody girls. Nancy's sisters were thirteen and twelve but already the lads were flocking and Nancy would have to watch them, for they hadn't half, nay a quarter, of the sound common sense she had. Easily led they would be, preening over a bit of flattery and though Nancy looked after them like a mother hen with a couple of chicks she'd have to have eyes in the back of her head where their Rose was concerned.

"Now then, my lass, what's all this about yer leavin' Monarch? Yer can't be serious. You an' yer sisters are't best spinners in't mill. I wouldn't say this ter anyone else but yer even better 'n me." She leaned against Nancy's shoulder and parted her lips in an almost toothless smile. "Now then, chuck, that's sayin' summat so think on an' keep it ter yersen. But, lass, yer can't leave," she went on in a more serious vein. "Yer well thought of by't gaffer an' yer well paid, the three on yer. They'd be right sorry ter see yer go an' so would I. An' what I can't fathom is why? 'Ave yer got a better job then?"

She leaned forward to peer into Nancy's lowered face as though the secret of it all lay there but Nancy sighed and shook her head.

"No, not really."

"Well then, what's ter do? Is someone botherin' yer?" meaning a man, of course, for Annie had seen the way they watched the tall, straight-backed, gracefully swinging stride of Nancy Brody as she walked by, head up, that tempting, thrusting bosom of hers catching every male eye in the mill.

"No, and if there was I would soon deal with it, you know that," Nancy answered scornfully, her eyes narrowed and gleaming.

"Aye, I suppose so, lass. Well then . . . ?" Annie waited while Nancy drew breath and sorted out her thoughts. She had a crust of bread in her hand which she crumbled to bits then threw them to a couple of sparrows pecking hopefully at the cobbles.

"Well . . . ?" Annie prompted again.

"There's nowhere to go here, Annie."

"Eeh, what can yer mean? Nowhere ter go."

"If I lived to be fifty I'd never get any further than a spinning frame."

"I'm over forty, I reckon . . ."

"There you are then."

". . . an' I've bin at that same pair o' mules since I were ten." Annie's voice was sad and yet not humble.

"You see what I mean, Annie," Nancy cried. "Oh, I'm not sniffing at what you've achieved. You've worked hard and are well respected and that's a wonderful accomplishment. To be well thought of. To have pride in yourself."

"Aay, 'old on, lass. Anyone'd think I'd bin made Lord Mayor o' Manchester."

Nancy laughed but there was a break in her voice. Her face was like marble with the intensity of her feelings and without being aware of it she took Annie's old, calloused hand between her own, which were equally calloused, but young, strong, enduring.

"It's not enough for me, Annie. I want to get on. I want to be someone. I don't want to wait until I'm forty to have Mr Hayes tell me what a loyal and conscientious worker I've been."

"No chance o' that, chuck. Some lad'll snap yer up an' wed yer an' before yer know it—"

"That'd be worse still, Annie, don't you see?" Nancy's voice had dropped so that it could barely be heard. She looked about her at the busy yard. Men in soiled cotton shirts and trousers, sprawled on the cobbles or lolled against the high wall surrounding it, smoking their pipes, most of them eyeing the lasses who tossed their heads and fluttered their sparse eyelashes in a show of coquetry. Most would be married before they reached seventeen and had no greater future than a child every year and a husband who spent his hard-earned wage in the beer house and probably gave her a good hiding if she objected.

"My mam was wed at sixteen, or at least she said she was but who knows. My pa ran off and she took to the streets."

"Eeh, lass, I didn't know. I'm that sorry."

"When she vanished a few years back I swore I'd be no man's wife, at least one of these men," looking about her at those in the yard, "and no man's whore. I'm going to be independent, respectable. I'm going to get on somehow and make a success of what I do and the only thing I know is cotton and the dozens of industries that come from it. I've read books, Annie. I've kept me eyes and ears open while I've been here and I know the time's come for us to move on. I know how to spin cotton. I've watched it right from the blow-room where the bales are opened and the raw cotton cleaned. I've stood in the combing-room and studied what goes on there and then I've spun what comes out of it on my frames. I've watched the winding, the knitting, the warping, the sizing and then the weaving and I reckon if I was asked to I could do the lot. There's only 'making up' left. I know a bit of decent cloth when I see it, Annie, and I'm going to put it to good use. It won't be easy. I don't know how our Mary and Rose'll take to it but I've made my mind up."

"Ter do what, Nancy?"

"As I said all I need now is to learn how to make up. To use a sewing-machine and make shirts, trousers, baby things, anything. Value for money for working-class folk to begin with. Good stuff but cheap."

"Eeh, lass." Annie was clearly flabbergasted. "I'm fair speechless. I can't tekk it in. Glory be ter God, a little lass o' your age tekkin' on them manufacturers from Brown Street 'n' Shude Hill."

"I'm going to take a stall on Smithfield Market, Annie. I know someone who'll help me. One of us can work on it while the others machine whatever we find sells best."

"Eeh, lass," Annie said again, shaking her head, her admiration for Nancy's courage warring with her instincts to tell her not to be so daft. Women like them didn't go into business for themselves. In fact women of any sort, as far as she knew, didn't go into business at all. That was a man's world. Women who were married to wealthy chaps, though how they lived and what they did all day was a mystery to Annie, stayed in their own homes, safe and protected. If you were poor like she was you got wed and had bairns and still worked in the jennygate, leaving the children to drag each other up, those that survived, and when they were big enough they followed you into the mill. Her old man had been a labourer at the market and between them they had managed but it was a hard row to hoe. How much harder for this bright-eyed lass who had no man behind her. Even one as feckless as Annie's had been was better than nowt.

"So where yer goin' then, ter learn all this stuff?"

"It's a shirtmaker's in Brown Street."

Annie was horrified. It might be hard work in the jennygate but compared to those deep cellars in Brown Street and the other streets in Manchester and Salford where making up was done, this was bloody heaven.

"Not in one o' them sweat shops, Nancy," she protested. "They'll work yer ter death there, lass, so I 'eard, an' in the most dreadful conditions. Not fit ter keep pigs in, some o' them places. Cellars, cold an' damp so that the girls are ill all the time."

"I . . . I saw it, Annie, when I went to ask for work and I agree it's not pleasant but we must learn the trade and we won't be there long. We're all quick learners and machinists are better paid than handworkers. As soon as we know all they can teach us, we'll leave and go to one of the factories in Shude Hill and learn how to make undergarments. How to cut out and . . . well, whatever is needed to set up on our own. You can hire a sewing-machine, Annie, did you know that?"

"No." Annie was in a daze, unable to keep up with the sharp flight of Nancy's mind.

"Oh, yes, I've been making enquiries so if I could hire one, or perhaps two, to use at home in the evening making up . . ."

"What about cloth, lass? Where yer gonner get it? They don't sell it by't yard, yer know."

Nancy's face fell. "Mmm, I know that." Then she brightened, unwilling to be put off by Annie's practical question. "I'll get over that when the time comes."

They sat for several long minutes staring bemusedly at the familiar scene before them, not really seeing it, for it was one their eyes happened upon every day of the week. Even though it was breakfast time the yard was busy, for several waggons loaded with bales of raw cotton just come from the southern states of America via Liverpool were in urgent need of attention. The bales weighed five hundred pounds each but the men, young and broad-shouldered, hefted them from the waggons as though they contained nothing more than feathers. They were sweating, their brawny, muscled arms rippling in the smoke-hazed sunshine, glancing across the yard to where the mill lasses were eating their "snap" and though most of the lasses smiled and looked away, then back again in the manner of young girls, the bonniest of the lot did not appear to notice that they were even there, let alone showing themselves off for her.

There was a shout and a sudden clatter at the mill gate and the gatekeeper ran frantically to unlock it. Every morning at six o'oclock it was locked against latecomers and was not opened again until eight o'clock and breakfast time. This was nearly over and those who had been allowed in a few minutes earlier had dispersed and the gates locked behind them again.

A fine chestnut mare cantered through. The animal was, even to their untrained eyes, a thoroughbred, dashing and wild and as good-looking as the man on her back; a beautiful animal with a rippling coat that looked as though it had been polished with a silk scarf. Her hooves crashed on the cobbles in alarm over something only she could see. She rolled her eyes in what seemed to be furious rage and her rider struggled as he strove for dominance. He rode through the crowd of men and women and children, scattering them like a flock of squawking chickens in a farmyard in a way that appeared to imply they either got out of his way or he would ride them down.

"Aay up, 'ere's our lord an' master," Annie muttered. "It's a bloody wonder 'e don't injure someone on that there bloody 'orse of 'is, the great daft sod."

They had both stood up since it was almost time for the engines to be switched on, shaking down their skimpy skirts and smoothing their hair back from their sweaty faces. They watched as the young master, apparently not in complete control of the lively mare, did his best to restrain her lively side-stepping.

"Steady, girl, steady," he was saying, his voice low and soothing, leaning forward to put a gloved hand on the animal's neck but she was young, new to him, new to the vigorous bustle of the yard and she continued to toss her head, to roll her eyes and dance her way sideways across the cobbles.

There were two enormous shire horses, which had just brought in a further waggon load of raw cotton, standing patiently awaiting their turn to be unloaded. Children darted about, so used to the gentle, patient giants they played almost under their bellies, and when one of the horses began to urinate in a long, yellow stream, after an initial cry of dismay, the children stamped and jumped in the warm and widening pool. They wore no shoes as they shrieked with delight at the game then, suddenly noticing them, they stopped and stared at the horse and rider.

There was one child, skinny, as they all were, dirty, as they all were, a little girl with a wild mop of uncombed curls who seemed to be transfixed as the tall mare loomed over her and though the man on her back shouted at the child to get out of the way, she continued to stand in her path, her eyes wide with shock.

Nancy was the nearest, and the quickest, and though she felt herself for several heart-stopping moments to be directly under the mare's belly, she snatched the child sideways, throwing her and herself to the pile of sacking she and Annie had been sitting on. Annie clutched at the child, holding her as she might one of her own, telling her with rough kindness that she was all right and to give over snivelling, for there was no harm done.

Nancy didn't think so. Her pale face had become pink with indignation.

"What in hell's name d'you think you're doing, riding that horse among a group of children. You might have killed that child or any of them, for that matter," she cried accusingly, and everyone in the yard surged forward enthusiastically the better to hear. "If you've no control over the bloody thing you've no right riding it in here where there are young children about. Children under nine years of age, I shouldn't wonder," she spat at him meaningfully. She shaded her eyes with her hand, almost falling over backwards in her attempt to look up into his face several feet above hers. "Have you no consideration for these babies you employ? Not content with endangering their lives in the mill beneath those lethal machines of yours, you ride them down in the mill yard."

She paused for breath as the young man threw his leg over the horse's back and leaped lightly from the stirrup to the ground. The mare was still nervous, inclined to jib at every sound and movement and when he shouted for someone to come and see to her, the reluctance to do so was very marked.

The animal was finally led away by the burly chap who drove one of the waggons and who looked as though he'd stand no nonsense even if the thing had a pedigree as long as her long legs. She went meekly enough, recognising authority, it seemed, her head hanging as though ashamed of her previous precocious behaviour.

They stood face to face. He saw a tall, slender girl with eyes like molten honey. A girl with full breasts, the nipples of which almost pierced the thin, sweat-stained cotton of her sleeveless bodice. Her skin was flushed at the cheekbone, whether with her indignation or perhaps where the sun had tinted it, he didn't know. Her mouth was wide, a ripe tomato red and her teeth were as white and even as his own. Her hair was a rich, gold-streaked brown fastened at the back of her head into a plait as thick as his wrist and yet it still managed to look unconfined. Crisp curls hung into her eyes and about her cheeks so that, like another man before him he felt the strangest need to put up a hand and smooth it back. Her jaw was strong, clenched to a defiant angle and her whole manner spoke of fearlessness, of her need to let him see that she was afraid of no one, and certainly not of him.

She saw a man, hard, tall, lean, arrogant as men of consequence often are, dressed in the manner of a young gentleman of business, his linen immaculate, his dark grey suit and dove grey waistcoat fitting him to perfection. His face was amber-tinted as though he spent a great deal of his time outdoors. His narrowed eyes were a smoky grey with strange flecks of darker grey in them, almost like stripes running from the iris to the outer edge of the pupil. They were surrounded by long, curling lashes. His hair was much the same colour as her own and just as thick but where hers was curly his was straight, spiky, standing up from his forehead where it had been brushed.

He was perhaps half a head taller than she was and in the tick of a second on the gold watch he wore across his waistcoat, less than a second, as their eyes met there was a flare of recognition, not from a previous meeting but of something in them both. So here you are, his spoke to hers. I knew you would come one day, and here you are. Yes, I'm here, the answer followed, then the strange moment was over, forgotten as though it had never been and they were just one furious combatant facing another who was more surprised than annoyed.

"And what the hell is this, then?" he asked, not speaking to the crowd of operatives in the yard, of course. "And who, may I ask, are you?" looking her up and down impudently, clearly amused and not at all put out, even if she was. The child who, to his credit, had aroused genuine alarm in him was forgotten. There was insolence in the way he stood and in the long, lounging line of his body, in the curve of his well-shaped mouth which was inclined to smile, if she would. She was a very lovely girl, his eyes said, though she was clearly maddened by something: was it to do with the child she had thrown, as though she were in great danger, to the pile of sacking? The child – and weren't there always children in his father's mill and beneath his father's machines, illegally so – was not harmed. Even if this furiously indignant and gloriously attractive girl had not removed her as she had done, he would not have run the child down. He was too good a horseman for that but it had been a close shave. Still, she had no reason, and no right to turn on him as she had done, ready to scratch his eyes out by the look of her.

"It doesn't matter who I am," she spat at him, "and I suppose that's about right. I don't matter, that child doesn't matter" – with a furious movement of her arm towards where Annie still held the little girl – "and nothing matters as long as the yarn is spun and you and your father, and the rest of you, make your first thousand pounds profit before breakfast."

His jaw dropped and the silence, except for the chomp of the horses' jaws and the stamp of their hooves on the cobbles, was absolute. There were faces at the rows of windows along the mill face, men with sheaves of papers in their hands, girls in aprons and caps, all looking out in astonishment to see what was to do.

He recovered quickly. "Well, I never." He smiled lazily. "What a firebrand," intrigued by this girl who was obviously a spinner in his father's mill. Not only was she very lovely, even in the dreadful rags she had on and which they all wore, but she had a decidedly odd turn of speech. For a mill girl, that is. Where on earth had she picked up the word "consideration", for instance, and "lethal" which were not words used in the general way of things by the uneducated labouring masses. And where had she heard that phrase about his father, and other mill owners, making their first thousand pounds worth of profit before breakfast? That was what his father did, of course. His father was Edmund Hayes, the owner of Monarch Mill, who, along with all the other "Manchester Men" considered himself to be successful. That was the name coined: Manchester Men! They were respected by their fellows and the accepted sign of such respect was membership in the Manchester Exchange where most of the city's business was transacted. They were hardworking, self-righteous, shrewd and not concerned overmuch in matters of art and culture which they considered to be a waste of time when they could be better employed making an even bigger profit.

And then there were the Manchester *Irishmen* of which there were many in the mill yard, for they were a different species from their masters. They were seen only as a source of cheap labour, Catholics for the most part, of peasant background and heirs to several centuries of hatred between themselves and their English rulers. They did not mix well, forming their own alienated community and though Nancy Brody was not Catholic, she was of Irish descent; she was one of them and they'd like nothing better than to see her triumph over the cocky bugger who was the son of the man they worked for.

"And where did you learn about such things, my girl?" he asked her, the patronising tone in his voice very evident.

"The same place as you, I'd say," she answered him, her eyes flashing defiance so that those in the yard prayed that the engines would be delayed in being turned on, for they would dearly love to see her have the last word with their young master. All except Annie who was certain Nancy would be sacked on the spot. Mind you, she was leaving anyway so that was perhaps why she was not afraid to square up to the master's son.

"Oh, yes, and where was that then?"

"From books, and from working in this mill, which I don't suppose you can claim to have done." Her glance moved contemptuously up and down his tall frame, eyeing his immaculate suit as though she'd like to see the day when it would belly up to the machines she worked. "I keep my eyes and ears open and when I . . . when I—"

She stopped speaking abruptly, glancing round her in surprise at the crowd of avid faces. She had been so incensed by the casual way in which the master's son had dismissed the child he had almost injured, just as though she were no more than a bale of raw cotton that had got in his way, indeed the cotton had more value, that she had overstepped herself. In all her muck and stink, her bare, oily feet and her sweated face, she had bristled up to a man who was so far above her he could step on her like a cockroach if he chose.

She could see he was amused and, naturally, he didn't take her seriously. She came from another world to the one he inhabited, no more than a pair of hands to work his father's machines, a strong back and legs – or weak; what did he care?

– to walk the miles each day in the operating of those machines. He was surprised, she could see that, that one of these faceless, illiterate, ill-nourished, often stunted creatures should have the gumption to stand up to him in the defence of a child but she'd only show herself up if she continued with it. She was already looked on by the others as a queer sort who had forgotten her place and she had said more than enough already. Best back down while she had the chance.

Joshua Hayes watched the play of emotions on her face. It was a strong face, he noticed with surprise, since it was not something one said about a woman, but it was the way she spoke, articulate and open, that took him aback and made him want to find out how she had become as she was.

As he opened his mouth to suggest, amazingly, that she follow him to his office on the first floor, since for some reason he felt the need to question further this extraordinary girl, the engines thundered into life and at once it was as though an ant-hill had been kicked over by a careless foot. Everyone in the yard turned and flew towards open doorways, for a minute not spent on a machine might mean a copper less to spend on the necessities of life. In a moment the yard was empty, the girl gone with the rest of them. Only the men loading and unloading waggons remained and when he asked them the name of the spinner who had stood up to him they all gazed vacantly at him. They didn't know, they said. Aye, they'd seen her around, who wouldn't notice a bonny lass like her but as for her name . . . They scratched their heads and exchanged glances and winks behind his back as he strode away from them and up the stairs to his office.

Mick was waiting for them, as he had formed the habit of doing ever since Whit Monday, his hands in his pockets, leaning against the high mill wall just outside the gate. He nodded and smiled at lads he knew, and winked at girls he knew, but he straightened up slowly as Nancy Brody walked towards him. He was quite amazed at the effect she had on him, not just at his natural male instincts to possess, to dominate her body with his, which he hoped to do soon, but by the strange, unfamiliar and tender feelings in him to protect her, feelings he had shown to no woman before. At the sight of her, tall, gracefully swaying, her head proudly tilted, he could feel himself fall into a state of what he could only describe as the "jitters": a dryness of his mouth that made it hard to speak, a racing of his heart that amazed him, alarmed him and that he did his best not only to suppress but to hide from others, since it was not something of which he was proud. He had never been in thrall to a woman before. His prowess with the opposite sex was legend among his cronies and if it got about that his feelings for Nancy Brody were more than just a desire to lift her skirts his reputation would be in tatters.

As he fell in beside her he winked suggestively at several of the lads and they grinned behind their hands, wondering how long it would be before Mick O'Rourke got Nancy Brody to lie down for him.

"All right, my lasses?" he said to the Brody sisters, swaggering a little as they moved with the crowd of be-shawled, be-clogged women along Victoria Parade, moving past Chetham's College towards Long Millgate, which, in turn, took them through the narrow alleyways and courts to Angel Meadow. Their way led past a hideous, unplanned sprawl of dilapidated cottages, broken pavements, rutted tracks and open drains but they were accustomed to such sights and such smells, sauntering along in the mild dusk as though they were walking a fragrant country lane.

Mick kept up a monologue of lively chatter, his Irish need to hear the sound of his own voice, to see the interest and admiration in the eyes of the three pretty girls, to listen to their laughter, which he caused since his wit was deliberately wicked, very strong in him. He was a born story-teller, a clever mimic with a sharp eye for detail and a good memory. He was putting himself out to be entertaining and he was succeeding, particularly with the younger girls, though he sensed Nancy was not quite as impressed as he would have liked her to be. She was not like the other two. She had a more serious side to her which baffled and yet intrigued him and it would take more than a few jokes, a few laughs and the several small jobs he had done about their home in the last few weeks to win her over to . . . well, to his way of thinking! She needed softening up, something he achieved quite easily with most lasses but this one required a different approach. It was a challenge that he rose to eagerly. He loved a challenge. Anything won easily was not worth having, in his opinion, which was why he so quickly tired of the girls who fell like ripe plums into his greedy hands.

"An' what're the three of yer up to this weekend, then?" he asked casually as they turned into Church Court. They were watched by the usual sprawling figures of men and women enjoying the fine spell of warm weather, including his own mam who pursed her lips and hitched up her sagging breasts with crossed arms, displeasure in every line of her at the sight of her son with Lady Muck. It was evident that Nancy Brody was not yet broken in then, her expression said.

"Nothing much, Mick," Nancy answered. "We usually go over to the market to do our shopping and I wanted to have a rummage on the second-hand clothes stall. Our Rosie grows out of her clothes so quickly."

For a moment Mick was diverted by the evidence of Rosie Brody's "growing out" of her clothes, which displayed itself in the budding of what promised to be tits as splendid as Nancy's, but Nancy was still speaking.

"And I want some paint. Them window frames are a disgrace and I thought—"

"I can do them for yer, acushla. Just say the word and . . ."

"I can do them myself, thanks, Mick," Nancy answered tartly, for now and again, though she enjoyed his company and he made her laugh, Mick's male belief that she was helpless without a man to do these things for her irritated her. She had been managing her own life and the lives of her sisters all these years and yet he insisted on the pretence that she'd be lost without him. And in such a short time, too! "Anyway, what d'you mean about the weekend?" she added to distract him.

His face, which had begun to frown, cleared and he grinned, pleased with himself over something.

"Well, I 'eard yer mention the Art . . . somethin' or other . . . show."

"The Arts Treasures Exhibition?"

"Aye, that's the one."

"What about it?"

"Yer said yer wanted ter see it."

He was most gratified by the way her face lit up and when her hand clutched at his arm, pulling him to a stop to face her he thought she was going to kiss him, right there in the street under the fascinated gaze of their neighbours.

"Oh, Mick," she breathed and he was bewitched, with her and with himself who was so bloody clever.

"Does that mean yer do?" He grinned mischievously.

"Oh, Mick."

He preened himself, looking about him to see if the spectators had noticed the way Nancy Brody, who bothered with no one, was clinging to Mick O'Rourke's arm.

"Well, I reckon if it's good enough fer 'Is 'Ighness Prince Albert, an' I 'eard tell t'Queen's comin' in a week or two then 'tis good enough fer Mick O'Rourke an' Nancy Brody."

"What about us, Mick?" Mary and Rose clamoured, and with an expression of false sorrow he told them the lie he had prepared.

"Eeh, darlin's, I only wish it were possible, so I do, but only two at a time the chap told me." He turned to Nancy. "I've bin over there terday ter mekk enquiries, yer see."

Nancy withdrew a little and her face became uncertain. It was all right to go about with Mick with her sisters accompanying them but to go somewhere, just her and Mick, seemed to her to be making a declaration on which the wrong interpretation might be put. She had no interest in the impish young Irishman, much as she liked his company, for he played no part in her future plans. In fact, when the time came he would only stand in their way. But surely just this once it could do no harm? There was nothing she wanted more than to see what was described in the *Illustrated London News*, which she had read at the library, as the "scene of an event almost unique in the history of art in England and perhaps the world". She was still no more than a cotton spinner, no matter how she bettered herself; and in all her life, until Mick took them to Belle Vue, she had known nothing beyond the perimeter of Angel Meadow. Was she confident enough to go alone, or with Mary and Rose, to walk among what she was sure would be the gentry, in her second-hand cotton dress and straw bonnet? Would it cost more than she could afford or was willing to part with? Would they even let her in? Her ignorance of the world outside books was enormous but she had to start somewhere and this might as well be it.

Her smile was radiant and Mick's heart swelled with some emotion he did not recognise and ignoring the sullen muttering of Rose and the sigh of envy from Mary he pushed open their front door and ushered them inside.

At once, knowing exactly how he should treat this lovely, shining, grateful girl, he stayed on the doorstep, smiling.

"I'll see yer then, Nancy," he told her, curbing his need to be bold and manly, then turned and whistled his way to his own front door.

6

Joshua Hayes ran lightly down the back stairs, along the passage and through the enormous kitchen where half a dozen women were working. He winked at several on his way, before striding out into the sunlit yard. A pretty girl in a frilly mob cap and a snowy apron, with a laundry basket on her hip, sauntered towards him across the yard and at once, on sight of him her rosy face became even rosier. She dimpled and lowered her long lashes, then peeped up at him knowingly and yet innocently.

"Mornin', sir," she said softly, a wealth of meaning in her voice.

"Mornin', Evie," he answered just as softly. No more than that but the air about them seemed to warm and colour like the sunshine that fell about them.

"Lovely day, sir."

"Indeed it is, Evie."

"The washing's dry already," she went on, sticking out her hip to draw his attention to the basket of snowy linen, and at the same time to her small waist.

"I'm not surprised. Let's hope the rain keeps off."

"Oh, yes, sir," she answered, with what seemed heartfelt emotion.

They were walking away from one another by now, she towards the kitchen door, he to the arch let into the high wall over which already roses were beginning to clamber. The arch led to the stretch of rough grass that stood before the stables. They were in full view of the kitchen window where stood a ramrod-backed woman with iron grey hair drawn into so tight a bun at the back of her head it dragged the skin of her forehead taut. She wore a floor-length black frock of great severity and she frowned as she watched the little exchange beyond the window. She could not hear what was said and if she had could not have taken exception to its content but it was apparent she did not at all care for what she saw.

She tutted to herself, then, as Evie entered the kitchen, turned towards her, rattling her housekeeper's keys menacingly.

"You've taken your time, my girl," she said, as though even before the laundry-maid spoke she was prepared to call her a liar. "Don't ask me to believe that it takes ten minutes to unpeg a line of washing."

"I 'ad ter peg out another lot, Mrs Harvey," Evie protested.

"Don't you argue with me, girl," Mrs Harvey hissed, her flinty eyes narrowed suspiciously, for though there had been nothing untoward in the appearance of the laundry-maid and the master's son, Evie's smile had been too warm for Mrs Harvey's liking.

Evie bit her lip to prevent the next words of protest from tumbling out. She stood, her head hanging, her poppy mouth clamped mutinously shut and in the chair by the fire where she was smacking her lips over her mid-morning cup of tea, Cook shook her head sympathetically. Cook was younger than the housekeeper, with a lighter spirit, an inclination towards good humour, a bit of a laugh and, she admitted it to herself, would have allowed the maidservants, if they had been in her charge, which they weren't except the kitchen-maid, the scullery-maid and the skivvy, more leniency than Mrs Harvey showed. More freedom to gossip and giggle and stand about idly which would not have done at all, but then she had been married and, despite her use of the title, "Mrs" Harvey had not. Cook had found in her long career that women who had never known a man's touch were often harsh on those who had. Not that young Evie was married and, as to the other, it had not gone unnoticed that the laundry-maid and the master's elder son smiled at one another a lot. Mind, Evie was a good girl, a bonny girl, an innocent girl, Cook would have sworn to it, with glossy dark curls that constantly escaped the severe cap Mrs Harvey insisted upon, and the loveliest laughing blue eyes. She had cheeks on her like a ripe peach and a mouth that looked as though it had just been kissed, which it probably had if the young master's smiles were anything to go by, and it was as well that Mrs Harvey was as strict as she was. No followers, she told the maidservants, and it was a rule that was strictly adhered to, though who they met, or where, on their day off, was their own business.

"Now, if it's not too much trouble I'd be obliged if you'd get on with the ironing, girl," Mrs Harvey told Evie sharply, "or the morning will be gone and not a blessed thing done." This despite the fact that Evie had been at the washtub for the past three hours.

"I haven't had me cup o' tea, yet, Mrs Harvey," Evie was unwise enough to say and at once Mrs Harvey's face flushed a bright, brick red and for a moment Cook thought she would strike the girl but she quickly controlled herself.

"You've the impudence to expect to sit about drinking tea after wasting half the morning idling in the yard! I've never heard the like and what girls of today are coming to I don't know. In my day we were lucky if we managed to sit down for our meals let alone a cup of tea. Many's the time I took my dinner on the move we were that busy. Now, Jeannie's seen to the fire for you and brought in the box irons to be filled. The embers are ready and so should you be. Now, not another word, d'you hear. I've to go up to see Mrs Hayes about the arrangements for the dinner party at the weekend but when I come back I want to see them shirts done at the very least. Is that understood?"

"Yes, Mrs Harvey."

"Very well, now get at it. Keep an eye on her, will you, Cook?" Just as though the minute her back was turned the laundry-maid would be lolling in Mrs Harvey's chair in Mrs Harvey's sitting-room drinking tea from one of Mrs Harvey's china teacups.

Evie got her cup of tea, though she had to swallow it down quickly before Mrs Harvey came back or not only she, but Cook, who slipped it to her in the laundry-room, would have been for it.

The cause of it all was at that precise moment thundering round the loop in the River Irwell which ran at the back of his home. In fact it was so close it almost passed through the garden of Riverside House. Riding low on the neck of his new chestnut mare, which he had named Copper for obvious reasons, he galloped beside the river, then turned right abruptly, racing across field after field, putting the high-spirited mare to hedges of hawthorn and may, the fragrance of the newly opened blossom disturbed into a haze about him as Copper's hooves clipped the top of the hedges. The fields were a spring miracle of silvery green, crimson, white and yellow where poppies and kingcups mixed with field mouse-ear in the tall grasses that brushed the horse's belly as she and the rider hurtled onward.

When he reached Kersall Dell, a dense grove of beech trees which were already clothed in their bright, pure, spring foliage, he checked the mare slightly, for the smooth, silver grey trunks of the trees, like the soaring columns of a cathedral, were very close together. The trees, forced to grow tall in their constant struggle to reach the light, made a perfect hiding place and he smiled reminiscently at the memory of some moment pleasing to him. The grass was short and soft, as he well knew, muffling the mare's hooves and he slowed right down to a walk. Layer upon layer of leaves circled each tree-trunk and as summer progressed the dense shade cast by the foliage would strip the ground of growth, leaving only the rotting carpet of last year's dead beech trees.

Josh slowed only for a moment then turned the mare south towards the small pedestrian bridge at London Place Print Works which stood on the northward loop of the river. He crossed it, the animal's hooves making a great clatter, causing heads in the print works yard to turn curiously.

He was down to a graceful canter now, both he and the horse sweating in the warm air. He wore no jacket or tie, just a fine pair of caramel-coloured doeskin breeches, a cream, open-necked shirt with the sleeves rolled up and well-polished riding boots. His back was straight but not stiff as he rode, his head up, his feet straight forward, looking every inch the superb horseman he was.

When he reached Suspension Road he urged his mare into a gallop again, clattering over Suspension Bridge until he was on his own side of the river once more. He was riding through water meadows now which led down to the river and backed on to the houses on Lower Broughton Road, houses with long gardens, growing longer as the river took a lazy turn away from them. There were no cotton mills or dye works here, for this was where wealthy men of cotton had built their homes and his father was the wealthiest of them all. His house, when his son came to it, stood on a rise of land twenty acres in total, consisting of lawns and flowerbeds, terraces lined with potted shrubs, stone steps leading here and there, a small pond in which golden fish lazily turned, a walled vegetable garden, a herb garden, with woodland and fenced paddocks which ran down to the water's edge.

Josh slipped from his mare's back, leaving her to crop the sweet grass, her head lowered, for she was tired after her wild gallop. He sank to his haunches, his arms across his knees, staring sightlessly into the slipping, silvery river, his expression thoughtful, then he smiled, as he had done earlier, as though at some pleasing memory.

She had almost let him do it last night, the deliciously pretty young girl who was his mother's laundry-maid, and though he knew he shouldn't play so close to home – all his instincts and the oft-repeated advice of his friends told him so – he had been unable to resist the rosy innocence, the dimpled sweetness, the soft adoration in her vivid blue eyes which was directed at him whenever he appeared. She was so lovely, soft, full-breasted, with a handspan of a waist and a full womanly hip. She came up only to his chin, her arms clinging about his back, her face lifting to his, her mouth opening beneath his in a way he found quite irresistible. She loved him, she told him so a dozen times as his hands pushed the bodice of her gown off her shoulders and his mouth found her full, rosy-peaked breast. She moaned softly in her need but he could get no further with her than that. Despite her status as a maidservant in his mother's kitchen she was a decent girl, as well brought up and guarded, as pure and ignorant as his own eighteen-year-old sister, Milly. She had been protected as savagely by her labouring father as Milly was protected by Edmund Hayes until she had been forced by circumstances and the yearly increase in the size of her family to become laundry-maid at Riverside House. Her mother was a laundress, she had told him naïvely in one of the "conversations" she liked to have before he melted her into his arms with soft kisses and laughter, and had taught Evie all she knew. God almighty, he had groaned to himself a dozen times, he knew he should leave her alone, for the risk was great, not only for him but for her if they were found out. At best she would lose her position, flung out without a character; at worst, the same but with a child inside her.

He was playing with fire, and it was not the first time, and if his father became aware of it there would be hell to pay. The last time it had been the compliant daughter of a small farmer up towards New Town, and only his father's influence and the fifty guineas that had changed hands, enabling her to buy a farm-labourering husband who was willing to father the child, had kept him out of trouble. He liked women, and not just for the pleasure their bodies gave to his, and they liked him but try telling that to the old man as an excuse for what his father described as his wild and licentious ways and which, so his father told him, would break his mother's heart if she knew.

He sighed deeply, straightening his tall frame and turning to click his tongue softly to the horse. He took the bridle and began to lead her towards the house, the chimneys of which could be seen above the trees that stood at its back. He moved through the small patch of woodland and on to a well-mown lawn, skirting the rose gardens and another row of trees, pines this time, which shielded the stables from the house. The mare went with him amiably enough, crossing the wide, gravelled path to the stable yard.

"Miss Millicent's bin lookin' for yer, Master Josh," Charlie, who was head groom at Riverside House, told him, taking the mare's bridle from him and leading her away across the yard.

"Did she say what she wanted, Charlie?" he asked, perplexed.

"Summat about an exhibition that you was—"

"Jesus Christ, I'd forgotten all about the bloody thing." Josh stood for a moment with a look of comic dismay on his face then he pushed his hand through his thick hair, fingering it off his brow so that it stood up like a yard brush. "God almighty, I'll be in bloody hot water now," he muttered as he set off at a furious clip across the stable yard.

"Aye, yer will, lad," the groom murmured softly against the mare's neck, "an' 'appen if yer were ter let yer brain lead yer instead o' yer cock yer might do better," for Master Josh's fondness for milk-maids and laundry-maids was well known among the men-servants. He turned to stare disapprovingly after his master's son.

They were in the hall, his parents and his sister, his father looking wrathfully at his watch, his face nearly purple with his rage, his mighty bellow at the front door heard by every servant, inside and out.

"Where in hell have you been, damn you? Do you realise that your mother and sister have been waiting for ten minutes? Your manners are appalling, lad, and if it wasn't for your mother's intervention I would give you a thrashing, big as you are."

"I'm sorry, sir, I . . . well, I . . ."

"Daydreaming as usual, I suppose, but I'll take no excuses, so save them for later and I warn you they'd better be good. Now, go and change. We'll give you five minutes then we're going without you."

"I wish to bloody hell he would," Josh murmured in an aside to an astonished maidservant who was coming down the stairs and who pressed herself against the wall as he ran lightly up to his room. It was only the thought of his mother's distress that kept him from saying it out loud, from defying his father. His father's threat of thrashing him was an empty one, for it was a long time since Joshua Hayes had been of a size to take a beating from Edmund. Instead of visiting the damned exhibition he would dearly have like to idle and daydream about in his room, take his time and stroll downstairs, defiant in the face of his father's wrath, but it would only upset his mother of whom he was deeply fond. Sighing, he stripped off his breeches and shirt, struggling with his boots until he was naked. He had a beautiful male body, with long, graceful bones and flat muscles that flowed smoothly from the curve of his chest and shoulder to the concavities of his belly and hard, lean thighs, a horseman's thighs. He had a sprinkling of fine dark hairs on his chest and belly, growing into the thick dark triangle that protected his genitals. Though he was not powerfully built he was strong and arrow straight, each part of his frame in perfect proportion to the rest, his legs long, his feet narrow.

Within the allotted five minutes he had changed into a morning coat of fine grey merino, under it a matching waistcoat, the coat with broad tails and a velvet collar. His trousers were tight, showing off the fine calf of his leg and he wore an immaculate lawn shirt with a large and fashionable neckcloth. His hair was brushed and, as he kissed her cheek in repentance his mother whispered, "Very nice, dear."

"Never mind that, Emma," his father said irritably. "Can we please get into the carriage now, that is if our fine gentleman is quite ready. See, Milly, sit by me, lass," his tone softening, for he loved and was proud of his plain but well-brought-up daughter who, unlike her older brother, was not a scrap of trouble to him and it pleased him to have her on his arm.

It was Saturday and the exhibition, opened several weeks before in the presence of their good Prince Albert, was a seething, babbling, excited mass of folk who had come to be amazed. There would be a million and a half middle- and working-class folk who were to see it, come on special excursion trains from Chester, Liverpool, Birmingham, Crewe, Bradford, Halifax, Huddersfield and Leeds, in one day alone 13,664 of them. They could think of no reason why they shouldn't see this wonderful spectacle which was being likened to the Crystal Palace, the Great Exhibition of 1851 in London.

When it was being decided where to place the great building it was felt that its position would be of the utmost importance, the deciding factor being the desire to avoid the nuisance of smoke. The cricket and racing grounds at Old Trafford along the Irwell and two miles south-west of the city centre were finally chosen, for the executive committee noted that this was one of the few places where flowers would grow.

And so did the building, a wondrous thing completely constructed from glass, gracefully rearing out of an enormous garden filled with trees, shrubs, flowers and fountains surrounded by a smooth sward of velvet grass where benches were placed and where families could picnic.

Josh was so bored it was all he could do not to yawn directly into his father's face but again, to please his mother, he did his best to appear interested. There were works by Botticelli, Raphael, Titian, Gainsborough and Constable and many other well-known European and British painters, all tastefully arranged and exclaimed over by his mother and Milly. But not just paintings were on display, for there were engravings, glass and enamel, gold and silver, armour, fine clocks, watches, brasswork, bronzes, furniture and sculpture. He admired them dutifully, his eyes glazing over with the sheer tedium of it all but aware that if he was not once again to suffer his father's wrath, which did not worry him but would distress his mother, he must not let it show.

"Is not the decor lovely, Millicent?" Mrs Hayes asked her daughter. "Such a warm shade of maroon and how well it goes with the green."

"Indeed, Mother. Oh, do tell me that really is Alfred Tennyson strolling by. One never knows who one is to see next. Fanny Tompkinson told me that Lord Palmerston was here only last week."

"How thrilling. And is it true, d'you think, that the Queen of Holland is to be a visitor?"

"So I have heard. What a wonder it all is."

"But tiring, dearest. Let us persuade your father to take us to the lounge for refreshments."

Josh caught his father's eye, surprised by the gleam of amusement in it, realising that Edmund Hayes was as bored as he was. They smiled ruefully at one another, for once in total agreement. They were both aware, for despite his wild ways, Joshua Hayes was his father's son and learning to be a businessman, that this sort of exhibition, like the one at the Crystal Palace in London, could only be good for trade. Though it displayed only art and not the new developments in science and technology that had been shown in London in 1851 it brought men of business to Manchester, put Manchester on the map, so to speak, which could harm no one. Most of the middle and lower classes eagerly attended to keep in step with the latest fashion, to educate themselves and simply to be amused. Men such as Edmund Hayes were keen to display their wealth and to boast of their achievements, for they were self-made men and proud of it.

They were not the only ones to be bored by the endless rows of paintings, room after room of them, by the crush of people among whom he kept losing Nancy, by the lack of anything lively with which to relieve the monotony of watching the cultured classes enjoying culture at its finest. Mick O'Rourke could see that Nancy was quite enchanted with it all which, instead of pleasing him, since to enchant her had been his aim, had begun seriously to offend him. The trouble was she seemed to be scarcely aware of him and the great sacrifice he had made on her behalf as she stood and gazed for what seemed hours on end at every bloody painting, most of which were, in his opinion, absolutely and monumentally dreary. She shook off his hand when he attempted to draw her on, turning away from him as though she hadn't heard him when he made one of his witty Irish remarks which had always made her laugh before. She even "shushed" him at one point when he told her he'd seen better in the sporting prints, the pictures of which were the only ones he cared for. Boxers and horses and greyhounds and that sort of thing.

"Really, Mick, it's all so lovely I can't see why you should say such a thing. Look at those wonderful lions. D'you think they're made of gold? And those fountains and trees and all flourishing so magnificently indoors. I've never seen such lovely things, and what about the painted figures on those columns. D'you think they're Egyptian?"

"'Ow the 'ell would I know," he answered irritably, telling himself he'd better get some reward for all this tomfoolery he was putting himself through. Thank the Blessed Virgin none of his mates were likely to see him or he'd be sneered at at every ring or public house he attended.

"I think they must be," Nancy was saying. "I saw something like them in a book at the library."

"Begorra, will yer be fergetting yer old books fer five minutes an' let's go an' get a drink. D'yer reckon they sell ale in this God-forsaken place?"

Nancy turned to him in surprise. She had been so bewitched by the beauty that was all about her, by the cleverness and talent displayed, by the lovely swishing gowns of the "quality" and the aura of grace and good taste that surrounded her, she had been scarcely conscious of the growing moodiness and ill-humour of the man who had brought her.

"Aren't you enjoying yourself, Mick?" she asked him, concern in her voice. "I thought when you asked me you wanted to see it as much as I did."

But even as she spoke Nancy wondered at the foolishness of the remark, for what on earth would a down-to-earth, fun-loving, uneducated Irishman like Mick O'Rourke find to entertain him here; and even as the thought entered her head she knew she must not associate with him any longer. He was not for her and she must give him no reason to believe that she was. He had no place in her life which was aimed like an arrow from a bow to the point where one day these lovely things would be a part of her world, not exactly taken for granted, for who could take for granted such loveliness, but as much a part of her life as . . . her own hair, or skin. She knew it as positively as she knew the words in the books she read which had led her to this. She had seen this now, seen these lovely paintings, these glorious exhibits, these fashionable and even lovely women, the courteous way in which they were treated by their escorts. On her way in she had gloated over the spick and span carriages and polished, high-bred horses that pulled them and the smartly uniformed grooms who tended them. One day . . . one day . . . She could not finish the sentence, not even in her head, but it nestled there inside her, the knowledge that she was meant for something better than to be a cotton spinner at Monarch Mill.

It was then she saw him and it was then he saw her and for a fraction of a second, as it had done at their first meeting, time seemed to come to an abrupt halt. Again there was that flame of recognition, not the recognition of people who have met before and are meeting again but a strange *knowing* that had fleetingly touched them at their first encounter. And there was a moment of pleasure too, lighting velvet grey eyes and golden, and something that could only be described, if it was described at all, as a movement of the heart.

They both stopped and, behind them, as they came face to face, people tutted irritably and collisions seemed imminent.

"What is it, dear?" she heard an attractive, well-dressed lady ask him, turning both herself and the young woman on her arm in his direction. The thickset gentleman who had almost walked into his back glared about him as though to ask who dare hold up such an important man as himself, but not for a moment did he connect it with the poorly dressed couple, members of the labouring classes obviously, who in his opinion should not be allowed in at all and certainly not stand in the way of their betters.

"What's up, acushla?" Mick asked, as belligerent in his own way as Edmund Hayes, and as determined no one should block the path of Mick O'Rourke who was cock of the north in his own small patch.

The wide doors to the refreshment lounges were directly opposite one another, standing open to allow the press of people who, having tramped round for hours admiring – most of them – the marvels on display, were determined on something to give them fresh energy for a further onslaught. One lounge, described as providing rest and refreshment for the upper classes and the other, a "second-class" facility for workers.

It was very evident to which one Joshua Hayes and, Nancy supposed, his family, were headed. Still she seemed unable to look away from him nor he from her, and at her side Mick was beginning to bristle belligerently, not really understanding what was going on, only knowing he didn't like it. The toff, long, dandified thing he was, was staring at what Mick considered to be *his* property and if he kept it up Mick O'Rourke, no matter who the toff was, would deal with him as he dealt with bigger chaps than he was in the ring. Bloody nerve, standing there with his mouth open, and when he turned to say something to her he was dismayed to find that Nancy, *his* Nancy, was looking just as gormless.

" 'Ere," he said roughly, taking her arm and propelling her towards the working-class tearoom so that she was forced into tearing her eyes away from those of Joshua Hayes, "I'm not 'avin' any bloody feller-me-lad eyein' my girl, an' more to't point I'll not 'ave my girl lookin' at other chaps, so think on."

If anything was needed, which it wasn't, to make up Nancy Brody's mind, it was those few words. She didn't know what had happened back there between her and young Mr Hayes, really she didn't, and she felt extremely foolish about the whole strange episode. The Hayes ladies, with Mr Hayes ushering them forcefully away from the curious little crowd that had gathered, had disappeared into the first-class refreshment room, but behind him his son turned for a moment just as Nancy did, and Joshua was in time to see the big, handsome chap she was with put his arm about her shoulders and was quite bewildered by the feeling of anger it aroused in him. Then they were out of sight and he did not see her shake the arm off, or hear her sharp words which were, though he did not know it at the time, the end of Mick O'Rourke's "seduction" of Nancy Brody.

7

If she had not kept a tight hold on Mary's hand she was convinced her sister would have turned tail and made a run for it. Even Rosie, who was of a stronger constitution than Mary, blanched and held her hand to her mouth as though she were about to be sick.

It was the smell that first assaulted their senses. They had come straight off the street which was by no means bright, even at six o'clock of a summer morning, not with the usual pall of dirty brown smoke that hung over it, and at first Nancy could see nothing beyond a few vague shapes moving about or sitting at tables. She had worked in a cotton mill since she was nine years old and, as Annie used to say cheerfully, that didn't exactly smell of roses, but this was a mixture of the secretions of the human body, women's bodies, which, at certain times of the month were particularly rank if unwashed, of overflowing privies and the accumulated years of a mass of humanity living and working together without the benefit of an open window. There was a strong odour of gas, of scorched cloth, of rotten food and some other indefinable aroma that reminded Nancy of the foetid stink caused by damp. The cellar was below ground with no windows except a skylight which she could now make out at the far end of the large, rectangular room. It was low-ceilinged inside the entrance at the bottom of the rotten steps which led from the street but expanding irregularly upwards and outwards to the skylight at the other end. The walls were lined with match-boarding which might have been a pleasing light shade when it was put up but now it was black and greasy with age. Placed at regular intervals along the room were hooks on which hung shawls and bonnets, and beside them, casting a flickering, evil-smelling light, were several gas lamps. In a prominent place, framed and under glass, hung the Factory and Workshops Regulations which, it seemed to Nancy, had never been adhered to in all the years they had been in force.

"You can't mean us ter work here, our Nancy," Rosie said in a loud voice, her horror making her aggressive, and a man whom they had not noticed hovering over a child at a table turned menacingly so that they all three shrank back.

"Nobody's mekkin' yer work 'ere, lass, so if yer not satisfied, sling yer 'ook. There's plenty lookin' fer decent jobs like these so 'op it if yer not suited."

Nancy recognised the man as the one who had agreed to employ her and her sisters, very reluctantly with respect to Mary and Rosie since none of them was a trained machinist, he added, but he was prepared to take them on, looking her up and down with that particular gleam in his eye that she was beginning to recognise in men.

"We're quick learners, Mr Earnshaw," she'd pleaded with him. "We want to learn to be machinists but you can put the other two on as hand finishers to start with if that suits you better. They can both sew a decent seam." Which was true, for they had helped her to alter many a garment gleaned at the market. "We're willing to do anything, really we are, to get a decent job in your establishment."

"Where you learn ter speak like that, lass?" he had asked her suspiciously, just as though she were trying to put one over on him.

"Does it matter, Mr Earnshaw? We . . . we all went to Sunday school so . . ."

"Aye, that must be it but I want no high-falutin' pernickety lasses 'ere. I told that to 'er," nodding in the direction of a frail-looking girl who was staggering between the tables under a load of what looked like half-sewn shirts in her thin arms. "She talks all lah-di-dah an' all but as long as she does what's needed she can speak chinee for all I care. You an' all. It's 'ard work an' long 'ours so delicate ladies 're no good ter me. If yer not prepared ter work when I want yer to work then yer'd best look elsewhere."

"No, really, Mr Earnshaw, we'll do whatever you say."

They had no choice. She knew Mr Earnshaw of Earnshaw's Fine Shirts would exploit them, as he exploited all the girls in his employ, but he was the only one who had been prepared to take on all three of them. She had not been willing to let Mary or Rosie, or even both of them, find employment on their own, Mary because she was too timid and Rosie because Rosie needed a firm hand and God knows what she might have got up to. This place was wretched but as soon as all three of them had learned the trade she meant to get out of it and start what had been her dream, at least the start of her dream, ever since she had been old enough to formulate it in her childish mind. She had in the hole behind the spare brick in the upstairs room, beside her precious hoard of money, a letter from a firm of sewing-machine manufacturers in Oldham by the name of Bradbury's which told her that they would be pleased to hire her one of their splendid sewing-machines at a cost of one and sixpence a week. If she kept up the payments and did not fall into arrears, it went on, the machine would ultimately be hers. If she could afford it she meant to have two, or even three. She had spoken to Mrs Beasley who had promised to enquire about the possibility of a stall on the outskirts of the market, providing it didn't interfere with *her* trade, of course, for there was no place for sentiment in Mrs Beasley's line of work.

"Right then," Mr Earnshaw said briskly, "let's get yer started."

Close by the door and well within reach of the gas stove that was used for heating irons, were two small, high tables which served the pressers. There was a long, low plank-like table furnished underneath with a wooden rail on which those sitting at it might rest their feet, with forms on either side of it and a chair at the top and bottom end. This was where the shirt finishers were seated and this was where Rosie and Mary were placed with instructions to wait there until Jennet came to set them off. Those already seated were diligently cutting out and making buttonholes on shirt fronts already machine sewed. The girls sank to the form, huddled close together, their faces showing their trepidation, for it seemed their Nancy, who had always looked after them, worked beside them, decided the very pattern of their lives, was to be whisked off with Mr Earnshaw.

"It'll be all right," she whispered to them. "Just do as you're told and it'll be all right."

Along two high tables, one against each wall leaving a passage down the centre of the room, were clustered women who were basters and this was probably where "them two", Mr Earnshaw said, indicating with a nod of his busy head Rosie and Mary, would begin, since basting was very simple. Directly under the skylight and at the far end of the room, again lining each wall, were rows of sewing-machines, each one on its own treadle stand with a small table between on which were piled cut-out shirts ready to be made up, and the rapid movement of the machinists' feet was already in progress. Beyond this, at the extreme end of the workshop, was what appeared to be a private kitchen, for a woman stood at a stove and several children were sitting round a filthy table eating what looked to be a decent breakfast of bacon and eggs. There was another door which led to a small yard with an outhouse and, near to it, a tap and a sink for the use of the inmates of the establishment.

Nancy counted forty hands in a space that seemed barely big enough for a dozen but so crammed together were tables, machines and humans alike they all appeared to be working, despite the conditions, in some sort of haphazard harmony.

"'Ere, this'll do yer," Mr Earnshaw told her, nodding at a machine that stood idle between two others at which girls of about eighteen were industriously engaged, their feet going ten to the dozen, the treadle a blur of movement, their hands the same as they whisked the cotton cloth across the cloth plate and under the needle. "Ivy, show this lass – what's yer name again? Nancy. Right, show 'er what ter do an' then keep an eye on 'er. An' don't pull faces at me, me girl, or yer can 'op it. There's two more up along waitin' ter get on't machines," nodding towards Rosie and Mary who were bent over the table with the frail little girl standing over them. "You 'ad ter be taught an' so's this lass so get on wi' it."

Mr Earnshaw stamped off in the direction of the kitchen where presently he could be seen eating what was evidently his breakfast. Nancy sat down at the machine and, without a word being spoken, Ivy left her work and, with a face like thunder, shoved a pile of unfinished shirts at Nancy, taking one in her none too clean hands and proceeding to feed the material across the cloth plate.

"Treadle," she hissed venomously. "It won't work unless yer use treadle."

"I appreciate that," Nancy began tartly, for it was not her fault that Ivy had to stop her work, thereby losing precious minutes in which she could be earning money. Machinists were the best-paid workers in the industry but they had to labour practically non-stop to earn their wage, she knew that.

"An' what the bloody 'ell does that mean?" It was plain Ivy was nonplussed, not only by the word which she didn't really recognise but by the fearless defiance in the new girl's manner.

"It means that even you had to be taught so if you'd just show me how to get this machine going, what I am to sew and how it is done, I will continue from then on by myself."

"Oh, one o' them, are yer? Know bloody everything, is that it? We've met your sort before, ain't we, Doris? If yer so bloody clever get on wi' it yerself."

Ivy smirked at Doris and several other girls who had overheard the exchange, then sat down at her machine and began furiously to set the treadle in motion.

"I don't think Mr Earnshaw will be very pleased if he comes back to find I've spoiled his shirts, do you, particularly as I have been put in your charge. It seems to me that you will be held responsible. I had better call him over and ask him if—"

"Yer little bitch." Ivy was so incensed she missed her footing on the treadle and her machine came to an abrupt stop. "Yer'd bloody tattle ter 'im an' before yer've bin 'ere five minutes?"

"No, I won't. Just show me what to do and I'll leave you alone. I'm a quick learner, Ivy, and I promise not to hold you up for long. In fact, when I get the hang of it I'll do a few for you so that you won't lose any money over it. How's that?"

Ivy was astounded, though somewhat mollified, but she would not let the new girl see it, so with a pretence of irritation she bent over Nancy and guided her on her first steps to becoming a machinist. It was apparent in her demeanour that she thought the new girl was a real facer and no mistake, even the way she talked confusing her, but if she was prepared to make up Ivy's time then she didn't mind giving her a hand.

It seemed that the frail-looking girl, whose name was Jennet, was not only a machinist, a hand finisher and an exquisite needlewoman, which was not really needed in Mr Earnshaw's line of business, but also Mr Earnshaw's right-hand "man". It turned out that she had been with him for four years and he trusted her. As Nancy was to find out later, Jennet could have run Mr Earnshaw's business as well as, if not better than, he could. There was nothing she did not know about the business of shirtmaking from the purchase of the cotton cloth to where to sell the finished product and every process in between. There was a Mrs Earnshaw who rarely emerged from the back realms of the workshop, even sending her eldest, a child of ten, to do what shopping was needed for her and Earnshaw, as she called him, and the nine children who came after the ten-year-old.

Nancy was in trouble within the first hour, not only with Ivy, who had soon calmed down when she realised that Nancy was going to be no bother to her, but with Mr Earnshaw. There were several young girls, no more than ten or eleven, standing at the basting table carefully tacking the seams which would then be hand sewn. They were not allowed to sit down, for if they did they could not comfortably reach the high table. For hours on end they sewed, their heads nodding now and again and it was Mr Earnshaw's practice to give them a crack about the ears to keep them alert.

She stood it for no more than an hour, cringing every time his heavy hand cracked a child's head to the bench in front of her. She had seen overlookers in the cotton mill give a child a clout to keep it from dozing off but it had been no more than a cuff round the ear and nothing like the heavy-handed treatment Mr Earnshaw doled out.

"Surely there is no need to be so brutal with that child, Mr Earnshaw." Her voice was heard even above the racket of the machines, but it was noticeable that not one female, from eleven years old to fifty, lifted her head. "Can not a more humane method be used to keep them awake? I would have thought so."

So far neither Mary nor Rosie had faltered and God knows what she would do if they did, for she would have no truck with him slapping them about as he had done with several others. It was barely nine o'clock in the morning. What would these children be like by six tonight?

Mr Earnshaw turned in astonishment, ready to do a bit of slapping in her direction, then he began to laugh. It was not often someone, especially a female, caused a flicker of interest in his busy and often worrying life, for there was a lot of competition in the making up trade, but this lass was proving to be a real diversion. Not that he would take any notice of her, not in that respect anyhow, but it might prove interesting to see, if she wanted to keep her job, that is, how she would respond to a bit of . . . well, he wouldn't mind feeling her up in the outhouse in the back. She was a bloody good-looking girl!

"Well, will yer listen to Lady Muck 'ere. 'Umane'! Where d'yer pick up words like that, my lass? Not in Angel Meadow, I'll be bound. But there's one thing you an' me'd best get straight or yer might as well bugger off right now an' tekk yer sisters with yer. You mind yer own business, see, an' stop stickin' yer nose inter mine. That way you an' me'll get on fine. I dunno, talk about bloody cheek." He walked away, quite entertained, it seemed, by the new girl, smiling and shaking his head. Nancy bent her head to her work, conscious of the smirks and soft whispers around her. She had made a mistake and though it would be very hard to restrain that quick flare of temper which now and then afflicted her she would damn well have to do it. It incensed her to see these fragile little creatures, who, but for her own hard work, might have been her own sisters, misused by men like Earnshaw, and, she supposed, the thought popping uninvited into her head, the young master at Monarch Mill, but there was nothing, absolutely nothing she could do about it. She had her own future to think about, her own carefully planned and dreamed-of future to safeguard, so she must learn to keep her head down and her trap shut.

At dinner time some of the women left the workshop and turned out into the street but the majority pulled dirty newspapers from under their tables wrapped around bits of bread and butter, cold sausages, salt fish, slabs of bacon or herrings. There was a tin teapot stewing on the stove where the irons were kept hot and from this those who wished to pay into the collective purse might purchase a cup of tea coloured with skimmed milk. Nancy, Rosie and Mary caused quite a sensation when from a small wicker basket Nancy brought out a red checked cloth wrapped around pieces of fresh bread, cheese and pickle, three apples and a jug of fresh milk. The bread, bought on Saturday from the fresh bread stall on the market, was two days old by now, of course, but a hell of a lot more appetising than what the rest were eating, though the milk had been purchased only that morning from the milk dray that did business in St George's Road.

"You and your sisters eat wisely," a soft, gentle voice said in Nancy's ear. "No wonder you are all so attractive."

Nancy turned in surprise. They were seated on the forms round the sewing table, she, Rosie and Mary and several other girls who were staring in amazement, and whose mouths salivated as Rosie bit deeply into a fat pickle. On Nancy's other side was the girl called Jennet and from a small but clean packet she was nibbling on a piece of bread which had smeared on it what looked like thin, colourless dripping. She had a bottle with a screw top and in it was a clear liquid which could only be water and which she poured daintily into a small cup with roses painted on its side.

"Well, that's nice of you to say so . . . er . . ."

"Jennet."

"Jennet, what a pretty name. I've not heard it before."

"No, it was my mother's name and when she died at my birth my father, who loved her, gave her name to me. But please, won't you tell me about the contents of your picnic basket? It is most unusual."

Nancy smiled. "Well, I found early on in life that if you are careful in what you eat there is less likelihood of being ill. My mother used to make us drink milk, I didn't know why at the time but it seems it builds good teeth. The same with cheese. I've come to the conclusion that all . . . all natural foods are better for you. Dear Lord, will you listen to me giving you a lecture on what to eat. Most people think I'm simple-minded. Besides, I'm sure you must know all this." For it was very evident from the way she spoke and acted that Jennet was not of the same class as the other girls in the workshop. Though she had not said much, really only to give orders and speak here and there to another hand, her voice was like no other Nancy had heard. *Except one!*

"Well, I'm afraid it's a case really of having little choice. When you have no more than a few shillings a week left to spend on food after rent and—"

"Oh, no, Jennet. I go to the market every Saturday and if you leave it until late you can buy food at knock-down prices. Poultry, meat, fish, stuff that won't keep until Monday, and the choice of vegetables and fruit . . . I've brought my sisters up on such a diet and they've not ailed a day."

"You!" Jennet looked astonished.

"Yes, you see our mother . . . died when I was nine and so I had no choice but to . . ."

Dear God in heaven, why was she rattling on like this to a perfect stranger, one she had met only hours before? Jennet was no bigger than two pennorth of copper, with bones on her like a bird and looking as though a puff of wind would have her over. And yet Nancy had seen the amount of work she had got through with no word of complaint. The help she gave unstintingly when asked, her quick replies to Mr Earnshaw about this or that bit of business, her knowledge which Mr Earnshaw appeared to rely on. This was the first time she had sat down, except when she was untangling some mistake one of the other machinists had made. She was eating what looked like bird crumbs; in fact there were scarcely enough to keep a sparrow alive. Her face was thin, pale, her nose was too big for it, her forehead extremely high, her mouth too wide with scarcely more colour in it than her cheeks. Her eyes were an enormous silvery grey, and her soft, pretty hair, a pale golden blonde, was scraped back from her face into a tumbling knot of curls. She wore black, unrelieved, plain, coarse, beneath which her black boots twinkled with polish. A clean, neat little person and Nancy approved of that. Perhaps it was why she had taken a . . . yes, she must admit it, she had a taken a fancy to her.

"I tell you what, when we've finished here on Saturday why don't you come with me and my sisters to Smithfield and we'll do our marketing together. I bet I can make your few bob go further than you can." She grinned and was rewarded by a shy smile of pleasure.

"Oh, would you? I'm afraid I'm not much of a housekeeper. You see until my father died there was—" She stopped speaking abruptly, colouring up from her neckline to her hair.

"Where d'you live, Jennet?" Nancy asked her, realising that there was something vulnerable and mysterious about this girl and that she was not willing to divulge it.

"I've a room in a house on Fennel Street, just over the river."

"Why, that's on our way home. We can walk together, but I have one condition." Nancy kept her face very serious and she could sense Jennet's withdrawal. She felt enormously protective for no good reason towards this slight little girl. Well, she was really no girl. Probably about eighteen or nineteen but the size of her gave the impression she was no more than a child.

"Yes?" Jennet said warily.

"I want you to teach me to speak like you do. I know the words but until I heard you" – and someone else – "I didn't know I wasn't pronouncing them properly. Is that a deal?"

Jennet gave a little gurgle of laughter, the first Nancy had heard, leaning for a moment against Nancy's shoulder.

"It's a deal."

She was the first friend Nancy had ever had. Her sisters were part of her, loved and protected, but it was her instinct to love and protect them, like a mother with her children, her own flesh and blood, her responsibility which she had no choice but to take on. She knew she would guard and direct them until they were old enough and mature enough to make their own decisions but with Jennet it was entirely different. She liked her. She loved her sisters because it was natural to do so but she liked Jennet with no strings attached. Jennet was hardworking, conscientious, honest, good-mannered, shy and yet willing to share all she knew, and was, with Nancy. Rosie and Mary were a bit stiff with her at first, inclined to feel left out of the friendship that bloomed between their sister and Jennet. They couldn't see what Nancy saw in her, they said, not realising that for the first time in her life Nancy was holding conversations with another person who was as well read as she was. Who understood what Nancy understood, who could share views with or argue with her, on many subjects that did not interest her sisters in the least. They could read and write and add up, since she had made them learn, not because they wanted to but because she wanted them to. It had been a chore to them, not a love of learning as it was with Nancy and she knew if she wasn't there behind them they would probably drift off to the sort of life that would lead them to become a Mrs O'Rourke or a Mrs Murphy, living in Angel Meadow or somewhere like it for the rest of their lives. At the moment they were prepared to follow quite cheerfully where she led but already there were lads hanging about outside their front door, calling out and whistling after the Brody girls and both Mary and Rosie would giggle and preen and glance back over their shoulders at them; how long would it be before they began to chafe at the bonds Nancy kept firmly about them? When they did she wanted to be long gone from Church Court, even if it was only to some small place, perhaps another cottage but in a better part of the city.

One of those lads was Mick O'Rourke. Not that Mick hung

about outside waiting for her to appear. Not he! He would boldly knock on the door and take it as his right to be invited inside, since it was well known in the area by now that Nancy Brody was his girl. Had he not taken her about, first with her sisters and then on her own to the exhibition at Old Trafford. Though he had been disappointed by her response to the sacrifice he had made in taking her to the bloody thing it in no way deterred him from pursuing her, from inviting her to go to the Annual Manchester Fair on Liverpool Road, for a Sunday walk among the flowers in Peel Park, to Belle Vue and the dancing that took place there and which would surely lead to better things and even to the Music Hall where there were some damn good turns to be seen. He was willing to spend money on her, for Christ's sake, so what more did she want?

He didn't like it when she said no; he didn't like it and he didn't believe it, for handsome Mick O'Rourke could have any girl he pleased and so he persisted. He knew she was different to the other girls of his acquaintance; that's what fascinated him about her, apart from her looks which made every male head turn as she walked with that straight-backed and graceful stride of hers down Church Court. He couldn't understand it, really he couldn't and he told her so every time he got inside the house. They had been getting on so well, so why was she trying to break his heart like this? he asked her, grinning audaciously, for he had learned that if he could make her laugh she would relax and smile back at him which made him try all the harder.

"Mick, you're a lovely chap, really you are."

"Well, then, why won't yer come to Belle Vue wi' me on Sunday?"

"Because I've things to do."

"What things?"

"I've a friend coming."

He frowned ominously. "What friend? 'An' if it's a bloke I'll knock 'is bloody block off, so I will. Yer my—"

"Mick, it's not a man and if it were it would not be your concern. I am not . . . not your anything, so please, won't you stop believing that I am. We are friends, if you like, and I was very grateful to you for taking me to the exhibition."

"Show it, then."

"I don't know . . ."

"Yes, yer do. Stop pretendin' yer not interested in me, acushla. Come on, let's—"

"No, Mick, you must stop this."

But it did no good. His face would grin at her when she opened the door, his charm, which was beginning seriously to get on her nerves, oozing from him in the belief that he had only to persevere and Nancy Brody would fall into his arms like every other girl he had known. He was a problem and one that she would have to address resolutely very soon. He had even taken exception to her friendship with Jennet, his face stiff with indignation, asking her what she wanted with such a milksop when she could be with him.

Jennet had begun to spend Sunday with them, since it seemed she lived alone. She knew the city like the back of her hand, she said, as she and her father had lived in and explored it ever since she was a child, and though many of the places, art galleries, museums, a concert at the Free Trade Hall where the Hallé Orchestra was playing, were not to the younger sisters' taste, at least they were going out, not exactly meeting people but *seeing* them, which was nearly as good, and better than sitting at home reading a book.

Mr Earnshaw, though he wasn't much on handing out compliments, was pleased as punch at the way the Brody girls got on. All three were soon on machines, earning, since they were on piece work at the rate of twopence halfpenny a shirt, over ten shillings a week each. He did not tell them, of course, what *his* profit was on every shirt they made up, though he might have been somewhat more generous with Nancy if she had been more generous with him. No matter how hard he tried he had not yet cornered her in the outhouse. He was unaware that Ivy and Doris, both not unattractive, had warned her the first week she was there, since he had tried it on with both of them. In fact with every girl with a claim to looks.

"Not that Jennet, o' course. There's not a man in Manchester 'oo'd want a feel of 'er, poor, skinny little bugger, but yer want ter watch them sisters o' yours, Nance," Ivy told her. "He don't care 'ow young they are."

Nancy and Ivy had taken measure of one another by now and had formed a tentative alliance and had it not been for the troublesome business with Mick O'Rourke, which was beginning to turn nasty, Nancy would have gloried in the way her plans were taking shape.

8

The sound of a human voice pealing up among the full, interlocking branches of the heavily leafed beech tree lifted a flock of rooks from their nests and sent them spinning in an ever widening circle above the woodland. The sound came again, this time deeper, full-throated and in the foliage that grew there, yew, holly and wild cherry, small animals such as badgers, squirrels, mice and rabbits, come to gather the harvest of autumn nuts, burrowed deeper into the dense shade.

The trees were quite magnificent, positively glowing with colour, a brilliant mosaic display of flaming orange, russet and gold as summer departed and though the sun could barely reach the woodland floor through the dense foliage a narrow shaft of light beamed down through a break in the canopy to touch the entwined figures of a man and woman who gasped and floundered on a soft bed of wood anemone.

"Dear God, Evie," the man got out at last, "that was bloody marvellous. You really are wonderful." His sweated cheek was pressed to the full and lovely breast of the woman, his body, naked but for his shirt and, incongruously, his riding boots, slumped in the boneless devastation that comes after making love, nailed to hers in a way that seemed to say he didn't think he could ever stand again.

They lay still for several minutes, the woman, a girl really, lovingly smoothing the rough tangle of the man's hair, her eyes dreaming up into the branches of the trees. Her bodice had been thrown to one side along with the man's breeches, leaving her naked from the waist up and her full skirt and froth of white petticoats had been pushed to a position where the man could have access to her body with his. She wore white stockings to just above her knees and might have looked somewhat foolish, but she was an exceedingly pretty girl with shapely legs and skin like silk on her thighs and belly. The dark patch of her pubic hair, which was revealed when the man rolled off her, was damp and crisp and curling.

At once, as if now that his body no longer shielded hers, though there was no one to see but the birds and animals of Kersall Dell, she pulled her garments about herself, looking away with what seemed shy modesty as the man struggled to get his breeches over his boots and draw them up about his lean hips.

When they were both decently clothed he turned to her and pulled her into his arms, holding her against his chest and fondling her cheek and smooth throat. He breathed in the sweet aroma of her hair which tumbled in a glossy mass about her shoulders and down her back, then sighed quite dramatically. Josh Hayes was not in love with this sweet girl, he knew that, but she certainly possessed him, body if not soul, at the moment. Not only was she gentle and good-hearted and ready to laugh whenever he did, she was as lovely and fresh as the wild flowers that bloomed in the fields about his home. She was made for love, too, now that she had given in to his pleading, as passionate and eager as he was himself in the delights of the male and female body and what they did together.

But the loving thoughts only came to him in the moments after he had made love to her. As soon as they had parted, she with many a backward, yearning glance, he with light-hearted kisses blown to her across the privacy of the walled vegetable garden that they slipped through, he barely gave her another thought, since he had such a lot on his mind these days. His father was putting more and more responsibility on to his shoulders, pleased with him at last and the way he was shaping. He had begun to send him to Liverpool to see to the business interests they had there and there was even talk of him going to America to get a first-hand look at the growing of the cotton that was their livelihood. His father had more or less put the warehouse in Moseley Street, where their cotton goods were not only stored but displayed and sold, almost totally in his charge. Mr Jonas, the warehouse manager, was still in charge in name but it was only as a supervisor and Josh knew that at last he was beginning to enjoy the challenge his father had, daringly for him, flung his way. It was what he needed and he had risen to it and was proud of himself and he knew that privately his father was too, though he wouldn't have said so for the world.

The end of May, just after they had all been to the art exhibition, seemed to have been the turning-point in his life, and he couldn't for the life of him think why, though in some strange sense, daft as it seemed, he had begun to think that it was something to do with that girl.

It had been a strange experience and even now, at times, just before he fell into a deep, dreamless sleep he saw behind his closed lids the golden-lit eyes and soft, parted lips, as though in surprise, of the girl who worked in his father's mill. He didn't know why. She was remarkably lovely, refined-looking, he could remember that, and he could also remember the strange feeling that had come over him at the sight of her lover; he supposed it was her lover, putting his arm possessively about her shoulders. He had not liked it. It was as though he were disappointed in her. She had been so brave and fearless in the mill yard, and, yes, different from the usual girls who were employed at the machines, and to see her with that big, coarse chap with the bold strut of a prize fighter seemed to have demeaned her. Still, it was not his concern, was it, he had told himself and after that he had other things to think of.

It had been the following week that Evie had been coaxed and kissed into finally giving way, allowing him to take her into an abandoned workman's hut on the other side of the river and remove her clothes.

God, what a moment that had been. She had been shy, distressed almost, but the love she spoke of continuously as though that made what they did acceptable had so overpowered her she had not stayed his hands as they began their leisurely exploring of her virgin body.

"Will I have a bairn, sir?" she had whispered, for her mother did, every year, the result of the regular coupling with Evie's father. "I'm afeared of havin' a bairn." The words were anguished, pleading, but what man can think of that when his male body is totally aroused and will not be denied its natural conclusion. He thought of it at other times, naturally, but not at that precise moment and when she reassured him a week or two later, her face crimson with embarrassment, that she had not "fallen", he had drawn her tenderly into his arms, his kisses persuading her that if she had escaped the consequences she dreaded once, then she would do so again.

That was nearly four months ago.

"D'you love me, Josh?" She sighed, burrowing her face into the curve under his chin. She looked quite glorious, flushed and dishevelled and at that moment, as he looked down at her, he did.

"Of course I do, sweetheart," he murmured, bending his head to kiss her parted lips. "In fact, if I wasn't pushed for time I could start all over again."

"I didn't mean that, Josh." And at once he felt the familiar spurt of irritation. She always asked him the same question whenever they lay in the aftermath of lovemaking and it always made him feel resentful and, yes, he supposed, guilty because he knew just what she meant and just what she wanted him to say, and, of course, he couldn't. Surely she knew what she was and what he was. Surely she could not truly believe that something could come of this liaison of theirs. He was the son of one of the most influential and wealthy men in Manchester and she was his mother's laundry-maid. He wished it could be different but it wasn't. One day, he supposed, he would be expected to marry some suitable young lady of his own station in life who would be just like his mother. One day he, and, he imagined, when the time came, his younger brother who was fourteen and still at school, would own and run the business his grandfather and father had built up, and this delectable young girl had no part, could have no part, in his future life. She was not simple-minded so why did she ask the same question of him as though she hoped that one day he might say, "Yes, I love you and want you to be my wife."

His mare, who was tethered to a tree a few yards away, lifted her head and blew through her nostrils and they both turned to look at her. It was as though it were a reminder of their separate duties, he as the son of a great house, she as its servant. A familiar story and one Josh himself would have smiled over if it had not concerned him.

The autumn sun as it dropped lower in the sky was turning to flame, lighting a few drifting clouds to gold-rimmed apricot. An owl, hunting early, swooped through the branches of a tree, its startled cry at the sight of the human creatures carried away into the approaching dusk. Birdsong, which had piped up in the ensuing silence, died away again to a soft, fitful murmur and with a muffled oath Josh stood up then leaned down to help Evie to her feet.

"We'd best be getting back, sweetheart. We can't talk now. Mother's got people coming to a dinner party and I'll be in hot water if I'm not there to greet her guests." He smiled as he fiddled with buttons and buckles, not looking at her; but though, as she always had done in the past, the girl wanted nothing more than to leave the subject alone, for could she really believe that his answer would be any different, something in her tightened and strengthened and made her sharp. She knew it would do her no good, that it would only make him truculent if she pushed him into a corner, but this time she could not stop herself.

"I asked you if you loved me, Josh. You didn't answer."

"I did. You know how much I think of you, Evie. Now, please, I must go or my—"

"Yes, I know, your mam is having a dinner party. I should know, I washed and ironed the tablecloth and napkins that're to be used."

"Well then, we should go."

"So you say, but . . ." Suddenly she crumpled, putting her face in her hands. "Oh, please, Josh, please . . ."

He turned to her at once and took her into his arms, kissing her wet cheeks and smoothing her tumbled hair back from her forehead. This was how he loved her. When she was sweet and submissive, not making demands he could not possibly answer. He loved her when she trembled beneath the touch of his hands, when she moaned as he entered her, when she cried out as he brought her to a fluttering climax and when she clung to him afterwards, not asking him to love her but just to hold her in his arms. He loved her when she laughed with him, when she listened to him talk about what he meant to do, quite spellbound when he described the ships in the port of Liverpool, the shops there, his journey on the train, and his plans to visit America. Then he loved her, for she made him feel like a . . . like a what? He didn't know, only that it was special, to him and to her.

"Come, lovely girl," he said tenderly to her now. "We really must go or not only will my mother be searching for me but Mrs Harvey will be scouring the house for you."

"Kiss me, Josh."

Willingly he did so, sorry really that he had to go, ready to say the words to her she wanted to hear, for she was so sweet and docile under his hands, but somehow he couldn't. They were words he had spoken to no woman and never would until it was the truth. Amazingly a flushed face glimmered across his vision and it was not the face of the girl beside him. Not blue eyes but a deep, golden brown. Hell and damnation, he groaned to himself, what was wrong with him, thinking about a girl he had seen only twice in his life and at a time like this as well. He must have lost his wits. He turned blindly towards his mare. It was nearly dark.

It was dark once she had left the gas-lit thoroughfare of St George's Road and Angel Street, just like plunging into a gloomy tunnel. The candlelit windows, which were let into the scabby walls of the cottages on either side of the narrow length of Church Court, were barely visible. She could hear voices, some of them talking quite normally inside their one-up, one-down boxes along Church Court, others quarrelling, screaming even, as the usual family evening took shape. Mothers would be screeching at squabbling children; husbands and fathers lifting heavy fists in frustration, or flinging open flimsy front doors in their escape to the beer house at the corner: crashes and cries of pain, for they were poor and Irish with tempers to match in Church Court and they were not quiet, at play, at work or in the squalid sanctity of their own homes.

She had sent Mary and Rosie home, with Mr Earnshaw's permission, of course, since they had finished their quota of shirts, as she had, but at the last minute Mr Earnshaw had offered her and Jennet a shilling if they would just put the buttonholes in half a dozen shirts between them. A last-minute order and they were the quickest and neatest sewers in the workshop and so, unable to turn down the chance of an extra shilling which, after all, was almost the price of the hire of a sewing-machine for one week, they had agreed.

They had sauntered out of Brown Street and into Chapel Street together, crossing the river at Old Bridge to Cateaton Street and on to the end of Fennel Street where they had bid one another an affectionate goodnight. They had talked all the way, telling one another it would not be long, perhaps the spring of next year, before they would start up the business they planned together because, of course, she would not dream of leaving Jennet behind in this new endeavour. Nancy found it quite glorious to have someone . . . well, sensible, practical, to discuss things with, for with the best will in the world, though they worked hard and willingly, her sisters did not have the sharp mind and shrewd intelligence Jennet had. Before the winter set in, though why that should matter they didn't know, for the trains were very reliable, they meant to go over to Oldham and have a look at the sewing-machines they would hire, and there would be a workshop to find, for once they got under way the downstairs room at Church Court would not be big enough for them all. Jennet would move in with them, naturally, since it was not practical to pay the rent on two places. In fact, they had talked about her coming to Church Court soon for this very reason. Nancy's secret hoard behind the loose brick in the bedroom continued to grow, penny by penny, helped by a surprising contribution from Jennet who had been left a tiny sum by her father. Andrew Williams had been a parson in a poor parish in Pendleton, Jennet had told Nancy, and, though she did not know how he had done it since they lived like church mice, he had passed on what he had saved, for an emergency, he had told her as he lay dying. She had not touched it yet, though God knew she had been tempted to do so many times in the hard days of working for Earnshaw's Fine Shirts. Now, since she was to be partner in this enterprise it was at Nancy's disposal and . . . Oh, dear Lord, as Jennet would say, for she did not care for swearing, they got so excited they could hardly speak, holding on to one another's arm as they strode out towards their wonderful future. Nancy gave thanks every day for Jennet. Oh, she would have done it on her own. She'd come this far, hadn't she, but without Jennet to encourage her, to give advice, to advocate caution, generally just to be there to listen it would not have been the same.

There was a ginnel between the Finnigans' cottage and the Murphys' which led on to Style Street and it was as she was hurrying past it, hoping that Mary had remembered to put the beef stew on to warm, her mind already winging on to her own place no more than a dozen yards away, that a pair of brawny arms came at her from nowhere, a hand was clasped over her mouth and she was dragged into the total darkness of the passage. She knew who it was, of course, because hadn't these same arms done their best for the past three months to get themselves about her whenever they had a chance. She wasn't even particularly alarmed, for she had always been able to evade Mick O'Rourke's advances, to talk or laugh him out of the foolishness he directed at her every time he caught her in the street or knocked on her door and blustered his way inside. He had even spoken of marriage, for God's sake, the last time, backing her up to the window of Ma Siddons' gin-shop, from where he had just come, capturing her between his arms, his hands flat on the window, begging her to stop this bloody nonsense, which was how he saw her daft refusal to let him court her. Yes, that was what he had said. Court her! He had been drunk, of course, and it had been this that had allowed her to push him aside in disgust and run for her life to her cottage.

So what the devil he thought he was up to now she couldn't imagine. He wasn't drunk or she would have detected it on his breath. His big hand over her mouth smelled of onions which made her want to retch as she fought silently to escape him. She heaved and kicked against him, doing her best to get the heels of her boots into his shins, but he was strong and determined, dragging her backwards through the heaps of refuse that had piled up over the years in the passage, then, to her surprise, across Style Street, which was deserted, and into the narrow alleyway that led to the burial ground at the back of St Michael's Church.

He let her go then, flinging her forward on to a stone-edged grave so that she fell against the headstone, putting out both hands to save her face and badly grazing her palms.

She turned and like a wildcat just let out of a bag and furious about it she flew at him, spitting out all the foul words she had learned through her childhood, reaching for his eyes, ready to draw blood, to feel his skin break beneath her nails, to blind him or cripple him in any way she could, but he merely reached out and grabbed her by the wrists and held her, saying nothing, the whites of his eyes and his teeth, which he seemed to be baring like a wild beast, the only things she could see in the darkness.

"I'll have the bloody law on you for this, Mick O'Rourke," she hissed, struggling to get her hands free, aiming at him with her feet but he was a large man with muscles built up in the prize-fighting ring, agile and quick on his feet and though she herself was not fragile she was no match for him. "Let me go, yer lousy, stinking bastard or I swear I'll scream me bloody 'ead off."

"Scream, is it? Go ahead, acushla," he said quietly, the softness of his voice, where she would have expected bluff and bluster, surprising her. "Sure an' there's no one ter 'ear yer an' if they did 'oo'd tekk any notice round 'ere?"

Which was true, for in this part of the city husbands frequently thrashed their wives, or children, there were set-tos outside the gin-shops and beer houses where not only men but drunken women took exception to one another, raising their voices to the skies. One more would scarcely be noticed and if it was, would be ignored.

"What in 'ell's name d'yer want?" she screeched at him, knowing she sounded like a fishwife but unable to hang on to the calm, well-modulated voice Jennet was teaching her.

"Ye know what I'm wantin', m'darlin'." She could see him more clearly now that her eyes had become used to the diffused darkness which seemed to hang like a veil about the leaning, lopsided headstones. He was holding out his hands placatingly in a way she had not seen before, pleading, begging her to listen to him, since there was no one in this dark place to see charming, handsome, winsome Mick O'Rourke humble himself.

"I've never said this ter any woman before, Nancy Brody, but . . . I love yer, yer see, an' well . . . I reckon we'd be 'appy together. I'd do me best, acushla. As the Blessed Virgin's me witness I swear yer'd not want fer owt. I . . . Jesus, Mary and Joseph, I wanter marry yer, lovely girl, so what d'yer think ter that?"

He stuck his chest out. His pride in himself was very clear, his willingness to put aside all other considerations, like the amazement of his mates, evident in his tone of voice. His belief that though it had cost him a great deal of soul-searching, if the only way he could have this mysterious, fascinating, irritating girl was to wed her then so be it. In his eyes and in the eyes of Angel Meadow he was considered a good catch. He was strong and healthy. He had a steady job and didn't mind hard work. He could provide for her in a grand fashion, by the standards of those hereabouts, for not only did he have decent employment he earned many a purse in the prize-fighting ring. There wasn't a girl in Angel Meadow who wouldn't jump at the chance to marry Mick O'Rourke and he had convinced himself that the reason Nancy Brody had been so bloody elusive was because she was not aware of his grand intentions. His mam would have a fit but what did he care. He was a Catholic and went now and again to mass since he had been taught that he would undoubtedly go straight to purgatory if he transgressed and, though he didn't believe it, just to be on the safe side he showed his face to the Blessed Virgin on the occasional Sunday. His and Nancy's children would be brought up in the true faith, naturally, even if Nancy wouldn't come over and his mam would have to be satisfied with that.

"Well?" He grinned, his teeth a white slash in the darkness of his face, cocky and pleased as punch and glad, really, that he was to make the great sacrifice of his freedom, for would that not prove to her what his feelings for her really were. "Let's 'ave a kiss then, acushla. All these bloody months when we've bin . . . friends I've never even kissed yer. That shows 'ow much I respect yer, darlin'. 'Ave yer any idea 'ow 'ard it's bin for me, watchin' yer go by wi' that way yer walk what sets all't lads off? A real teaser, so yer are, but I'll say nowt more. So, 'ow about it, darlin', come over 'ere an' give us a kiss."

She made a mistake. Mick O'Rourke was not a violent man, not with women at any rate. He meant her no harm. He had dragged her out here because it was the only place he could think of where they could be totally alone and uninterrupted. Everywhere they met there had always been someone about but here she could not escape him. She would be forced to listen.

His cocky assumption that she had only to be offered marriage to fall into his arms infuriated her and she made no effort to keep the contempt and loathing out of her voice.

"Dear sweet Jesus, why won't you listen to me, Mick O'Rourke," she snarled, white-hot with anger and rage. "I wouldn't marry yer if yer were the last man on earth, d'yer hear. I don't love yer. I don't even like yer, yer cocky bastard. Yer never see any further than the end o' yer nose, do yer? Are yer so puffed up with the belief that yer God's gift ter women yer think every lass yer smile at's bound ter fall inter yer filthy 'ands? Well, 'ere's one who won't, so just step aside. Go on, get out o' me way, yer jumped-up piss-pot, fer yer must be drunk if yer'd imagine—"

"Yer little bitch, don't yer dare speak ter me like that. 'Oo the 'ell d'yer think you are. I'm offering marriage, yer daft cow," just as though she had misunderstood him and needed further explanation.

"I don't bloody care if yer ter be made King of England and want me ter be Queen, Mick O'Rourke. I don't want yer. Can't yer get that inter yer thick Irish 'ead. *I don't want yer!* Now get out o' me way fer I've 'eard enough o' this bloody nonsense."

His fist came out of the darkness with the swiftness of a bullet from a gun, catching her on the point of her jaw where, in a dozen fights, Mick had learned to knock his opponents to the canvas. His eyes were blind in the darkness, with an uncontrollable anger, a frustration at the contemptuous smashing of his hopes and dreams and longings, for he truly loved Nancy Brody, a destruction of what he had believed to be the rightness of his proposal. She had belittled him and his aspirations. She had spat on him and his longing to do the right thing by her and in that moment, a moment of rejection he had never known before, his mind went blank, empty of everything but his male desire to hurt, to possess, to humiliate, to subjugate; in other words to show Nancy Brody who was boss.

She fell away from him in the dark, landing spreadeagled on the grave, her head, as it thumped downwards, catching the corner of the headstone. The darkness, which was a kind of sombre grey all around her marked here and there by the deeper darkness of the headstones, dragged her downwards into an inky black hole and the last thing her anguished eyes saw were the onion-smelling hands of Mick O'Rourke reaching out for her.

He was gone when she came to. She was alone in the dead of night among the sneering ghosts of those who must have come out of their graves to mock her. In her arrogance and belief in the absolute rightness and strength of Nancy Brody she had taken one step too far and it had knocked Mick O'Rourke far from the whimsical, good-humoured, fun-loving Irishman who had pursued her for the last few months. She had taken something from him with her contemptuous refusal of the honour he was doing her, the honour of marrying the best catch in the Irish community and he had . . . Oh, dear God in heaven, what had he done to her? While she had been unconscious – the aching of her head and her jaw told her she had been unconscious – what had he done to her? She hardly dare stand. She hardly dare raise her head from the weeds on which it lay, for she could feel the cold and the damp and the mossy slime, not with her hands which were still outspread as though in crucifixion, but on her . . . on her . . . Dear Lord . . . Oh, dear Lord, help me . . . on the backs of her bare legs, on her belly and thighs, on her buttocks and the small of her bare back which was pressed down on to the cold stone and rotting vegetation of the grave. She ached from head to foot as though she had been given a beating and she was sore in that private place she had defended so fiercely. There was something wet and sticky on the inside of her thighs; aah, dear God . . . oh, please not. Please, sweet Jesus, help me . . . help me.

She knew what had been done to her, of course she did. She had been knocked down, forced on to her back and while she was there, dazed and semi-conscious, held like a bitch and raped. Mick O'Rourke, allowing his wild rage to overpower him, had taken what she had denied him.

She was a strong woman; circumstances and her own resolute will had made her so and despite the hardships ahead of her she had not been afraid. She had confidence and pride in herself, a belief that she would succeed. She also believed she was a woman of warmth and humour with an inclination to do a kindness where she could to those who deserved it. She had in her a capacity to do things that would not only help her family but others whom she hoped to employ to escape the trap of poverty. A woman then, of consequence, in a small way. A woman who had a joy in her own self-esteem, for she knew it to be justified.

She was not that same woman when she finally got to her feet. She had been weakened. She trembled in deep shock and her hands fluttered uselessly as she made an attempt to smooth her clothing about her abused body. She felt frail, not just physically but in her woman's mind which flinched away from the horror of what she had suffered. Indeed it could not believe it. Her stunned senses could not seem to function on the level she had become used to, wandering confusedly among images that she could not remember. She wanted to weep. She wanted to run home and be gathered in some strong and protective arms, shushed and petted and told she would be all right but there was no one in Nancy Brody's life to do that for her. There had never been anyone in Nancy Brody's life to do that for her. Ever. And if there were, would she let them? Did she want anyone to know that Mick O'Rourke had finally had his way with Nancy Brody? She was pretty sure he would tell no one, even if he wanted to boast of it, since he would be too afraid she might tell the truth of it, show him up not only as a rapist but as a man who had been contemptuously refused by a woman, which would be worse in his eyes. A woman he had to rape to get!

She would keep it to herself then. She was helpless and ready to stagger like a toddling child at this moment of vulnerability but give her a few minutes and, by God, she would be herself again. Not the same, but strong again. She would not let this . . . this desolation drag her down as Mick O'Rourke had dragged her down; but she'd not forget it, not if she lived to be a hundred, and neither would Mick O'Rourke!

9

Though the sun was shining from a cloudless blue sky, the blue the colour of a duck egg, it was bitterly cold with a crackling coverlet of hoar frost underfoot. The frost even helped to disguise the ugliness and filth of Angel Meadow, painting the roofs and window ledges, the piles of rubbish, the cracked pavements and cracked doorsteps with a shining silvery white which dazzled like scattered diamonds in the sunshine. It was a Sunday and there was no one about, for even those who were to attend mass had decided that the later one would do when perhaps the streets would be "aired". They huddled together under their thin coverlets or sat over carefully nursed nuggets of coal on fires that were barely alight, cursing the winter and all its tribulations. Life was hard at all times of the year, wages earned, when not poured down the throats of the men in the beer house, eked out to keep body and soul together, but in the winter it was malevolent. They fought it, some more savagely than others, but it was hard going until spring came to ease the burden.

Nancy Brody's fire leaped cheerfully up her chimney and had they seen it would have caused serious envy among her neighbours. She sat with her feet on the fender, brooding into the flames, her face pale and sombre. The room was warm, since she had left the fire in last night. She had banked it up with clinkers and ashes saved especially for the purpose in the ancient bucket Mick O'Rourke had mended for her mam many years ago and which was kept at the side of the chimney breast. Nothing was wasted in this household, not a scrap of food nor a scrap of material, not a button nor a pin nor a spoonful of water, not a farthing spent unnecessarily; and as soon as spring came she and Jennet were to hire three sewing-machines and move them in here. There had to be enough money to keep all four of them until the business began to make a profit. There was cotton cloth to be bought, thread, needles, oil for the machines and money enough to rent a stall in the market on which to display and sell their goods. Initially she had intended that she and the girls would move on from Mr Earnshaw's in Brown Street, where the business of shirtmaking took place, to the production of undergarments and baby clothes in the sweat shops on Shude Hill. But it appeared there was no need, for Jennet knew all there was to know about such things, since she had been employed in their manufacture before being taken on at Earnshaw's. Jennet was invaluable with her knowledge of the trade, knowing exactly where to purchase what was necessary, especially the fabric. They must make every farthing count, for if they failed it would be back to the sweated trade of shirtmaking for Mr Earnshaw or someone like him. *They must not fail.* She repeated the words over and over again, trying to regain the enthusiasm, the sheer, overpowering excitement that had surged through her for a long time now, but despair, something she had never allowed herself to suffer before, swept it all away on a wave of hopelessness that she could not seem to swim out of.

She sighed deeply, allowing her glance to wander round the room in which she had taken such pride. She had made it what it was. She had overcome the filth, the squalor, the misery, though she still lived, with the rest of the denizens of Angel Meadow, in unpaved streets, strewn with offal and refuse, airless cul-de-sacs and noisome alleyways. Among huge, unsightly, shapeless mills, towering chimneys which tainted the sky to a dull, leaden colour, the cesspools and ash-pits which were a familiar part of her everyday life. But her determination, her sheer bloody-minded determination had lifted her out of the life the others led, the life they saw no chance of changing nor had the will to try. It had given her the resolution to sweep aside all obstacles that might stand in the way of what she wanted for herself and her sisters. It had made a shining path that was hers to follow. It had got them this far but now . . . now, how was she to survive this last and fatal blow? This room was a symbol of all she had achieved. Nobody else in Church Court had strips of matting spread on a floor from which you could have eaten your dinner, nor two armchairs and a settle. None of the neighbours except

Mick O'Rourke had been inside in all the years the Brody girls had lived alone, but if they had they would have been open-mouthed with wonder at the sight of the whitewashed walls, the cupboard in which were displayed her precious assortment of mismatched crockery, her skillet and stewpan, her teatray, her clock and the pictures, cheap prints, that hung on her wall, her cracked ornaments, all costing next to nothing but loved just the same. Upstairs were two iron bedsteads with spotless feather mattresses and regularly changed bedding, warm blankets and even, bought in a dreadful fit of extravagance, a couple of worn patchwork quilts. She shared one bed with Jennet and the second was occupied by her sisters.

She had come so far, she, Nancy Brody, daughter of Angel Meadow's whore and now that was what they were going to call her. Like mother, like daughter, they would say, which didn't matter, for what did she care what people thought or said? What had she ever cared about the opinions of the people who lived beside her? What mattered was the enormous extra burden, the impediment, the strain this would put on not just her but on Jennet and the girls.

She leaned forward and grasped her knees with both hands as though in deep pain, gritting her teeth until they ground together. Great God above, what was she to do, what was she to do?

A sound behind her made her lift her head hurriedly and turn, doing her best to smile at Jennet who stood hesitantly at the foot of the stairs. Like Nancy she still wore just her nightgown. She bit her lip and half smiled, waiting for Nancy to say something, for Jennet was a private person who believed that others deserved to be private too. Then, as though it were not really her business – but how could she ignore what was obviously Nancy's pain? – she came forward and, sitting in the chair opposite, she leaned forward and took her hand in both of hers.

"What is it, Nancy? What's bothering you? You haven't been yourself for weeks now. Can you not tell me what it is? I'm, I hope, your friend. You have done so much for me I long to repay you in some way."

Nancy gripped Jennet's hands fiercely and her face spasmed with some deep-felt emotion. "God almighty, don't you think you haven't done that already? I couldn't have done . . . anything without you."

Jennet didn't even wince at the blasphemy nor the vice-like grip of her friend's hands. "Of course you could, Nancy Brody," she said quietly. "I wasn't here when you achieved this," looking round the cosy room. "I wasn't here when you found work for yourself and your sisters. I wasn't here when you went to Sunday school and learned to read and write. *You* did all that, you alone, for your sisters merely followed where you led. Now, something has happened and it is dragging you down, tearing you apart, I can see it and I want you to tell me what it is. I . . . well, tell me to mind my own business if you want but I'm your friend. I . . . I'm very fond of you, Nancy, and friends, true friends, help one another."

"You can do nothing to help me with this, Jennet Williams, so go back to bed and . . ." Nancy's voice was harsh in her effort not to weep. This was what she was afraid of. Weeping, crying her eyes out, and Jennet's soft sympathy was about to start her off. She had sworn she wouldn't cry. She wouldn't let any man make her cry but it was Jennet who was doing it and she resented it.

"Don't be so bloody foolish." The words were spoken coldly and Nancy lifted her bent head in astonishment.

"Why, Jennet, I've never heard you swear before."

"You're enough to make a saint swear, my girl, and it's no good looking at me like that. You're in trouble and I'm—"

"Yes, the worse sort, Jennet," Nancy interrupted sadly. "The worst sort of trouble an unmarried woman can be in and I'm sure I don't have to tell you what that is."

For several seconds Jennet stared at her uncomprehendingly then her pale face became even paler and her eyes grew wide with shock.

"Yes, you may well look amazed and so was I, though why that should be, I don't know. When a woman lies with a man it is a natural consequence."

"*Nancy*! You have . . ." Jennet gulped, for it seemed she was incapable of repeating the words Nancy had spoken.

"Aye. Oh, not voluntarily, believe me. I wasn't going to tell you, or anybody, if nothing had come of it but I'm afraid I won't be able to hide the result before very long. I was raped, Jennet."

"Dear Lord above!"

"Yes, on a grave in the churchyard."

"Dear sweet Jesus!"

"Oh, He was no help to me, Jennet, I can assure you. I was on sacred ground but there was no help from that quarter. I was dragged off the street, knocked unconscious and raped. Before he . . . he did it he offered to marry me which I suppose was very generous of him but I refused, which he seemed to think gave him the right to . . . Oh, Jennet, what am I to do? Jennet . . . Jennet."

With a soft cry Jennet swept Nancy into her arms, clutching her tightly, smoothing her cloud of curly hair, letting her weep the tears that had been dammed inside her for weeks. She said nothing, for what was there to say at this moment? Nancy was desolate, but if Jennet knew her friend, and she did, she would get over this in time. She would need the strength of others now, at least until she had regained her own and Jennet meant to be one of those others. She was horrified, repelled by the act that had brought Nancy to this; brave, courageous Nancy who had struggled so resolutely to escape from Angel Meadow. Jennet had been brought up in the gentle refinement of the vicarage and had, somehow, despite her squalid years in the sweat shop in Brown Street, and her bare room in Fennel Street, kept her gentleness and her refinement, for inside her bird-like frame was a core of steel without which she would not have survived. Now that steel was at Nancy's disposal.

Nancy wept for ten minutes, silently but savagely and all the while Jennet rocked her and soothed her, much as Nancy had wanted on the night Mick O'Rourke had taken her down. She wept a little herself, for she was a woman too and with that sense that women possess could imagine, as though it had happened to her, what Nancy had suffered. She produced a clean handkerchief, a relic of her days as parson's daughter, handing it to Nancy who blew her nose vigorously, then sat back in her chair. She looked at the handkerchief and with a touch of returned humour, grimaced. "What the devil is this bit of nonsense? It's scarcely big enough for a sparrow."

"I know, but it's all I had."

"Thank you." They looked into one another's face, both searching for something and, finding it, sighed then smiled.

"You'll do, Nancy," Jennet told her softly but sternly.

"I know that, lass. I know that now."

"We make a good team."

"I know that, too."

"I'll make a cup of tea."

"That'd be nice, then I'm going out."

Jennet, who had stood up to reach for the teapot and caddy, whirled about to face her. Her face was afraid for a moment as though she suspected Nancy of hurrying to the nearest back-street abortionist of whom there were plenty in Angel Meadow. Nancy smiled and reached for her hand, then in a rare demonstration of affection, placed her cheek along the back of it.

"I won't do anything stupid, Jennet. I just need to collect my thoughts, be on my own for . . ."

"Let me come with you."

"No, Jennet, not this time. When I get back we'll sit down together and make our plans. I'll . . . I'll have to tell the girls and that won't be easy. They liked him, the man who did it and I'm sure you know who that was."

"I guessed. He's been bothering you for a long time."

"He won't bother me again, I can tell you, but as sure as God's my witness, I'll bother him."

She skirted Strangeways Park until she reached the quiet, tree-lined thoroughfare known as Bury New Road. Here the frost had laid a delicate finger along branch and bush and dying leaf, turning the everyday world into a magical glory of white and glittering silver and at each step she took Nancy felt her heart lighten. Here was space and purity, a world she had never seen before, since, except for the walk along Hyde Road when *he* had taken them to Belle Vue, she had never walked a country road. There were fields on either side all crisped over with the white dazzle of the frost and here and there along the way high walls that hid the grand houses of the cotton princes of Manchester, their fancy wrought-iron gates shut against intruders. Beyond the gates she could see neatly raked gravel drives, massed shrubberies, trees which hid the house and now and again a broad sweep of immaculate frosted lawn edged with flowerbeds, empty of colour at this time of the year. She stood like a child at the window of a toy shop, her hands gripping the gate, her nose pressed between the bars, staring in wonder, her sigh of rapture expelling a cloud of breath about her head.

She turned left along a lane which advertised on a neat sign that it was Broughton Lane. It was as deserted as Bury New Road except for a milk float, the driver of which raised his cap politely.

"Nippy this mornin'," he told her and she smiled despite herself.

"It is that."

She let her shawl slip back from her head and her hair, which this morning she had brushed vigorously, fiercely, as though brushing out some demon, clouded about her head and down her back in its usual mass of ringlets as she flipped it outside the shawl. There were more houses surrounded by fields and she imagined what it must be like to wake up each morning, draw back the curtains and see nothing but greenery, meadows carpeted with wild flowers, the clutter of mill chimneys and factories far away and hidden from view. One day . . . one day!

There was a bridge and on the right beyond it a stretch of woodland, the bridge spanning what she supposed was the River Irwell. She stood for five minutes, her arms on the parapet, looking down into the sliding waters, her face serene now, for what was the use of mourning for what was gone, for despairing over what was done. She had Jennet and the girls. She had the small hoard of coins behind the brick in the bedroom. She had her health and strength and she had her plans which no man, least of all Mick O'Rourke, would be allowed to interfere with. She did not let her thoughts wander to the coming child nor to what was to happen to it, and her, when it arrived. It would have to be fitted in to their lives somehow, she supposed. She didn't want it, naturally, but it would be hers, her responsibility like all the others she had accumulated in her young life and she would not shirk it. She would survive it and one day . . . one day . . .

Those magical repeated words made her smile, then, her feet slithering down the frosted bank, like a child on a helter-skelter, she stepped between the dark trunks of the trees. It was enchantment. Every tree and bush was as sharp as ebony against the pale blue of the sky, the low sunlight shining through the bare branches and slanting across the slight, lavender-coloured mist that drifted above the ground. There were long shadows of deep purple stretching across the woodland floor, formed by the sun shining through the lace of the thin branches. Every stalk of what she thought must be fern or bracken stood to attention, frozen in a patina of glittering ivory and across a smooth carpet of white were the imprints of a small animal. She was bewitched, frozen herself to the spot where she had entered the woodland, wanting to weep, not this time in desolation, but in joy. It was as though the wonder, the beauty, the sheer magic of this tiny piece of what was still, really, her Manchester, had finally and irrevocably delivered her from her dread of what was to come, revealing to her another side of life, bringing her out into what could only be the fulfilment of her dreams. She was quite shaken, not only by this revelation but by the hushed beauty of the white and shaded world that had caused it.

She stepped carefully between the trunks of the trees as though it were sacrilege to leave a mark in this perfect place and when she came to the other side she let out her breath on a long sigh of sheer delight. It might not last, this feeling. There would be troubles enough and to spare in the months ahead but now, at this moment, she knew she was perfectly capable of dealing with them all.

The river lay to her right and, holding her shawl loosely about her shoulders, she strode out on the path that ran beside it, her head constantly turning to look about her. There were houses on the far side of the river, their gardens running right down to the water, trees sheltering them along the water's edge. She walked for several minutes wondering, as she stepped out, what the old, ruined building ahead of her was. There was a narrow lane to the left of her, leading, or so it seemed, to the ruins which were half hidden behind a screen of mixed trees, beech and, she thought, hornbeam. Since their visit to Belle Vue and the lovely walk she had shared with Mary and Rosie and *him*, she had taken to dipping into books on trees and flowers, and even birds and had begun to recognise some of those she had seen there.

She skirted the castle, thinking perhaps she would bring Jennet and the girls out here for a picnic in the spring, assiduously avoiding the matter of how she herself might be by then. Her shape and size and . . . well, whatever. There were several flat-topped stones that looked as though they might once have been part of a wall, sheltered and yet in a scrap of sunshine. She sat down on one and leaned her back against another higher one and with a contented sigh closed her eyes and let the peace and stillness and total emptiness of the space about her seep through her pores into the centre of her.

She had no idea how long she had been there but it had given the sun time to move across the sky and leave her in the shade and she was cold, but it was not this that had wakened her. She was not awfully sure she had been asleep, just in a light daydream, but there was the sound of boots crunching in the crisp frosted ground, the rattle of something that might be a bridle and the blowing snort of a horse that has been ridden hard. She didn't know how she recognised these sounds since she had no knowledge of horses but when her eyes sprang open she was not surprised to find she was right.

There was a man, tall, with a big flowing cape which seemed to billow out like a bat's wings behind him and for a moment she shrank away as he strode towards her, leading the horse by the bridle, a horse she seemed to recognise. It was a lovely polished chestnut colour, rich and showy and still, she had time to notice, pulling at the restraining hand of the horseman and fractiously tossing her handsome head.

"You've not got the better of that thing yet, I see. I would have thought that by now it would have learned who was master."

Josh Hayes shrugged but did not smile, nor had she meant him to. He led the animal to a denuded silver birch, tying her to a low branch to allow her to crop the stiff grass, then walked back and sat down beside Nancy as though it were the most natural thing in the world to do. He leaned forward, his elbows on his knees, his chin cupped in his hands, studying pensively the white, glittering world ahead of him.

In contrast to her he was richly dressed, his cape a warm wool, his polished boots expensive, his jacket, which she could see beneath the cape, a double lining against the bitter cold. And it was cold now, for the sun had moved behind them leaving them both in the shade. Neither spoke for several minutes and yet the silence was not oppressive.

"I seem to see you in the strangest places," he said at last, "and yes, Copper still fights me for her own way. But she has a lovely nature and I will not give up on her."

"She's a beautiful animal."

"Yes. But won't you tell me what you're doing out here? You must be a long way from home." Meaning, she knew, that one didn't expect to see a mill girl in this splendid area.

"Am I trespassing?" she asked abruptly.

"No, I don't think so."

"Well then, I have as much right as you to be here."

"Of course, I just meant—"

"That I am out of my proper station in life."

He frowned, turning to her and she saw the pale smoky grey of his eyes darken. He had the most beautiful eyes surrounded by long, dark lashes of which any woman would have been proud, she found herself thinking, set in a face that was young and arrogant and yet humorous, ready, she thought, to smile if she would. The last time she had spoken to him in the mill yard she had given him the rounds of the kitchen for his carelessness with his horse among the children. The last time she had seen him she had been with Mick at the Arts Treasures Exhibition and she remembered the strange communication that had passed between them. It was as though they would have spoken but she had Mick's arm possessively round her and his family had been about him and he had been hurried away by the man she knew to be his father, the owner of Monarch Mill, Edmund Hayes. Since then she had not clapped eyes on him, had not even given him a thought, but then why should she? He was nothing to her and she was nothing to him and why she should have such a curious thought was beyond her.

"Are you warm enough?" he said at last. She had begun to shiver, for despite the good shawl she wore it was not really the most practical garment to sit about in in January.

Her face was cold and unsmiling. "Yes, thank you, but I must be getting home."

Before she could stop him he stood up and with one swift movement lifted his cape from about his shoulders and settled it round hers. "There, that's better," he told her, seeing nothing strange, it appeared, in a gentleman giving a lady his cape, even if she wasn't a lady. She felt the warmth and the softness of the lining drift about her and smelled some pleasant fragrance, but just the same she struggled to refuse it.

"I'm quite warm enough, thank you," she told him curtly, "and as I said I must be getting home. My sisters will wonder where I've got to."

"Please, just for a moment, keep the cape. I'm as warm as toast." He grinned disarmingly. "Now, won't you tell me what you're doing out here? And I'd like to hear about your sisters. I have one sister and one brother, younger than me. He's still at school." His frown had completely gone now, like a cloud drifting away to reveal sunlight. She watched as the corners of his mouth lifted, fascinated against her will by the crease that appeared at each side, then turned away impatiently, wondering what in God's name she thought she was doing. She was three months pregnant and yet here she was admiring a man's smile, listening to his chatter, she who had told herself a hundred times since Mick O'Rourke had raped her that as far as she was concerned men had no part in her life except later perhaps, in the line of business. This man had something, she didn't know what, that seemed to draw her to him, even if it was in anger, as in the mill yard. And what the hell was she doing sitting here with him with his cape about her shoulders as though they were equals? It was seven months since she had left Monarch and she didn't suppose for a moment that he'd noticed she'd gone. And yet in the most odd way she felt comfortable with him. They'd said nothing much to one another, nothing of great weight or importance and once again she asked herself why they should?

"Won't you tell me where you live?" he asked her, turning his smoky-eyed gaze on her.

"Why, are you thinking of calling on me?" She could not help but smile.

"It's only a question, dammit." He slapped his riding crop against his booted leg. "I'm doing my best to be polite, that's all."

"Why?"

"Why not?"

"Very well, I live in Angel Meadow, at least for the moment." She lifted her head imperiously.

"I see. You are about to move then?"

"As a matter of fact, I am." She was saying more than she should, she knew that, but then what did it matter. It was good to talk to someone, apart from Rosie and Mary and Jennet, of her aspirations.

"Oh, and may I ask, without getting my head bitten off, where you are going?"

She drew back then, for as yet they had no idea where they were going, or when, but still she felt the need to tell this man – why, for God's sake? – of the grand plans Nancy Brody had for herself and her family.

"I . . . I don't know yet. We're . . . I'm waiting . . ."

"When you say 'we' do you mean the young man I saw you with at the exhibition?"

At once she was appalled. "Dear God, no."

"He's not your . . . ?" What name could he put to it and why should he care anyway?

"Dear God, no," she repeated, a look of such loathing on her face he was quite amazed. "I mean my sisters and Jennet. Jennet is my friend and we intend . . ."

"Yes?" She had his complete attention now and without meaning to he put out a warm hand and took her cold one in it. Amazingly she made no objection.

He did not wait for her answer. The words came out of his mouth before he could stop them, or even think about them. "You're very lovely," he said to her, his eyes a soft and velvety grey, stating a fact, no artifice or false regard in it and for several long seconds they looked at one another in what could only be called total surprise, then she snatched her hand away and stood up. His cape was flung at him in what seemed to him to be contempt, a contemptuous anger that he could not understand, for he had meant no offence.

It seemed she was offended, deeply so.

"I'll bid you good-day," she almost snarled at him, turning away and beginning to stride off in the direction from which she had come. He watched her go, amazed at the emptiness her going had left in him, then, leaping to his feet, he moved towards his mare. When he was mounted he galloped away with what appeared to be the same sort of indignation that was in her. Damn the woman, he cursed, then wondered why, for she meant absolutely nothing to him. Did she?

10

She felt as though there were rock inside her, pressing down inexorably but uselessly to a point just between her legs, but no matter how hard she heaved and pushed and struggled she could not rid herself of it. She could sense the anguished figures of Rosie and Mary and Jennet hovering about the bed but she was so exhausted her eyes could not focus on them properly. She knew they were there because she could hear their voices, though at a great distance, and she longed to tell them she was sorry to be putting them to such trouble and really, if she could do anything about it, she would, but even a whisper was beyond her.

Hands touched her face and a voice – was it Jennet's? – told someone else she was burning up and that she'd just slip down and get some fresh water and whoever it was she spoke to begged not to be left alone.

"You're not alone," Jennet said harshly. "You have Mary with you."

"But we don't know what to do," the voice wailed. "Oh, Jennet, she's not going to die, is she?" and despite the agony she was in Nancy felt a small smile tug at her lips at the sound of a sharp slap administered by an exasperated hand.

"Don't you say that, Rosie Brody. Of course she's not going to die. She's having a baby, that's all. Women all over the world have babies and don't die of it so don't let me hear another word. Now, if you don't want me to leave her you go and get the water. Dash down to the tap and let it run for a while then it will be nice and cool but be quick about it."

Though she did her best to feel confident, to show confidence, not only to the younger girls but to the labouring woman on the bed, Jennet could feel the terror grip at her insides, for, like Rosie, she didn't know what to do either. They were all unmarried girls and as far as she knew none of them had ever seen the birth of a child. Well, she certainly hadn't but even she, ignorant as she was, could not believe that it was normal to take so long. Over thirty-six hours and though at first Nancy had been cheerful, saying the pains weren't so bad, that things were moving along nicely, that it wouldn't be long now and reassuring things like that, for the past four hours nothing further had happened, despite the pains that continued to harrow her. In between Nancy seemed to doze but even Jennet could see she was weakening, moaning feebly, her body fighting to relieve itself of its burden but failing for some reason.

Doing her best to overcome her reluctance to expose Nancy's body, not only to her own gaze but that of her sisters, for surely it was an invasion of Nancy's privacy especially when she was unable to protest, she had opened her legs and peered into that secret place from which the baby would come but there was nothing, nothing but blood and stretched flesh which looked as though it would tear apart. To encroach upon another woman's innermost recesses was against all the precepts with which she had been brought up, for a motherless girl does not talk to a father about the embarrassing workings of a female body, but she could not help to bring a child into the world without . . . without looking at that part of Nancy's body from which it came, could she?

But that had come later. At first she had kept Nancy decently covered under a clean sheet, giving her sips of water, wiping her sweat-streaked face, holding her hands even though Nancy's grip felt as though it were breaking every fragile bone in her own. She had made broth from ham bones, lentils and carrots, spooning the liquid into Nancy's reluctant mouth, telling her that she must keep her strength up and all the time at the back of her mind had slithered the unpleasant truth that soon she would be forced to help her friend to bring the child into the world. There was a cord to be cut, Nancy had told her and she'd need plenty of clean sheets and to keep hot water ready, for what purpose Jennet was not awfully sure. She had dreaded the very thought of it; now she prayed fiercely that it would happen, no matter how embarrassing she might find it, how frightening or mystifying, if only it could be got over and Nancy relieved of the suffering that was, Jennet was sure, slowly killing her. The baby *had* to come out, there was nothing surer but when, and how . . . please, please, dear Lord, let it be soon.

Rosie hurried in with a jug of clean, cool water and in her eagerness to help tipped it too far over a piece of clean linen so that half of it splashed on Nancy's skull-like face. She slowly opened her eyes which were sunk in great muddy holes of pain and with an effort lifted a hand which, even in the past thirty-six hours, seemed to have wasted away, to have become thin and claw-like. Her cracked and bitten lips parted and with deep and painful compassion, ready to weep in sympathy, Jennet wet them with the cloth.

"Yes, darling," she murmured brightly, "it won't be long now and then the baby will be here." On the other side of the bed Rosie and Mary hung over her, wishing they could believe Jennet but knowing instinctively that it was not true. They were so afraid. Nancy had been their mainstay for a long time now, providing them with food and warmth and decent shawls and clogs; how would they manage it all without her? Besides, they loved her. Though they might have thought her harsh in her determination to make them learn to read and write, to be clean and fastidious so that it was second nature to them now, expecting the standards she had set to be kept up, she had done it only for their sakes, and her own. Even when that awful thing had happened to her last year and the grievous months that had followed when they had suffered the derision of their neighbours who had been delighted to see the Brody girls pulled down, she had kept them steady, calm herself, saying it would soon be over. They would leave Church Court, she had promised them, so what did it matter what its denizens shouted after them.

"Sticks and stones might hurt my bones but words can never hurt me," she had quoted at them cheerfully and they had got through it. She had got them through it. They could not bear to lose her now.

Nancy was trying to say something. From inside her, where that reservoir of strength lay, the strength that had kept her going for the past nine months struggled through the layers of pain, through the layers of bone and muscle to get to the surface of her and speak the words that she must. Her glorious fighting spirit, which had battled through death and disaster, hunger, cold, poverty and hardship, and now the hardest labour she had ever been asked to perform, inched its way to her lips and the words she must speak.

Her breath fanned Jennet's cheek but no words escaped and they realised that her exhausted body was almost beyond itself.

"What is it? What is it, dearest?" Jennet was weeping and Mary began to moan, for surely her sister was dying and what was there to be done about it.

It was Rosie who caught the faint, sibilant whisper and at once her face cleared.

"Annie . . . she's asking for Annie. Annie'll know what to do for her."

"Who is Annie?" But Rosie, without shawl or bonnet, was already racing down the stairs and out into the street and all those who were gossiping there, it being a fine day in July, watched in astonishment as she raced like a greyhound in the direction of Angel Street. They knew, of course, what was happening to Nancy Brody, for like all small communities such things soon got about. How, no one could have said, but Nancy's first labour pains had been known of almost before she felt them herself. It looked as though there were some problem, they told one another, feeling no sympathy, the way their Rosie was going hell for leather down the street but it was *their* problem, theirs and that stuck-up cow who'd moved in with them. In the ordinary way of things they would have rallied round any woman in trouble but those Brody girls and their airy-fairy friend had made it quite plain right from the start that they wanted none of them. Course, that Nancy had been like that from the day her mam vanished!

If the inhabitants of Church Court were amazed it was nothing to the sheer, jaw-dropping consternation that afflicted every minder at Monarch as the fleet foot of the girl they recognised as Rosie Brody flew down the narrow aisle between the spinning frames. The gatekeeper, against his better judgement, even though he remembered her, had opened the gates in answer to her frantic cries, calling after her as she sped across the yard and up the steps to the floor where Annie Wilson worked. His shout lifted every head in the yard but it was too late, for Rosie had already gone.

"Wha' . . . wha'?" Annie gawped, breaking at least half a dozen threads as Rosie's hands pulled at her. "'Ere, what the 'ell are yer doin'?" she managed to gasp, then, before she could even turn round to stare at her co-workers, Rosie had switched off her machine and was tugging at her to go with her.

"Give over, yer daft cow." She slapped at Rosie's hands, convinced the girl had lost her senses, but all the while Rosie was drawing her towards the door at the end of the spinning-room, her feet and Annie's slipping in the grease and oil that slicked the floor. The overseer was beginning to stride towards them, his face like thunder and all over the room women were staring, open-mouthed, more threads breaking and the place in an uproar; all the while Annie struggled and all the while Rosie, being younger and stronger, drew her forward. She was shouting, her face like a flame, for she had run all the way, her hair standing out from her head in a cloud of tangled curls.

"You've got to come, Annie. Please, you've got to come. There's no one else . . . and Jennet can't manage and Nancy's going to die."

"Will yer let go o' me arm, yer little madam," Annie panted.

"I can't. We have to run."

"I'm runnin' nowhere. Bloody 'ell, at my age . . ."

"Please hurry, Annie. Our Nancy's dying."

"What yer talkin' about? Dyin'? Will yer let go o' . . ."

Suddenly Rosie stopped, turning to face the distressed figure of the older woman. They were out in the yard by now and a dozen men watched with considerable interest. Annie gasped and floundered, her hand to her breast, her face as red as Rosie's, her own hair all over the place. They were nose to nose and it was plain that Rosie Brody had no intention of allowing Annie Wilson any choice in the matter of where she went in the next moment.

Her words were bald. "Our Nancy's having a bairn."

"A bairn?" Annie put her hand to her mouth. "Dear God in 'is 'eaven. Bu' why?"

"It won't come, Annie. It's stuck. Thirty-six hours and it won't come."

"Bloody 'ell, lass. But is there no other woman 'oo can 'elp?"

"She won't have them, Annie. She wants you. Besides, they wouldn't come."

It had been April before Kate Murphy, who had eyes like a hawk, even if her Joe did black them regularly, noticed the curious fullness of stuck-up Nancy Brody's body, and even though she narrowed her eyes, squinting in the pale sunshine, she could not quite believe what she saw. She *knew* what she saw, all right. Bloody hell, she'd had enough of her own and there wasn't a moment went by in Church Court when some woman or other wasn't up the spout, but just the same . . . *Nancy Brody?* Lady High Mucky Muck who hadn't the time of day for anyone, who considered herself so far above any of them it was a wonder she condescended to walk on the same rotten flags that they did. There was a rumour she was to leave Church Court taking her lah-di-dah friend and sisters with her and good riddance to the lot of them; but the fascinating evidence of her own eyes as Nancy's shawl slipped for a moment could scarcely be believed. Was it real? Was it a bairn in that slightly distended belly and if so who was the chap? Not Mick O'Rourke who had been hanging about her last year, for he'd taken up with Marie Finnigan and there had been no one else about or someone would have noticed. Happen someone where she worked in that sweat shop in Brown Street or . . . or . . . Well, it was no good standing here gawping.

With a delighted cackle she let herself out of her front door and ran like a ferret to spread the news, starting with Eileen O'Rourke. They turned the corner into Church Court, Nancy and Jennet in front and Rosie and Mary behind them, and before she had taken a step or two she became aware that they all knew. She had been expecting it, of course, but because of the cold winter and spring had contrived, with the help of a capacious shawl she had bought from Mrs Beasley, to hide her changing shape. She was tall and had an upright carriage and though she had got to six months she had managed to carry on undetected, at least in Church Court, though Mr Earnshaw had had a thing or two to say about it when he found out, inferring in his sneering way that if he'd known she was a girl like that he'd have had a go himself. Oh, aye, he'd keep her on for she was a bloody good worker but the minute she showed signs of falling off in her work she was out on her ear, so think on. She didn't tell him that they were to be "out" the minute this baby was born. She and Jennet had discussed it endlessly after the girls had gone to bed, realising sadly that they must postpone their plans, for she could in no way get over to Oldham, inspect and order the sewing-machines, find a workroom and, hopefully, a new home, not to mention the stall in the market which she herself must set up and she couldn't do it with her belly sticking out to here, she said, making Jennet wince.

The girls had been remarkably good about the baby, though they seemed to find it hard to understand what had happened to her.

"But who was it? And what were you doing in Style Street?"

What indeed?

"The man dragged me there and . . ."

Mary had cried. "Oh, Nancy . . ."

"There's no use crying, our Mary, it's done now and, like everything else that has happened to us, we just have to get on with it." Even though her very soul cringed at the thought of carrying Mick O'Rourke's child, of bearing Mick O'Rourke's child, she could not let it get in the way of her firm belief that even now, she and her family and her dearest friend would get to that magical place she had dreamed of, an insubstantial, ephemeral place but real nevertheless to her, ever since her mam went. It was Mam who had started it, which sounded odd, but if it had not been for her disappearance she and Rose and Mary would have drifted into a life not much different from the women in Church Court. The mill first probably, their wages handed over to Mam to pour down her throat, some neighbourhood lad picked, for want of anything better, for a husband and the father of the dozen children she would bear. She had escaped it only because Mam had left them and Nancy had no choice – and a growing and burning desire to do better than Mam, let's face it – but to get up off her arse and fight for what she had discovered she wanted.

Her sisters, being the daughters of Kitty Brody, knew exactly what had been done to her. They had been devastated when she told them about the events in the churchyard, wanting her to go to the police and report it, thinking it to be a stranger who had done this to her and she had let them continue to think so. But that was the very reason why there was no use in reporting it, she said. Did they remember how the sergeant had been over Mam's disappearance? she asked them. Had he given a tinker's toss? No, he bloody well hadn't, and he'd be the same over this. He'd probably think no decent girl would be out and about at that time of night on her own and besides, were there any decent girls in Angel Meadow? He wouldn't think so and looking for such a man would be like looking for a needle in a haystack.

Now Church Court was to get its revenge. "Well, if it ain't 'Er Majesty 'erself, come ter see 'ow the riff-raff live," Eileen O'Rourke shrieked gleefully from her doorstep where she stood with her arms akimbo. "But what's that under yer pinny, Yer Majesty? It can't be a babby, fer Queen Nancy wouldn't let any chap put his dick in 'er, not wi' 'er 'avin' her legs fastened tergether at top. Or is it a cork yer keep there, Yer Queenship? Gawd, I never thought ter live ter see the day when Kitty Brody's lass would go the same way as 'er, but I might've known better. Like mother like daughter, they do say, an' it's damn well true. Are yer ter set up a 'ore 'ouse then, 'cos if ya are I can send yer round a few likely chaps 'oo'd like a go at yer."

"Now then, Mrs O'Rourke, don't be so 'ard on't girl. I reckon she didn't know which end of a chap was which she's that refined and when he offered ter stick it in 'er she'd no idea what it was."

"Nay, 'tis a virgin birth, Mrs Murphy. Any man what touched that frozen bitch would get 'is thingy turned ter bloody ice."

The men watched with the women, sorry in the way that men often are, not being as spiteful as their women, that Nancy Brody was suffering such insults. True, she had no truck with any of them, which was why they resented her, and then on top of that she had committed the sin of being successful. She had started with no more than they had but she had worked her fingers to the bone and achieved bloody miracles, so it was said, with her home, her family and the work she did. But she was a lovely-looking lass and had done no one a bad turn, but some lad had done her one and there were more than a few of them who turned their gaze in Mick O'Rourke's direction. He was standing next to his mother, his own arms folded across his brawny chest. His eyes were narrowed, his mouth thin-lipped, his jaw jutting ominously as though he would like nothing better than to cross the road after Nancy Brody and give her a bloody good hiding, though God knows why. Perhaps because some chap had got what he had chased after for months! When he felt their gaze on him he pulled his mouth into a wide smile, then went indoors as though the spectacle of Nancy Brody's humiliation were of no particular interest to him

They were all weeping when they reached the safety and privacy of their cottage, all except Nancy who kept her head high and her chin firm, passing every doorway and every jeering woman as though they did not exist, even managing a smile of pure contempt which rather took the wind out of their sails, for they had been convinced that at last they would see Nancy Brody get her comeuppance. Rose and Mary huddled together behind the door as it was shut and Jennet collapsed, white-faced and shivering, on to the settle but Nancy turned on them like a cat who has faced and outfought a pack of howling wolves. Her face was stiff and savage. Her voice trembled but it was with rage, not fear and they recoiled from her as they had done from the crowd beyond the closed door.

"Never let me see you cry again, d'you hear me?" she snarled. "Never give them the satisfaction of knowing that they are hurting you. That's what they want, to hurt you because you have something they could never have and that's hope. They won't let up, believe me, so you'd best get used to it."

"But, Nancy, why? Why?" Jennet quavered. "What have you ever done?"

"You can see what I've done, Jennet Williams, and so can they and they resent it. If, when my mam went I'd gone snivelling to them for help they would have been only too glad to give it. Only too glad to see me in the same bloody pickle they're always in and always will be in for the rest of their lives. But I didn't. Now then, let's have a cup of tea. See, Mary, put a match to the fire and stop that grizzling; and you, Rosie Brody, put the kettle on."

She relented then and took her sisters in her arms, leaning her head against theirs. "It won't be for ever, my lasses. Just as soon as this soddin' baby comes we'll go, so cheer up. We're in this together. We – Jennet and I – will always be with you in the street and I don't think I need to tell you never to go out alone. Oh, I don't think they'd physically hurt you but . . . well, you know what I mean."

They never gave up on her: they never tired of it, taunting not only her but her sisters and Jennet.

But now that "sodding" baby was about to be born and within a few weeks they'd be away from it all in a decent neighbourhood.

For thirty-six hours they had believed this to be true but it seemed they were wrong, for Nancy Brody, brave and courageous Nancy Brody, was slipping away with her child fast inside her and unless Annie Wilson could perform some magical thing their grand future, not to mention Nancy's life – bugger the baby – would slip away as Kitty Brody had slipped away.

"Let t' dog see t' rabbit," Annie gasped as she stumbled into the room, "and open them bloody windows. The stink in 'ere's enough ter choke t' cat," and at once it was as though a heavy pall had been lifted from the devastated room. Annie's cheerful instructions, even though Nancy still lay like one dead on the bed, put new life in them and they hurried to obey her, even though Nancy had told them to keep the windows closed just in case she screamed out loud!

Whisking off the sheet that Jennet had discreetly placed across Nancy's flaccid body, Annie pried open her legs and poked her nose almost up into Nancy's insides.

"Fetch me some water an' carbolic soap, I want ter wash me 'ands."

This was done, the three girls falling over themselves to fulfil her every wish. With no more ado than if Nancy had been a piece of meat on a butcher's counter, Annie thrust her hand high inside her and though Nancy twitched and moaned feebly it didn't faze Annie.

"It's arse about face, that's what's up wi' 'er," she announced firmly, turning to smile confidently at the three hovering figures.

"Pardon?" Jennet asked politely.

"Bum first."

"Bum first?"

"Aye. I've seen a few in me time an' it'll not be easy but I reckon us can turn it." And again, as though Nancy were not a person, which at the moment she wasn't, Annie thrust one hand deep inside her body, the other placed on the enormous dome of her belly, feeling, listening, kneading, massaging and all the while Nancy whimpered feebly though she was too weak to protest.

"Pepper, fetch me't pepper pot," Annie barked.

"Pepper pot?" Jennet whispered.

"Listen, lass, if all yer can do is repeat what I say ter yer you an' me's gonner 'ave words. Just do as yer told."

It was a miracle from God, at least Jennet thought so and was ready to fall to her knees in prayer to that being to whom she and her father had offered their thanks every day. The pepper, heaped in Annie's bloody hand, was thrust beneath Nancy's nose and with half a dozen hefty sneezes from its mother the child leaped out into the world, complaining lustily at the inconsiderate delay.

"Never mind that, lass," Annie snapped at her as Jennet sank beside the bed. "We've more ter do than gerron our bloody knees. See, gimme a 'and; and you two" – turning to glare at Rose and Mary who were edging forward to get a view of the child – "pass me them scissors an' 'ave yer some 'ot water? Good lasses. There's just t'cord ter do an' then she'll be right as bloody ninepence. Good strong girl like 'er. Now, go and fetch 'er a cuppa tea, an' me an' all while yer at it. And a basin o' warm water fer't babby 'oo'll need a bit of a wash."

And so, for the first time in her life Jennet Williams witnessed the beginning of life and from that moment when Nancy Brody's daughter, still covered in the muck and blood of birth, was placed in her trembling arms, she loved her, which was just as well for her mother didn't. She wanted to sit down and nurse her, gaze into the blood-streaked, indignant face, inspect the quivering, vulnerable gums, the mouth which was wide in a yell of disapproval and yet at the same time was beginning hopefully to suck on the empty air. Tentatively she placed the tip of her little finger in the baby's mouth and at once the gums clamped down on it and began to suck vigorously.

"Oh, Lord," she whispered reverently, "oh, thank you, dear sweet Lord."

"Never mind that, Jennet Williams," the weak voice from the bed told her. "The Lord, whoever He might be, had nothing to do with this. It's Annie you should be thanking. And where's that cup of tea?"

11

Josh Hayes allowed his mare to pick her way wherever she pleased, guiding her only between the tree-trunks of the several small patches of woodland through which he rode, following the bridle path leading from Higher Broughton towards Cheetham and Harpurhey. Though Copper wanted to gallop and work off the energy that lay dormant in her, Josh kept her to a walk since he needed all his wits about him to mull over the dreadful predicament in which he found himself. And should he be surprised at it, he sighed, for he had been Evie's lover for a year now and the consequence to that could not be unexpected, nor his father's reaction to that consequence. Their relationship had begun last summer and in January she had told him she was with child. And now it was July and though he had not set eyes on her for weeks he knew she still hoped for something he could not give her. She held a place in his heart, did his loving Evie, for not once had she reproached him but had taken the burden he had placed on her as though it were all her fault. But he knew, even as late as this she hoped for . . . for . . . something though God alone knew what.

The sun shone from a cloudless sky at the zenith of which a skylark sang its heart out but he did not notice. In the fields, knee-deep in rich grass and clover, cattle turned their heads to watch him go by, their jaws chomping rhythmically on the juicy sweetness in their mouths. A farm labourer crossing the meadow with his dog raised his cap respectfully, recognising quality, not only in the young gentleman, but the fine animal he rode. His dog slunk at his heels, its tail down, but the man on the mare did not notice. The air was drenched in fragrance, for the hedges were a tangle of wild flowers with a fine festoon of dog roses and honeysuckle about them, but Josh Hayes did not notice. He put the mare to a small stream which she took elegantly, crushing under her hooves the delicate water figwort and water forget-me-nots which grew there in great abundance, but again, still deep in his reverie, he did not notice. Men and women were haymaking, the men scything in ordered rows, their weather-beaten faces set in lines of concentration, the women gleaning and gathering and stooking, their faces deep in frilled sunbonnets. Though the women nodded pleasantly, again he did not notice.

Beside a placid stream which wound through a stand of trees he reined the mare to a stop and slid from her back, then, leading her by the bridle, walked on, the mare lifting and shaking her head at the restraint. Though she had steadied since he had her last year she was still inclined to skittishness if her energy had not been run off.

"Whoa, lass, whoa. Calm down, will you. We'll have a gallop on the way back, I promise you. Now stand, stand, I tell you."

Josh kept his arm around the horse's neck, leaning against her as though weary unto death, and together they studied the serene flow of the water.

"I don't know what the bloody hell to do, Copper, and that's a fact," he told the animal. "I feel I should be doing more than I am but there are so many people to consider. Father's right but that doesn't help Evie."

He seemed to find nothing unusual in speaking thus to his mare, not here, at any rate, where there was not another human soul in sight to hear him. It was nearly three months now since Evie's condition had been discovered by a triumphant Mrs Harvey who acted as though she were pleased to have had all her worst suspicions about the laundry-maid and the master's son confirmed, for who else could be the father, though she did not say this to Mrs Hayes when she brought the appalling situation to her attention. Mrs Hayes had been justifiably upset, for no mistress likes to think that a girl in her employ has been "carrying on" and, of course, the girl must be dismissed at once, for she had an unmarried daughter of her own and it was not proper nor decent to have a fallen woman under the same roof. In fact, none of the maidservants could be expected to work with disgraced Evie Edward who must be sent home to her mother at once.

"Don't worry, Evie," he had whispered to her, holding her trembling figure in his arms the last time they had met in Kersall

Dell. It had not been an agreeable moment. All the times he had held and delighted in her slender body were swept away by his awareness of the swollen bump that pressed against him and he felt the guilt strike like a knife, but there was nothing he could do except give her some money to tide her over until he could think of some way out of this mess.

"Don't worry, sweetheart," he murmured again into her hair, "I'll always take care of you." Though at that moment he wanted nothing more than to see her set off across the fields towards Park Meadows and the small cottage where her family lived. She had trailed her bundle of clothing behind her, looking back at him disconsolately again and again, her face still wet with her tears and he had felt something wrench inside him, for what a tempest of recriminations she would face, a disgraced daughter come home to bear an illegitimate child.

He had his own recriminations to contend with when he got home.

"So, you've been at it again, have you, lad?" his father had thundered, his fury so great he could not keep still but strode the study from window to desk and back again. "Can't keep it inside your breeches, can you? Sniffing after every bitch that crosses your path like a randy dog. I told you the last time I would not stand it again and now I come home to find your mother in tears since it seems the laundry-maid has been dismissed and it doesn't take much reckoning to come to the right conclusion on who the father might be. You've been seen hanging about her. Oh, yes, I made it my business to ask a few questions of the servants and though they didn't like it I got it out of them. Now then, what have you to say for yourself? Though as far as I can see there's not a lot to say."

Breathing heavily his father had glared at him, drumming his fingers on the desk in an ecstasy of rage.

"Well, as you so succinctly put it, there's not a lot I can say, is there, sir? I am condemned before I have had a chance to speak a word in my own defence."

"Are you telling me you are not the father of the slut's brat?"

"She is not a slut but a young girl," keeping his temper with great difficulty.

"Who dropped her drawers for the master's son and God knows how many others."

"No, Father, only for me and . . ."

"Yes?"

"I think I should marry her. She comes from a decent family."

"A labourer's daughter!" His father was slack-jawed in amazement. "A decent family! You must be mad. You seem to have lost your mind along with your ability to show restraint. Dear God, lad, could you not do as other men do and go to some decent place where the women know exactly what is expected of them and are a trouble to no one. But let's get one thing straight. There'll be no talk of marriage, d'you hear? Your mother is distraught enough as it is. Can you imagine how she would react if I went to her and told her she was to have some common labourer's daughter, her own laundry-maid, as a daughter-in-law? No, I won't have it."

"I don't see how you could stop me, sir. I am over twenty-one, after all, and can do as I like."

His father had become quiet then, his face like cold, grey granite, his mouth so tightly clamped he could barely speak.

"Is that so?" he managed icily. "Well, my lad, you're right, you can do as you like and so can I. Let me warn you that trollop will never come over my doorstep as your bride, and neither will you if you marry her. I have another son, Joshua Hayes who, though he is still young, can take over from me in time, for there's nothing surer than the truth that *you won't*."

His face had softened then and his voice too, ready to implore his lad not to give up all he had for nothing more than a bit of "sport" which, he supposed, all young men indulged in. He'd done it himself at the same age and even now he had a pretty young woman set up in a smart little villa on the outskirts of Newton Heath, far enough away for discretion and yet near enough for him to visit whenever he had the need. Mrs Hayes, of whom he was very fond, did not care for that side of marriage which was what he had expected when he married her, for she was a lady. She had given him his two sons and a daughter and he had left her alone after that.

"Son, I know you think you are obliged in some way and it does you credit but you are . . . you need not feel responsible. She can be taken care of. Like the other one. A husband will be found for her, if that's what she wants but I'm sure you will discover that she will settle down among her own sort, who, let me add, are not at all as particular as you seem to think about the need for marriage. If you feel the urge to help her and the child then that's up to you, perhaps a cottage of her own and money to support her, but surely you can see that marriage between you would be disastrous, and not just for the pair of you who have nothing in common but for your family. How do you think she'd fit in here in our home among women with whom she was once a servant? And even if your mother and I were to accept her no one else would. We'd be shunned. Your mother and sister would no longer be welcome among our own kind. Your sister's marriage prospects would be seriously harmed. So you see there is not just yourself and . . . and her to consider."

The more his father placed before him the good, logical reasons why he should desert – he could think of no other word – Evie, the more reasonable it all seemed. But still he could not forget her woebegone face, her dragging figure, the slump to her shoulders, hampered by the bundle of her clothing as she set off across the fields towards her father's cottage. He wished now that he had gone with her. Would he beat her, her father? God almighty . . . he couldn't stand the thought nor the picture his father painted of the treatment his mother and sister would suffer at the hands of their acquaintances should this get out. Nor could he cope with the idea that his father, who always kept his word, would totally disinherit him if he followed Evie across those fields. He was just beginning to get a good grip on the business and he revelled in his own growing knowledge and expertise. He was to go to America in the autumn and there was talk of markets in other parts of the world where Hayes cotton might be sold and he was to go and look for them. His father was giving him more and more freedom to make his own decisions, trusting him, and he found he liked it.

Edmund Hayes sensed the indecision in his son. Josh had been foolish and Edmund had been furious, but at the same time he did not want to lose him. He was becoming an asset to the firm and he would miss him, apart from any family ties which would be painful if they were broken. He watched his son's face and, like the clever adversary he was in all matters to do with business, he drew back a little, not pressing any advantage but letting it simmer quietly.

"Don't do anything hasty, lad. Give it a day or two. Let it settle, then, if you think it necessary you can ride across to . . . to her home and do as you please with her. *But think about it first*. You've a lot to lose and I promise you she'll be well looked after."

So, taking the coward's way out, he was well aware, he had

done what his father asked and was rewarded, not only by his mother's discreetly whispered but nevertheless heartfelt relief and gratitude at his sensible view of the matter but by his father's approval. A weekly sum of money was to be settled on Evie so that if she felt the need she could be independent of her family but he had been told that she remained with them and had been seen laughing in the lane outside the cottage with a labouring man.

There was a path of sorts but it was hot in the midday sunshine so Josh took the mare to the shade of a group of trees and tethered her, though she was not pleased. She snorted and sighed dramatically, then, as her master drifted away from her, as though sensing his abstraction, she bent her head and began to crop the thick grass.

Josh slowly sank to his haunches, his arms round his knees and stared into the slow, clear water of the stream, watching intently as though his life might depend on his description of it as a small twig floated by in the tiny ripples. The child was due any day now, so he had been told by a sympathetic Mrs Cameron who was cook to the Hayes family and who had made it her business to keep in touch with Evie of whom she had been fond. A nice little thing Evie had been in her opinion, good-natured and kind-hearted which was probably the reason she was in this pickle. But she had known the consequences of making free with the young master of the house and should have kept her hand on her halfpenny, a thought Cook had kept to herself. None of them blamed Master Josh for not marrying her; the very idea was ludicrous and surely even she had not expected it of him. She wasn't the first to become involved with the young man of the house and wouldn't be the last and in one way she was lucky in that she was to be looked after financially by the family, which didn't happen to most. Turned out by employer and family alike, many of them drifted away and into menial jobs until they could no longer work, then took up prostitution as the only way to support themselves and their infants. At least poor Evie had been spared that.

He sat for an hour or more while the sun moved across the sky and the shadow cast by the trees crept over him and dappled the water in shades of pale blue and grey. Copper blew noisily through her nostrils then stamped her feet impatiently, shaking her bridle as though to say what the hell did he think he was up to hanging about in this place and her longing to be free and galloping across the fields.

"All right, lass, all right, I know you want to be off so let's have a good gallop and then make for home. I've some papers to go over with the old man so we'd best make a move."

He raced through field after field, going north, taking hedges and fences and even five-barred gates as though they were no more than a foot high, tearing on until great drools of spittle fluttered and trailed from Copper's mouth, her heart pumped and her flanks heaved. As they galloped over a rocky stretch at a place called simply Hill Top, her hooves dashed like great hammers against an anvil, sparks flying. It was as though devils were after him, devils of remorse and guilt and sadness, for he knew he had used innocent little Evie Edward for his own pleasure and yet had not been asked to pay for that pleasure, as she was paying. It was a man's world his father was fond of telling him, but surely a modicum of compassion . . . Dear sweet Jesus, was he never to let up on himself? Was he never to forget sweet Evie and get on with his life as his father had advised? He must and, he supposed, he would in time but it was bloody hard. Why could he not just put it behind him, forget Evie and her predicament, which after all, he was putting right as far as money was concerned, and let up on himself?

He arrived in the stable yard an hour later. Charlie ran to take Copper and on his face was a mixture of emotions, the first being massive disapproval, for what man, what horseman would treat an animal as the mare had been treated.

He spoke up before thinking. "Nay, Master Josh, what in hell's name 'ave yer done ter't beast. Poor lass . . . poor lass. Look at 'er, she's all of a dither and can yer wonder. I'm surprised at yer, I really am. I thought yer knew better. Come wi' me, my lass," he said tenderly to the mare, then, as though Josh's treatment of the animal had taken all thought from his head, but which had now returned, he turned from the mare and faced his young master. Another expression had come to replace the first, one that Josh could not read.

"What's up, Charlie? Apart from Copper, I mean, for which I'm truly sorry. I just got carried away and kept on going. I'm sorry."

"Eeh, Master Josh, there's such a to-do up at th'ouse." Charlie shook his head in what seemed to be sad bewilderment, a bewilderment that his own simple soul could not unravel.

"A to-do! What sort of a to-do?"

"Yer'd best get up theer, Master Josh. Eeh, I'm that sorry . . ."

"Sorry? What the devil for?"

"Nay, 'tis not fer me ter say, sir. 'Tis not my place."

"Bloody hell, man, you're beginning to alarm me."

Charlie shook his head sadly then turned away and began to lead the exhausted horse back towards the stable and Josh had no choice but to let him. He began to run. He was himself soaked in sweat, his hair sticking about his forehead and ears in wet spikes. His shirt clung to his back and chest and even his breeches were sweat-stained. Should he go directly to his room, which had been his first choice, get washed and changed before facing whatever "to-do" had taken place in his absence or should he go straight to his father's study, for if some drama had exploded while he was out his father would know all about it? He did not want to upset his mother if . . . if what? What could have happened in the few hours he had been riding like a whirlwind so to distress even the bloody groom, for goodness' sake?

His boots clattered across the cobbles in the yard. The door to the kitchen stood open to let out some of the heat, for the preparation for the evening meal was well under way, but as he almost ran into the enormous room which was always filled with some activity, even if it was only Cook making work for idle hands, as she called it, he was struck full in the face and chest by the absolute lack of any movement or sound. The maidservants were in a huddle, some with their arms about one another as though for comfort, one or two weeping silently and the most terrible fear gripped him, for surely, while he had been out trying to rid himself of his own ghosts, death had come into the house and helped itself to one of the household.

"Dear Lord," he whispered. No one heard him say the words but as one they turned and looked at him, their faces blank and shocked, even that of Mrs Harvey who, he would have said, had no feelings at all. Cook leaned with what appeared to be a great weakness against the enormous dresser where the everyday crockery was kept and with her face pressed into Cook's full, maternal bosom a little girl sobbed and sobbed. But all with no sound.

"What is it? Dear God, what has happened? Mrs Harvey . . . Cook . . . what . . ."

Mrs Harvey found her voice but it sounded hollow and toneless.

"You'd best go through to the study, Master Josh. Your father's there and . . . your mother."

"But won't someone tell me what's happened. It's . . . it's not Arthur, is it?" His young brother was away at boarding school but perhaps some awful thing had happened to him, word reaching his father while Josh had been galloping about the countryside filled with his own self-pity.

Cook lifted her head from that of the little girl – was she the scullery-maid? – and spoke sadly.

"No, lad, not Master Arthur."

"Thank God. I'll go and . . ."

"Aye, Master Josh, you go an' . . . well, your pa's waitin' for you in the study."

He strode across the kitchen, aware that one or two of the maids scurried to get out of his way as though afraid he might touch them. As he opened the door that led into the passage and the front of the house he noticed there was a basket on the table over which several of the housemaids were beginning to hover. With the part of his mind not harrowed by fear he wondered what was in it to arouse their strange interest.

Two days later he announced his intention of going to the funeral, though his father threatened him with the hobs of hell if he went.

"Can you not see, lad, that it's an admission of guilt if you go."

"I *am* guilty, sir. I killed her. She was bearing my child when she died and I can do no more for her than go to her funeral."

"But what will folk think, lad?" his father pleaded. "What of your mother and sister?"

"Don't threaten me with that again, sir. I'm sorry if they are to be made to feel social outcasts just because . . . Sweet Jesus, will you listen to me? I was going to say just because a working girl has died, as though she were nothing. We . . . I did her a wrong and if the admitting of that wrong is to hurt me then so be it. I . . . I have a son."

"And that's another thing. An illegitimate child can't stay here under the same roof as decent folk."

"He's three days old, sir, and can harm no one and as for his being illegitimate I shall adopt him and make him my legal son."

"Goddammit, I won't have this, I won't. Your mother is on the verge of a breakdown and your sister won't come out of her room for the shame of it. You realise it's all over Manchester by now."

"You must do as you think fit, sir, as I must. Mrs Cameron has found me a nurse."

"Mrs Cameron?"

"Your cook Father, who was friend to Evie Edward and—"

"The bloody woman will be sacked."

"For what? For finding someone who can feed the child who would surely die like his . . . like his mother if . . ."

He nearly broke then, the youth who had grown up overnight and become the man. He wore black. His face was gaunt and haunted, even the warm amber tones of his skin, put there by his outdoor pursuits, seeming to have faded. His eyes, a soft smoky grey once, had become flinty, deep, his feelings hidden, his grief hidden, his guilt, which racked him hour after hour, hidden from those who could not understand his madness.

From that appalling moment when he had entered the study to find his mother wilting in hysterical tears and his father like a man demented, he had been the same. When he was told that gentle Evie Edward had died of a haemorrhage, the tide of which her own experienced mother could not stop, he had for a moment gone wild, flinging himself dangerously against hard objects in the study until even his father had been afraid. His mother had screamed and Billy, one of the grooms, had been sent hell for leather for the doctor. Wrapped tenderly in a basket, his rosy, pursed lips sucking hopefully on nothing, Evie's son, *his* son, lay where his maternal grandfather had laid him on the kitchen table, to the consternation of the kitchen-maids.

"Theer's nowt us can do fer 'im," he said, absolutely no emotion in his voice, though his face was grey with grief, "so I reckon 'is pa'll 'ave ter see to 'im."

Without another word he had turned on his heel and left and though Edmund Hayes had sent Jack from the stables to fetch him back he had refused to come and that was that.

"If you keep this child it will kill your mother, you know that, don't you?"

"I don't believe that, sir, and if he offends you I shall arrange that he and I will live elsewhere."

"Christ, Josh!" His father was appalled. "You can't do that to us, you can't. Keep the boy by all means but put him with some decent woman who will look after him. You can visit when you want and though it will cause talk . . ."

"I mean to have him with me, sir," his son said quietly. "I killed his mother and surely every child deserves one parent. He is a healthy lad, so the doctor, whom I took the liberty of asking to look him over, tells me, and he is handsome too." There was an astonishing expression of pride in his voice. "If you won't allow me to put him in the nursery upstairs . . ."

"*What!*" His father's bellow could be heard all over the house and Clara, the kitchen-maid who was nursing the baby by the kitchen fire, pulled the blanket up protectively about his head which was covered in tiny whorls of dark brown hair. For the moment, and Edmund Hayes had made it very clear it was a temporary thing, the child was spending his nights in his basket beside Clara's bed and his days beside the kitchen fire, the wet-nurse, who had several bairns of her own to see to as well as her new babe, coming in every four hours to feed him and he seemed to be content enough. Well, there were enough of them to nurse him, weren't there, Cook said, and all fighting with one another over who was to hold him whenever he so much as whimpered.

Josh Hayes stood at the edge of the churchyard of the little chapel in Pendlebury where Evie Edward was laid to rest. He had not loved her, not as a man can love a woman, but she had left something of herself, beside her son, in his heart which no woman would ever dislodge. He stood almost hidden by the broad trunk of an ancient oak tree, for he did not wish to distress her family, but if they had turned and spat at him he knew he must be there to pay his last respect to the girl, she was no more than that, who, if he had not loved her, had loved him.

When they had all gone he moved slowly through the steady drizzle to stand beside the raw earth of her grave, his head bowed, his face drenched with what could have been rain but was not. For several minutes he stood, then, raising his head, he let the rain wash across his face before turning towards his mare whom he had left tethered in the lane.

12

They called her Kitty. Well, Jennet and the girls did, for Nancy said they must do as they pleased since she was far too busy to be bothering with christenings and the like. Of course she'd *be* there, she said impatiently, if Jennet wanted to arrange it, Jennet being quite horrified at the idea of the child not being made known to God, but with the journey to Oldham to be fitted in and the machines they meant to hire to be installed she was run off her feet as it was. It took up time she could barely spare just to feed the infant, which she felt compelled to do, since she had enough milk to nourish every newborn in Angel Meadow, she said, somewhat bitterly, but it was not long before Kitty Brody and her feeds were determined by the needs of her mother and not the other way round. If Nancy could not be there she drew her milk from her breasts with a pump, the milk then being put into an infant feeding-bottle with an india-rubber teat, all purchased from a good druggist in Deansgate, and one of Kitty's other "mothers" fed her. She was not what you would call a placid baby, but she took the teat or the nipple with great forbearance, which astounded her mother in view of who her parents were, in particular Mick O'Rourke who had a temper on him that could turn nasty, as Nancy knew to her cost, and she herself was no shrinking violet.

For a moment, when the name of Kitty was suggested, Nancy had looked quite haunted as though the ghost of her poor mam had come back to grin drunkenly at her, then she shrugged, for it was as good a name as any, she supposed.

From the first she could find nothing in her to give to her child, except the sustenance of her milk, that is. How could she, she asked herself, when she remembered the way in which the baby had been conceived and who her father was. She hated Mick O'Rourke with a venomous loathing that grew inside her, blocking the way along which her maternal and protective love might have flowed. She knew she was damaged in some way by it. She knew it was not normal for any woman to feel the total indifference for her child that she felt towards Kitty. Even her own mam, drunken whore that she had been, had loved her and Rosie and Mary, protecting them as best she could from the filthy hands of the men who had grabbed for them, doing her best to feed them and clothe them and warm them in the depth of the dark Manchester winters. Not that Kitty would suffer as she and her sisters had suffered, for she was petted and pampered like a little princess by her Aunt Mary and by Jennet. They adored her and fought with one another over who should pick her up if she cried – which was often – and she thrived on it, not really caring who her mother was, since she had two others. A child needs love to grow. It needs nourishment and that Nancy gave her in abundance but the love she received came from elsewhere.

Rosie was not quite so obsessed by the charm of the infant as the other two and Nancy was beginning to notice a certain restlessness in her sister, an inclination to prowl about the house and peer from windows as though outside there might be something more exciting than what was to be found in a house with four women and a child. She was a mature thirteen, two years younger than Nancy and very pretty, which she knew, of course. She had always been bolder, more wayward than Mary, more difficult to lead in the way Nancy wished her to go but Nancy put that down to the fact that she was longing to get away from Church Court, as they all were, and would settle down when they did. Not that she ever totally rebelled against the bridle Nancy put on her and Mary but she was often surly and muttering and now and again, for a whole hour, she would be missing and when questioned would say vaguely she had gone for a walk. Where? Nancy had asked her. To look at the shops in Deansgate, the answer came and though Nancy didn't know whether to believe her or not, it did sound the sort of thing that Rosie might be interested in. Lovely shops, fashionable ladies, impeccably dressed gentlemen, shining carriages pulled by shining horses. It had worried her, but short of tying her to the bedpost there was nothing much Nancy could do about it except work all the harder and strive all the quicker to get them all out of Church Court.

On the day after Kitty's birth Jennet, Rosie and Mary had gone down to Brown Street and Earnshaw's Fine Shirts and presented themselves for work to Mr Earnshaw, who had looked at them as though they were beings from another world, his coarse face working in spluttering indignation.

"Oh, yer've condescended ter come back then, 'ave yer? Yer ready ter work are yer after yer two days' 'oliday? Bin anywhere nice? Blackpool, 'appen. An' where's her ladyship if I might be so bold as ter ask?" Mr Earnshaw was the picture of injured sarcasm, turning round to the rest of the girls and women in his employ in order to assess their reaction to his heavy-handed wit. "She 'avin' another few days, like, or is she . . ."

Jennet drew herself up, her small figure looking as though it were doing its best to protect the tall, well-fed frames of the Brody sisters, one of whom was totally intimidated by Mr Earnshaw. Mary was so used to Nancy defending them, standing up for them, speaking out for them, she was at a loss on how to face Mr Earnshaw. Not so Rosie! In a sense, though the sisters were working girls who had been flung into life at the deep end, so to speak, at a very early age they had led a remarkably sheltered life, dominated by their older sister in all things. Since they had left the mill where there had been young men to tease and flirt with they had come into contact with no man but Mr Earnshaw and so their development in that area had been halted temporarily. But Rosie Brody had seen the way the lads in Church Court looked at her, one in particular, and she was well aware of her own charms in that direction, *and* her worth as a machinist, and if this old bugger thought he could look her up and down as though she were something one of the girls had brought in from the street on her shoe, then he was sadly mistaken.

Lifting her head in a fair imitation of their Nancy she gave him a withering look of contempt, since she did not have her sister's ambitions nor the intelligence to realise that at the moment they were still beholden to a man like this and must therefore be polite to him.

"Well, you've only to say the word, Mr Earnshaw," she began, but before she could continue Jennet had her arm in a grip like a vice, halting the "mouthful" Rosie was just about to let loose.

"Nancy had her baby yesterday, Mr Earnshaw," Jennet said in her courteous way. "A little girl. She had a hard time of it and so will be unable to return to her employment with you."

"Is that so? Well, yer can tell 'er she's not wanted anyroad. I've replaced the four o' yer so yer can sling yer 'ook an' all. I can't run me business wi' girls comin' an' goin' ter suit theirselves so yer'd best—"

"You knew Nancy was with child, Mr Earnshaw, and she worked for you as diligently as any other girl here, despite her condition, right up to the day before the birth. Now, obviously she can't return but we can and so—"

"Did it tekk three o' yer ter act as bloody midwives, then? An' it's bin three days since—"

"We're here now, Mr Earnshaw and we are all three willing to work without pay for two days to make up any losses you might have incurred."

Rosie muttered sullenly at this but she kept her mouth shut.

Mr Earnshaw was quite taken aback, but he was not a man to turn down an offer such as this one, since the Brody girls and Jennet Williams were his best workers. He told a lie when he said he had replaced them and the chance to make up what he had indeed lost was too good to miss. Besides, though Nancy would be missed the three of them standing before him looking suitably chastened were as good as any four or even five others.

"Well, I dunno . . ." He pulled on his lip and pretended to hesitate.

"Very well, Mr Earnshaw, we will take our labour elsewhere," Jennet told him politely, beginning to turn away and at once he began to bluster.

"'Ere, there's no need ter be like that. I 'aven't said I wasn't willin', 'ave I? No. Right then, get on them machines an' no messin' about, d'yer hear?" just as though they were about to sit down and engage the other girls in gossip.

They had decided before Kitty was born that three of them would continue at Earnshaw's until the new machines came from Oldham. They needed every penny they could earn to pay for the hire of them, to replace the wages they would no longer earn when they left the sweat shop, for the rent of a stall on the market, and eventually, when the time came, for the rent of a workroom in the shirtmaking district of the city. Nancy had to stay at home until she was recovered from the birth of the child, which would not be long, she promised them, and then Jennet would leave Mr Earnshaw, probably pleading her health as an excuse, for he must not as yet be aware that they were to set up in competition with him. Mary and Rosie would stay on until they were needed, along with Jennet, on their own new machines in the downstairs room at Church Court which was to be the workroom. Among all these arrangements the child had to be fitted in. Nancy was to spend four days a week on the stall in the market and on the other two do all the things that she was sure their new business would require: buying the shirting material, the thread, oil for the machines, needles, embroidery silks and, later, when her plain stuff was selling well, the lace, fans, bonnets, gloves, parasols, shawls and fancy goods which she would display in the smart little shop she meant to have in St Ann's Square in the best shopping district of the city. Nancy Brody did not mean to be a stall holder for the rest of her life, like Mrs Beasley.

At times in those long months of pregnancy, quite frightening her sisters and Jennet, Nancy had sworn obscenely, describing in graphic detail what she would like to do to that part of Mick O'Rourke's anatomy that had got her into this bloody mess. Had it not been for him and his beastliness their young business would have been up and if not exactly running, then tottering on increasingly strengthening legs months ago. All had had to be postponed until after the child came but now, with Kitty's arrival, their plans, discussed endlessly through the spring and early summer months, could be set in motion.

Two weeks later she and Jennet took the train to Oldham to keep an appointment with a gentleman at the premises of a firm called Bradbury and Company, who had been manufacturing commercial sewing-machines, among others, for the past seven years. Both the girls – for they were still only girls – were dressed tidily and soberly in summer-weight tarlatan, the separate bodices well fitted to their breasts, Jennet's small like a child's, Nancy's full and deep with her new maternity. The waists, even Nancy's, who had regained her trim figure very quickly, were neat, flaring out over the fashionable crinoline, flounced about the wide hem. Nancy was in a soft shade of blue and Jennet in the dove grey she favoured, both gowns, thanks to Jennet's cleverness with a needle, having been cut out and sewn over the last few months in readiness for this day. Mrs Beasley had found them the material and even a cream straw bonnet apiece with a low flat crown and a brim on which they had sewn cream silk lily-of-the-valley. It was amazing what came Mrs Beasley's way, Nancy had murmured in an aside to

Jennet when the bonnets and flowers had been triumphantly produced. Nancy's growing bulk had elicited nothing from Mrs Beasley, not even a sideways look, for even in this, the stall holder kept her own counsel, minding her own business as she expected Nancy to mind hers.

Nancy had not been outside the house since Kitty's birth. It was a Saturday, planned so that Rosie and Mary could be at home to look after the baby, and Church Court was out and about in droves in the pleasant warmth of the summer's day, the usual pastime of gossiping and spying on their neighbours occupying the women at least. They sprawled on doorsteps and even in the gutters, for more than one was drunk. Children screamed and squabbled and scrabbled about in the filth that floated down the drain in the centre of the alleyway, but the sight of the two elegant young women, their noses high, their skirts held up out of the filth, as usual brought the whole fascinated lot of them to open-mouthed silence. They had seen the Brody girls go by a thousand times since their mam vanished and they had decided to go it alone but no matter how many times it happened their appearance never failed to stupefy them.

They came out of their trance with a start. "Bloody 'ell, it's 'Er Majesty an' 'er lady-in-waitin'," screeched Mrs O'Rourke, the first to recover. "Yer dropped yer load then, I see. An' is it all right ter ask what yer 'ad? Not that we're interested, are we, lasses?" squinting round at those who were within hearing. "'Ave yer told its pa yet, 'ooever 'e may be or don't yer know?"

She cackled at her own joke. She was leaning against her door frame and where her shoulder rested on the wood it could be seen that over the years a groove had been worn. She was dressed in her usual assortment of grubby and dilapidated garments and, incongruously, a large grey pinny – which once might have been white – as though to protect them from the filth all about her. Her feet were encased in a pair of men's clogs, worn and encrusted with something she had picked up in the street, and on her head she wore a man's cap. For a shuddering moment Nancy allowed herself to imagine that this woman, if Mick had had his way, would have been her mother-in-law, wondering at the same time why Mick and Marie Finnigan, who it had been rumoured was also carrying his child, were not yet married. Had she had the child yet? The horrifying, terrifying thought slipped into her mind that when she did it would be half-sister or -brother to her own. Great God above, the sooner she got herself and her family away from this place the better. None of their neighbours had seen Kitty yet but when they did, especially this old biddy, they would recognise at once who her father was, for it was there in the baby's face even at two weeks old. Perhaps that was why she couldn't seem to take to the child, she brooded, because of her likeness to Mick.

As though the thought had conjured him up, Mick O'Rourke appeared from the depths of the cottage, elbowing his mother aside to lean his broad shoulders against the door frame, his mother protesting volubly. His face was closed and expressionless, his vivid, Irish blue eyes narrowed with what might have been a warning as he swept them offensively up and down her body. She gave him no more than a glance, but it was a glance filled with her loathing before she turned away as though he were no more to her than the filth beneath her feet. Just the same she had time to register that when he saw her look at him it seemed to please him, for the corners of his mouth began to curl up as if in amusement. His smile broadened into a grin and a feather of ice ran down her spine, though for the life of her she could not think why. She was not afraid of Mick O'Rourke. She had never been afraid of Mick O'Rourke, but something in that smile seemed to say he could be dangerous to her. She supposed he could still tell the world that he, Mick O'Rourke, had fathered her child. That he had laid the high and mighty Nancy Brody on the ground and taken her, impregnated her, but he must be aware that if he did she would reveal to the street, to Angel Meadow itself, that the only way he could get her was by force. Rape! That handsome, popular, charming Mick O'Rourke who all the girls loved had had to resort to rape to get what he had lusted after for months.

She could feel their eyes like knives in her back all the way down the street, hear the jeers floating after her and though they reckoned to hate and despise her, which she knew was laced with envy, she had the strange feeling that when she left they would miss her, for hadn't she and her family entertained them all for years.

The trip was a huge success. She and Jennet took the train from Victoria Station to travel the six and a half miles to Oldham, the pandemonium of Church Court and the sneering of its occupants completely forgotten in the excitement, the exhilaration of this day for which Nancy, at least, felt she had waited all her life. At least since her mam left. This was the start of it. She could go forward now, she thought, as the train whipped them towards Oldham, her very first train journey which was thrill enough on its own. She sighed but there was no sadness in that sigh, only the sheer joy of satisfaction.

"I do hope Mary remembers to get Kitty's wind up after her feed," Jennet said, breaking into her thoughts. "That bottle of hers is inclined to make her—"

Irritation prickled Nancy's skin and her voice was sharp, since she wanted nothing to get in the way of this splendid day.

"Please, Jennet, can we not leave Church Court behind for a couple of hours. This is very important."

"And so is Kitty," Jennet answered sharply. "Mary is not as adept as she might be with the baby though she does her best and loves the child devotedly."

"As you do."

"Of course." No more was said, for Jennet was well aware that Nancy was obsessed at the moment, not with her child but with the start of her new venture.

When they reached Oldham, flushed and quite intoxicated by the short train journey, they stepped out along Manchester Street towards King Street where Bradbury and Company was situated and where Mr Bradbury himself was waiting to meet them. He was quite mesmerised by the beauty and intelligence of Miss Brody and the sweet calm and courtesy of Miss Williams, not to mention their intimate knowledge of the sewing-machine. After their business was done, the contract signed for the hire of the machines, which if they kept up the payments would eventually be theirs, he invited them to take lunch with him at the Albion Hotel.

It was the first time that either of them had eaten in a public place, and especially one as fine as the dining-room of the Albion Hotel. They had nothing with which to compare it, of course, but it seemed very luxurious to their unsophisticated eyes. The flowers, the attentive waiters, the sparkling white tablecloths, the gleaming cutlery, the shining elegance of the glassware from which, again for the first time, they drank a delicious wine of Mr Bradbury's choosing. They ate something that Mr Bradbury told them was salmon, followed by roast pigeon, tiny potatoes and artichokes, which Jennet said afterwards she had heard of but never tasted. There was fruit – figs, melon, nectarines, peaches and some myterious thing they were told was pineapple – all so mouthwateringly delicious they would have liked to wrap some up and take it home for the girls to taste.

They were quite overcome with Mr Bradbury's kindness and attention, in their innocence believing that all his customers must receive the same treatment; but it was not until the end of the meal, as he led them out of the hotel, taking their hands and bowing over them, that it dawned on them that it was not their custom he was after but Nancy Brody herself.

"Perhaps you will allow me to call on you when next I am in Manchester?" he asked her, his eyes warm and admiring, and for the first time Nancy began to realise the power her own female beauty was to give her over the male. Then the picture of this fine gentleman, who must be forty-five if he was a day, knocking on the door of the cottage in Church Court almost undid her. She was afraid to catch Jennet's eye, for she knew if she did they would both burst into hysterical laughter.

"Why, that's very kind of you, sir, and I would be glad to renew our acquaintance," wondering where the words came from, then remembering the many fine passages she had read in *Sense and Sensibility*, in *Pride and Prejudice*, where Elinor Dashwood and Elizabeth Bennett expressed such sentiments. "Perhaps, when my business is on its feet, I may invite you to dine with me."

"And when will that be, Miss Brody?" the gentleman asked ardently.

"A few weeks, no more. I will write to you, if I may . . ." For it did no harm to keep on the right side of a man of business.

"I would be enchanted, Miss Brody. But perhaps I may come over when the machines are delivered?"

"Mr Bradbury." She let her voice become a shade cool and at once he retreated. "I shall be very busy for the next few weeks so . . ."

"Of course, forgive me. Until the next time then."

"Indeed" – warmly – "and may I say how grateful Miss Williams and I are for your help and your hospitality. You have been most kind."

Even when they got home they were still inclined to break into giggles at the image of Mr Bradbury, probably in a hansom cab that would be unable to squeeze between the walls of Church Court, picking his way through the filth and debris to knock on her door. Mrs O'Rourke would probably give him the time of day in her own inimitable way and the children, screaming abuse if they were ignored, would beg for farthings at his coat tails. The picture was enchanting!

Rosie was green with envy, inclined to glower as they described their day, their wonderful day, but Nancy, too overwhelmed with their success, did not notice it, or if she did, believed it would all blow over. Just wait until they moved from here to a better workroom, to a better home, to all the things she had promised herself and them. Rosie would be satisfied then, flowering as Nancy had always imagined her sister would when they lived among decent folk. Fine husbands for both her sisters, comfort and even a little prosperity. Just give her a year or two and it would all happen.

The question of where to leave Kitty while she and Jennet went to purchase the shirting they would need proved to be a problem that seemed insurmountable and once again Nancy cursed Mick O'Rourke with the fluency she remembered from her mother's days. They mulled over it, she and Jennet, for it would have to be a weekday and they simply could not afford to keep Rosie or Mary from the sweat shop. They had given Mr Bradbury a hefty deposit for the sewing-machines, which were to be delivered at the end of the week and every penny must be made to count. Mr Earnshaw had lost Nancy and then Jennet, the best of them in his opinion, and if either Rosie or Mary was to take a day off he would most likely sack the pair of them.

"I saw Annie the other day," Mary proclaimed out of the blue as she came downstairs from where she had been putting Kitty in her little bed, which was no more than a shallow cardboard box lined with scraps of soft blankets.

Both Nancy and Jennet looked up in surprise.

"Oh?"

"Mmm. She didn't look very well."

"Oh?"

It was a month now since Annie had saved not only Nancy's life, they all firmly believed, but Kitty's, and she had seemed well enough then.

"She was just off to the market as we were coming home from Earnshaw's. She laughed as she told us she was looking for the leavings though she didn't seem very amused. Remember how we used to?"

"And still do."

"Yes, I suppose so."

"But what was Annie . . . Well, did she say she was poorly?"

"Oh, she's not poorly."

"Dear God, Mary, will you get to the point? It's like trying to draw teeth. What's the matter with her if she's not ill?"

"She's had an accident. Hurt her hand so Hayes put her off."

There was a deathly silence then, "Nay, never!" from Nancy, reverting to the speech of her young childhood in her shock. "She's been there for years and was the best spinner they ever had and then just to turn her off. Poor Annie. How will she manage? She only knows spinning."

"And looking after children," Jennet added quietly.

"Yes, she had enough of those, I remember, though—" Suddenly she stopped and swivelled to stare at Jennet, then they both smiled as Nancy's thoughts caught up with those of her friend.

"D'you know where she lives?" Jennet asked.

"No, but I can soon find out," Nancy answered, while Mary looked from one to the other in honest mystification.

"It would be ideal, for she is a kind woman and could be trusted to care for Kitty as we do." This from Jennet, since it was the most important factor in this.

"And we would all be able to work uninterrupted," Nancy added, glowing with good humour, stating what to her was the nub of the matter. "Not to mention putting a few pence in Annie's pocket which I'm sure she'd welcome. See, Rosie," turning to her sister who lolled indolently on a chair by the window, staring at something in the street, not taking a great deal of interest in what was being discussed, "will you run over to Monarch? The girls who worked with Annie will know where she lives and then when you've found out go there and ask her to come and see me. As soon as she can, there's a good lass. Tell her . . . tell her it's to her advantage."

If she was surprised at the alacrity with which Rosie set off up the street, suddenly as cheerful and sunny as a summer's day, Nancy did not voice it. She knew her sister became easily bored with what she called "hanging round the house" and was always eager to run an errand, or indeed was glad of any excuse to get out. But then she was young and pretty and should have been out having fun, like girls of her age did. Not in *her* class, Nancy realised, but then Rosie had been brought up differently to girls in her class and must feel sometimes that she was neither one thing nor the other. But that would change soon.

And with Annie Wilson to help they might make it happen all the sooner!

13

They did not call Manchester the warehouse town for nothing, since the warehouse played a vital role in its economic life. There were cotton mills in abundance, multiplying from the one built by Richard Arkwright in 1783 on Miller Street near Shude Hill to the hundreds of steam-powered spinning factories in Ancoats, New Cross, Beswick and Holt Town and the new industrial zones along the Rochdale and Ashton canals to the east and astride the Irk Valley to the north. As the River Irwell wound its way through Salford it brought industry in its wake.

But there was more to the cotton trade than its mills. Never more than a few streets away was the main warehouse district. The demand for commercial premises grew with the development of the mills themselves, spreading from King Street to Cannon Street, High Street and Moseley Street where the quite magnificent warehouse belonging to Edmund Hayes and Sons was situated. The great architect Thomas Worthington was so impressed by this building and by the many others built by Manchester's merchant princes he named the city the Florence of the nineteenth century, for they were indeed as glorious as many an Italian *palazzo*. The palatial edifices had rows of regular windows to four storeys and sometimes more, with a central doorway at first-floor level reached by a flight of steps. The tops of the buildings were marked by prominent cornices.

Nancy and Jennet, though they knew their business here was as legitimate as that of any of the gentlemen who hurried up and down the steps, hesitated at the bottom, overawed by such magnificence. They themselves were as carefully and neatly dressed as any lady in the outfits they had worn to Oldham, but beneath their bodices their hearts beat rapidly for it was very obvious this was strictly male territory. Even just standing here at the bottom of the steps looking up at the impressive open wooden doors, they were exciting some interest and not a little irritation.

"Madam," said one gentleman, addressing Nancy, which gentlemen tended to do, "are you to go up or not?" He clearly expected the answer to be in the negative as he did his best to brush by them. He was seriously alarmed when, with a polite nod, Nancy took Jennet's arm and walked her gracefully up the steps ahead of him.

"Can I help you, ladies?" he ventured to ask as they moved through the wide doorway at the top of the steps, politely removing his top hat, fully expecting that, like ladies the world over, they would find themselves to be in the wrong place, thinking this to be the Portico Library which was further along Moseley Street.

"Thank you, you are most kind but we can manage," Nancy told him, giving him a smile that quite bowled him over. He was not to know that she hadn't the faintest idea what she was looking for nor how to proceed with her business when she found it. There was a massive central staircase leading to the upper floors and again gentlemen dashed up and down as though they had not a minute to spare and with another flashing smile she proceeded towards them, propelling the speechless Jennet with her.

"I thought you knew what to do in the purchase of materials," she hissed at her friend. "Mr Earnshaw . . ."

"Mr Earnshaw did not buy quality stuff, Nancy. We bought from back-street merchants, anywhere it was cheap and plentiful."

"Then how are we to know what the devil to do in a place like this? It's like a bloody palace."

"Oh hush, Nancy, please, we are supposed to be ladies, after all."

"You are a lady, Jennet. I'm not."

"Don't be silly. You are the same as me in every respect. If I'm a lady so are you. But if one of these gentlemen should hear you swear they wouldn't think so and might call someone to put us out and that would be the end of our venture before it began. Now smile at me and pretend that we do this every day of the week."

"But what shall we do? Where shall we go?"

"Let's have a look round first. Perhaps we'll get some idea of what we should be doing."

Arm-in-arm, just as though they were strolling round the department store, Kendal, Milne and Faulkners, two ladies out to do a morning's shopping, which was what they were but not the sort usually done by ladies, they wandered from floor to floor doing their best to be calm and unhurried, the only females among the male visitors to the warehouse. Everywhere they went they were met by amazed stares and open-mouthed curiosity, though none as yet had the nerve to question their right to be there, since, for all they knew, the two ladies might be relatives of the Hayes family.

On the upper floors were the sample-rooms where customers might inspect goods by the light of the tall front windows and this was packed with jostling men who threatened to take the coats off the backs of one another in their eagerness to get a good look at the sample of what was on offer.

It appeared the ground floor was taken up with offices and the basement used solely as a packing-room, which Nancy and Jennet discovered when they stumbled inadvertently into a room jammed with astonished workmen. This must surely be the hub of the warehouse, for Nancy believed she had never seen such frenetic activity taking place in one area, which covered the whole of the basement. There were men in shirt sleeves working hydraulic presses and porters with great brawny arms and shoulders, reminding her of the men in the mill yard at Monarch, groaning under heavy bales of cotton. Clerks perambulated about holding notebooks in which they checked and noted this and that; beyond them, leading on to a side street, was an enormous open loading bay crammed with waggons, each one in turn receiving pack after pack of goods until they were made up, when the whole lot rolled away like moving mountains.

It seemed there was to be a public auction that day, not only of a range of cotton goods but of textile machinery which was apparently being viewed prior to the auction later in the morning. As the two women sauntered here and there, quite enjoying themselves now that they seemed to have their bearings and nobody had interfered with them, the scenes about them began to take on a frenzied atmosphere. Warehousemen scrambled up the stairs with rolls of material on their shoulders, placing them on a clean white cloth spread over the floor of the top room before racing down again to fetch another. Nancy and Jennet were roughly pushed to one side and it began to be obvious why the customers had looked so astounded, for this was no place for the niceties shown by gentlemen to ladies. They were pressed back against the wall and it was only with the greatest difficulty that they extricated themselves and fled down the stairs to the floor on which the offices were situated. It was quieter here and for a moment they leaned against a wall and fanned themselves.

"Well, it's no good expecting anyone to ask us what we want to buy, Jennet, because they're not going to do it. It's just a free-for-all and unless we press ourselves into it we shall go home empty-handed. If only there was some likely employee from whom we could find out . . . well, where to start."

They were in a relatively quiet corridor off which there were several doors, splendid highly polished mahogany doors. After the frenzy of the upper floors it was almost silent down here, just the muted sound of voices beyond the doors, presumably those of the clerks, the office staff, the managers and whoever helped to run this vast enterprise, for surely it must have many employees.

"Well, I don't think we're going to get what we want down here, do you?" Nancy murmured, straightening up from the wall against which she had been leaning. "The action is on the top floor so I suppose we'd better get up to it. Let's hope all the best lengths have not already been sold while we've been dithering down here."

Jennet squared her narrow shoulders and lifted her head as though she were about to march into battle. "You're right, Nancy, though I must admit the notion of forcing my way back into that room among all those men fills me with alarm."

"What can they do to us, love? A few shoves won't hurt us and if they do shove we must just learn to shove back."

They linked arms and though Jennet's stride was shorter than Nancy's she kept up with her, skimming along the corridor and up the several flights of stairs that led to the top floor. It was just as frantic as it had been before, with men elbowing one another aside to get their hands on pieces as they were brought up, so frantic that, as Jennet said, one could be forgiven for thinking that what was on sale was the last cotton ever to come off a spinning frame.

They circled the room, looking for a way into the fray but

these men were here on business; if the two women were also buying they must take their chances with the rest of them. They shouldn't be here, the men's disapproving expressions said, and if they were jostled then it was their own fault.

But Nancy Brody had not come this far only to have her dream of success pushed to one side by a bunch of hooligans, for that was how she saw them and she'd dealt with enough of those in her time. They could not be worse than the guttersnipes in Church Court who she had dispersed with many a sharp word and even a clout or two round a filthy ear. If she had to clout the ear of an impertinent fellow here, then clout it she would and be damned to them!

"Excuse me," she told two of them in a firm voice. They stood shoulder to shoulder and as she tapped them on their smooth broadcloth backs with a peremptory hand they turned and parted to stare in amazement.

"Thank you, you are most kind," she told them, smiling her most dazzling smile. Dragging Jennet with her through the small gap she forced her way to the front of the circle and, ignoring those about her who muttered ominously, as she did those who clustered about the stalls at the market, she took off her glove, bent down and lifted the end of a roll of creamy cotton, fingering it knowledgeably.

"Feel this, Jennet," she told her bemused friend. "This seems of good quality. What d'you think?"

"I agree. Has this come off the spinning frames at Monarch, do you think?"

"I suppose so, but let's not decide on the first we see. There are other pieces that look suitable and there may be a difference in price. We must find out all we can before we buy. A farthing saved, you know the saying."

Now that they were in the inner circle of the heaving, pushing, shouting, gesticulating men they found it easier to move round the room, watched with slack-jawed astonishment by the men who had not at first noticed them. They seemed to want to say or do something, perhaps eject these interlopers, but as yet they were unsure how to go about it. It was quite unprecedented. They even stood back to allow the two females to circulate more freely and Nancy smiled at them which further increased their dismay. A woman in their midst was mystery enough, but a well-dressed woman of great loveliness, a woman with a smile that they would have liked to respond to, a smile that asked for and deserved some show of gentlemanly attention was very pleasant, but this was neither the time nor the place and they resented it fiercely. And not just one woman, but two, though the second was hardly worth a glance she was so plain and childlike. Ladies did go about in pairs, for it was only proper, but they certainly didn't wander about a male-dominated warehouse, nor were they so bold and presumptuous as the lovelier of the two was. She seemed to find nothing strange in being among men of business and was busy studying lengths of cotton, pointing out this and that to her companion as though she had as much right to be here as they did. Something should be done, for how could business be transacted when all were distracted by this phenomenon.

A tap on Nancy's arm, polite, respectful but determined, turned her to face a large man dressed in a clean white shirt, a neatly knotted tie and dark trousers over which he wore a green canvas apron tied at his back.

"Madam," he said in a low voice, "you really should not be here, you know. These gentlemen are here to do business and it is no place for a lady. I must ask you, and your companion," turning to nod politely at Jennet, "to come with me."

"I'm sorry, but we have not completed *our* business as yet. Perhaps you could tell me the prices."

"Madam! I must repeat, I cannot allow . . ."

"Yes?"

"This is a warehouse, madam, and these gentlemen are here to buy cotton goods and—"

"As I am, sir, so if you would just tell me to whom I should address my needs I will—"

"No, madam, you will not. This is not the way to do business."

"Then tell me what is. I am a customer with cash in my pocket who wishes to purchase your goods. Are you telling me that because I am female you will not sell them to me?"

He had taken them both by the arm by now, mortified, angry, for all about him business had come to a standstill as the gentlemen, all dressed in shades of dark grey and white and wearing silk top hats, smiled and dug one another in the ribs at the spectacle. Their own indignation was gone now, since the two intruders were being dealt with and they were prepared to enjoy the fun.

"Take your hands off me, you impudent scoundrel," Jennet

was saying, proving she was not the little mouse they had first thought her. "There is absolutely no need for violence. We are doing no harm."

"Perhaps not, madam, but this is not the place for you. If you wish to buy cotton goods or a length or two of fustian or jaconet then I suggest you go to one of the drapers in Deansgate or Market Street. This is a wholesale warehouse."

"We wish to buy *wholesale,* you fool, and if you don't let go of my arm and that of my friend I shall fetch a constable."

Nancy's face had turned a glowing pink and there were not a few gentlemen who conjectured on how pleasant it would be to make her acquaintance, though in different circumstances.

"How dare you molest us," she went on hotly. "*We are customers.* We have come to—"

"I don't care *why* you've come, madam. This is no place for . . ."

They were almost at the door by now, for the man was strong and determined, red-faced with indignation and given a helping hand now and again by a chappie or two who did not mind putting his hand on a pretty lady, who was *not* a lady, of course, else she would not have been here.

A quiet voice in the doorway brought the three of them to a halt, for short of shoving the two women through the man who stood there, the warehouseman had no choice but to stop.

"What's going on here, Burrows? I could hear the commotion at the bottom of the stairs."

"Don't worry about it, Mr Josh. They're just going. What the devil they thought they were up to in the first place I don't know."

Expecting Mr Josh to move aside, the man took a firm grip of Nancy's arm with one hand and with the other tackled Jennet, but neither Nancy, Jennet or Mr Josh was willing to move, or be moved, and he was forced to let them go, his face a bright scarlet, his eyes almost starting out of his head with vexation. He'd never felt such a fool in his life and left to himself without the intervention of his employer's son would willingly have dragged these two down the stairs and thrown them into the street.

The man in the doorway was young, tall, lean, leaner than Nancy remembered, immaculately dressed in the sober suit of the businessman. His face was unsmiling. His eyes were a clear grey, almost colourless, with no expression in them that could be recognised and his well-cut lips had no hint of humour or warmth. It was a quiet face, sombre even, impassive and preoccupied, as though far greater things needed his attention than this. Nevertheless he was attending to it. Nancy was quite taken aback, not that he should have intervened, though she supposed that was natural in this man's world into which she and Jennet had blundered, but by the dramatic change in him since she had seen him last. He didn't look ill exactly, for he still had that sun-tinted face that spoke of outdoor pursuits but he seemed to be lifeless, as though that rather engaging . . . well, charm, she supposed she would have called it, had been squeezed out of him, leaving him empty and without substance. They had met three times before and on each occasion he had been young, as he still was; an inclination to be reckless, arrogant certainly, but with an engaging, half-hidden light-heartedness that she had found she responded to, a readiness, or so it had seemed to her, to be friendly if he was allowed. Now he looked as though he had lost a dear member of his family, grave and brooding and ready to scowl should he be displeased.

Well, it was no good dwelling on the change in him, for it was nothing to do with her. Here was a chance to get past this damned warehouseman, perhaps to overcome the vexing problem of how to obtain the material they needed, and to clear the way for further transactions. If they were not to be allowed to come to this place, or any place where cotton goods were sold, how were they to proceed with their enterprise which was just getting under way? The machines were ordered. In the cottage all the furniture except the settle had been crammed upstairs so that there was barely room to move. The two beds and Kitty's sleeping box were jammed against the wall, the rest of their stuff – and Jennet's – piled up about them to the ceiling and they just hoped that it would not come crashing down about their ears as they slept. Downstairs had been left empty, awaiting the arrival of the sewing-machines. As Nancy said, they must work where the warmth was, for with autumn and then winter coming on it would be too cold to work upstairs.

Nancy elbowed aside the warehouseman and, with her hand on Jennet's arm, stepped forward haughtily while all about her men gawked and the silence was so tangible it could almost be felt.

"Mr Hayes: it is Mr Hayes, isn't it? I wonder if my partner and

I might have a word with you. This . . . this fellow," giving the warehouseman a look of contempt, "seems to think we are up to no good."

"And what are you up to, Miss . . . ?"

"Brody. Nancy Brody and this is Jennet Williams," turning to smile reassuringly at Jennet as though to say she must not be afraid. "We are not 'up to' anything, Mr Hayes, for that seems to imply dishonesty. We are here to buy cotton, that's all, but if you would allow it I would rather discuss it where these gentlemen" – she waved her hand dismissively at the crowd of men at her back – "cannot hear my business."

"There is nothing hidden here, Miss Brody. These are all men of integrity who are doing an honest day's business with this firm."

The men in question shuffled their feet and looked at one another in agreement, glad that this impudent hussy was being taken down a peg by Josh Hayes, as she deserved, but they had reckoned without Nancy Brody who, for the past six years, had moulded her own destiny which she was following and nothing, *nothing* was going to stand in her way. If she had to get down on her knees and beg this unsmiling young man for the cotton she needed, and in front of them all, she would.

"Mr Hayes, I am here for the same purpose as these gentlemen. I wish to do business with you. Are you so prosperous that you can afford to turn it away? Once your father, and all these gentlemen," turning a passionate face to the men at her back, "began their own ventures and because they worked hard and risked everything they had they have succeeded. Won't you allow me the same chance? I am to start . . . I'm going into business for myself in the textile trade but I must have your co-operation if I'm even to get under way. I know there are other warehouses selling what I want but I know the quality of your cotton and so I have chosen to buy it. You know where I started. Oh, yes, sir, you do, for you saw me there a year or two back and I have come some way since then. Will you stop me now?"

There was absolute silence in the enormous room and even those standing outside it, gathering in the hallway and on the stairs, for word had got about that something unusual was happening on the top floor, made not a sound.

Josh Hayes remembered her and he remembered the strange sense of recognition he had felt on each of the occasions they had met. She was not a lady, of course, and these men knew it. The first time he had seen her had been in the yard at the mill. She had been a spinner then, clothed in the drab garb of a mill girl. Last year she had been dressed in decent but humble garments when they had almost bumped into each other at the Arts Treasures Exhibition. She had been accompanied by a rough-looking labouring chap and he recalled his sad feeling of . . . well, he could only call it disappointment that such a fine-looking young girl should associate with such a man. The last time they had met among the ruins of Castle Irwell she had been wrapped in a working woman's shawl. So what had brought about this transformation? She spoke with the careful enunciation of a woman who has taught herself to speak as the upper classes do although there was still a trace of her Manchester heritage in her voice, but to look at her a man who did not know her background could be forgiven for thinking her to be a lady born and bred.

He was intrigued, though he did not let it show in his face. He had learned in the last few weeks to let nothing show in his face. He knew his family were perplexed and worried about him, for Evie Edward had been no more than a young man's fancy and had been taken care of before her death so why should he appear to mourn her so? The child, his son, still remained at Riverside House, installed in the nurseries there with a nursemaid, his father allowing it because Josh had told him that if the child was sent away, quite simply he would go with it. It, that was all it was to him, without even a name as yet and he knew that he must pull himself out of this quagmire Evie's death had flung him into if he was to get on with his life, and make one for the child. The infant was made much of by the servants, he was aware of that, and even his mother had ventured up to the top floor to peep at her grandson, though she had said nothing to him about it. The servants knew, naturally, all that went on in the household, marvelling when, with Mrs Hayes's permission, the nursemaid began to push the child about the gardens in the old Hayes baby carriage. He had seen it himself. It was the talk of the polite society his family moved in, but it seemed none blamed him, for young men must sow their wild oats and who else to sow them with but one of the lower classes. It was a constant source of amazement to him that though two people were involved, the man and the woman, it was the woman who was condemned as wicked. Evie had not been wicked. She had been an innocent and he had taken advantage of it and he could not forgive himself, but at least he could make it up to her son. As soon as he felt up to it he meant to call on his father's lawyer to arrange the adoption of the child, when, presumably, he would be christened, given his proper name and be brought up as the son of a gentleman.

For the first time since Evie's death he felt a stirring of interest as he looked into the glowing golden eyes, the passionate face of the girl before him. What must it be like to have such enthusiasm, to show such ardour over what was really only a day's business? The men about them were nudging one another and murmuring, fully expecting, he knew, that he would tell her that this was a place where men, and *men* only carried on their transactions and that he would be obliged if she would leave his establishment at once; but that something that had stirred in him grew stronger, lifting his heart a little, warming some place that had been cold and distant since Evie's death. He had not loved Evie, not as a man loves the woman of his heart. He had never loved a woman, except in the physical sense and, his heart being as it was, cold and stern and unforgiving, of himself, he did not expect ever to experience what was called "true love".

What it was he did not know, nor, at the moment, did he care but this woman had, three times, four if you counted this meeting, come into his life, challenged him, if you like, and he thought he might like to take up that challenge, see what she made of herself, give her the chance she asked for. Why not? It might not be to the taste of his other customers but they would not go elsewhere, for the cotton though coarse that came off his father's frames was the best in Manchester, in Lancashire and they would not want to lose it for the sake of a principle. Profit was their god and they would not give it up lightly.

They faced one another, Josh Hayes and Nancy Brody, while the whole room held its breath. Though Josh was tall so was Nancy and she had not far to look up into his eyes. A message of some sort passed between them, of what sort neither understood, but it was something neither had experienced before and without knowing it, without knowing why, they both sighed.

"Well, Miss Brody, it seems you are determined on a career in the textile trade and who am I to stand in the way of anyone's career, man or woman, so, if you will follow me to my office we will discuss what we can do for one another."

He turned to the warehouseman who stood with his mouth

foolishly open, since he had been fully expecting to escort the two young ladies off the premises.

"Thank you, Burrows, that will be all, and in future when Miss Brody or Miss Williams call, will you bring them to me."

14

"I think we should go for a picnic. It really would be a sin to waste such a perfect day; besides which, Kitty has never seen real grass or wild flowers—"

"You're always taking her to Vauxhall Gardens," Nancy interrupted absently as she studied the pattern for an infant's dress that she was about to cut out. "Anyway, I'm too busy. Mrs Underwood wants these dresses by the end of the week and if they're not ready she'll go elsewhere. And you promised you'd do the embroidery."

"And so I will but not today. It's too nice. This evening, when Kitty's in bed, I'll make a start and I won't stop until they're all finished, even if I have to sit up all night."

"You might have to. There are two dozen."

"But all with a simple satin stitch joined by a chain stitch. White on white. What could be simpler? Even Kitty could do it if we let her and Mary has promised to help me. Oh, come on, Nancy, do let's go. We've all worked so hard without a break and you promised ages ago to show us that ruined castle."

"Heavens, Jen, we couldn't carry Kitty all that way, even between us. She's getting too big. And there'd be food and such to bring, blankets . . ."

"We could get a hansom."

"*What!*" Laughingly Nancy turned to look at her friend, the scissors poised in her hand. "Are you out of your mind? A hansom indeed. You'd think we were made of money. You know every penny counts and even if I wanted to pay the price, which I don't, you'd never get a hansom to come into Church Court. Remember all that pandemonium when the machines were delivered. You'd have thought we were putting on a show for the benefit of the neighbours. No, why don't we wait until we move house then we—"

"When will that be, Nancy?" Jennet interrupted quietly. "We have been in business for almost a year now and we have done well, but still you won't get out of this place. We need the extra space, you know we do, even though we have a workroom in Shude Hill. If we had another room Annie could move in with us now that she lives alone and save herself the rent on her place, which would be so much more convenient and, frankly, if you don't do something about getting away from here you're going to be in trouble with Rosie. Oh, I know she's a good worker and turns out more than her share but she needs to be got away from . . . well, you know who. It doesn't bear thinking about that she might . . ."

"Don't, Jen, please don't." Nancy's face was a picture of remembered despair and she turned away and put her head in her hands. The room in which they were working was now restored to what it had once been before the machines came, with the furniture brought down and arranged as best they could in the space there was. It was clean and tidy and had a certain degree of snugness, but it was far from what those who lived in splendid isolation in Broughton or Cheetham Hill might call even comfortable, though compared to their immediate neighbours it was the very height of luxury. On the floor, now decently covered with a bit of worn carpet, the little girl played with some empty bobbins and a tin box, carefully placing the bobbins in the box, then taking them out again. There was room only for six but she was doing her best to force in a seventh, her tongue sticking out from between her rosy lips, her fine dark eyebrows dipping in a scowl of concentration.

She was a beautiful child with the best of both her parents in her, not only in looks but in temperament. Her impish charm and her colouring came from Mick O'Rourke. She had eyes the shade of a speedwell and glossy hair as dark as a blackbird's wing. It was curly, tumbling about her small head, not in the crisp curls of her mother and aunts but like Mick's, deep and loose and thick. Her skin was cream and peach, like her mother's, and her features, unlike the somewhat coarse countenance of her Irish forebears, were refined, delicate, her nose still retaining the blob of babyhood, her mouth like a rose petal. Though she was not yet a year old she was quick and vivid and soon those about her knew she would become impatient with the bobbins and look for something more challenging. She was a lively child, strong-willed but friendly enough, sitting on whichever lap was available to her, not feeling the lack of a devoted mother's care, for she was loved by her Aunty Jennet, her Aunty Annie and her Aunty Mary. But now and again Mick O'Rourke's fierce temper and her mother's vigorous competitiveness came out in her, showing itself in a determination to have her own way, as in her increasingly impatient resolve that the seven bobbins could be made to fit in a box big enough only for six.

"No, darling." Jennet kneeled down beside her and attempted to take the box from her. "The box isn't big enough for all the bobbins. See, let Aunty Jennet show you." But Kitty set her face in a mutinous frown and wilfully jerked the box away.

"No." It was the only word she knew but she said it frequently. Sometimes Nancy caught a glimpse of the first Kitty in her, a curl at the corner of her mouth, a movement of her head and for a moment was saddened for the dreadful life and, one supposed, death, that her mother had suffered. And yet, if her mother had shaped herself, as Nancy had done, could she not have made more of her life than she had? There was work to be had in this vast cotton city, Nancy herself had proved it. Gritting her teeth and ignoring the jeers and laughter of her neighbours she had dragged herself and her sisters from the mire her mother had wallowed in and now look where she was. Getting above herself, they still shouted after her but she had shown them all and now had a small but increasingly successful business of her own, a bank account with money in it, premises in Shude Hill, six sewing-machines with six girls, including Mary and Rosie, turning out shirts and waistcoats, baby garments, ladies' undergarments such as petticoats and shifts, and indeed anything that she thought might sell on the market. While Jennet supervised the work and attended to customers in the workroom Nancy stood behind a stall for the three busiest days of the week and sold the garments that had been made in her own workroom.

She remembered that first day with quiet amusement. How afraid she had been and yet not for a moment would she allow it to show, holding her head high and her shoulders squared against whatever might come her way. She was not awfully sure what she had been afraid of, unless it was that she might stand there for the full day and sell nothing. She didn't care what anyone thought of her, or the way the men eyed her, for she knew she was not unattractive, or that the decent women who shopped in the market might have heard that she had an illegitimate child and so condemn her and her merchandise. She didn't care what they thought of her personally as long as they liked what she was selling, the attractive, well-made garments she and her sisters, with Jennet, had spent hours over. Wearing a plain grey skirt and bodice, a snowy muslin apron and a shawl wrapped about her shoulders, she had arranged her goods on her stall on a wide length of clean cotton, the shirts, the baby garments, the undergarments, all in a plain creamy cotton, of good quality, well made and even a bit of embroidery on some of them. They were within the price range of the careful, thrifty housewife, those who shopped in the market not at the end of the day when produce was cheap, since it might not keep until tomorrow, but early in the morning when it was fresh and therefore cost more. These were the customers Nancy wanted. They had husbands who were in decent work. They came not from Angel Meadow but from better districts, still working class but decent and hardworking, limiting their families to the size they could afford. They might be shabby but they were clean and proud and required the best for the prices they could afford. Nancy meant to give it to them. Mrs Beasley, opposite whose stall Nancy stood, catered to the poorest of the poor, selling second-hand clothing that sometimes was no more than tattered rags. Nancy knew, for Nancy had once worn them, so she and Mrs Beasley were not in competition with one another.

That first day many of the women had stopped and fingered her goods, looking for a bargain, studying the seams, the embroidery, the buttonholes, the hand finishing over which she and Jennet and the girls had laboured, nodding pleasantly enough before moving on. Their circumstances meant that they could not afford to buy the first thing on offer but had to circle the market on the lookout for value, for every penny must be made to count. But one by one they drifted back. They were not to know that Nancy had herself gone round the market on many occasions, stopping at every stall that sold children's clothing, shirts and undergarments, matching the quality and prices to her own and by charging a penny less, sometimes even as much as sixpence, she undercut them all and the housewives could not resist.

By the end of that first day she had sold everything on her stall and had orders from women who had been slow in returning but were prepared to wait until the following week for what they wanted.

In those first weeks it had been chaotic at the cottage in Church Court and Annie had threatened to throw herself in the Irwell if they didn't do something about the space.

"'Ow can I look after't babby, cook a bit o' grub and run a cloth over't place wi' three o' yer goin' away like maniacs on them bloody machines. I 'aven't room ter turn round an' I can't sit upstairs all day, it's too bloody cold. That babby'll freeze up there in't winter."

"Oh, please, Annie, can we not just make do for a few months?" Nancy had pleaded with her. "I daren't spend more money on a workshop just yet. I know things are going well, better than I ever hoped. I had no idea what an opening there was in the market – did you, Jennet? – for better-class clothing but at a price they can afford," turning in a delirium of enchantment to Jennet, then back to Annie, "but we must walk before we run."

"That's all very well, Nancy Brody, but there isn't bloody room ter even sit down on yer bum, never mind walk about. That babby—"

"Never mind the baby, Annie. As long as she's fed and warm she'll be all right," Nancy was unwise enough to say carelessly to the woman whose job it was to look after her while the rest of them worked. Annie was made up with her new position and Nancy had lifted a great burden, possibly even a death sentence from her when she put her in charge of her child. Annie's right hand had been badly damaged by a moment of carelessness – or was it old age? – on her part and could no longer manage a spinning frame. Her old man had died long ago of the consumption that was rife in the disease-ridden world of Angel Meadow and her sons had long since left home. Then Nancy had sent for her and Annie would never, if she lived to be ninety, be able to thank the lass for rescuing her; but just the same she would not have her speak about the child, of whom Annie was becoming increasingly fond, as though she were a puppy who could be left in a basket and fed three times a day.

She drew herself up and her mouth thinned. She had lost most of her teeth and her lips disappeared completely.

"Now listen 'ere, lady. That babby needs—"

"Annie, dear Annie, I know what she needs, believe me. Jennet never lets me forget, but surely there are enough of us to give her everything that is required. Perhaps you could take her to . . ."

"Where? Tell me an' I'll tekk 'er." Annie screwed up her eyes and glared into Nancy's face.

"Dear God, haven't I enough to contend with, Annie Wilson, without planning your day as well. I'm trying to make a living for six people here. To get a business going and I haven't time to be bothering with a baby, for God's sake."

"Then why did yer 'ave the poor little mite? Some chap must've took yer fancy an' . . ."

Annie was amazed when Nancy bowed her head and began to cry. They were alone, for it was a Sunday and Jennet and Mary had taken Kitty to Vauxhall Gardens. God knows where Rosie had got to, though Nancy had her suspicions. Both Jennet and Mary wore a shawl and, taking it in turns, carried the baby in it. She had been six weeks old then and was not yet too heavy to be taken about this way, though as yet her mother had never done so. She was too busy, she said. She had too much on her mind but if they wanted to take a turn about the gardens, which were only a ten-minute walk away, then she'd stay at home and go over the accounts which she kept faithfully in a big red ledger.

For a moment Annie was astounded, for she had never seen Nancy Brody other than steadfast, confident, strong and ready to tackle anything. Now, here she was crying like a child who has been unfairly thrashed. But Annie was not the sort of woman who could be swayed to sympathy by a few tears. Tears were an indulgence she had rarely allowed herself, and she wasn't about to be got round by Nancy's.

"Now then, what's up?" she asked sharply, just as though Nancy were doing herself no favours by acting this way and she'd best pull herself together.

"*Some chap must have taken my fancy*," Nancy wailed, allowing herself for the moment to weaken, allowing herself, though she despised herself for it, to feel self-pity, then she sniffed, wiped her nose on the back of her hand and threw up her head, her curls bouncing independently.

"You should know me better than that, Annie Wilson," she cried. "You've known me since I was a nipper. You've seen me struggle on a spinning frame when I could hardly reach the bloody thing. You've seen me work towards one goal. To better myself and my sisters. To *be* somebody. To be respectable. To drag myself from this bloody muck-heap I live in. Do you honestly think I would casually let some chap up my skirt? Dear Lord God, Annie, you should know me better than that."

"Then 'ow?"

"I was raped, Annie," she hissed into Annie's horrified face. "I was dragged into the churchyard and raped by that bastard who . . . who still is doing his best to . . . to . . ."

"What, lass?"

"Oh, never mind, Annie. We'll be gone from here soon, all of us; oh, yes, you included, and the problem will be solved. But you must see why I cannot consider anything else, even my daughter and where she is to spend her day. As long as she's in your care while we are working I know she's safe and looked after. Please, Annie, do your best, please."

It was after Christmas when Nancy knew she could no longer manage to juggle the complexity of her growing needs. They had more work than could be done on the three sewing-machines and she knew that a business that stands still, that does not expand when it is needed, is going backwards. Space, she needed more space. Only last week a Mrs Underwood, who had a small but respectable draper's in Market Street, had stopped at her stall and examined every article on display. She had turned each one inside out, studying the seams, the buttonholes, the dainty bit of embroidery, even sniffing the fabric as though to ascertain where the garments had been made, her attitude saying that if it was among dirt she was not interested.

"What time do you finish here, Miss . . . er . . ."

"Brody . . ." she replied suspiciously.

"I am Hetty Underwood. I have a small shop in Market Street and I think, if you are willing and we can come to some arrangement satisfactory to us both, we might do business together. May I call on you?" she had asked abruptly.

As she had done with Mr Bradbury when he had suggested he would visit her when next he was in Manchester, Nancy had a mental picture of this sober, decently dressed woman, a working woman but very respectable, picking her way along Church Court, but she managed to control herself.

"I think not, Mrs Underwood. We are rather crowded at

home. I have sisters and . . . well, it would be more convenient if I called on you; that is if you don't mind."

Though Hetty Underwood liked to see the premises from which her merchandise was purchased she made an exception for Nancy Brody, since the girl was so immaculately turned out and her goods could not be faulted.

The upshot was that within a month the baby garments manufactured in the stinking alleyway known as Church Court were being displayed in the shop window of a small but well-respected draper's window in Market Street. They sold and they sold well to the wives of the lower middle classes, ladies who would not dream of frequenting a market but were glad to clothe their infants from a good shop like Mrs Underwood's. The orders grew and Mrs Underwood wanted more and it was then that Nancy and Jennet began to look around for a decent workshop, for decent machinists and to send word to Mr Bradbury that they would require more machines.

She could have done none of it without Josh Hayes. From that first day when, to the mortification of every man in the sample-room who could not believe it of him, he had led her and Jennet courteously down the long flight of stairs to his office on the ground floor, he had made it possible for her to obtain whatever she required in the way of materials. He had seated them in splendid leather chairs, rang a bell and when a cheerful little messenger boy popped his head round the door, ordered coffee for three. He questioned them vigorously while they drank it. There was no polite small talk, for these were potential customers and as such did not require it. Time was money to them all and so they had none to waste.

"So what would your requirements be, Miss Brody?" he asked her, watching, though she was not aware of it, the excitement of her smile. It was a deep smile in which her eyes changed colour from pale amber to a rich gold. Her eyelashes meshed together, dark and silky and long and her full mouth parted in what appeared to be delight over her even white teeth. A faint flush of colour tinted her creamy white skin at the cheekbones. About her forehead, from beneath the tilted brim of her straw hat, and in front of her ears, a small cascade of tight curls, which had escaped the severe chignon she had devised at the back of her head, danced enchantingly as she leaned forward, her eagerness lovely to watch.

"Mr Hayes, we want no more than you give to your other customers. We want to be able to come in here and buy our cotton, or whatever else we might need, without interference from your staff and from the other customers. We want no privileges, or special attention. We want to be treated as though we were . . . men, in fact."

"That might be difficult, Miss Brody." He smiled coolly to take the sting out of his words. "You are not a man and my other customers won't like it. But if you can stand their hostility then so can I."

She positively glowed with rapture. It was quite extraordinary, for it was very little that he had given her. Somewhere to purchase the cloth she needed, that was all, but she was acting, and looking, as though he had given her the key to the Kingdom of Heaven where treasures of a sort never before seen were to be offered her. She turned to clutch at her quiet companion who was so exactly the opposite of herself. Small, plain, mousy, he supposed men would call her, colourless, from the neat grey gown she wore, her hair which he could see beneath her undistinguished bonnet that was so fair as to be almost white, to her cool grey eyes. An oddly matched pair but with some link between them that showed itself, not with words but with the look they exchanged. Golden eyes blazing into silver as though relaying a message of jubilance, of joy, of triumph over adversity; and when he remembered how he had seen her, the lovely one, over a year ago now, in the mill yard, could you wonder that she should be so exultant. For a mill girl, a young mill girl at that, for she could be no more than eighteen even now, to rise to such dizzy heights was quite extraordinary. He would have been astounded to learn that she was still only fifteen! He had never come across a woman involved in the cotton trade, not in all the years since he had entered his father's business, not one who wished to compete with other men, that is, and he found his curiosity was aroused though he did not let it show in his face.

He knew he was watching her with rather more interest than one man of business shows to another. She really was a beautiful creature, even more so now, for she had let down her guard, thrown off the defensive stiffness with which she had held herself together during the last few minutes. She had become soft, warm, sweet-faced, girlish even, letting her emotions be seen, and they were overflowing like a river in full flood towards her friend who was patting her hand, doing her best to recall her to this transaction they were discussing. But for this fraction of time she could not contain it. Some wonderful thing had happened to her and her eyes were dewed, great golden pools from which he was sure tears would soon flow.

"Nancy, dearest . . ." Miss Williams was saying to her, her voice low, warning her that this was neither the time nor the place for emotion and at once she pulled herself up, turning back to him with her head held at an imperious angle, giving the impression that she was doing him a favour and not the other way around. How fascinating she was. How dazzling, how . . .

Abruptly he took hold of himself, lounging indolently, deliberately in his chair, hoping to God that none of the upheaval that was taking place inside him had been revealed to either young woman. Good God almighty, he must not fall into that trap again, he told himself with a shiver of self-disgust. Look where the last indulgence had led him and, more to the point, where it had led poor Evie. A lovely face, glowing eyes, a wide smile, just like Evie had once had, and he was allowing himself to be led into the same sweet meshes, deliberating on the attractions of a woman who had come here to do business with him. In a small way, she was saying now, for their business was only just begun but she hoped that before long they might be purchasing . . .

He barely heard her, regarding her with a cool, watchful look, his eyes a frosted grey, his face expressionless, seeing her mouth form the words, waiting for her to go with some impatience, and, when she had finished speaking and was turning to her friend in some bewilderment, standing up and offering her his hand in a way that seemed to speak of distaste.

"I'll have a word with my head warehouseman, Miss Brody, Miss Williams," bowing in Jennet's direction, "letting him know that you are to be allowed to buy whatever you want from my warehouse." Despite his previous words when they met he did not mean to do business with her himself. He did not mean to see her again if he could help it. There were enough complications in his life as it was and this sense of being drawn to her, as he had been strangely drawn to her on the other occasions they had met, was not something he wished to investigate. He could see she was surprised by his attitude of impassive neutrality, his lack of anything that might be called enthusiasm. Not that she cared, her own expression told him, for she was here on business only and now that their business was done then she'd be on her way.

Her gloved hand, how he did not know, for he had made no deliberate attempt to hold on to it, seemed to linger in his, their fingers linking in a curious way and their eyes met in surprise. Her lovely face flushed a little and she seemed to hold her breath then the moment was over and they pulled their hands apart, turning away from one another with a sharpness that held them both silent for a moment.

"Thank you, Mr Hayes," Miss Williams said to him and he was glad to look back to her, quite bewildering her with the warmth of his smile, not recognising it as relief.

"Thank *you*, Miss Williams. I wish your business every success."

"Thank you again, Mr Hayes. You have been most kind."

In an effort to cover his chagrin he almost conveyed Miss Williams to the door without her feet touching the rich depths of his carpet. Nancy was ahead of them, opening the door herself in her effort to get away from him, though she could not for the life of her have said why. A strange moment, a frisson of positive dislike from the man and yet he had given them what they wanted so what did it matter? He was merely a means to an end. He was not a man, not in the sense women mean when they speak of such things, but a tool, a tool that she would use to make what she was building. She had done with men. She had done with them on the night Mick O'Rourke had thrown her in the muck and raped her. She had no need of them, or their filthy ways. She and Jennet had reached their first goal. They were there, at the beginning of the road, at the foot of the ladder, whatever damned stupid cliché she wished to use for what lay ahead. It was all there, waiting for them, but at that moment she did not care to believe that had it not been for the man who was bowing over Jennet's hand, it would have been like mist, there to see but impossible to catch.

15

He heard the laughter first, female laughter, high and pealing, young and infectious, so filled with merriment he felt the corners of his own mouth lift in an involuntary smile. The laughter seemed to come from somewhere ahead of him, though he could see nothing but the tumbled stones of the ruined castle. Among the ruins grew scattered coppices of small hazel trees sheltering against the walls, the seeds from which they had grown dropped there by birds. The dense, deep green of the leaves quivered on the branches as though disturbed by the passage of something, though he supposed it could have been caused by the slight breeze which pleasantly cooled his skin. A small dog that ran beside him, darting hither and yon in the summer grasses as the fancy took him, following every scent that promised to be of interest, hesitated with one paw raised, looking towards him questioningly, waiting for his command. He was a somewhat scruffy dog, though his owner preferred to call him rough-haired, a mixture of colours and breeds but attractive, with a good-natured face and bright, intelligent eyes.

The horseman frowned and reined his mare to a halt, listening intently and the laughter rang out again.

"Who the devil can that be?" he asked his companion somewhat irritably but, getting no reply, nor expecting any, he put his heels to the mare's side and continued on towards the ruin that lay across the water meadow at the back of his home. He had hoped to have the place to himself. He had brought a blanket, a tin of Cook's almond biscuits and a bottle of milk which was kept cool in a nest of ice. He had brought a change of small clothing, for it was usually needed and had even smuggled out a bottle of dry white wine and a fluted glass, which he knew the nursemaid would not have approved of, hiding it with the milk in the ice. He had intended settling down in the grassy ruin, which was a favourite place of theirs, and having a pleasant hour or so without the confining hand of those at the house. Now it looked, or at least sounded, as though someone had got there before him. He didn't want company and it would hardly be possible to keep out of anyone's way, for the ruined castle was small.

"Damn and blast," he muttered and was just about to turn his mare towards home when a girl with no shoes on ran out from behind a portion of broken wall, her flight so precipitous his mare shied nervously and his dog began to bark. She almost ran into him, skidding along in the tall grass in an effort to stop, gasping, not just with her exertions but with shock. It was obvious she had thought herself to be alone and the sight of him brought her to a stunned and speechless standstill.

"God love us," he roared angrily, hanging on to his passenger, trying to calm the alarmed horse, signalling at the same time to the dog who was barking ferociously, though his tail wagged a greeting.

"I'm sorry," the girl gasped. "I didn't know there was anyone else here. We were playing . . . a game and . . . I do hope you are not hurt – you or the . . . the . . . Mind you, it was not really my fault, was it? That animal has always been flighty as I remember. She almost ran down the children in the mill yard." Her head rose. She had recovered her composure. "It seems its manners are in no way improved."

Living with Jennet Williams for so long had given Nancy Brody a greater command of the English language and taught her, without exactly recognising it, how to speak as the gentry did.

For a moment Josh Hayes was speechless himself. Christ, he wouldn't have recognised her, not at first, had she not mentioned the mill yard. Dressed in a plain gingham gown, the fabric come from his own warehouse, he noticed, the colour somewhere between rose and apple blossom with a broad cotton sash of deeper rose; her hair unconfined and flowing in glorious disarray to her waist, thick and curling, her cheeks crimson with her exertions, her golden eyes gleaming with enjoyment, she was a different being to the cool Miss Brody who, almost a year ago, had begged him to sell her his cotton. Her feet were stained green with the juices of the grass, long and slender, her sleeves had been pushed up above her elbows to reveal the creamy white satin of her arms and the neck of her bodice was unbuttoned almost down to the high, full curve of her magnificent breasts.

He knew he was what he could only call "gawping", like any yokel at a pretty girl and the knowledge made him even more irritable. At once his face set in stern lines of disapproval, though he didn't really disapprove at all, and she saw it and was immediately, and with the same degree of acrimony, as displeased as he was.

"Well, Miss Brody, I'll disturb you no longer. Get on with your . . . game." He was about to turn his horse, in what direction he did not know, for he had set his heart on the castle, when two more females hurtled round the corner of the wall, one of them carrying a laughing child. They were also barefoot and equally as dishevelled as Miss Brody, careering to a halt at the sight of him, their expressions comical, only the child seeming to be unconcerned. His dog barked again, since that was his position in life but this time his mare, as though she had become accustomed to these human foibles, stood her ground patiently.

"Mr Hayes," one of them stammered and again he was amazed to recognise Miss Williams. The other he did not know.

"Miss Williams." He bowed as best he could with his burden, ready to turn and bid them a polite good-day but the child in Miss Williams's arms pointed to the one in his and smiled broadly. From her mouth came a jumble of baby words, none of them recognisable, except by Freddy, who returned the words then craned his neck to grin broadly into her face.

"What a beautiful boy, Mr Hayes," Miss Williams said, recovering her composure and moving forward. "And so like you. How old is he?"

Mollified somewhat, he looked down at his son and his stern face softened out of all recognition.

"He is almost a year. A year in July."

"Why, so is Kitty. She was born in July, weren't you, darling? How odd, but they seem to have taken a liking to one another. Won't you join us for a while? We were having a picnic and then . . . well, we became silly and started this game and . . . But please, bring your son and introduce him to Kitty. Oh, and you have a dog as well. Kitty has never met a dog, have you, sweetheart? We would like her to have one, wouldn't we, Nancy, when we find the right house, but until then she must make do with a toy."

The whole time he and Miss Williams smiled at one another Miss Brody stood like a frozen pillar of ice in exactly the spot in which she had come to rest five minutes since. Her face was rigid with what seemed to be displeasure. She did not speak again and neither did the third girl who was obviously her sister.

"Oh, dear, where are my manners," Miss Williams exclaimed. "You have not met Nancy's sister, have you. This is Mary." She drew the girl forward, kindly and smiling, and Josh felt himself warm to Miss Williams who evidently had a good heart. "And this little handful is Kitty, Nancy's daughter."

If he was taken aback, which he was, he managed to keep it to himself.

"Miss Brody." Again he bowed, this time to Mary, thinking it wise to say nothing, to or about the infant. Then, as Freddy began to struggle in an effort to get to his new friend, he put his left arm firmly round his plump body, threw his left leg over the mare's rump and slithered to the ground.

"Oh, careful, Mr Hayes," Miss Williams said breathlessly. "See, Mary, you take Kitty and I'll hold Mr Hayes's boy while he does . . . well, whatever one does with a horse. Perhaps you could tie him to a tree, Mr Hayes."

"She, Miss Williams. Copper is a mare."

"Really, she is a lovely animal, isn't she, Mary? My, your son is heavier than Kitty, Mr Hayes," as the child wriggled companionably in her arms, looking up into her face with that intent, wide-eyed stare of the infant.

"Shall I . . . ?"

"No, I can manage him. See, we are just over here in the shade of the trees. We have spread a blanket for Kitty but I must admit it is the dickens of a job to keep her on it now she is crawling. She seems to find it so much more interesting to explore what is beyond it and whatever it is goes straight in her mouth."

Josh laughed, liking this young woman more and more, not only because she was so open and natural but because he knew there would never be the temptation to be more to her than a friend. She was not flirtatious or coy or coquettish as most young women are with a member of the opposite sex and so he could relax with her. And then there was the sympathy between them brought about by the children who seemed to be of an age, the shared interest and concern, his own pleasure at and love for his son and what was obviously a strong bond of affection between Miss Williams and this beautiful girl child who was not hers but the wooden-faced Nancy Brody's.

He turned to Miss Brody who had begun to follow them slowly across the grass, still having nothing to say on the matter, or indeed any matter, dragging her feet, her head down, the gleeful excitement that had been in her a few minutes ago completely gone.

"I'm sorry to have interrupted your picnic, Miss Brody." His voice was cold, for it was very evident she resented his intrusion into what was a family outing. "You have only to say the word and we will go. Freddy is—"

"Does your wife not accompany you when you take your son for a ride, Mr Hayes?"

Dear God. Dear sweet Jesus, what on earth had provoked her to say that? It was nothing to her whether he had a wife, a son, indeed a whole nursery full of children at home, though she thought him young for that, but from somewhere had sprung the stupid words, displaying an interest that she certainly didn't feel in his personal life, or indeed in any part of his life. She had not seen him since that day in his warehouse. She had been sincerely grateful for what he had done for them, knowing that without his aid and personal intervention they would have struggled to get where they were. He had helped to smooth their path, taken away the worst of their problems and yet, for some reason, she resented him and she resented feeling obliged to him. She was being rude, petty, childish even and she must stop it.

"I do apologise, Mr Hayes," she said stiffly. "That was impertinent. What you and your wife do is—"

"I have no wife, Miss Brody." His voice was abrupt, still inclined to be unbending and certainly, his expression said, disinclined to discuss private matters with her.

"I'm sorry, I really am. I had no idea . . ." For at once she had jumped to the conclusion that, young as he was, he was a widower.

"There is no need, Miss Brody. Now, shall we join the others? It seems my son has taken a great fancy to . . . to . . ." His polite voice was not sure how to go on.

Nancy's was harsh as she finished his sentence for him.

"To my daughter, and I have no husband." Her face was like granite, pale as marble, turning away from his censure, for surely that was what she would see in his eyes, then she whirled to face him again and he could see the turmoil in her, the stormy challenge that told him she was prepared to give him no explanations and certainly no excuses.

He had nothing to say. What could he say? he asked himself as he flung his rug on to the grass and, politely waiting until she was seated, squatted down next to his son.

They all four tasted a sip or two of his wine and even several of Cook's almond biscuits which they agreed were delicious, wondering as they bit into them what it must be like to have a woman in the kitchen whose sole purpose in life was to cook for you. The babies drank their milk and scrambled all over the patient little dog who was hardly more than a puppy himself. Josh explained that he had acquired the animal from a local farmer when his son was a few weeks old, for though he had not had one himself he believed that all children should grow up with a pet of their own. They digested this bit of information, pondering on the strange image of this young father bringing up his child on his own, making decisions in which no woman figured, and yet it was very evident that the child felt no lack of affection, for Mr Hayes, when the child allowed it, frequently held him in his lap and hugged him fondly.

Had it not been for the children and the dog, who entertained them, made them laugh, excused them the task of making polite conversation and eased the hour they spent together into a pleasant interlude, Nancy's quietness, coupled with Mary's shyness, would have made the situation impossible. Of course, had it not been for his son and her daughter, he would not have considered sitting down to a picnic in the first place and at the end of the hour when he stood up and indicated that he must go, it was with evident relief.

He got on his horse and Mary passed his protesting son up to him. There were fulsome remarks on all sides – except one – on how much they had enjoyed themselves. The dog frisked about among his new friends and the babies cried, for they did not want to part with one another.

"By the way, what day in July was Kitty born, Miss Williams?" he asked her out of politeness, wondering why he should address the question to her and not the child's mother. Perhaps because during the whole of the hour he had spent in their company she had made no attempt to take hold of her own child, though she seemed quite happy to retrieve Freddy when he crawled off the rug in the direction of an enticing clump of daisies, calling him a scamp and firmly kissing his round cheek. Even now Mary was cuddling the little girl to her, murmuring in her ear and kissing away the tears caused by the loss of her new friend.

"The twenty-third."

His face must have shown his astonishment.

"What is it, Mr Hayes?"

"Freddy was born on the twenty-third."

Even the expressionless face of Nancy Brody melted into open-mouthed wonder. They looked at one another, the mother and the father and for a second or two, no more, allowed one another to see what was hidden deep inside them both, and which had been there since that first day in the yard. Then hers closed up and his followed and their polite murmurs of surprise, their blank-faced unconcern for such a coincidence took them over once more.

Nodding in a gentlemanly fashion at Mary and Jennet, with one hand he took a firm hold of his son who sat before him, with the other grasped the reins and with a word of command to his two animals set off in a careful walk in the direction of Broughton Ford which would take him back to his own side of the river. His son was wailing dismally and so was Kitty.

"Well, thank God for that," Nancy said briskly.

"Why don't you like him, Nancy?" Mary asked curiously, for she had thought Mr Hayes to be a grand chap and so handsome and rich, too. What more could a girl ask for in a gentleman and yet their Nancy had made it very plain she was glad to see the back of him.

"Who said I didn't like him?" Nancy coldly defended herself. "All I feel for Mr Hayes is total indifference and," being honest at least about this, "a certain gratitude."

"But how strange that his wife should have given birth to Freddy on the same day as Kitty. His wife must have been very young. I didn't know he was even married, did you?" Jennet was busy gathering up the remains of their picnic, stuffing bags and tins and cups into a large basket and preparing to wrap the baby in a light shawl which she would fasten about herself.

"I can carry her, Jennet," Mary protested, for wasn't she a

big, strapping girl and Jennet no bigger than two pennorth of copper.

"It's only five minutes' walk to the cab rank on Lower Broughton Lane, sweetheart. I'll take her as far as there and then you can carry her at the other end."

Neither of them seemed to think it strange that Kitty's mother made no attempt to carry her own child.

The two-wheeled, leather-lined hansom cab had turned into Camp Street which led in to Bury New Road when Nancy let out a shriek that almost had the cabbie off his box at the back of the cab and caused the two girls to jump out of their skins and the baby to howl.

"What?" Jennet quavered, doing her best to soothe the baby.

"There . . . just there on the corner."

"What is it, for heaven's sake? I nearly had a seizure."

"It's to let."

"To let! What is?" Both Jennet and Mary peered round Nancy's shoulder as she leaned over the padded half-door of the hansom, craning her neck to look back.

"Stop here, please, Cabbie," she was shouting, much to the cabbie's annoyance, for Bury New Road was busy at this time of day with a fair number of horse-drawn vehicles nudging him from behind.

"What's up?" he protested, wondering on the ways of women. First she wanted St George's Road and now she was telling him to pull up in the thick of the traffic to the danger of not only himself, his cab and his horse, but the other vehicles.

They all leaped out, baby an' all, standing gawping at the end house of a modest row of terraced villas as though it were the gates of heaven but he couldn't hang about here, for he was blocking the road, which he told them stoutly.

"Never mind. What do we owe you?" the tall, haughty but quite gorgeous-looking creature asked him, putting the coins in his hand when he told her without even looking at them.

"I can't wait," he threatened her.

"It doesn't matter. We'll find another cab."

"Not at this time o' day, yer won't," he warned her, but she either didn't hear him or she didn't care.

It was on the corner of Bury New Road and Broughton Lane and pronounced itself to be Grove Place. There were about a dozen houses all with a minute front garden surrounded by a low wall and what appeared to be a yard at the back. Each house had a bay window on the ground floor, with a bay window above, and next to that a flat sash window over the front door. The front door itself was protected by a neat porch which was reached by three steps. It was empty.

Silently they walked a little way down Broughton Lane towards the back of the house and were at once standing among green fields, other pleasant houses and further on a walled nursery garden where they could make out trees and climbing plants. Bubbling merrily under a narrow hump-backed bridge that spanned Broughton Lane, evidently a tributary of the River Irwell, was a narrow, singing brook. They stood in awed contemplation of the wonder of it, exchanging glances and sighing, since it was all so perfect.

None of them spoke. Even the baby seemed impressed, quietly looking about her until after some minutes both Mary and Jennet turned to Nancy who appeared to be in a dazed trance. They waited.

At last she spoke. "This is it," she said in a low, dreaming voice. "If we can afford it, this is it."

"What d'you think the rent on a place like this would be?" Mary asked longingly, hopefully, tentatively.

"God knows, but there's only one way to find out."

"How?"

"By getting in touch with the person who put that sign up in the window."

Mary walked back along the length of the side wall of the house and the others followed her until they were at the front again. They stood at the gate, not daring to go beyond it, though it was obvious there was no one living in it. It had a slate roof and was clean and tidy-looking, the paintwork having recently been given a fresh coat of green paint. The garden was laid out with a small lawn which badly needed trimming and round its edges was a profusion of colourful flowers. On the opposite side of the road were more fields and a sign that said "St Ann's Square, 1 mile".

They were just about to turn reluctantly away when the front door to the neighbouring house opened and a brisk little woman in an immaculate apron stood there, a duster in one hand and a jar of what smelled like beeswax polish in the other. Nancy loved her at once.

"You interested in renting the house, chuck?" she asked, coming down her gleaming steps to the gate where, as though it were a habit she could not break, she gave it a brisk rub over with her duster, then, smiling, she tickled the baby under her chin. Without hesitation and as if she knew exactly what was expected of her, Kitty put out her arms and the woman, gratified beyond measure, laid her duster and the polish on the dividing wall and took her from Jennet. Kitty beamed right into the woman's face and with some aversion Nancy could see Mick O'Rourke in her roguish smile.

"Well, aren't you a little beauty?" the woman said. "And what's your name, then?" as though the baby might answer.

"We call her Kitty," Jennet told her proudly. "And she is beautiful, isn't she?"

"She yours?" the woman asked her, turning round to study all three of them and at once Nancy felt the apprehension rise in her. She wanted this house. Her instinct told her that this was to be the next step along that rocky path to success, to the respectability she craved, but these were decent people living in this terrace who took pride in themselves, in their status and in their homes. Respectable folk, that was evident, still working class, like them, but very far above the human debris beside whom they lived in Church Court. This woman's husband probably held down some artisan's job, or was perhaps a supervisor in a mill or in charge of a small warehouse. A clerk perhaps, or a man who had been apprenticed to a trade and now worked for himself. A man who had taken advantage of the educational opportunities that were now available to any man who had the guts and tenacity to take hold of them. And she wanted them to . . . to respect her, to accept her, to be a neighbour with whom she and the girls and Jennet might mix on an equal footing.

But she couldn't take this next step with a lie. She hadn't lied to anyone during the last seven, going on for eight years. She'd stood her ground, laboured until she dropped and drove those about her to do the same. She was proud of herself, and of them and she wasn't going to tell this woman a cock-and-bull story about a husband lost at sea or in an accident in the mill yard. They must take her as she was and if it upset them and the others then she was sorry. She had an illegitimate child through no fault of her own and she wasn't about to apologise to anybody for that. She would not offer information. She would not fabricate some story, but if she was asked she would tell the truth.

"She's mine," she said shortly, stepping forward and taking Kitty out of the woman's arms. For some strange reason she found hers wrapping themselves protectively about her child. Kitty, as though sensing something in her, some link that bound mother to daughter, leaned against her and rested her head in the curve of her shoulder.

"Aah, I can see that now, lass. She's the spit of you." The woman turned smilingly to Mary. "And this'll be your sister. There's a real family likeness." She nodded pleasantly at Jennet as though to say she didn't know where she fitted into this family group but she was willing to give her the time of day. No more than that. No questions about their position in life, the existence, or not, as the case may be, of menfolk. She picked up her duster and polish and with a last nod turned and left them and with great vigour attacked her front door.

But, having jumped the first hurdle, so to speak, and survived it, Nancy chanced another.

"Er . . . pardon me, but . . ."

"Yes?" The woman turned, not exactly irritably but telling them plainly she was busy and could not spare the time for idle gossip. Nancy felt her admiration for her deepen.

"I was wondering if you happen to know what the rent is on a house like this?"

"Well, if it's the same as ours it's seven and six a week. That includes the rates, water and such. There's a privy in the yard and tap in the scullery."

She turned back to her task, her elbow going ten to the dozen, her head nodding up and down with her exertions, her back telling them quite clearly that she had finished fraternising.

A privy of their own! A tap in the scullery! And what other luxuries did the spring-fresh façade of the house, the smiling house – Nancy could see it smiling quite plainly – hide from their hungry eyes?

"Thank you, you have been most kind. I do hope we will see you again," she told the woman's back and was rewarded by a brief, hurried smile.

They had walked almost to St Ann's Square, all three of them in a daze of delight, their feet barely touching the flags, which seemed in any case to be as soft as the drifting fleecy clouds in the sky, before they came down to earth. Kitty had fallen asleep in Nancy's arms, her dark head nodding against her shoulder and again, for some strange reason, Nancy was reluctant to hand her back to Jennet or Mary as they were expecting her to.

"There's a cab on the corner," she said briefly, for like Kitty they were all tired. As she spoke her voice was quiet, for she felt a great unwillingness to break the magic spell that the house had put on them, holding her breath almost as though afraid to draw the three of them to the attention of God or the Fates or whatever powers ruled their destinies. Tomorrow she would know. Tomorrow would decide how the next chapter of their future would read. If she had been a praying person she would have asked whoever was up there to let it happen in Grove Place. But then Jennet would be speaking to that God of hers so perhaps it would be all right. Who could resist the goodness of Jennet?

The house was quiet, as quiet as they were, all busy with their own thoughts, for this was one of the most important moments of their lives. Jennet had lived in the genteel poverty of the vicarage until her father died so had not been subjected to the squalor and filth into which the Brody girls had been born, though she had seen it all around her recently. But tomorrow, if the house in Grove Place had not already been let and if the rent was within their means, they were to leave this place of abomination and move to what, in comparison, seemed like paradise.

"Put the kettle on, Mary, there's a good lass," Nancy said, her voice low and hushed as she placed the sleeping child in a little nest of cushions on the settle. "The fire's just about in and a cup of tea would be most welcome." She turned away from her distracted contemplation of her child and looked about her. "I wonder where our Rosie's got to? She should be back by now. I hope she and that Nell haven't got up to any mischief."

Nell was one of their machinists at Shude Hill, a lively girl of sixteen to whom Rosie had taken a liking, it seemed, and the two of them went about together, though Nancy was not sure she approved. Nell was a nice enough girl and sensible but Nancy was not happy about it. Still, Rosie was fourteen herself now and could not be tied to Nancy's apron strings for ever.

A sound from upstairs lifted their heads and brought the three of them from their brooding thoughts. They looked at each other in surprise.

"Rosie? Is that you, Rosie?" Nancy called out, standing up and going to the foot of the stairs, smiling as her sister began to descend them. Rosie's feet were bare as though she had just come from her bed and she wore nothing but her shift.

"Rosie, what are you—?" Nancy began then her voice shrivelled in her throat and her hand went to her mouth. Every vestige of colour left her face, for coming down behind her, grinning triumphantly, was Mick O'Rourke.

16

Rosie was flushed and defiant, Mick wickedly elated, his handsome face split in a wide grin. Jennet and Mary were open-mouthed, wide-eyed, stunned and speechless, then they both turned as one to see what Nancy was going to do. She didn't at first know herself, for the shock was so great it took her senses, her thoughts, her ability to function, froze her quick mind and rooted her to the spot at the foot of the stairs, blocking them so that Rosie and Mick could not come down further. Mick lounged indolently against the whitewashed wall, his shirt open to the waist to reveal his broad, hairy chest, his hands on Rosie's shoulders as she stood on a step beneath him, proprietorial, challenging, sneering as though provoking Nancy Brody. If she thought she could do anything about it she was mistaken, for it was all too late.

The silence went on and on, for the shock had taken the voices, the power to move, the ability even to think coherently, of the three young women who had just come in and it needed something electifying to fetch them out of it.

Rosie provided it. She stepped forward boldly.

"Well, I suppose you had to know about it some time, our Nancy. Me and Mick's been going steady for a while now. Nell was only a cover-up. And let me tell you I think it's disgraceful the lies you told about being raped. Mick said you were always willing—"

Mick interrupted hastily. "Hush now, mavourneen, are we ter stand 'ere for ever chewin' the fat or will we sit down an' 'ave a cup o' tea? To be sure, let's be civilised about it, fer are we not ter be related as soon as may be. Now, if I'm not mistaken, that kettle's about ter boil, Rosie, me love, so will yer be making us a brew. I'm thirsty after . . ." He winked and leered at them over the top of Rosie's head, leaving them in no doubt as to what had made him thirsty, putting his brawny arms about her, one hand coming to rest familiarly on her breast.

Nancy stepped back from the horror of it, the horror of him, inclined to shudder and twitch as the shock raced through her, wanting to turn away and run screaming out of the house, wanting to get away from it, for it was obscene in its shame. Her sister, her little sister for whom she had had such high hopes, for whom she had worked so hard, to be caught like some helpless fly in the web of Mick O'Rourke's clever charm. Oh, yes, there was no doubt about it, he had charmed and tricked Rosie and he had done it for only one purpose: to get back at *her*. He was a devil, beastly, evil, loathsome and if she had a knife handy she would have killed him then and there.

But strength was returning to her. She was beginning to recover and with recovery came a rage, a loathing so great it gave her strength so that she felt she could do ten rounds in the prize-fighting ring with this brute of a man and emerge victorious.

With an oath she sprang forward and tore her loudly protesting sister from his arms, throwing her with such violence across the room she fell to the floor by the front door where she crouched, dazed. He was next, though it made her stomach heave to touch him.

"Open the door, Mary," she screamed, "and let me get this filth out of my house," and Mary leaped to do her bidding, pushing aside her sister who still lay in a heap on the floor.

"Now then . . . now then, yer daft bitch, what d'yer think . . ." he began to splutter but, despite himself, Mick O'Rourke, six foot two and fourteen stone of hard muscle and bone, probably carried more than anything by the momentum of his own weight down the last few stairs, was propelled across the room and through the door into the street where he staggered like a drunk come from the beer house which, from the look on his face, enraged him even further. Mick O'Rourke was proud of himself, of his strength and obvious manhood, of his reputation as a fighter and a lover of women and to be bested by a woman, to be thrown out of a house by a *woman*, was more than he could bear. He was incensed to madness to have his masculinity mocked by this shrieking virago, and in front of his friends and neighbours, but she would not let him speak.

"You filthy sod . . . you bastard. You're the scum of the earth, that's what you are and if I catch you hanging about my sister again I'll kill you. I'll stick the bread knife in you and gladly hang for it."

"'Ere, don't you be talking ter me like that, Nancy Brody, fer yer as bad as yer sister." He shook his fist, wanting to use it on her, that was very evident, wanting to hurt her, to knock her down as she had almost knocked him down. "A hot little bitch, that's what yer are, liftin' yer skirts fer any man what wants it. 'Aven't I had a taste meself and that kid in there ter prove it. Oh, aye, 'tis mine all right," feeling better now that he thought he had scored a point or two, turning to grin at the rapturous onlookers who had gathered to witness what promised to be a right old ding-dong, and involving, of all people, Lady Mucky Muck herself, the stuck-up Nancy Brody. Oh, they all knew about her bastard, for hadn't she flaunted it for the past year and some had privately thought that it might have been Mick Brody's get, but, since he'd said nothing and took no interest in her or the child, the gossip had died away. Now here he was shouting to the world that he'd stuck it in not one sister, but two. A right devil with the women, was Mick O'Rourke and you had to hand it to him, he had style.

"If you come within a mile of any member of my family again I'll have the law on you, you filthy bugger," Nancy hissed. She stood like any common street woman on her own doorstep, arms akimbo, face contorted with fury, her hair wild about her face and was ashamed, but was powerless to stop herself. "You're saying that child in there is yours but are you man enough to tell these . . . these friends of yours how you got it on me?" she snarled, a vixen showing her teeth, defending what was hers, gasping for breath, her self-control, on which she prided herself, totally gone. "Do you think they'd like to hear how you dragged me into the churchyard and—"

Mick's face was contorted with his rage and his voice shook. "Yer lyin' bitch, yer were as eager fer it as that one," pointing a shaking finger at Rosie, who was fighting with Mary and Jennet to get out to him and in the background the baby wailed in terror.

The audience was enchanted. Men and women and children edged closer, forming a semicircle almost at Mick's back, for he was one of them and this hoity-toity bitch, though she had been born in this very alley, was not. They were elated to see her getting what they thought of as her comeuppance. But they did not really know Nancy Brody, any of them. *Really* know her, that is. They thought she was bested, but she wasn't. Not by a long chalk!

"Do you honestly believe I'd be satisfied with a piece of trash like you, Mick O'Rourke? You're the dregs of the earth, scum, riff-raff" – there were not enough words to describe what she felt about him – "and it makes me shudder and want to be sick when I think of what you did to me." She looked over his head at the open-mouthed faces of her neighbours. "He wanted to marry me, did you know that?" she asked them. "Oh, yes, and when I refused, for I mean to do better than an illiterate, feckless, workshy Irish bucko, he took me anyway. Now he's sniffing round my sister—"

"More 'n sniffin', Nancy Brody. You ask 'er. You ask 'er what me an' 'er's bin up to this last few months. Go on, tell 'er, Rosie," even though Rosie had already confessed. "All this time when yer were serpossed ter be wi' that mate o' yours, tell 'er 'oo yer were really with, so. An' tell 'er 'tis yerself I want ter be marryin', not 'er. She's jealous, that's what's up wi' 'er."

With a screech Nancy launched herself across the cracked cobbles at him and, since he had not expected it she had scratched both his cheeks almost to the bone with her clawed fingers before he could defend himself. The blood sprang forth and he screamed a curse before lifting a fist, a fist that could fell a man as heavy as himself and smashed it against her cheekbone. She fell like a stone.

They stood like pillars of frozen ice, every man and woman in the street. They had been enjoying the spectacle and had been rooting for Mick, since there was not one of them who had not felt Nancy Brody's contemptuous eye upon them at some time since her mam vanished, but this was just a bit too much for even them to stomach. They stared at her crumpled figure, so pretty in her rosy pink frock, her hair falling like a living curtain across her face, her arms flung every which way, her legs the same. They began to shake their heads and as though at a signal her sister, Mary that is, not Rosie, and that friend of hers, flew out to her, crying her name, for surely he had killed her. The blow she had received had been enough to fell an ox. They watched in silence as the pair of them struggled to lift her, one at her head the other at her feet. The hem of her frock fell back to reveal her legs almost up to her thighs and one woman moved forward and compassionately pulled it down, then helped them to carry her across her own doorstep, placing her on the bit of carpet of which they were so proud. The baby hiccuped broken-heartedly on the settle but was, for the first time in her young life, ignored. The woman emerged and walked down to her own front door, shutting it quietly behind her. They all began to drift away then, turning back to look at Mick, and there was not one there, rough, uneducated, brutalised as they were, who did not believe that what Nancy Brody had said, much as they disliked her, was the truth.

The Brodys' front door opened once more and from it stepped their Rosie, carrying a bundle. She stood hesitantly in front of Mick who had his hands to his bleeding face. She waited submissively, as she was to wait for the remainder of their lives together, for him to tell her what to do.

"Don't just stand there, yer daft cow," he snarled. "Give us a 'and up ter me mam's."

Somehow they got her to Angel Street where they found a hansom cab who was willing to stop. The trouble was the cabbies who drove by looking for custom thought they were drunk as they heaved her along on her tottering feet, somehow carrying Kitty between them since they had no one to leave her with and had no time to fetch Annie. Kitty was whimpering in shock, reduced to an almost senseless state by the events of the past half-hour. Nancy's face had come up like a balloon. It was cut to the bone which showed white and shattered through her grey flesh and the scarlet blood which seeped from it; and though neither of them knew *how* they knew, Jennet and Mary were aware that if they didn't get help for her soon she might never come out of the state of semi-consciousness into which Mick's powerful blow had knocked her. She mumbled in pain as they bundled her into a cab, the driver of which, seeing the child and the women's decent clothing, the dreadful injury to one woman's face, decided to stop.

"The hospital, please, and quickly."

"Which one, lady?"

Which one? Dear God, which of Manchester's hospitals? Several of them were no more than infirmaries for the poor and needy, glorified workhouses which, though they served a useful purpose, would have no doctor to treat the terrible injury Mick O'Rourke had inflicted on Nancy Brody. Mary was of no use, only in as much as she provided strong arms and a strong back, for the whole appalling incident had frightened the wits out of her and though she obeyed Jennet's instructions to the letter she could not be said to be thinking with any degree of comprehension.

Then, her brow clearing, Jennet remembered an article she had read in the *Manchester Guardian*. Two gentlemen, Doctor Merei and Doctor Whitehead, had taken a lease on premises at number 8 Stevenson Square, which was not far away, where they had established a hospital specifically for women and children. The article had spoken of medical and surgical treatment of children and certain forms of disease peculiar to women: surely this fitted into one of these categories?

"Stevenson Square, please, Cabbie. Number eight."

Nancy lay in a spotlessly clean bed for almost a fortnight, in what was known as the Clinical Hospital and Dispensary for Children, which stood between Ancoats and Angel Meadow. Her face was wrapped about from brow to chin with bandages, from which her slitted eyes glared at Doctor Whitehead and his nurses as though they were personally responsible for this catastrophe that had struck her down.

"I can't stay here," she told them, or at least that was what they thought she told them, for her mouth was partially covered by the bandages and the words came out in a sort of muffled gasp.

"Sip your broth, Miss Brody, and stop trying to talk," the nurse told her briskly. "Doctor Whitehead won't like it if you don't take nourishment."

"I don't care what Doctor Whitehead would like. Let him drink the bloody broth. I must get out of here. I have a business to run."

"So you keep saying, Miss Brody," the nurse answered absently, not in the least concerned with Miss Brody's business.

"If you'd just loosen these damned covers and let me up."

"Miss Brody, will you please keep your mouth shut. I don't mean to be rude but if you don't relax your face and give it a rest it will never heal. Your cheekbone was fractured quite badly and you were lucky to find Doctor Whitehead here when you were brought in. He's wonderful with bones."

"And I'm grateful, but nurse, I have so much to do. The constable who came on the night I was admitted said I was to give a statement when I was well enough."

"And so you shall, when you are well enough and Doctor Whitehead will decide when that is."

"But the bastard who did this to me—"

"Miss Brody, there are children in this ward and I will not have language."

"I'm sorry."

"And so you should be. Now go to sleep."

They came for her in a cab, Jennet and Mary. They had left Kitty at home with Annie, they said, their faces glowing with some inner excitement, begging her to be careful on the stairs and telling her how well she looked even with the dressing which had been reduced to a thick, well-padded patch on her cheek. Though one or the other of them had visited her each day she had been wrapped about in her bandages and they had not quite realised the extent of her injuries. They were considerably distressed by the bruising that still showed, and her eyes which reminded them, they told one another later, of a picture of a panda bear they had seen in a zoological magazine in the reading-room of the library. Set in deep purple sockets, they were, and even her nose seemed out of true, forced to one side by the damage to her cheek. Would she ever be the beautiful girl she had once been? they agonised, but not in her hearing.

She had not seen her own face since Mick had broken it, and didn't want to, for it didn't matter what she looked like, did it, unless it frightened her customers. She cared not a jot for what a man might think of her or her appearance, for there was not one in this whole world who concerned Nancy Brody, except Mick O'Rourke, and the moment she was well enough she meant to see him incarcerated in New Bayley gaol. Doctor Whitehead was to give evidence for her. She had given a statement to the constable from the police station on St George's Road, as had Jennet, and Mick O'Rourke was to be taken into custody. Had he gone easily? she had begged Jennet and Mary to tell her but they seemed curiously vague, saying they had not seen him go and she was not to worry about it now. She was to rest and get herself better, for that was all that mattered and she could get nothing else out of them.

The cab moved smartly along Thomas Street but, when it came to Shude Hill, where she meant to insist they stop so that she could slip into the workroom and check on her business, instead of turning right it turned left.

She twisted in her seat, peering out of the small window at the rear.

"Where are we going?" she demanded.

"Home," they told her and it was then that the truth and wonder and incredible rightness of it, of where they were to go, washed over her and from her poor, swollen eyes tears of relief and happiness welled. She would never have to see Church Court again!

"You got it?" she breathed reverently.

"We did."

Always the business woman. "At what rent?"

"Seven and sixpence a week but if it had been *seventeen* and sixpence I would have taken it to get us away from . . . well, you know."

"You would not." But she held Jennet's hand tightly, for she knew what this was to mean not only to her and her family but to Jennet who had known better things.

"And . . ."

"It is all ready for you, dearest. There's not much furniture but we though you might like to . . ."

"Dear sweet God . . . oh, dear Lord, what a day that was when I found you, Jennet Williams. And what a blessing you have been to me, my sweet Mary. Was ever a woman so fortunate. And Annie?"

"She moved in when we did. She . . . well, you will see when we get there."

The cab drew up to the front gate of the house in Grove Place. As though to welcome her, to remind her that this was her special day, for she had made this happen, the sun shone in a haze of golden light, reflecting in the windows which Annie had evidently polished, on the newly painted front door, which opened as she stepped from the cab. The lawn had been cut and though it was still a bit rough it was green and fresh. Whoever had cut the lawn had weeded the flowerbeds which bloomed in a rainbow of colours. There was a lovely fragrance in the air, fresh and clean, or was it just the absence of the bad smells that had been in her nostrils for sixteen years? There were curtains at every window, just bits of remnants run up by the girls at the workroom in Shude Hill, Jennet told her, holding her arm solicitously as she opened the gate.

A shriek of joy came from within the house and from the narrow hallway tumbled a laughing child, her child, who called her "Mama", as she floundered on unsteady legs to meet her.

"She's walking!"

"Of course," Jennet said proudly, as though it were all her doing. But the biggest surprise of all was the fat, laughing puppy who followed Kitty in a jumble of precarious legs and wickedly gleaming eyes down the steps.

"Who on earth . . ."

"Would you believe, Mr Hayes was passing on his mare, since as you know he lives in Broughton, and when he saw us in the garden he stopped and . . . well, he wishes you a speedy recovery and yesterday we found this little scrap on the doorstep. She's to be called Scrap so . . ."

"Dear God, what next?" But she was not displeased as her child clutched at her skirts and the puppy at once began to gnaw at her boots until Annie, clean, neat and proud in her enormous white apron, the symbol of her new position in life, came out to rescue her.

"Lass," was all she said, then put her arms about Nancy and held her gently for a moment; then she sniffed and wiped her nose on the back of her hand as she drew her up the steps.

"Mind that dratted aminal," she told her sternly. "Blasted thing's just done her business on my clean kitchen floor."

"Oh, Annie . . ."

"I know, chuck, I know. 'Appiness is sometimes as much ter cope with as sadness but yer'll be right now. Let's get that face o' yourn better an' then we'll see. That bugger. I'd like ter cut 'is balls off, 'onest. They give more trouble than they're damn well worth. If men didn't 'ave 'em women'd be a sight better off all round."

"Oh, Annie." Nancy was laughing weakly, ready to cry as the comforting arm led her down the long narrow hallway, from the end of which a shaft of sunlight gleamed. There was a narrow, uncarpeted staircase with a polished banister to the right. There was a door off to the left but Annie led her past it, saying they would look at that later, moving towards the sunshine that filled a kitchen of such wonderful proportions and so splendidly equipped Nancy just stood looking round her with her mouth agape.

It sparkled in the golden light, its walls festooned with all her precious things from Church Court: with pictures and pans on hooks, with skillets and kitchen utensils and unfamiliar things that must have come from Annie's own kitchen. There was a magnificent blackleaded kitchen range with a side oven on which a pan of something smelling delicious bubbled, teasing the palate, and Nancy was aware that she was hungry for the first time since Mick O'Rourke had walloped her. There was a new wood coal box with brass handles and a hand scoop. The two old armchairs that had been her mother's sagged on either side of the fire in the range, a patchwork of neat mending keeping the upholstery together. Above the mantelpiece, which Annie had edged with a pelmet of red plush, was her little Dutch clock, its pendulum swinging busily as though it were made up with its new position in life, as Annie was. The dresser, twinkling with her old crockery and looking grand with her highly glazed teatray placed proudly in its centre, stood against the wall next to the door leading out into a long, narrow scullery which had its own sink and a tap from which water dripped. *Their very own water!* There was a window at the end looking out on a small yard, at the bottom of which was a door enclosing their own private, *exclusive* privy. There were flowers in glass jars on the table and windowsill and it was all so perfect and just as she imagined it, better even, she wanted to break out afresh in tears.

"Oh, Annie . . ." she said for the third time.

"I know," Annie said proudly, folding her arms across her bosom, while at her back Jennet and Mary smiled in satisfaction at one another and said nothing, the baby fell and picked herself up, talking ten to the dozen, not a word recognisable, and the puppy wandered and sniffed and finally made a neat pool on Annie's scrubbed floor.

"Little devil," she shrieked, scooping her up and putting her out into the back yard where she began to howl. "That's where yer go or you an' me'll not be friends. Fancy bringin' a puppy! That's men for yer, though 'e did ask after yer and said 'e'd call as soon as . . ."

Nancy's face, which had been smiling beneath its layer of padding, at once became fixed in granite. Her eyes, what you could see of them, darkened from gold to amber and she drew herself up imperiously.

"I hope you told him he was not welcome, Annie. We want no men."

"I did not. 'E were perfeckly polite so why should I say such a thing?"

"Because he's *not* welcome, Annie. We have enough to do without entertaining gentlemen. Call indeed! You'd think we'd nothing better to do than sit about like his mother does and serve tea to anyone who knocks on our door. I won't have it, Annie, and you shall tell him so when he calls. Dear God, I've a good mind to send that damned dog back, for she'll be nothing but a nuisance, making a mess and . . . Just listen to the thing."

Mary moved across the kitchen and scullery to the back door, opened it and picked up the shivering puppy, holding her in protective arms, looking at Nancy with pleading eyes. The little animal greeted her ecstatically, her rough tongue all over Mary's face and neck until, despite her distress, Mary began to laugh. Kitty half crawled, half tumbled to join her and in a minute the three of them were a mad scramble of arms and legs and shrieks of laughter on the bit of carpet which Annie had refused to leave behind at Church Court.

"Eeh, will yer look at them three. It's a while since I saw our Mary laugh like that." For already this family belonged to Annie.

Nancy did as she was told, watching her sister play with the puppy and it was then she realised that not once had Mary ever *played*. Played like a child, laughed and giggled as she was doing now, with that lovely abandon that children forget when they become adults. She had steadily walked behind Nancy, supporting her in everything Nancy had wanted to do. Mary's serious nature had given her an insight into what Nancy was after and Mary had never let her down, for it was what she wanted too. How could she deny her this one small joy? For though the puppy was meant for Kitty it was Mary who would have the caring of her.

Mary, her sweet, loyal sister. Bowing her head Nancy asked the question she did not want to ask but must and waited for the answer she did not want to hear, but must.

"Rosie?" she asked quietly.

"She's . . . with him."

"And him?"

"No one knows, dearest," Jennet told her sadly. "When the constable went to pick him up for questioning he had gone."

17

She did her best to ignore all their pleadings to stay at home and rest, saying she had to catch up on a lost fortnight and had to make good the deficit as soon as possible. It was not that Jennet and Mary had not done wonders, they had, she told them approvingly, bringing smiles to their faces. Jennet had even overcome her natural reserve, taking Nancy's place behind the market stall while Mary supervised the girls at the workroom, which was a credit to them both, but she must see it all for herself, she said emphatically.

"But Nancy, you have just suffered a serious injury which has kept you in hospital for two weeks and even now you are not healed. Doctor Whitehead has not said so but I know he is very concerned that if you try to do more than you are able, in view of what happened, you may have a relapse. And there is still a risk of infection, so will you not have a few days at home?" Jennet pleaded with her, her little pointed face drawn and tired, her eyes drained of all their usual colour in her anxiety, Nancy noticed.

"Jennet, you have kept the business going, you and Mary between you, while I have been away, for which I thank you but there is so much that needs bringing up to date. Things that I have always done and with which you are not familiar. There are the account books to be done up, bills to be paid, invoices, profit margins to be worked out before ordering more cotton, existing stock to be gone over, a hundred and one things that must be seen to and I can't do them lolling about in the fireside chair, can I?"

She was seated in one of them now, her head resting on the chair back and in the one opposite Annie nursed the child who, like children do, had simply fallen asleep where she was playing, not waking when Annie lifted her into her lap. Mary and Jennet sat side by side on the old settle and in Mary's lap the puppy slept and twitched and yipped. Mary's hand rhythmically stroked her soft coat. She stared into the good fire that Annie had stoked up the chimney back, for though it was summer the evening had turned chilly, her face peaceful and dreaming, content in this new environment but with no real conception of what it had taken her sister to get them here. She worked hard and long and willingly but she was no leader, no innovator, happy to do as she was told without concerning herself with what she really didn't understand. She knew her machine and could expertly sew a shirt or a baby's little dress, or any plain seam, but that was the extent of her talent. She was a good girl, a girl without the complex mind of her sister, a girl better educated than any of her own age but totally unable to look after herself since, quite simply, she had never needed to. She depended utterly on Nancy and Jennet. She loved them and Kitty and Annie but until Nancy found her a good husband, which she meant to do one day, she knew Mary would be her child, her responsibility just as Kitty was. It drove her on, even beyond her own strength. She could not let down her guard for a second but must push those dependent on her, and herself, to the very limits. And even then would she be satisfied, would she feel secure, would she relax? she asked herself as she looked into the three concerned faces of the women who were her family.

"Will you compromise?" Jennet begged, leaning forward into the firelight which painted a false and rosy hue on her tired face.

"What does that mean?"

"I suppose you are intending to set off tomorrow wherever it is you decide. Would you not wait until the end of the week?"

Nancy frowned. "But it's only Tuesday. I can't possibly."

"What if Annie were to go and see Mrs Underwood and ask her to call here?"

"Jennet, that is ridiculous." Nancy's eyes narrowed above the pad of her bandage, gleaming through the purple slits of her lids in a way they all recognised, for Nancy Brody had had no one to oppose her for nearly eight years and wasn't about to start now, her expression said.

"Why is it ridiculous? She has been asking me when she could speak to you for the past week. Apparently there are women queueing up in her shop for our goods."

"Really!" Nancy was delighted, smiling and wincing at the same time.

"So it seems, but I am not used to that side of the business and apart from telling her you were . . . not well, I didn't know what to say. She was not especially interested in what was on the stall since she wanted a better quality, something fancier with drawn threadwork, smocking and embroidery, perhaps in fine lawn or even silk and was prepared to pay for it. If Annie was to take a message to her shop . . . You know where it is on Market Street, don't you, Annie?"

"Oh, aye, I've passed it times an'—"

"Now just a minute, I haven't agreed yet."

"This house is perfectly decent for anyone to call so why—"

"I *know* that."

"Then why are you—?"

"Will you stop bullying me, Jennet Williams. I am perfectly capable."

"No, you are not. You are not yourself but you will insist on having your own way all the time. Beside the fractured cheekbone you were concussed, Doctor Whitehead told me. It would do you the world of good to sit in the garden and get some sun on you."

"I do not wish to sit in the sunshine in the garden while every man and his dog peers inquisitively over the wall at me. Anyway, I'm already recovered," she told them testily, "and that is the end of the matter."

Yes, she agreed explanations of some kind would need to be given to the next-door neighbour – Mrs Denby, was that her name? – about her injuries and indeed to every other curious person with whom she came in contact over the next few days but that was not her concern, for they must make of it what they would. An accident, was all that needed to be said and they could like it or not as they pleased.

But she was weakening, for even sitting in this comfortable chair with her head resting on its back was exhausting her. Her head ached, which Doctor Whitehead had warned her would happen for a few weeks, and her fractured cheekbone was on fire as it knit together so, having had her say to show them that she would not be bullied but would make up her own mind, perhaps she would do what the others begged, which was simply nothing for a day or two. She must get down to Shude Hill as another machinist must be found to replace Rosie, she went on, bending her head and biting her lip in anguish at the thought of what might have happened to her sister, while Jennet leaned across and took her hand and Mary and Annie looked on compassionately.

It was perhaps this hurt, more than the physical one, that cut into her most deeply. Rosie had always been headstrong, more like herself really, she supposed, but the underhand and disloyal manner in which she had associated with Mick O'Rourke, knowing the way he had pursued Nancy, was pulling her to ribbons. Though Nancy had never told either of her sisters that it had been Mick who had raped her, she was pretty certain that they had both guessed who it was and yet Rosie had met him secretly, lying to them all, allowing herself to be seduced by his wit and charm and swaggering arrogance. Where had she gone, the sister for whom she had such hopes and plans, as she had for Mary? Probably living in some hovel dancing to Mick O'Rourke's tune, for though Rosie was strong-willed she was no match for Mick O'Rourke. A child every year like the rest of the women in Angel Meadow, that's if she was still there, for that would be the fate of a woman marrying him. If he married her! A black eye every Saturday night when he came home with drink in him, ground down like their mam had been ground down and just when the Brody girls were beginning to amount to something. It didn't bear thinking about but she could not stop thinking and worrying about it.

As though divining her thoughts the three women leaned towards her, Jennet patting her hand soothingly.

Annie spoke sadly to her bent head. "There, there, lass, she's medd 'er bed an' she must lie in it. It don't do ter brood over it since there's nowt yer can do."

"I know that, Annie, but after all we've gone through; to get this far . . ."

"P'raps if . . . p'raps if 'e were put in prison she'd come back."

"Dear God in heaven, Annie! She'll probably be pregnant by now with his child. What relation will it be to Kitty? No! no! it doesn't bear thinking about. Like you say, she has made her bed."

She choked on the tears she would not shed, then, standing up, she leaned forward to kiss Annie's cheek in a rare show of affection. She was tired. She was longing to climb into the bed in the front bedroom, the one with the bay window, which she was to share with Mary and which she had been shown earlier. There was nothing else in the room except the bed but it was spotlessly clean with a deeply polished floor and was as peaceful as a summer meadow. The curtains were drawn and even a small fire glowed in the grate. There were candles on the mantelshelf: extravagant, Jennet admitted but just for this once in honour of her homecoming and her first night in her new home, let them be so. She knew that they must be careful with their money with all the extra outlay, she said resolutely. There was the rent which was six shillings more than they had paid at Church Court and six shillings was a week's wage to some men. There was the additional food for Annie, who refused absolutely the wage they had offered her, no matter how they argued with her, saying they could pay her when their ship came in! There would be no more cabs, of course, which had been necessary now and again in the past, for they were only a mile from St Ann's Square. They were all strong and healthy and well fed and would make nothing of such a short walk and was not the green of the open countryside right on their doorstep. They had only to wander down the lane at the side of the house for their recreation, which would cost them nothing.

Lodge's Nursery Garden, a few yards along, was approached by a long, wide pathway. There was a small running brook inside its high walls and scattered about were summerhouses and arbours where visitors, if they wished, might sit and have tea and watercress sandwiches. A further saving was the fact that they could still eat economically, for Annie now had time to shop at the market where value for money might be had, and not last thing at night either, though knowing Annie she would make one penny do the work of two! Not a farthing wasted on anything inessential until Nancy felt that the tiny account in the bank on Piccadilly had grown large enough; that the work they had was to come in steadily enough for them to be able to let out their breaths on a sigh, knowing they were secure.

The three young women went up the stairs together, Jennet carrying Kitty while Annie had a last potter round her miraculous kitchen. It seemed that Annie could not quite believe her good fortune and had to wander about touching her rolling pin or her skillet, wiping her pine table and her window bottoms for the hundredth time since they had moved in, ready to give the blessed pup a quick clean about her pretty face if she would let her. They could hear her telling Scrap to "be'ave yerself, fer if I find a mess in 'ere when I come down in't mornin' yer'll get a leatherin', so think on!"

In the second bedroom at the back of the house was the bed Jennet was to share with Kitty.

"I though it best for the moment," Jennet had said hesitantly, for after all Kitty was Nancy's child, not hers, "since Kitty might wake in the night and you need all the rest you can," and Nancy knew that Jennet was telling her as diplomatically as she could that as they had not known how Nancy would be with her daughter they were leaving her with the woman who had practically brought her up in Nancy's stead. "Annie will have the small front bedroom to herself. Is that all right? She is old," she whispered, for she did not want to offend the woman without whom they could not have done this, "and she snores. Besides, we are used to sleeping together and I know Annie relishes the idea of having her own bedroom."

Nancy put her arms about Jennet and Kitty. She said nothing, merely held them both for a long moment, then turned to smile at Mary.

"Come on, sweetheart, help me out of my clothes and into bed." And they knew she was telling them that she really was not yet completely well and would let them have their way for a few days. Just a few days, mind.

Mrs Denby next door had informed Annie that there was no need to walk into town as there was a horse-drawn omnibus that passed the house and ran regularly into Manchester centre. At the corner of Bury New Road and Knoll Street were stables for "Greenwoods" horses which was a stopping place for their omnibuses. If Mrs Wilson waited at the Grove Inn, a short walk from Grove Place, Mrs Denby told her, and was a favourite last "pull-up" before their journey's end into town, she would find that there was a regular and convenient service.

Annie did indeed find that the service was very efficient, and exciting too, for Annie had never been on an omnibus in her life. She and Kitty stood and stared at the mighty draught horses that pulled the vehicle, overcome with awe by their size and patience, the polish on their glossy coats and the chinking and gleaming of their harness.

"Eh, dids't ever see such beauties?" she asked Kitty, who studied the great beasts with admiration.

"Is't off ter town then, my lasses?" the driver asked them comfortably. "Then 'op up, fer we're away now."

They hopped up and both enjoyed the ride enormously!

Mrs Underwood, upon receiving Annie's message, followed almost on her heels to the house in Grove Place. She had been impressed by the clean and tidy woman in the carefully darned shawl, highly polished clogs and snow white pinny who told her politely that she was Miss Brody's housekeeper, a title Annie quietly relished.

"And is this your . . . grandchild?" Mrs Underwood asked her, smiling and holding out her hand to Kitty who, on cue, took it, dimpling with the charm of Mick O'Rourke, whose true child she indeed was.

"No, ma'am," Annie told her, smiling herself but venturing nothing more, for it had always been Annie's philosophy that folks' business was nowt to do with anyone but themselves.

Half an hour later she was opening the door to Mrs Underwood. A cab was just drawing away from the front gate, joining the stream of horse-drawn traffic that hurtled up and down the busy, tree-lined road from Manchester centre to Broughton and beyond. Bury New Road, as its name implied, was the main road to Bury and at certain times of the day, when the manufacturing gentlemen made their way to their offices, mills and warehouses, it was exceedingly busy. Because both Higher and Lower Broughton were totally unaffected by the explosion of what was to be called the Industrial Revolution, more and more families were moving there from inner Manchester. Higher Broughton had been chosen by the Manchester merchants, merchant princes who wished to be seen by other merchant princes as successful and therefore well able to afford their country homes. They joined the landed gentry by purchasing large estates and building spacious mansions in private parks, living among country meadows and yet within driving distance of their warehouses and factories. From the edge of Strangeways an extensive meadow spread as far as Broughton itself, covered with rich grass, the air scented with nothing more than the hawthorn's scent from the hedges still bordering the new roads and the wild flowers whose spirited fragrance nothing could quench. If you stood on the high ground in Bury New Road in the springtime it was possible to see the magnificent orchards of pear, apple and plum trees laden with blossom so thick it looked as though it could be walked upon.

And yet it was not just the middle-class families who began to move out of the urban sprawl, the dingy, uninviting hovels in the alleyways that cobwebbed the centre of the city. Neat terraced houses were being built at the lower end of Broughton, and the white-collar workers, who worked long hours for low wages but regarded their jobs as steadier than mill work, settled in them.

It was to a house such as this that Mrs Underwood called.

Mrs Underwood was a handsome woman of large proportions, with sleek black hair, a proud easy carriage, a clear skin and excellent teeth, for she came from a family who had never known want. She was dependent on no one since her husband, the one her father had married her to at the age of eighteen, was dead. He had left her well off but she was a woman who found no satisfaction in sitting at home doing her embroidery, so, since she had no children and was beholden to no one, she had bought herself a small business in the drapery trade. She was a woman of means and had no need to work but she did it just the same and her life was busy and satisfying. She had taken a liking to the beautiful girl who stood so proudly behind her stall on the market, knowing it was because she reminded her of herself, not in looks, for who could match the market girl in that, but in strength of character. But not only that she found her merchandise well made and good value, which proved itself by the way it walked out of the door of her shop. Everything she had bought from her sold at once and she was prepared to buy more. Indeed she had this in mind when she called at Grove Place that morning.

She gave a gasp of horror when, as Annie, in her position as housekeeper, showed her into the shining kitchen, she caught her first glimpse of Nancy's face.

"We've only just moved in," Annie was telling her in that way she had: take us or leave us, it's all the same to us, "so yer'll 'ave ter mekk do wi't kitchen. Parlour's got nowt in it just yet. Now mind that dratted animal. Thing's allus under yer ruddy feet," picking up the prancing puppy and depositing her on the step outside the scullery door. "I'll put kettle on, shall I, my lass?" she said to Nancy, placing an affectionate hand on her shoulder. "Well, sit yer down." This to Mrs Underwood who was still standing by the door, her hand to her mouth, her eyes wide and stunned.

"Oh, my dear, whatever has happened to you? When your housekeeper said you weren't well . . . I had no idea what caused . . ."

Suddenly from some back recess of her mind, where perhaps instincts are formed, Nancy became aware of a sureness, like a soft and drifting image, that told her this woman could be trusted. That she need not hide the truth of her previous life, for she would not be judged by it but by what she had done with it. What she had achieved. Mrs Underwood was a woman of the world who would not faint or shudder or scream at the appalling circumstances that had brought her to this moment. She had been raped and later beaten by a man, none of it her fault, as many so-called respectable women would believe of a girl such as herself. She should not have been out after dark on her own, since none of them would dream of it. She had asked for trouble, they would tell one another, having no regard for the fact that she was forced to support herself and her younger sisters, since she had no man to do it for her.

She lifted her head, smashed, bruised but unbowed, and as they sipped the strong, hot tea Annie had brewed before she wandered off into the garden with Kitty she told Hetty Underwood how she had come from Angel Meadow to Grove Place. Mrs Underwood said nothing but her eyes, almost black in the amber smoothness of her face, never left Nancy's and when she had finished speaking there was silence for several minutes. Nancy stared into the small fire. She would be sorry if this woman took offence and refused to have anything more to do with her. More than sorry, for a good deal of Nancy's merchandise was sold in Mrs Underwood's shop. She would find other buyers, she had made up her mind to that; indeed, when her face was healed she meant to walk the length of Deansgate, Market Street, St Ann's Square, King Street and Exchange Street, in fact anywhere respectable shops were to be found, and look for other customers.

Mrs Underwood took a deep breath, then placed her cup and saucer on the kitchen table. Nancy still kept her face averted, not from a misplaced sense of guilt or shame, far from it, but she felt that if she looked up and saw revulsion on Mrs Underwood's face it would hurt her deeply. She didn't know why, really, for the woman was nothing to her. And yet she was. There was a strange bond between them, of what sort she didn't know, but it was there just the same. There were not many people in this world whom Nancy took a liking to, whom she held in respect. She loved her sisters, of course, and Jennet meant as much to her as they did. Annie was almost like a mother to her, fond, scolding, always ready to speak her mind, protective and sharp-tongued but Nancy knew Annie loved her and she loved Annie. Into this equation the baby face of her daughter glowed and something unfamiliar warmed her heart. She was a charmer, there was no doubt about it, like her father; but also in her childish character was a steadfast will, a resolute determination and strength which showed itself even at this tender age and Nancy found she liked it. And now there was this woman who seemed to have found a place in Nancy's . . . should she say heart? No, that was too fanciful but she really liked her and would be distressed if she proved weak and false.

"Will you look at me, Miss Brody . . . or may I call you Nancy?"

Nancy turned her head in astonishment and delight.

"Of course you may, Mrs Underwood."

"I feel we are to be friends, Nancy, and though I know I am a good deal older than you that does not matter. Your tale horrifies me, for though I am from the working classes I have lived a sheltered life, a privileged life and confess I have never come across violence. Now, tell me, is your face to heal?" For like the others she felt a real sense of loss for the beauty that had once been Nancy Brody's.

Nancy shrugged carelessly and Hetty Underwood realised that the girl was still in a state of shock. No woman likes to lose her looks and Nancy's attitude of indifference could not be real. It was apparent that what had been done to her had left her scarred, not just on her face but in her inner self, and to cover that wound she was affecting not to care. Men were anathema to her now, so what did it matter whether she was plain or pretty, or even downright ugly. Her work was the most important thing in her life, her business that she had built from nothing and with very little help. Hetty Underwood could not conceal her admiration.

"What are you to do, my dear, when you resume work?"

Nancy stared in surprise. "Do? What can you mean? I shall do exactly what I have always done. Jennet is working the market stall today and until the end of the week. Mary has kept the workroom going, though she is very young for such a responsibility. They have done wonderfully well but they need me, Mrs Underwood, and I cannot afford to stay at home for more than a day or two. I am to go to the hospital on Friday, when Doctor Whitehead is to remove the rest of the bandages, and every day the bruising to my face fades a little. I intend taking over the stall on Saturday which is our busiest day—"

"You need more staff," Mrs Underwood interrupted abruptly. She leaned forward and her face was alight with some private enthusiasm.

"More staff: you mean machinists?" Nancy was plainly astonished.

"I do."

"But I have only six sewing-machines."

"You need more of those as well."

"But I have not the room."

"And bigger premises."

"Mrs Underwood!" Nancy's face showed her bewilderment, even under its layer of padding. She and Annie had brushed back her hair as best they could, knotting a length of scarlet ribbon at the end of the plait Annie had fashioned, but it had not been washed for over two weeks. It looked drab and lifeless and though the nurses had done their best there were still streaks of dried blood here and there. As soon as her dressings were gone she would wash it, she had told Annie this morning. The plait hung over her shoulder and across her breast and her hands were busy with the ribbon, tying and untying it in her consternation, then she sat up straight, looking stern and somewhat aloof.

"Mrs Underwood," she said again. "Believe me, if I had the wherewithal I would do all these things you suggest, and one day I shall, but at the moment I am hard pressed to—"

"I know, that is why I am here, apart from wishing to ascertain the state of your health. You have a talent for business, Nancy, for making money, but you need money to *make* money. I see you as a good investment and so I wish to invest in you. If you agree, that is," she added somewhat hastily, for Nancy's face was a picture of amazement. "You must look for bigger premises, rent more machines, employ more girls and I guarantee you will expand beyond all your wildest dreams. I know you have had plenty of those, my dear. So what do you say? Will you accept my offer? You could manufacture not just shirts and baby clothes but blouses and even dresses."

"Oh, Mrs Underwood, stop, stop, I can't think." Nancy's eyes glowed with excitement, ready to brim with tears but already there was that reflective look on her face which told Hetty Underwood she was weighing up this and that and the other and would not be found wanting when it came to the details.

"You agree?" She took Nancy's hand in her large capable one and squeezed it. She did not need an answer as Nancy stood up and, throwing off her hand, stretched her arms to the ceiling, tipping back her head in what looked like ecstasy. Then she became still and an expression stole over her face that Kitty Underwood was to see many times.

"This will be a proper investment – is that what you call it? – with contracts and . . . and whatever legal arrangement are necessary. Lawyers and . . ."

"Of course, my dear," and she smiled. "I see you are not a woman to be trifled with, Nancy Brody. I think you will go far."

18

Josh Hayes was deep in thought, his mind only half occupied with the task of steering his chestnut mare through the Saturday midday traffic, which is perhaps why the accident occurred.

It was warm, sultry, the air trapped beneath the inevitable pall of dirty brown smoke that would hang about over the city for the rest of the day even though the chimneys from which it poured were now at rest. The factory hooters and whistles had signalled the end of the shift, since, after the introduction of the statutory establishment of the Saturday half-day, the pavements were crowded with workers making their way home, their clogs clattering on the cobbles as they darted almost under the belly of his horse. He scarcely noticed.

It was June 1861 and since the beginning of the year affairs in North America had assumed a more and more unhappy and alarming character, so much so that the British government had last month felt compelled to issue a proclamation of its neutrality. The exact nature of the dissension between the northern and southern states that led to the war between them was never quite understood by those not involved, many of them believing that it was merely over the abolition of slavery, but there were many other factors tangled in its complex history. For years estrangement had gradually been building up between the northern and southern states, grounded on a number of differences, some, not all, on the continual collisions to which the question of slavery gave rise. In November of last year Abraham Lincoln had been elected President of the United States of America and, beginning in December and continuing to February 1861, seven southern states had withdrawn from the union and Jefferson Davis had been sworn in as President of what was known as the Confederate States of America. In

April Fort Sumter, situated on an island in northern hands-off Charleston in South Carolina, was fired upon by Confederate troops and President Lincoln called for the rallying of union forces and proclaimed a blockade of all southern ports.

It was on this that Josh was dwelling as he picked his way along the narrow congestion of Moseley Street in the direction of the considerably broadened Market Street, for if southern ports were blockaded how were the cotton planters of the southern states to get their raw cotton to market? Manchester was known as the spinning centre for the finest of all cotton yarns and most of its production found its way into the city's own weaving sheds. It was the world's largest market for cotton goods. Ready-made clothing and the rising influence of the fashion cycle were changing the dress habits of the lower middle classes. There was a steady growth of a working-class market for ready-made clothes, most of the making up carried out in small, ill-regulated sweat shops where underclothes, shirts, and collars were made up, though of course there were exceptions.

The firm of Brody and Williams, begun no more than twelve months ago, was, besides its baby garments and shirts, becoming well known for its good-quality blouses and dresses. Its merchandise was aimed at the lower middle classes in the first instance, but it had rapidly become popular with that in-between class that was neither upper nor lower, consisting of self-made men who were enterprising and knew how to set that enterprise and their own ambition to good advantage in the world of business opportunities which abounded in Manchester. They had wives who wished to be considered fashionable, despite the fact they could not yet afford the bigger and more expensive fashion houses, and they were happy to make their purchases at Mrs Underwood's, a smart little shop, recently extended, on the corner of Market Street and Brown Street in which the blouses, dresses, undergarments and baby clothes made in the small factory owned by Brody and Williams were sold. Josh had heard that they intended branching out into other areas of ladies clothing: shawls and fans, lacy garments to be worn in the privacy of a lady's own boudoir – for those ladies who had a boudoir – bonnets, gloves, parasols and a host of fancy goods. He knew, of course, who the Brody was in Brody and Williams, for did not she and her companion, Miss Williams, still cause something of a stir whenever they called into his warehouse to view his textiles. Their orders had grown by the week, not just in plain cotton but in the other fabrics he had introduced since his father had trusted him with the management of the warehouse: batiste, a dressed cotton muslin; dimity, a stout cotton with a raised pattern: fustian which was coarser; jaconet, fine and light; nankin and sateen; all made from cotton but with a different appearance and use. It was said, for men were just as inclined to gossip as women, that the Misses Brody and Williams bought silk from many of the silk manufacturers in the city, ribbons, artificial flowers, feathers and all manner of materials in the making up of their goods; and there was a rumour that Miss Brody and her partners were so successful new premises were even now being looked for to accommodate her machinists.

And in all this time he had not once seen her, on his premises or off. He passed the draper's shop in Market Street and her home in Grove Place on the New Bury Road on his way to Broughton and though he could not say he deliberately searched her out he often cast an eye at the small house where she lived. He had seen the child in the garden, her daughter who was the same age as Freddy, playing some game with the dog and an older woman, and had nodded politely at the woman who had nodded back. She was the one who had told him a year ago that Miss Brody had suffered an accident, no details, but that she was not at home to callers; and since he was disinclined to call anyway he had – inexplicably – left the puppy and enquired no further. It was best that way. She was a beautiful woman and for some reason had aroused a certain feeling – interest: what could he call it? – in him, and God knew where it might lead if he was to investigate it. He was older and wiser since his affair with Evie, the tragedy of her death, the birth of his son, and he meant to keep well away from any temptation of that sort. He had immersed himself in his warehouse and the mill his father was encouraging him to take charge of, in the delights of parenthood which gave him all that was required for the softer, affectionate side of his nature. He knew he had withdrawn into himself over the last two years, hidden his emotions, buried them with Evie, which was strange since he had not loved her. Only his little son was allowed to see the gentleness, the sweetness, the tenderness that lay dormant in his heart, even the humour that had once made him tease and flirt and laugh, since he had nothing to trouble him then. It was gone now, leaving only the serious concerns of business, of profit and loss, of balance sheets and expanding markets for his cloth – which might not expand so easily with the situation as it was in America – and it was very clear that before long these matters which nibbled at his half-attentive mind would need to be concentrated upon and appropriate action taken.

And it was not just the home trade that would be affected by this war between the states in America. The export of textile goods to Australia, New Zealand, Canada and South Africa was growing rapidly. It was a boom time: so what was to become of the boom if there was the cotton shortage that Josh and other men of cotton knew would come? Unless another supply of raw cotton could be found it looked a bleak prospect for those who made a living from cotton, and there were many hundreds of thousands of those, not only in Manchester but all over Lancashire.

Market Street was a teeming mass of people, all crowding the pavements, jostling one another good-naturedly, since it was the weekend. Some were hurrying to get home after their morning's labour, others drifting in a leisurely fashion from shop window to shop window, most of them of the working classes, the women in shawls despite the heat, and clogs, the men in caps and mufflers. Today was their day, for the ladies of the upper classes would not dream of shopping on a Saturday, preferring to mix with their own sort, those who had wealthy husbands and therefore no need to work and so could visit Kendal, Milne and Faulkners and other smart shops during the week. Those here today were of the class that, for generations, had worked in the stifling, dangerous and overworked environment of the mills and factories, their ill-nourished bodies, stunted legs and bowed shoulders proclaiming their lack of anything that might be called fresh air, decent exercise outdoors, and bone-building, body-building food. But rising real wages had stimulated a popular demand for goods of all sorts and since they had a penny or two to jingle in their pockets they liked to wander along Market Street or Deansgate and peer into the shop windows. They might not be able to afford what was in them but they could look, couldn't they?

There were carriages, leather-lined, polished to a high gloss, pulled by carriage horses of splendid pedigree with high-nosed, smartly uniformed coachmen snapping their whips and doing their best to keep on the move, and in the carriages, gentlemen in top hats, those who did not wish to hazard themselves in riding a horse into the business quarters of town. There were drays piled high with bales of cotton, barrels of beer, sacks of coal, corn and vegetables, fish, fruit and flowers and meat heading for the great iron and glass-roofed food market of Smithfield off Shude Hill. The congestion was considerable and getting worse, for Saturday was the busiest market day of the week and from six that morning there had been hundreds of horse-drawn "lurries" and carts, heavy laden, heading there, pulled by magnificent horses, great in size and shoulder with glossy bowed heads and well-brushed manes. There were horse-drawn omnibuses, one after the other along the street, with their destination written in large letters at the front of the vehicle: Belle Vue, Hyde Road, Longsight, Alexandra Park, Hulme, Miles Platting, Broughton. As his mare took a prancing and supercilious step or two away from one of the shire horses that were used to pull the omnibus, whether from nerves or indignation, Josh became aware of a tall, well-dressed young woman who was just leaving the doorway of a shop on the corner of Brown Street.

She seemed unaware of any danger, stepping briskly from the shop doorway, whisking through the dawdling crowds across the pavement and stepping into the gutter with the evident intention of boarding an omnibus heading for Broughton. It was perhaps the crowds that hid him from her view. She was keeping a lookout for the drays and carts and carriages, but the smaller figure of a horseman, of which there were more than a few, seemed to be invisible to her.

He was upon her before he could draw on his reins. His mare shied, tossing her head, her hooves landing somewhere in the pleats of the woman's full skirt. The woman sat down in a most ungraceful way on the kerb, where her pretty hat fell over her eyes. She immediately began to abuse him in a most unladylike fashion.

She was beautifully dressed in a gown of wheat-coloured jaconet, the bodice fitted closely to her swelling breast, the skirt full and billowing out over a crinoline. There were touches of white at her neck and wrists. Her bonnet, from underneath which came her highly indignant voice, was of wheat-coloured straw with a ribbon as wide as her hand fastened under her chin. Her only concession to frivolity was a tiny bunch of violets at her throat.

There were shouts, the harsh noise of wheels scraping on cobblestones, the sound of his mare as she whinnied in fear. In a moment, and from God knows where, a great many people at once gathered round, bending over her, arguing quite ferociously with one another as to whether she had walked into the horse or the horse had walked into her. Was she blind, or deaf, perhaps drunk or even slow-witted, for surely anyone could see an animal of that size? She was still holding forth, he knew, on his stupidity and carelessness, his total lack of anything that might be called horsemanship and for a moment he felt a great desire to laugh. She really was the most diverting woman he had ever met, or was that too insipid a word to describe Miss Nancy Brody who, in the several times he had met her had, if not physically then metaphorically, collided with his horse head on. There was the incident in the mill yard when she had rushed to defend a child he was about to ride down, or at least *she* said so! There had been the day at the ruined castle when she had mocked his attempts to control his mare.

And now it was she who had stepped into the direct path of his mare and yet she was holding forth in such a furious manner one might believe he had set the animal to the pavement and deliberately run her down. But really he could not sit here studying her, listening to her, smiling at her indignation, which she obviously thought was justified, when she might be seriously damaged, though from the force of her abuse he did not think so.

Still inclined towards laughter, he leaped from his mare's back, throwing the reins to a startled lad in a cap, striding across the cobbles, which were strewn with horse droppings, to her side. He put his hand to her elbow, not sure which part of her might be damaged and therefore painful. His touch was gentle and so was his voice, though there was still a smile in it.

"Miss Brody, will you ever learn to look where you are going, I wonder? You really could have a serious accident the way you dash headlong—"

"I might have known it would turn out to be my fault. Will you ever learn to look where *you* are going, Josh Hayes," she spat at him while all eyes turned with interest to look at him. "Or at least teach that blasted animal of yours to go where you tell it. Every time I step out of doors there you are charging down on me as though you were leading a cavalry troop. No, I'm not hurt, no thanks to you."

But when he had helped her to her feet and then, when he found she could not stand erect, picked her up and carried her back to the shop from which she had emerged, it seemed she was glad enough of his strength as her own faded away. Her ankle, which the mare had caught with her sharp hoof, was swelling badly. She needed her boot removing, he told her sternly, and would she for God's sake be quiet for a moment while he found someone to apply a cold compress.

"Mrs Underwood can do that, if you would kindly put me down. There really is no need for all this fuss," though her arms were inclined to cling about his neck and he could feel a small tremor shake her slender figure.

"And where the devil is Mrs Underwood?" peering about him as though fully expecting whoever she was to be at his elbow where he needed her.

"In the shop," indicating the sign above the splendid double-fronted window which said: MRS UNDERWOOD LADIES' FASHIONS.

A young woman dressed in black stood behind the counter arranging something in a box. She looked up smiling as the door bell pinged, then put her hand to her mouth in dismay.

"Miss Brody. Oh dear . . . oh dear, whatever is to do? Mrs Underwood . . ."

As she gasped and floundered, a large and capable-looking woman came from the back reaches of the shop, her face displaying her own horror at the sight of her young partner in the arms of a strange man.

"Dear Lord, Nancy, what now?" she began, ready to flutter and wring her hands as her assistant was doing; then, pulling herself together, she drew back a red velvet curtain and led the way into whatever back room she had come from.

"Stay calm, please, Miss Jenkins," she called over her shoulder. "Stay here and see to any customers who – or perhaps Nancy needs a doctor. Shall Miss Jenkins run for a doctor?" she asked Josh anxiously.

He did not answer. Following the woman who was presumably Mrs Underwood, he carried Nancy Brody in arms which, for some reason, decidedly did not want to let her go. And when her ankle was bandaged quite expertly by Mrs Underwood and she had sipped the glass of brandy he had demanded, he told her firmly that he would not hear of her going anywhere without him. A cab would be called and he would see her to her home. It was the least he could do after so rudely riding her down, he told her bent head, his mouth curling in a wry grin.

And it was as she raised her face to his and he looked up from the neat bandage Mrs Underwood had applied to her ankle that he first got a clear look at her. He did his best not to gasp. He did his best not to stare or reveal in any way how shocked and . . . yes, how grieved he was at the puckered scar that twisted her once smooth cheek but his eyes, over which he had no control, darkened in his distress and compassion. She saw it and at once she lifted her head with quite regal imperiousness, her back, which had been inclined to droop, arching majestically, her look saying she wanted no man's pity, and certainly not his. What right had he to pity her, her manner asked and he looked away in confusion, which he realised at once was the worst thing he could have done. She would believe he could not bear to look at her which was not true. At once he lifted his head and met her eyes. It must be spoken of at once or it would for ever lie between them, though what exactly he meant by that he was not awfully certain.

"How did you . . . ? Please, I don't mean to be rude or unfeeling but . . ." he began and for some reason her eyes became less frosty and he was aware that she was grateful he had asked her and not simply turned away as though he had noticed nothing.

The wound must have been deep, taking with it the fine flesh that thinly covers the cheekbone, and though it was evident a clever surgeon had done his best the skin had been drawn together in a long pucker. The cheekbone, which must have fragmented, had fallen in and when the flesh had been pulled together it had drawn up the corner of her mouth. It was not unattractive. In fact it gave her a decidedly lopsided but permanent half-smile, whimsical, impish almost, making the observer want to smile too.

"I was hit . . . by a man," she said softly, gazing into his face as though she were sorry if it distressed him. "He was a prize fighter. He broke my cheekbone."

His face hardened and so did something inside him, something that now felt it could do murder on her behalf. There was something about this woman that had fascinated him from the start, drawn him to her, unwillingly let it be said, but he had told himself that it made no difference, his life was set on its course, with Freddy, and he wanted no more complications. But how could he simply ignore the damage that had been done to her lovely face? Walk away and pretend it meant nothing to him when the simple fact was, it did. Anger was boiling up inside him, a rage so great he could feel it thicken in his throat. Though she was tall with a magnificent bosom, there was a look of vulnerability about her, a slender, swaying frailty like a flower caught in a merciless wind. He knew she was strong. He knew a bit about her by now, for a woman like her was talked about and it had got around that she came from a poor background but by her own endeavours and sheer gritty determination had dragged herself, and her family, to this point in her life, which could only be called successful. But some man had attacked her, for a reason he was sure she would not speak of – and did he really want to know? He was a prize fighter, she had said, which implied a big bully of a man, for that was what prize fighters were. Why should he suddenly think of that swaggering, broad-shouldered lout he had seen her with at the Arts Treasures Exhibition, it must be three or four years ago now? He found he could not bear the images that formed in his mind, violent and sickening, of this lovely girl being battered to the ground by the fists of that brute, but he could not seem to blot them out and it appalled him, as did his own reaction to it. He would be appalled by any attack on any woman by any man, he was aware of that, but this, what had been done to this woman filled him with a savagery that would not be appeased until he had ground the perpetrator into the mud beneath his feet. His jaw clenched and so did his fists until his fingernails cut into the palms of his hands and his breath rasped in his throat.

He stood up and lurched away from her, leaning for a moment with both hands on a table which evidently was used for sewing, for there were piles of brightly coloured cottons and silks strewn about it.

"Mr Hayes?" she enquired wonderingly.

"Who was it?" he snarled at the table. "Who did this to you? If he's not in gaol I shall personally make it my business to see he gets there by the week's end."

"Mr Hayes!" This time in astonishment and yet in her voice was something that said she was not displeased.

"The bastard wants horse-whipping and if you will give me his name—"

Her voice when she spoke, interrupting what he knew to be none of his business, had cooled a little.

"Really, Mr Hayes, I can hardly think it has anything to do with you."

"Perhaps not, Miss Brody, but I would still be glad to hear that he had been punished." His voice was harsh.

"Mr Hayes, I am quite capable of dealing with my own—"

"Has he been punished?"

"Well, no, as it happens. He—"

"No, and may I ask why?" He began to stride about the small room, smacking his right fist into the palm of his left hand. Behind Nancy's chair, where she had been watching the scene played out before her, Hetty Underwood gaped in bewilderment. She knew who he was, of course, since she had accompanied Nancy and Jennet a time or two to his warehouse in Moseley Street. But these were not the actions of a concerned but impersonal onlooker to some stranger's troubles. This was not one male appalled at what another had inflicted on a weak and helpless woman. So what was it? Dear God, what was wrong with the man?

Nancy evidently had the same thought, for she drew herself up even further, presenting him with a full view of her disfigured face, her frosted eyes telling him that what had happened to her was none of his concern. But Josh Hayes was no longer the engaging, carelessly good-natured, happy-go-lucky young man who had swept Evie Edward off her feet. He had matured, shouldered responsibilities not only as a father but as a man of business with a standing in the community. This young woman was not his responsibility but could he ignore what had been done to her, the deed seemingly gone unpunished, and still call himself a gentleman? He could not.

"Miss Brody, I cannot rest . . . I beg your pardon, but I cannot rest easy in my mind knowing that a madman is still on the loose. You say he has not been—"

"He ran away, Mr Hayes, so there is really nothing to be done about it." Nancy's emotions were racing from her head to her chest and even down to her knees which, though she was sitting down, felt curiously weak, no doubt due to her fall, she told herself firmly without believing it. Some contrary female part of her, even while she was arguing with him, was noticing the firm but pleasing shape of his mouth, the clefts at either side of it and, whenever he stopped to glare at her, the black lines that striped his silver grey eyes from the pupil to the outer circle. But this wouldn't do. She had no time to play games with this fine gentleman who seemed determined to do battle on her part, which she supposed was what gentlemen of his class did for ladies. But she was no lady and though she would dearly like to see Mick O'Rourke brought to justice he – and Rosie – had been gone for the best part of a year.

Firmly she told him so, though she did not mention Rosie.

"Nevertheless I would like his name, Miss Brody. My family has some influence in Lancashire, contacts in all the cotton towns. If he is working hereabouts he would easily be found."

She sighed, for there was nothing she would like more than to have news of Rosie, and where Mick was there surely would be her sister.

"Very well. His name is Mick O'Rourke."

"Aah . . . Irish!"

"As I am, Mr Hayes. Or of Irish descent."

"I apologise, Miss Brody. I meant no slur to you. Now then, I think we had better get you home. You might have concussion, or worse." He was firm, sure in his male arrogance that, as a woman, she was incapable of getting herself anywhere without a male arm to support her, particularly now she was injured, not at all concerned about his mare which, apparently, was blocking the pavement to the annoyance of a constable. "I shall call a cab. Mrs Underwood, I presume you are Mrs Underwood?" And when Hetty Underwood, who had outfaced many a gentleman in her time, meekly said she was, he sent her scurrying into Market Street to hail a hansom cab.

"Really, Mr Hayes, this is ridiculous."

"Why is it ridiculous, Miss Brody? Accidents happen." His eyes were an incredible soft velvet grey and he was smiling as he knelt before her.

"You weren't looking where you were going."

"And neither were you."

"Oh, damnation."

"What is it now?"

"I don't know. I just feel so . . . so annoyed."

"With me?"

"I suppose so, and with myself."

"Don't be."

"I can't help it. I'm not usually such a fool."

For a brief second she drifted against him, her head drooping to his shoulder. His arms rose and his hands gently gripped her forearms and when she lifted her head their eyes met and acknowledged something that was there between them. He thought he might have kissed her and so did she but there was a bustle at the door as Mrs Underwood and her assistant came to help her to the waiting cab. He picked her up and cradled her to his chest, neither of them aware of anyone but each other.

"Your horse, Mr Hayes?" Mrs Underwood said faintly and was not surprised when he did not seem to hear her.

19

She knew something unthinkable had happened. She had felt it, she supposed, years ago, when they had exchanged angry words in the mill yard. She had felt it in the ruins of the castle where she had gone, in her devastation, after Mick O'Rourke had raped her, making her pregnant, and Josh Hayes had thrown his good warm cape about her shoulders. There had been some essence of him in the cape which had enfolded her, entered into the place that had been so sorely hurt: her heart, was that it, or the flesh and bones of her which had ached with weariness, and she had felt comforted by it, soothed; and something else that she had not been prepared to recognise. Deep down, unacknowledged, she had felt it again at his warehouse in Moseley Street when he had given her, for a reason she had told herself was merely kindness, though of course it wasn't, the key that had opened the door to her new venture with his willingness to sell her his cotton. Every time they had met something had flowed between them. Something she, at least, did not want and, she believed, neither did he if the coolness of his manner was anything to go by. And that afternoon when she and Mary and Jennet had taken Kitty for a picnic and he had come upon them, accompanied by his little son. What a bloody fool she had made of herself then. She could have bitten out her own tongue when she heard herself ask him about his wife, a question that had come from somewhere inside her that she had not even known existed. And with what incredible gladness she had received his answer. He had no wife, he had told her, looking at her as if to ask what the devil it was to do with her, which was as it should be, for what *had* it to do with Nancy Brody?

But he had put his hands on her outside Mrs Underwood's

shop, allowed her to feel the warmth and masculine vigour of him and from that moment she had accepted it, gloried in it, despaired over it and known it was too late. He had lifted her against his chest, lean and yet strong, held her close to him as he carried her into the shop, bent his head to her so that she had felt the warmth of his breath on her cheek and smelled the fragrance of expensive cigars mixed with his own particular male odour which seemed to be a combination of cologne and fine cloth. He had been alarmed and had wanted to curse her but his eyes had given him away, for they had been a soft, smoky grey, narrowed with his male impulse to hold her more closely than was necessary. His lean, dark face with its oddly slanting smile bewitched her and she felt her flesh warm with what could only be called desire as her hands felt the ripple of his muscles beneath the impeccable cut of his jacket as he lifted her effortlessly from the pavement. She had wanted the moment to go on for ever, for she had experienced a strange languor, warm and sweet and deep, cradling her in a most unusual need to be carried wherever he fancied taking her.

In the hansom cab he had arranged her to his own satisfaction against the faded, rather worn upholstery, keeping his arm about her shoulders as though to steady her and she had not objected. Telling the cab driver to go carefully, which was something of an impossibility in the midday traffic, he had directed him to take them to Grove Place, making no secret of the fact that he was well acquainted with her address. She had not explored the reason why, since she felt herself to be drifting in a hushed world of enchantment which lulled her into a state she had never before known. It filled her entire being, and his too, she knew that, erasing their busy, complicated lives with the one all-absorbing pleasure of looking at one another, of taking in odours, of hair and skin, the feeling of closeness, of female softness and male toughness so that the jolting ride from Market Street, along Victoria Terrace past the Collegiate Church and Victoria Station on to Bury New Road passed by them unnoticed.

The cab stopped at the front gate of her home and they dragged their eyes away from one another to stare foolishly about them.

"Oh, are we there?" she asked with slow dragging reluctance, for how could she bear the moment to be over.

"I'm afraid so," he answered without thinking, both of them

knowing exactly what he meant. It was not the time for speaking, for promises or declarations, but when his hard hand touched hers it burned her with a strange fire and she wanted him to go on touching her for ever. She felt drugged with happiness, a rare feeling; indeed she could not remember ever knowing it before. And in the midst of it all she found herself noticing what she had not seen before: the sweetness and humour in his firm lips, the quiet amusement behind his alert gaze. He was, quite simply, a beautiful man.

"I'll carry you in," he had told her and her heart had leaped, for his hands were a caress about her, going through her flesh to the bone, the length of his lean body an inch from hers, his slanting, enquiring smile like the sun warming her skin. His face was close to hers as he lifted her from the cab and, so separated had they become from the world in which they lived, again he might have kissed her, despite the fascinated stare of the cab driver, had not Annie, Jennet and Mary come hurrying down the steps and along the path. Kitty and the barking dog tumbled at their heels so that pandemonium reigned for several minutes. They surrounded her with cries of "what's to do now?" and "what next?" patting her, begging to be told what had happened, eyeing Josh Hayes with some trepidation as though whatever it was must be his fault.

It brought them both back from that dangerous bewitchment with a rapidity that made her gasp and she could see the confusion in Josh as he carried her up the steps and into the kitchen where, turning for directions to Annie, he placed her gently in the chair indicated. The dog at once jumped up and put her paws on her knee and Josh frowned.

"Miss Brody suffered an accident to her ankle," he told the twittering group of women, his voice suddenly distant. "Mrs Underwood kindly bandaged it but I . . . well, you might want to call in a doctor. Must that animal leap about at Miss Brody's knee like that?" They were astonished by his irritation, wondering what had caused it, though Nancy knew, naturally. "No," he continued, "please, it was no trouble. I must get back, my mare is still . . ." and he had gone.

She had not seen him since and the anguish was ferocious. She was in love. She who had resolved never, ever to get involved with a man after what Mick O'Rourke had done to her, who had sworn that she hated men, that she would concentrate her whole life on the task of making herself and her family respectable, wealthy, people of consequence with which an attachment of any sort to a member of the opposite sex would interfere, had fallen in love. She had fallen in love with Josh Hayes and she was savage in her anger, an anger directed not just at herself for allowing it to happen but at him who had encouraged it, or so it seemed to her. She was in a precarious position in her life, for Josh Hayes was not the only one to recognise what the civil war in America might do to the cotton trade. She and Jennet were laboriously building up a small but successful business, a growing business, for they sold their manufactured goods, not only on the market stall which Nancy insisted on keeping up, as a kind of insurance, but in a growing number of shops along Deansgate, King Street, Corporation Street and Piccadilly. Not of the class of Kendal Milne and Faulkner, of course, but respectable dress shops and drapers. But cotton was the sum and substance of their livelihood, their bread and butter, and if their supply dried up, as it looked increasingly likely it might, what was to become of their business? They were teetering on the edge of a precipice, so how could she add to the possible disaster by allowing herself to fall in love? She could not. Not now. Later, perhaps, when the cotton crisis was over and she would have time to think about it; but in the meanwhile she found herself torn most distressfully by a raging conflict of emotions. She suffered bursts of sheer joy at the thought of him, at the image of his lean, handsome face as it smiled quizzically into hers; then, abruptly, she would be caught up in an angry and urgent need to wish him as far away from her as possible where she hoped savagely he would stay. She didn't want this, did she? And her heart told her most definitely that she did and her head argued against it until it ached. There would be nothing more wonderful than the passion and folly – and love, did he feel it too? – that had vibrated from his body to hers and yet nothing more disastrous!

It was two months before she saw him again. A warm and sparkling Sunday in August with nothing above the roofs of the houses but a span of azure blue. The sunlight turned the plain red brick of the houses in Grove Place to a rich and blushing burgundy and struck diamond reflections from the well-polished windows, and even the donkey-stoned steps seemed all the whiter. The housewives of Grove Place, Annie among them, though she was not, strictly speaking, a housewife, were as proud as punch of their smart little homes and spent many hours on their knees scouring and deep scrubbing every surface, inside and out.

Couples were strolling arm-in-arm beneath the shade of the massive sweet chestnut trees that lined Bury New Road, planted years ago when the busy thoroughfare was barely more than a lane. Children in their Sunday best rolled hoops, skipping ahead of their parents, and a slow procession of omnibuses, taking town dwellers out to Castle Hills and Sedgeley Park for the afternoon, passed their door in stately splendour.

She and Jennet had taken Kitty and Scrap for a leisurely stroll down Broughton Lane where the hedgerows were thick with hawthorn, the dry ditches beneath them submerged by a rising tide of wild flowers. Sweet cecily, fragrant with the scent of aniseed, standing waist high, its full green foliage and luxuriant white blossom crowded side by side with hedge parsley, dock and nettle which would be followed, as autumn mellowed, by meadow cranesbill, ragwort, foxglove and willowherb. The fields beyond were just as rampant, a spreading carpet of blue and pink and yellow and white where periwinkle, buttercup, clover and meadowsweet grew riotously side by side.

Putting Scrap on her leash they turned into the long, wide pathway that led to Lodge's Nursery Gardens, and which was bordered by a small, running brook. They wandered along the paths between the extensive orchards of pear, apple and plum trees, all beginning to fruit, the colours quite glorious: apples of yellow and light red, the palest green, russet, orange and deep crimson; pears of the lightest green to the darkest; and the rich purple red of plums. Beds of antirrhinum bordered the paths, an explosion of colour from the palest lemon to the deepest red, delicate pinks and carnations, begonias and petunias in a patchwork quilt of colours. Roses of every sort, cabbage roses, pink and showy, the rich crimson of the red rose of Lancaster and many others, all neatly ticketed so that the novice gardener might have all the information needed to make his garden as glorious as the ones on show. There was a bed of buddleia bushes, known, the sign said, as a butterfly bush, the blossom varying in colour from white, violet-blue, pink to reddish purple and about them, as the name implied, was a cloud of dancing, skimming butterflies.

Nancy stopped, letting Jennet and Kitty go ahead, her heart pierced with the beauty and fragrance of the flowers and the graceful ballet of the butterflies above them, and something seemed to break inside her. His face swam before her eyes as though in a mist, one dark eyebrow raised, his silvery grey eyes smiling and the pain in her chest and throat became unbearable so that she could barely swallow. Dear God, what the devil was the matter with her? How could she have allowed this . . . this foolish thing to happen to her, for that was what it was. Foolish! Mad! Insane! Just the sight of the blossom and the butterflies had spiralled her into the memory of that day a few weeks ago when she had been held in his arms. And yet it was not just now, for wasn't it true that no matter what the time of day, or what she was doing in it, his face would dream into hers and his arms would rise to hold her so that sometimes she quite startled those with whom she worked or did business with her sudden distracted air. She must stop it. She must put him from her. She had no time in her life for dreaming like some silly girl and besides which, she had somehow to find a way to keep her business going if the promised cotton famine came about.

But with what joy she would have shared this lovely moment with Josh Hayes. Her arm in his, leaning on his shoulder, their heads close together, his face bent to hers, she could feel inside her a faint but persistent knowing of what it would be like. Just a wisp of an imagined joy like a curling mist in sunlight.

"Nancy . . . Nancy, dearest, are you all right?" a voice said to her and a hand came to rest on her arm and when she turned, disorientated, for in her trance Josh had been with her, she looked into the anxious face of Jennet. Beside her was Kitty with Scrap pulling vigorously on the leash, which the child was having a job to hold on to since Scrap wanted to go one way and Kitty the other. Kitty Brody, even at the age of two, was already showing the resolute will of her mother and it was a constant battle, or so Annie grumbled, to get her to do what she was told. She was demanding and obstinate. Only this morning, wanting to get out into the sun-filled garden with Scrap she had stood at the top of the stairs shouting, "D'yess me, d'yess me at *once*," her face crimson, her eyes a vivid brilliant blue so like her father's Nancy felt her heart shrivel. Her determination to have her own way was sometimes alarming but then, could you wonder, Annie added, for with a mother like Nancy she was bound to be self-willed, and with a father like Mick O'Rourke, though Annie had never met him, could the child be blamed for the temper she had. A bright and sunny-natured child when she had her own way but cross her and skin and hair flew, or so Annie was heard to say. She needed a man's hand to discipline her, or a mother's, she muttered behind Nancy's back, for Miss Jennet was too indulgent by far.

Nancy looked down at her and made an effort to smile and Kitty smiled back. Nancy was aware that the child did not exactly love her as a child loves its mother, for when had Nancy ever been that? She herself was not consciously aware of any degree of unusual tenderness for Kitty but she made damn sure she was well nourished and warm, protected and safe from harm, and knew, deep inside her where her motherhood lay dormant, that she would protect her child with her own life. She held out her hand to her and Kitty took it and on her other side Jennet put hers in the crook of Nancy's arm.

"Let's go and have some tea in the summerhouse, or perhaps over there in one of the arbours. They do say the watercress sandwiches are the best in Manchester."

They lingered for another hour, but over on the horizon, unnoticed, where the sky faded to a silvery blue, elongated puffballs of clouds had begun to appear, drifting and gathering ominously as they approached the city.

The first spots of rain caught the summer-clad crowds by surprise. Women clutched their bonnets and wished they had brought their umbrellas, running for shelter to the summer-house or one of the small arbours, while fathers gathered in wandering children and wished they had stayed at home to read the newspapers.

Both Jennet and Nancy were dressed in white, simple gowns made of leno, a transparent muslin-like material, over wide petticoats of white sateen. The sleeves were full, dropping from the shoulders in what was known as a "pagoda", wide at the wrist. The bodices were neat, fastened up the front to beneath the chin with tiny buttons covered in the same material. Each of them had a mesh hairnet enclosing a smooth chignon and a flat, mushroom-shaped hat, Nancy's decorated with a wide ribbon of duck-egg blue velvet, Jennet's of prim-rose. Kitty was dressed as all the other little girls – and boys of her age – were dressed, for up to the age of five or six both sexes looked identical in their little skirts and pantaloons. Kitty's calf-length white dress was covered with a sensible blue pinafore with a frill over the shoulder and on her small feet were black lace-up boots.

She began to scream as the rain, all of a sudden, came down in a deluge, demanding that Jennet make it stop, for she was getting wet and Scrap didn't like it. She begged Jennet to carry her, holding up her arms to be picked up and letting Scrap go to the devil for all she cared.

"Stop that silly noise at once, d'you hear?" Nancy told her, shaking off Jennet's clutching hands which would have reached for the child. "No, Jennet, she is quite big enough to walk the short distance to the house. There is no need to carry her. You take the dog."

"Could we not shelter in the summerhouse?" Jennet asked anxiously, eager to get her arms about the child who she loved above all others and who was shrieking in earnest now, for she was accustomed to having her own way with the other three women of the house. She had never been tackled by her mother and was crying more in amazement than anything else.

"The summerhouse is packed with people and so are all the arbours."

"The trees?"

"For God's sake, Jennet, we are no more than five minutes from home and if this child will stop dragging at my hand we will be there in no time."

"Aunty Jen . . . Aunty Jen, carry Kitty."

"Aunty Jennet is not going to carry you and neither am I, so pick up your feet or I shall simply drag you along on your bum."

"No, Mama. No, not walk," and she began to aim kicks at Nancy's ankle, wildly swinging her free fist in temper.

"Nancy, please. She is so small and is not used to . . ."

Somewhere deep inside Nancy knew Jennet was only speaking the truth but she was in some strange way dragging the ghost of Kitty's father at her heels. She could not be said to be punishing Mick – or the child, who was showing her true Irish heritage for the first time, at least to her – for what had been done to her in the past but in her present state of mind, which could not escape the shadow of Josh Hayes that had held her in its grip for the past eight weeks, she was not her usual fair and sensible self. For two years she had managed almost to ignore her own daughter, secure in the knowledge that Annie, Jennet and Mary gave Kitty all the child needed in the way of affection but suddenly, with this show of obstinacy, this flare of hot temper, a *paddy*, as Annie would call it, it was as though her daughter's father had returned to harass her. Kitty was, she had slowly become aware, being brought up in a household of indulgent women where her slightest wish was realised and though in her early months it had not mattered unduly now she was becoming unruly, unmanageable and it must be corrected.

They had got as far as the corner of the house, ready to turn into Bury New Road and the gateway to their own home when she saw him. By now they were all as bedraggled as wet hens in a farmyard, their long skirts trailing on the wet pavement and would they ever get them clean again, she was considering, still firmly gripping the hand of her shrieking child as she did her best to get her inside the gate. The rain dripped off the brim of her bonnet and at her heels Jennet was beseeching her to let her pick Kitty up and, in the turmoil of her emotions, she was not even sure for the moment that it was Josh Hayes riding by on his gleaming, copper-coated mare. As the rain pelted down he had hunched himself down in the saddle, for like the rest of the Sunday afternoon crowds he was not dressed for wet weather. The rain dripped off the brim of his top hat and was evidently running down the back of his neck, for he shivered even further down into his summer jacket.

She straightened up, letting go of Kitty's hand who immediately ran clamouring for the safety of Jennet's arms. They looked at one another. Her heart thudded so loudly and so fiercely in her chest she felt quite faint, just as though the thing were shaking her body to pieces. She wanted to reach out her hand for the gatepost, or lean her bottom on the wall, for surely she was about to fall, but instead, as though she knew exactly what he was going to do and must be ready for the agony of it, she straightened her back, squared her shoulders, lifted her sodden bonnet and stared at him as though he were a perfect stranger. He raised his hat politely, acknowledging her and Jennet and the rain in the brim spilled over his hand, then he returned it to his head and rode on.

"Wasn't that Mr Hayes?" Jennet asked in bewilderment, holding her precious, still sobbing burden to her, her precious burden who was proclaiming her disapproval of "naughty Mama" in no uncertain terms.

Nancy turned and shut the gate, doing her best to seem unconcerned, for it was of the utmost importance to her that no one should know that her heart was shredding itself to bloody pieces inside her chest.

"I believe it was," she murmured, lifting her hands to her wet face, glad of the rain which hid the true state of her tears.

"He was very cool," Jennet remarked as she struggled up the steps with the squirming child.

"Do you think so? I did not notice."

His thoughts were savage and painful as he continued his journey past the houses of Grove Place and the Grove Inn Bowling Green where the rain had scattered the players, leaving their bowls in black groups on the grass. His mare's head drooped and so did his, for he had never, even when Evie died, felt so dragged down and bloody miserable.

Nancy Brody. He had thought of no one else in the past eight weeks, his male body remembering her warmth, her sweetness and yielding in his arms, the surprise of her submissive compliance to his orders on the day he had run her down on Market Street. She had leaned against him, allowed him to hold her, to touch her hand, to place his arm about her, sighing and soft-eyed, her mouth ready to hover beneath his own and but for the presence of the others he would have kissed her and she would have let him. Damnation, why had he let this happen to him and yet, if he was honest, had he any choice in the matter? A man does not choose where he will love or the world would be filled with perfect marriages. Oh, yes, he loved her. He loved her as he had never loved Evie, he knew that now, had known it for weeks, months, years, he supposed, if he was honest. He could not get her out of his mind, or his heart, where she had settled and would remain for the remainder of his days. He knew that too but there was absolutely nothing, Goddammit, that he could do about it. His family just about managed to live with Freddy, who was now his legally since he had adopted him, the adoption giving the situation some degree of respectability. His mother had become fond of him, allowing the little boy to call her "Ganma" though his father was more difficult to soften. Those with whom the family mixed socially had forgiven him his sin, not the sin of impregnating a servant girl, for that was no sin at all and besides did not many of the young men of good families do that, but for acknowledging the child of that sin. Freddy would be brought up as the legitimate child of the Hayes family, for after all he *was* Josh's son. You only had to look at him, his cap of brown curls and the clear silver gaze of his eyes which came from his grandmother who had given them to Josh and to his brother Arthur, to know whose child he was. He was accepted and loved. Josh had his father's approval at last and was doing well in the family business, so how in hell's name could he introduce the woman he loved into this equation? Sweet Jesus, he himself did not know where she had got her daughter from. Not from any husband, that was for sure and even if she had, how would his father, who was ambitious for both his sons, and his mother, who had only just come to terms with Freddy, take to a daughter-in-law who had been born in the slums of Angel Meadow? It would tear the family apart and ruin any chance his son might have of growing up in the respectability a child needs. He had never forgiven himself for Evie's death but he felt he had atoned for it with his resolute determination, against strong opposition, to bring up her son in a way that would have pleased her and made her proud.

But Nancy . . . How was he to live for the rest of his life without her, without what he knew would be the sweetest, the most exciting part of it? For three years, ever since he had first seen her in the mill yard, she had invaded his thoughts in the strangest way and he had wondered why. Now he knew. He had, without consciously realising it, admired her tenacity, her spirit, her capacity to move forward despite appalling setbacks. Like the attack on her by the bully who had split her face and, though he knew no details, her illegitimate child, and, he was sure, many more in her journey from Angel Meadow. He liked her pride in herself, her belief that she was someone special, for she was. He wanted to guard her and keep her as a man does his woman. He wanted her to lean on him, *him* and was jealous of those who had her affection. He knew he would never be totally alive, totally enthusiastic without her, never totally whole. He would know other women but he would never feel like this again.

The pain in his chest was appalling but he rode on, knowing it would get worse.

20

The dependence of Lancashire on the cotton states of America was proved, if proof be needed, by the civil war which, as 1861 drew on, was slowly getting into its stride as the northern troops advanced deeper and deeper into the southern states. Names began to appear in the newspapers, names the people of Britain had never heard before but which were to become increasingly familiar as the year progressed: Manassas, Bull Run, the Battle of Chancellorsville and "Stonewall" Jackson, Fort Hatteras. All the major sea ports on the coasts of Virginia, Carolina, Georgia and Louisiana were stopped up tighter than corks in a bottle by squadrons of the union navy and slowly, slowly, the supply of cotton began to dry up. It was estimated that stocks of raw cotton could last only until December.

At the beginning of November forty-nine mills had closed and 119 were on short time, but the sad news the following month of the sudden death of the Prince Consort, Her Majesty the Queen's beloved husband, overshadowed even the distress which the American war was causing in the Lancashire cotton towns. There had been rumours that the Prince was dangerously ill and he was sinking fast, then that he had rallied and that no serious alarm was felt.

When the bell of St Paul's tolled at midnight on 13 December apprehension began to spread among the Queen's loyal subjects and the following day, a Sunday, when those who attended church noticed the omission of the Prince's name in the liturgy, the appalling truth was realised. Grief was universal, just as though each household had lost a dear and honoured relative; and on the day of his funeral every shop and factory and mill in the land was closed and every private residence drew its window blinds.

Annie wept inconsolably, much to the alarm of Kitty who sought sanctuary on the black-clad knee of her Aunty Jennet, who had felt it was only right to wear mourning, at least on this one day. She rounded fiercely on Nancy who, sitting restlessly in the darkened parlour which was now tastefully furnished, not with new stuff but with good second-hand pieces, was grumbling that she could well spend her time to better advantage in a trip to Liverpool and the Cotton Exchange.

"I know the Prince was a good man, respected and held in great affection by the people, but would he like to think that all over the north many thousands of his wife's subjects are starving? Even a day wasted might mean the difference between life and death to—"

"Don't be ridiculous, Nancy. One day will change nothing. And besides, do you think the Liverpool Cotton Exchange is somehow miraculously to produce the cotton you need? I heard that Hayes of Monarch Manufacturing is to go on short time next week and that the only cotton available will be that brought over from India."

The three women, Annie, Jennet and Mary, were so shocked by the tragedy that their Queen had suffered and by their own sense of sadness that they did not notice Nancy wince as the name of Hayes was mentioned. They *had* noticed, naturally, that she had been far from her usual brisk and confident self over the past few months but they had put that down to the slow dwindling of business, the need to put, first on short time and then no time at all, more than half of the machinists in her employ.

"And a fat lot of good that is to anyone," she answered bitterly, referring to the Indian cotton, "unless you want to make sacking. It's badly packed. It's dirty, knotty and full of seeds and leaves and at best is suitable only for coarse cloth. Manchester is where fine spinning is done. There is very little fine-quality yarn to be had and you know full well that is the only sort that is any good to us."

"I am aware of that, but there is little to be done about it, my dear." Jennet's voice softened and she leaned across the table to take Nancy's feverishly plaiting fingers between her own. "Perhaps this war will not last long. It seems there is little happening at the moment and if the two sides can settle their differences peaceably the supply of cotton will begin again."

"And in the meantime we do what? As soon as we are no longer able to get cotton yarn I shall have to let the machines go, since I can no longer afford to hire them. So, if what you say is true and the Hayes Mill is to go on short time there will be very little available and the chances of us getting any are very slim. We have a few pounds in the bank but that won't last much longer and we have to eat and pay the rent on this house."

"We'll manage, dearest, we always do."

Nancy could feel the irritation rise in her. It was all very well saying "we'll manage" in that soothing tone of voice as though Jennet were talking to a child, but when it came right down to it did Jennet have any ideas as to how?

She asked her.

"How?"

"We . . . we will find work, the three of us."

"There is no work, Jennet. Do you think that all those on poor relief, which will be us before long if we don't find jobs, would not be working if there was work to be had. Manchester lives by cotton. Every trade there is, is allied to cotton. We owe money to Hetty Underwood. I know she said it was an investment but she expected a return for that investment and so far has had none because we have put our profits back into the business. She will be one of the first to go under unless she can make a living out of her fancy goods. But then she has private means so will survive, but there are thousands and thousands who won't, us included. There were 583,950 operatives working full time at the beginning of this year. Do you know how many there are now?"

"No, but—"

"There are 121,129 and that is in the whole of Lancashire."

There was a long, sad, drawn-out silence and the child on Jennet's knee huddled closer, sensing the oppression of her elders. Mary, who was ready to go anywhere, do anything their Nancy told her, looked about her uncomprehendingly, her face anxious, wishing she could lift the spirits of the others but then it was a sad day anyway with poor Prince Albert passing away and all.

She lifted her head bravely. "I don't mind going back to the mill, our Nancy, just until things get better."

"Don't talk daft, Mary Brody," Nancy snapped. "There's no bloody cotton, not in the spinning-rooms nor the weaving sheds so how are you to work a frame, tell me that?"

"Nay, don't speak to't child like that, Nancy Brody. She's only a bit of a kid an' don't understand," Annie remonstrated, forgetting that Nancy herself was only seventeen.

Nancy gritted her teeth and did her best to find the patience that was needed to deal with this family of hers who confidently believed that she could put it all to rights. They relied on her. They had implicit faith that she would find a way. Hadn't she always? Even Jennet, who had more of a feel for business than Mary, who had none, believed that if they were patient, drew in their belts, cut back a little here and there, they would come through. A few months of hardship perhaps, and then, when the war in America was resolved and cotton began to flow once more into the port of Liverpool, they would regain the success they had known in the past eighteen months. But it would be longer than a few months. She and Mrs Underwood had discussed it. She had talked to men at the warehouse – the Hayes warehouse – and the opinion of most was that this crisis would not be resolved quickly.

Her voice was quiet but firm when she spoke. "We have to find a way to keep going until this war is over and cotton, good cotton, is available again. We've come so far . . ."

Nancy's expression became introspective as she considered just how far they had travelled in the past eight years, her memory reaching back to the three little girls who had found themselves abandoned by the woman who, though she had hardly been the kind of mother a child would choose, had, nevertheless, done her best. She recalled that squalid hovel in Angel Meadow which had been the only home they had ever known. She returned in spirit to the spinning-room in the mill where she and her sisters, though still no more than children, had performed an adult's job. Inch by slow inch they had dragged themselves, like small animals from a swamp, clawing and fighting for every fingerhold, out of the filth, out of the morass in which so many of those with whom they had lived side by side were trapped.

God, how had they done it? How had they found the strength, the will, the sheer bloody-minded determination, the nerve, to be somebody against such odds? To live decent, respectable, worthwhile lives. The hours, days, weeks, months, years they had spent learning to read and write, to find out from books how to better themselves, to feed themselves on nourishing food, to clothe themselves. They had lifted their heads and squared their shoulders and ignored the envious jeers of those about them who had not the gumption the Brody girls had. It was a bloody miracle, that's what it was; and yet, was it? A miracle implies that some being, some quirk of fate had stepped in and bestowed a magic phenomenon on three little girls, giving them a chance not afforded to others. And it had not been like that at all.

They had done it! They had made it happen. The Brody girls. No one else. They had slaved, coped, stirred themselves, planned, calculated, contrived, plotted, used cunning, resourcefulness, diplomacy – oh, yes, remember Mr Earnshaw of Earnshaw's Fine Shirts – and it had led them to this small house in a respectable neighbourhood, to the success of the factory, to her association with Hetty Underwood, to all the shadowed fantasies she had dreamed of, worked for, connived at since the day she had understood that Mam was gone for ever and the Brody girls were on their own. Was she any worse off now than she had been then? Of course she wasn't. Then she had been a child feeling her way instinctively through a maze of awesome hazards with no knowledge of how any move she might make would turn out. But she had done it. She had been lucky. She had found Jennet and Mrs Underwood and, of course, Annie and she had suceeded; her only sadness was that also on the way she had lost Rosie.

But now she was a woman. A woman of experience who, though it might take a while, would find her way back to where she had been at the beginning of the year. She would do it. She must not fall into a pit of despair. She, and the others, would do what had to be done, and she would succeed.

She sighed deeply and the others watched her, the dancing firelight playing across their anxious faces. It was dim and cosy in the small parlour with the curtains drawn. It was quiet too, for there was no traffic rattling up and down Bury New Road today. The people of Manchester, like the people in every town and city and hamlet up and down the country, were paying their last respects to the Queen's husband and the streets were deserted.

On the rug in front of the fire Scrap stretched and yawned noisily then shuffled herself into a more comfortable position. The child began to nod against Jennet's breast. A piece of coal fell into the embers of the fire with a small crash and sparks leaped up the chimney. The Dutch clock, which had been transferred from the kitchen, ticked musically and it seemed the company held its breath.

"Here's what we're going to do," Nancy announced firmly and was faintly amused when each of them relaxed and leaned back in their chairs. It was all right after all, their attitude seemed to say. Nancy would solve it as she always did, and so she would, a small but confident voice inside her said, the one that had spoken to her just after Mam disappeared.

The man behind the bar counter of the Grove Inn eyed her suspiciously as she hesitated on his threshold, for she was not the sort of woman who usually frequented his public house. The Grove Inn was a respectable place where working men, and sometimes their women, came to drink a pint of ale. A country inn of good repute for country folk but it had been known for the sons of manufacturers and even the gentry to stop, tie their thoroughbred horses to his fence post and take a glass of brandy in his bar parlour. For a bit of fun! A lark, as they called it. To mix with the lower orders, which they seemed to find diverting, and as long as they behaved themselves Sid Ainsworth did not object. Their money was as good as anybody's. They liked the food his Ginny cooked and served and he wasn't surprised, for it was the best to be had in any inn within a fifty-mile radius. Plain and nourishing and well cooked with the best ingredients to be had at Smithfield Market.

Nancy had never before been inside a beer house. Waited outside one, oh yes, many a time, looking for her mam, and had seen the men – and women – who drank and fought in such a place. Navvies and whores and local bullies, men full of ale who would take exception to the colour of another man's neckcloth, especially the Irish, or the cut of his waistcoat. Men like Mick O'Rourke who would take part in the bare-knuckle prize fights held in the yard. Places of ill-repute which the local constabulary steered well clear of.

She was pleasantly surprised by the low-ceilinged, oak-panelled bar-parlour which smelled acceptably of spirits and ale and tobacco. It was spotlessly clean, everything polished that could be polished, so that the pale winter sunshine filtering through the small, frosted, many-paned windows reflected, in brass pump handles, lamps, rows of pewter tankards, the glowing woodwork of the bar counter itself. There was a log fire of gigantic proportions roaring up the chimney like a lion on the attack and she felt a great desire to sidle up to it, for it was bitter outside. She had set off from the house cold, for already Annie had begun the stringent economies with which they were to beat this terrible time and the fire in the kitchen range had been meagre. A thick hoar frost was spread like crystals of sugar across every surface, roofs, gardens, cobblestones and even as she hurried up Bury New Road she had seen the pitiful sight of a horse drawing a hansom cab go down with a crash and a scream.

The man behind the counter was massive of shoulder though not tall. His bull neck, what there was of it, and bullet head, which was shaved almost to the bone, for what purpose she couldn't imagine, seemed to sit directly in the centre of his shoulders. His hands, which he placed threateningly on the bar top, were enormous, the size of dinner plates at the end of arms that were like young tree-trunks.

She smiled cautiously, unaware that her oddly slanted mouth, which had been held rigidly in nervous anticipation, relaxed, became fuller, softer and more appealing.

"Yes, miss?" the man said, smiling back, not quite sure how to address her, since she was not his usual kind of customer.

"Good morning," she said brightly. She had been in a quandary over what she should wear for this interview. She wished to appear decent, respectable but not *prim*. What did a barmaid wear in such circumstances? She didn't know, having seen only the slatterns who served in the beer house at the corner of Church Court, so she had decided on a plain, poppy-coloured cotton gown with short sleeves and a not too full skirt, achieved by discarding three of her starched white petticoats. The dress had been run up for her in the factory at the beginning of the summer, intended for country walks of a sunny Sunday. Over it, she supposed, she would wear an apron, but the colour suited her, bringing colour to her cheeks and highlighting her golden eyes. Her hair she had tied loosely back with a poppy-coloured velvet ribbon, leaving long, curling tendrils to drift about her neck and ears and a tumble of corkscrew curls on her forehead. She looked quite glorious, even the deep scar on her cheek giving her an air of individuality, apart from her beauty, which would catch any man's eye.

Slipping her warm cloak back from her shoulders and squaring her shoulders so that the man's eye went at once to her full breast, she stepped forward bravely.

"I heard you were lookin' for a barmaid," she lied confidently, widening her smile into what she imagined a barmaid might bestow on a customer.

"Oh aye? An' where d'yer 'ear that then?" he asked, but he was not displeased by what he was looking at.

"Oh, some lass in a public house in town. Can't remember't name." She deliberately roughened her speech, for the gentrified tones she had picked up from Jennet would not do here. It was ironic really, she had time to think. She had spent years improving her speech, cultivating the refinement of the upper classes and now here she was doing her best to revert to the way she had spoken in her childhood.

"Is that so?" He didn't believe a word but he was willing to listen.

As he spoke a short, plump little woman, who looked as though she dined all day on her own good food, came from a door at the back of the bar, a tray of golden-crusted meat pies in her arms. She was flushed, with a bead of sweat on her upper lip and her snow white cap was slighty awry. Putting the tray down with so resounding a thud all the pies jumped an inch into the air, she turned and glared at Nancy.

Here was the true "landlord" of the Grove Inn!

"What's this then?" she demanded, running her dark, shrewd eyes up and down Nancy's dress and cloak, eyeing her mass of tight curls with a distinctly disapproving air. There were several men drinking at the various small tables. Right from the start they had watched with considerable interest the entrance of the tall young woman with the unfortunate scar to her cheek, the buzz of conversation dying away so that they would not miss a word of any exchange that might take place. One chap, a farm labourer by the soil that clung to the soles of his boots, was even shushed impatiently by the others when he ventured a remark.

"This young woman's lookin' fer a job, Ginny," the landlord said mildly. "She 'eard there was one goin' 'ere."

"Did she now? Well, she were wrong, weren't she." The landlord's wife began to put the pies, piping hot and smelling delicious, out on to plates. "'Ere, Seth," she called out to a customer. "D'yer want mustard?"

The customer, the one with soil on his boots, which brought a frown to the face of the landlord's wife, at once sprang to his feet, reaching for his pie and taking the opportunity to get a good look at Nancy. His eyes lingered on her scarred face and you could see the regret in his eyes that such a bonny lass should be marred but as he took his plate, the pie on it covering it from edge to edge, she turned and smiled at him and at once he wondered what the hell he was bothered about. She was still bonny, scar and all.

"That looks good enough ter eat," she twinkled at him. She who despised all men, twinkling at one of them! If her family could see her they would be stunned but if it helped to get her a job, something to keep them going, something to hold on to until this bloody war in America was over, she'd smile and twinkle until her face ached!

The man looked bewildered for a moment, for was that not just what he was about to do then he saw the joke and laughed delightedly.

"Yer wanner try one," he said, winking at her with a wealth of meaning, then turning to beam at his open-mouthed companions. It was noticed that the landlord's wife was watching this small interplay with great interest.

"I will, if Mrs . . . Mrs . . . ?"

"Mrs Ainsworth," she offered stiffly.

"If Mrs Ainsworth'll sell me one. I've had no breakfast this morning."

But Mrs Ainsworth was not so easily taken in by a pretty face – if you overlooked the scar – and a warm smile and her stance, hands on hips, said so. Ignoring the pies she went straight into battle.

"There's no work 'ere, lass, only cleanin' an' I'm sure—"

"I'll take that, Mrs Ainsworth. I need a job. I have a child to support."

"Where's yer 'usband?"

Nancy lifted her head and dared Mrs Ainsworth to trifle with her.

"I have none."

"I see," Mrs Ainsworth smirked.

"No, you don't, Mrs Ainsworth. Ever since a man gave me this," pointing to the scar on her cheek, "I've had nowt to do with men like him. But I can be cheerful and polite to anyone who is the same with me which is all that is needed. Don't you agree, Mrs Ainsworth?"

She was telling Ginny Ainsworth that she'd have no trouble with Nancy Brody if she'd give her a chance.

Mrs Ainsworth studied her, liking what she saw, though for a different reason than her husband. The reference to the chap who had smashed her face was not lost on her. Not a husband, that was for sure, but if all the lass was going to do was scrub floors and wash pots she could surely be kept out of mischief, since there were always men who would try to coax her into it. A barmaid had to be saucy, pert, inclined to giggle, which you could see was not this woman's style, but then a scrubber of floors and a scourer of pots had no need of such accomplishments.

There was a long silence and the men at the tables found they were holding their breath.

Then, "When can you start?"

"How about now?"

"Yer'll find a bucket in't scullery and soaps on't shelf ter't right o't back door. Passage needs a good goin' over an' if yer shape, when Bella – she's barmaid – is on 'er day off, I'll try yer be'ind't bar. An' when yer've done there'll be one o' these pies keepin' 'ot for yer."

They managed, just! The lease on the factory was given up and the sewing-machines, apart from one, returned to Oldham, most of them almost paid for, which was a bitter blow since it meant they would have to start at the very beginning again when better times came. Mr Bradbury of Bradbury and Company was quite desolate, for he had taken a great liking to Miss Brody and Miss Williams, who were both ladies fallen on hard times, but he had assured them that when good times came again, which he was sure they would, he would do his best to let them have their machines back at a very reasonable price. He himself was in a similar position, for who wanted to buy or rent a sewing-machine when there was no decent material to sew on?

Those girls who were left after the closure of the factory were sadly let go to find work elsewhere, which would be hard, and most, like their families, would be on poor relief by the month's end. By the *year's* end, December 1862, half a million cotton workers in Lancashire were in the same condition: despite the fact that many "blockaders" managed to bring in thousands of bales of raw cotton, it was not enough. In Manchester and many of the cotton towns around the city, whole families were close to starving and had it not been for the good-hearted altruism of many Manchester men, mill owners who lost money every day of the week, many of them would have gone under. It was said that Edmund Hayes had lost his health and will to live as his businesses struggled to survive and had it not been for his elder son, Joshua, who had become as good a man of business as the old man, they might have lost everything they had. Despite this, young Mr Josh, as the older men still called him despite being the virtual head of the firm, and other mill owners of like mind made allowances or loans to their hands, ran soup kitchens without which many of them would have starved and did not press for cottage rents. Schools were opened for unemployed men, many a weaver gaining a decent education through the adversity of the cotton famine. Some learned shoe-making and other trades and never went back to their old jobs.

The gentry, Mrs Edmund Hayes among them, helped in the soup kitchen her son had opened and sat in classes of young girls where they were taught to sew. She formed a committee to raise a special fund to release from pawn the clothes and bedding of the distressed workers. Meetings were held in Manchester Town Hall with a view to extending loans to unemployed operatives and by the end of 1862 there was a relief committee, not only in Manchester but in almost every town in Lancashire. On reading of the plight of the mill workers financial help came from London and even from as far as the northern states of America who must have felt somewhat to blame.

The one remaining sewing-machine was installed in the parlour, the good furniture, which was held ready to pawn should it get to that, pushed back against the wall. Nancy had decided that any cloth they could manage to purchase, which was when Hayes or one of the other mills in the town had got their hands on some raw cotton, should be made up by Mary. She didn't want her sister to be wandering about Manchester searching for work, she said firmly, not adding that she thought her sister too immature, too sheltered, if you liked, to be out on her own. Mary sewed the cheap, good-quality baby clothes, the chemises and petticoats, the work shirts and vests that had been such good sellers when they had started out. It was not good enough for Hetty Underwood, who still managed to keep open her shop, but it was sold on the market stall behind which Jennet stood four days a week.

They managed, just, and each night Jennet prayed to her God that the war would soon be over, that they would all keep healthy and strong, for it only needed one of them to fall ill and the whole pack of cards would tumble about their ears. Nancy merely smiled grimly and looked at her chapped and chilblained hands which her new position in life had caused.

21

He watched her come up the stairs from behind the pillar where he was hidden from her sight, tall, slender – was she thinner than the last time he had seen her? – her back straight and graceful, her fashionably bonneted head held high. Beside her was her companion, Miss Williams, without whom she would not dream of venturing into this business world of gentlemen. She might not have been born a lady but she acted like the one she had worked so hard to become. She spoke to Miss Williams, bending her head a little, for she was six or eight inches taller and they both laughed. She looked serene, calm, composed, totally at her ease and he was not to know that her pulses raced, her heart was in her throat so that she could hardly breathe and her stomach was churning as it did every time she passed through the wide doorway of the warehouse.

In the year since the civil war in America had begun the average weekly consumption of four hundred- to five hundred-pound bales of cotton had dropped from around fifty thousand to fewer than twenty thousand but somehow Josh had managed to get his hands on a small share of it. Every week since the crisis had begun he himself had made the journey to Liverpool and the Exchange Building, along with dozens of other agents and mill owners from all over Lancashire, all with the same objective in mind. The hope was that a blockader might have slipped out of one of the ports of the cotton states of America, bringing a cargo of precious cotton to the distressed county of Lancashire. Josh had a man in Liverpool, a man paid solely for the purpose of hanging about the Liverpool docks to watch for ships, many of them steam-powered now, that carried the eagerly awaited bales of raw cotton. His vigilance had paid off and a couple of times he had managed to get hold of enough to keep his spinning mill and his weaving shed occupied on a part-time basis. Whenever more cotton was available full time production was resumed.

The cargoes of cotton, most shipped from Charleston which was the only port still unblocked by the union navy, had been steam-pressed before it left the port in order to squeeze the largest volume of cotton into the smallest possible space on the ship carrying it. The solid bales were then jammed into the hold with such force that Josh had heard the deck planking on some ships had been forced up. Even so, more were piled up on deck, three bales high, and a wall of cotton was built round the helmsman to protect him from bullets and shell splinters in the running fights that often ensued.

So was the precious cargo brought into Liverpool, the ships that carried it taking back cloth for uniforms, buttons, threads, boots, stockings, medicine, salt, paper, quinine, candles, soap, preserved meat and tea, all the goods that were in short supply in the beleaguered southern states, the rewards on these items, among others, so rich the blockader was willing to take the enormous risks to get them.

Josh had been lucky at the beginning of the month, arriving in Liverpool as a steam ship of the Hemingway Shipping Line had limped into Liverpool Bay. The bales of raw cotton she had carried had hastily been unloaded and transferred to the cotton sales room on the third floor of the Exchange Building ready for the buyers and Josh had been there among the huge crowd waiting to get their hands on it.

Cotton spins into hanks approximately eight hundred and forty yards in length and from a pound of cotton a hundred hanks can be spun. Depending on the fineness of thread required, the width of the cloth, the length of the piece, the pattern, and the speed of the loom, many thousands of yards comes from one bale of raw material. Over three million such bales had been imported in 1860. It was considerably less now! Josh had managed to procure enough bales, each containing four hundred to five hundred pounds of raw cotton, to keep his almost sixteen thousand spindles working for a fortnight at full time and the cotton yarn woven from them was at this moment being taken up to the first-floor salesroom of his warehouse where a scramble would then take place among the buyers.

He watched her hungrily, keeping well out of sight. It was almost a year since the day his mare had ridden her down in Market Street. Almost a year since his arms had held her and she had allowed it and in that year barely an hour went by when his thoughts had not drifted back to that moment. He considered himself fortunate that when he was conducting his affairs with other cotton men he had enough willpower to relegate her to the back of his mind, tearing himself apart with the hope that as time moved on it would become easier to forget her. Not if you spend your time hanging about like a besotted schoolboy for a glimpse of her, his foolish mind whispered to him, and in his quiet corner he smiled wryly to himself, for it would be easier to make the bloody rain stop at his command as miss the chance of seeing her, if only for a moment or two. God only knew what would have happened to his spinning-rooms and weaving sheds and all the processes that took place in his mill between one place and the other; to his warehouse and all the other concerns he had turned to recently had he not got a good grip on himself at such times. It might be said that his work, the long days he spent in his mill and warehouse, and his young son who was the hub of his life, were all that kept him from going mad with wanting her.

Just after Christmas his father and mother, on the advice of his father's doctor, had taken a house overlooking the sea at Lytham on the Lancashire coast. It was a pretty little fishing village, one street wide with no more than a handful of dwellings where the air was clear and wholesome. His father's lungs, ravaged by forty years of the smoke and filth that belched from Manchester's mill chimneys, spewing their foul fog over the whole city, obscuring the sky and covering every building with soot, had become so weakened that every winter his heart grew more weary as it struggled to cope with his efforts to scrape air into his diseased lungs. It was a mill worker's affliction which cared nought for a man's rank, whether he be owner or operative. The same engine fumes, the same factory smoke, the same six o'clock trek to the mill yard in the bitter depths of winter were killing him as they did them. He could barely speak at times as his exhausted lungs laboured to take another breath and so, reluctantly, he had given in to his wife's agonised pleas to spend at least the winter in the small but elegant house on the seafront at Lytham, leaving his empire, if only temporarily, he made it plain, in the hands of his son.

Their daughter, Millicent, went with them, since it would not have been deemed proper to leave a young, unmarried woman alone and unchaperoned in the company of only her brother.

It was raining, a thin drifting drizzle which misted the rooftops and partially obscured the busy traffic in a slanting pall of what looked like smoke. Pedestrains scurried along the pavements and across busy Moseley Street, jumping puddles, dangerously threatening to take out an eye with an injudicious umbrella. Those unprotected had their backs bowed, their heads bent into the rain, intent on getting wherever they were going with the greatest possible speed as though the quicker they moved the less wet they would become. The rain dripped from gutters and window ledges and the roofs of hansom cabs, forming great stretches of rainwater on the road. It sprayed up as vehicles sped through them, drenching even further those on the pavement who were not fast enough to get out of the way. There were heavily loaded waggons, drays, horse-drawn omnibuses, four-wheelers, even a curricle or two, for they were a great favourite among men about town, and as they cut through the downpour fists were shaken and the language was ripe.

At the top of the stairs he watched as she and Miss Williams paused, helping each other off with their waterproof capes, shaking their umbrellas, then smiling pleasantly at a member of his staff who hurried forward to unburden them. They seemed to think it quite normal, unaware that every man in the warehouse, from the humblest boy in the basement where the packing was done, the clerks in the offices who dealt with invoices and delivery notes, up through the floors where the sampling was done, to the senior warehouseman who was expected to supervise it all, had been charged with making the purchase of Miss Brody's cotton yarn as smoothly flowing as possible.

Keeping among the crowds of buyers, and there were a great many, he followed the two women to the sales floor where his warehouseman had stretched a great sheet of clean white cloth on the floor and placed the finished pieces across it. She and Miss Williams walked round the edge of the cloth, and he was annoyed to see that the men who had come here to snap up as much of his cotton as they could cared nought for the fact that she was a woman, a lady, and did not politely stand aside to let her through. She was a woman trespassing in their world and though most of them were accustomed to seeing her by now, if she was jostled then it was her own fault, their attitude seemed to say, and Josh could do nothing about it. His own men he could order to treat her respectfully, to make room for her where they could, to protect her from the rough bustle of the male buyers but he had no power over the buyers themselves. He wanted to stride over to where she and Miss Williams were struggling to sample a piece of fine cotton, elbowing aside the men who were attempting to do the same. To tell her to go and wait in his office where his Mrs Duckworth would fetch her and Miss Williams a dainty tray of tea or coffee, while he himself would personally fetch all the pieces she wished to purchase, have them packed and delivered to wherever she wished them to go, which he knew by previous delivery notes was her home in Bury New Road. He wanted desperately to help her, to smooth her path, for he was well aware that this cotton crisis, this cotton famine had wiped out her successfully growing business. That she had returned all her machines bar one to the manufacturer in Oldham and that somehow she was keeping her family on this fraction of cotton she bought from him and made up into garments which Miss Williams sold on the market. There was not much he didn't know about Nancy Brody. He was kept well informed by discreet men who had his ear and if she would have let him he could have made her life so much easier but he knew categorically that she would not allow it. So he did it secretly, making sure that whenever she came to his warehouse there was always something for her. That no matter how ferocious the struggle for his cotton became, she never went away empty-handed.

Even in the mêlée that was taking place over the square of white cloth and the cotton pieces that had been thrown down on it, she managed to look elegant, womanly, a lady going about her business with the least possible fuss, among the squabbling crowd who were like schoolboys fighting over a bag of sweets, or so her curling lip seemed to say. She wore a gown of dusky rose wool, the skirts wide, the bodice well fitted to her high, firm breasts. Her waist was tiny, supple and there was a thoroughbred arch to her back. Her bonnet, a marvel of dusky rose satin, ruched under its brim with cream muslin, was small and at the back of her head her hair was drawn into an intricate chignon which made her cheekbones appear higher and caused her great golden eyes to slant upwards a little at their corners like a sleek and haughty cat. The hairstyle and the small brim of the bonnet served to detract from the scar on her cheek and there were more than a few gentlemen there who made it evident that when they had finished their business they would be glad to further their acquaintance with her.

She was having some difficulty in attracting the attention of his warehouseman who was busy in the middle of some altercation with two buyers who both, apparently, wanted the same pieces. A man in a tall top hat and a rather shabby black suit was doing his best to remove from her hands the piece she had evidently decided on and, without thinking, Josh strode round the periphery of the room and, shouldering aside the two buyers who were taking up his warehouseman's time, spoke sharply to him, nodding in Miss Brody's direction.

She saw it happen and at once she became still, like a young animal that has caught the scent of danger, even allowing the man with whom she had been arguing to make off with his trophy. She straightened up and over the edge of the crowd they looked into one another's eyes and the message winged its way from one to the other.

So, it's still the same then?

Oh, yes, will it ever be any different?

No.

Dear God!

It was glorious! It was a disaster!

He was the first to recover. Tearing his gaze from hers he spoke briefly to the warehouseman, nodding in her direction but without looking at her. The warehouseman nodded and, leaving the two gentlemen staring after him in disbelief, began to make his way towards her. As she watched Josh Hayes he disappeared into the crowd.

"Miss Brody," the man said respectfully, as he reached her side. "Was yer wantin' something? I can fetch it to yer if yer care ter go an' sit on't bench by't wall. You an' the other lady. 'Ow many pieces did yer 'ave in mind?"

She wanted to run after him, push her way through this seething crowd of so-called gentlemen, grab his arm and shriek at him that she had no need of his help, no need of his charity, no need of *any* man to give her a hand with her own business. She was perfectly capable of managing her own affairs and did not want his favours, but how could she? She desperately needed this cotton to keep Mary busy on her machine in the parlour which would lead to Jennet standing behind her stall on the market where she would sell what Mary had made. Working men's shirts from the coarser, stronger fabrics, baby dresses and little nightdresses from the finer cotton. Well made and, to give them a little added something, the babywear beautifully embroidered with little motifs to appeal to a mother, done by Jennet of an evening. So she couldn't afford her pride, her rage that he should feel the need to give her preferential treatment, nor the scalding knowledge of why he did it.

Realising with intense annoyance that she was trembling, she turned away and did her best to give her attention to the confused warehouseman. She was dimly aware that Jennet was holding her arm as though to keep her steady and she found she was glad of it. She had not forgotten that strange day when he had ridden her down, lifted her up in tender arms, held her and carried her home, then vanished from her life as though what had passed between them had not happened, or if it had, he himself had forgotten it. But she had been so wrapped up in the crisis which had hit not only herself but the whole of Lancashire that she had made herself believe she had no time for the softer things in life, and certainly when they extended to a man, to men who had absolutely no part in her life.

"Nancy," Jennet whispered, "are you all right? Only everyone is looking at us. Will you not move to the bench as the warehouseman suggests and let him bring the pieces over to us?"

"I will not be beholden to him, Jennet," Nancy hissed, wishing it could be true, glaring about her at the men who, seeing her turn, all looked hastily away. It would create bad feeling now that they knew Josh Hayes was favouring her – a woman, and what might they deduce from that? – but there was nothing to be done about it now. She had her cotton and so, for a week or two, they would be safe. They had a life. The wolf was still at the door but there would be food on the table and coals for the fire. The rent would be paid and money for new boots for Kitty would be found. They managed, the four women, with what they had, wearing boots and last year's gowns, patching and darning, but the child grew so quickly, three years old already and her boots were too small for her before you could turn round from having just laced her into them. Little dresses could be let out, pieces put in, hems let down, but boots were a different proposition altogether.

"I know, dearest." Jennet's voice was soothing as she helped

Nancy to the bench just as though she were an old woman. She felt like an old woman at times. Scurrying frantically here and there, from this place to her place on her knees at the inn, from the market stall where she helped Jennet, who was not really cut out for shouting her wares, having been brought up to be quiet and retiring, then back again to the house to give Mary a hand. Life had become one long and constant tussle so that at night, though she was bone-weary, her body aching, her mind unable to switch itself off, she tossed on her bed from the moment she got into it until the moment she got out of it. She would savagely envy Mary who slept peacefully beside her, secure, she supposed, in the knowledge that she, Nancy, had it all in hand. Dear God . . . Dear God, let the war be over soon. Let the cotton come flooding in and let me forget the man who has just given me a few weeks' respite.

The rain was still falling, though in a steadier, heavier downpour as his mare walked dejectedly along Bury New Road. He bent his head to keep the rain out of his eyes but it only ran off the brim of his hat in a small waterfall so that he could barely see and down the back of his coat collar, soaking through to his shirt. He wore a waterproof cape but the water just ran off it into his boots but somehow he couldn't find the interest even to care. Jesus, what was he to do? She lived in his heart, in the pure agony of his mind and in his soul and no matter what he did he could not seem to wrench her out of it. He'd tried everything, even taking up with a certain attractive woman who lived in Cheetham Hill, the young and neglected wife of an elderly gentleman with a small engineering firm whom he had met in the way of business. He had been invited to dine and the young wife had made it perfectly clear to him that his attentions would not be unwelcome and though it had satisfied his physical needs he found it most distressing at times, just when he was about to penetrate her, to see Nancy Brody's scarred face on the insides of his closed eyelids.

He hunched even deeper into the chafing collar of his cape and so deep was his misery he did not even turn his head when he passed the small house where the woman who was in his thoughts lived. Goddammit, he would have to do something soon. He wanted more from life than a furtive hole-in-the-corner affair with a lonely and deprived woman who was the wife of another man, and though his pleasure in his boy, his love for him and the boy's love which was returned was a sweet joy to him, it was not enough. He wanted a wife, more children, a proper home, not the luxurious hotel his home had become since his mother and father left.

God almighty, he was cold and soaking wet. He wished he had taken up the gentleman's practice of carrying a hip flask of brandy with him. A good swig would put some fire in his belly and sustain him until he got home to a hot bath and a hot meal; but then why should he wait until he got home? There was the answer just across the road in the shape of the Grove Inn where he could take a glass of brandy and sit by the leaping flames of a good fire. He had taken a glass or two there before and his mare would be looked after in the landlord's stable which had been there, and still stood, since the days when the the premises had been a coaching inn.

The boy took his animal, promising to give her a rub down and a handful of oats until the gentleman came for her and to take his time since it was dry and warm in Mr Ainsworth's stable. He pocketed the sixpence Josh gave him and, whistling through his teeth, began to rub down the mare with a handful of straw.

She was on her knees, her arms bare, her back swaying, her head drooping, the brush in her hand sweeping in great arcs on the flagged floor and beside her was a bucket of hot, soapy water. She didn't look up as his feet stopped on the bit of floor she was just about to scrub, merely waiting patiently until he removed himself, for surely it was plain to any fool that he should get out of her way. Her hair had come loose from the chignon she had contrived earlier in the day and fell in a cascade of ringlets about her flushed face, and down the front of her short-sleeved blouse which was unbuttoned at the neck he could see the twin half-moons of her white breasts almost to the nipple.

"Won't be a minute, sir," a cheerful voice from the bar called out. "Some chap dropped his meat pies and there were gravy everywhere. Nancy'll be done in half a tick. 'Urry up, Nancy, there's a good lass, an' let the gentleman get by."

Still she did not look up. "Sorry, Mrs Ainsworth. I've nearly done. Sorry, sir, if you could just—"

Before she could finish the sentence and to the open-mouthed amazement of every man in the bar, the gentleman who had just come in bent down, took her by the forearms and dragged her to her feet on the slippery floor. She almost fell but he had her fast and when she looked into his face every last one of them saw the colour drain from hers.

"What the devil d'you think you're doing?" he hissed at her, his face so close to hers his saliva sprayed her.

She blinked, so amazed she seemed not to know who he was or what he was up to and so could not answer, even if she knew the meaning of his question.

"'Ere," Mrs Ainsworth said truculently. "Never mind what *she's* up to, what the 'ell's up wi' you?"

She might not have spoken.

"I asked you what you're doing here," he snarled dangerously, giving Nancy a shake that nearly had her off her feet and it was perhaps this that brought her to her senses.

"Let go of me, let *go* of me, you bastard." The fuse of her anger was lit instantly and was as furious as his, though neither of them was aware what had caused it, or if they were was not about to acknowledge it. She began to fight him, clawing to get away from his grip but his rage – was it rage or something deeper? – made him as strong as an ox and he shook her again as though she were a rag doll. The brush fell from her hand and her head lolled from side to side and the customers were mesmerised into total silence.

"What does this mean? Why in hell are you scrubbing this bloody floor?" he babbled, unable to form coherent words. "I won't have it, d'you hear. You'll come with me now."

"Take your hands off me." While from behind the bar Ginny Ainsworth unlocked her frozen mind and began yelling for her Sid.

"You're coming with me. I'll not have you working in a place like this. I presume you are working."

"Why else would I be on my knees scrubbing someone else's floor?"

"I don't know but I mean to find out. I'm taking you home."

"Let me go; *let me go.*"

But he was too far gone, too incensed, too horrified, too close to breaking down with shame and guilt and his love for her, to listen and before the fascinated gaze of the whole assembly he put his arms about her, lifted her bodily from the floor and carried her outside into the driving rain. In an instant she was wet through to the skin and so was he. He had removed his oilskin before making a dash from the stable to the bar and now the pair of them, still glued together by his determined arms, were as wet as though they had just come from a dip in the Irwell.

He drew her round the corner of the building into a patch of darkness which hid them from others but in which both could see the glitter of each other's eyes. He pressed her up against the wall, the clothing between them so plastered to their skin they might have been naked. Especially Nancy. Her breasts and the darkness of her nipples, even in the dark, were clearly visible to his ardent eyes and when her arms, which had been fighting to get herself free of him, went round his neck and clutched him to her the water in their clothing was squeezed between them, running down their bodies. He wanted her and she wanted him. It was as simple as that. Nothing else mattered, the past, the future, even the now, which meant that someone would soon come out of the inn to find out what had happened to Ginny Ainsworth's scrubbing woman. For a brief moment when both of them had no time to think about it, to consider what was important to them, they allowed themselves to rejoice in the ferocity of their gladness. Without thinking about it they allowed themselves to live, to think wholly and fully for themselves, knowing there could be nothing more wonderful anywhere in this cold world they had created, he for himself, she for herself, than the love and passion and wonder which each of their bodies generated for the other. Their mouths met, wet and slippery with rain which ran through their hair, which was plastered to their skulls, and across their faces. It filled their mouths, which were open and seeking, pouring off the gutters and on to them just as though they were standing beneath a waterfall. Heat flamed in them so that Nancy felt it would surely dry the rain that slicked her body. She was moaning with need and so was he and when his hard, wet hands went to the neck of her bodice and cupped her breasts she arched her back so that he would have easier access to them.

"Aah, my dear love . . . Nancy . . ."

"Josh, please . . ." and was she begging him to go on or to stop? Who was to say, for at that moment Sid Ainsworth lunged round the corner, almost cannoning into them, and it was over. The madness, the wonder, the flame of bewitchment had them both in a grip so tight it took several moments for them to acknowledge Sid's aggrieved presence.

"Well, call me a bloody fool but I never took yer fer a tart,

Nancy Brody, so if that's yer game yer can 'op it, fer me an' our Ginny run a respectable place 'ere."

With that he turned on his heel and disappeared round the corner.

22

They met her at the door just as they had the last time Josh Hayes brought her home. Annie, patient, enduring Annie, had an expression on her face that seemed to imply she was not surprised. Mary was wringing her hands, a habit she had when excited, and Jennet looked her usual self, anxious and loving. Mary, still a child in many ways, hopped about from foot to foot, her bright eyes going from their Nancy's face to Mr Hayes, knowing, of course, that something was up and waiting for Nancy to explain. But it seemed Annie and Jennet were curiously unamazed to see Nancy Brody and Josh Hayes arriving on the doorstep together, both in their oilskins and looking like a pair of "drowned rats", Annie was to say later. His mare was tethered to the gatepost and at once Scrap, who had run out when the door opened, began to bark hysterically at the shadowed, unfamiliar shape at the end of the path. Being almost mid-summer, it was not quite dark.

"Can't someone shut that damned dog up?" Josh said irritably as he dragged at Nancy's back towards the front door, with the evident intention of coming inside.

They had argued bitterly all the way home as he repeated stubbornly that he would see her to her front door.

"I can manage perfectly well by myself. After all it won't be the first time I have done it."

"Oh, I've no doubt about that, Miss Brody, no doubt at all." His voice was bitter. "And I can only say I am astonished that you should put yourself in such a dangerous position."

"Are you indeed? Perhaps you have heard of the saying 'the devil drives where the needs must', or something like that."

"Oh, I have indeed, but I cannot believe that—"

"If you don't believe me then there's no more to be said, so perhaps it would be as well if you got on that damned horse of yours and galloped off home. I don't need protection."

"Nevertheless, I insist."

"Mr Hayes, you have just lost me the only job I could get and where I am to get another I don't know. You are perhaps aware that there are thousands of people on relief in this city."

"Not you, Miss Brody, you can be sure of that."

"I don't know what you mean by that remark and I am not interested in an explanation, so if you would leave me alone I would be obliged."

"No doubt you would but I shall walk with you just the same."

"I am perfectly capable of—"

"Walking home alone? So you have just said but while I am with you . . ."

"You are not *with* me, Mr Hayes, so please, please, will you not just go on about your business." Her voice broke a little. "I am . . . upset . . ."

"*You* are upset? How d'you think I felt coming through that door and finding you on your knees scrubbing the bloody flags?"

"I don't know what you felt and anyway, what has it to do with you?"

"You can ask that after what has . . . taken place between us?"

"Nothing took place between us."

"Nothing! Miss Brody, if it was nothing to you, which I don't believe, then let me say it was something to me."

"You took me by surprise."

"Can I assume by that remark that any man who 'takes you by surprise' is as warmly greeted as I was?"

"No, of course not. It was just that . . ."

"Yes, Miss Brody?" But by this time they were at the gate and at the lighted window were her family, watching out for her as they always did even at this early hour. She was not expected home until after closing time and it was far from that but, still, one or the other would sit at the window looking for her, ready to welcome her, to pet her a little, to put a cup of hot tea in her hand, weak with no sugar these days, to let her see that they thought she was very brave to work in such a place.

She was terrified, enchanted, appalled, bewitched by that moment of loveliness at the side of the inn, remembering how she had wanted to take his hand as they walked side by side along Bury New Road, to lean against him sighing, to turn her face up to his to be kissed again; in other words to act like some silly, simpering female who has just been kissed for the first time. Which she had! And liked it. She had never known the rapture of touch, of a caress, of a hand on her that she welcomed, of soft kisses and fierce kisses which whirled to her head like the wine she had once drunk with Mr Bradbury when she and Jennet went to Oldham to hire their sewing-machines. The feelings had spiralled to other places as well, places she had known existed but had been innocently unaware could . . . could be aroused to such sensations. How could she explain it? even to herself. There were no words, at least she knew none, to describe how she had felt in Josh Hayes's arms, none. She had accepted a year ago when he had brought her home from Market Street that she loved him. It was a deep, quiet thing, hidden from him, kept safe and warm in her heart where it would remain until the end of her days, she supposed. She had cradled it to her, in silence, keeping it from cold and noise as one might a newborn child. It was certainly not to be talked of, or shown to others, especially not him, and now, for the space of five ecstatic minutes, she had clung to him as though he were a rock in a stormy sea, held his hard, male body as close to hers as possible, felt his need, acknowledged her own and, she was only too sadly aware, would have lain down for him in the mud and muck of the inn stable yard and let him do to her, gloried in letting him do to her what Mick O'Rourke had forced on her in St Michael's graveyard.

In the name of all that's sensible, what had come over her? After all she – and her family, remembering poor Mam – had suffered at the hands of men, how could she have allowed it? Not only allowed it but actively encouraged it, bold as brass, as the saying went. Not that she had had much choice in her forcible removal from the bar parlour of the inn. He had simply picked her up and carried her out into the downpour, but she had not cried out for help, had she? She had not turned to the other men in the bar and begged them to rescue her, had she? No, she had gone with him, not willingly, but making no objection just the same and . . . oh, dear God above, what was to become of her? Apart from losing her job and her wages, which were needed so desperately, what had she done? More to the point, what had *he* done to her?

She walked resolutely up the steps just as though she and Josh Hayes were in the habit of coming through storm and tempest in one another's company every day of the week, and into the narrow candlelit hallway. Rainwater ran down her body and dripped from every bit of her, her hair and chin and the end of her nose, her hands, the hem of her oilskin and on to the strip of carpet of which Annie, and she herself, was so proud. Others had linoleum in their hallways, scrubbed and polished, let it be said, but the Brody sisters and those who lived with them had new carpet; would it ever be the same again? she remembered thinking distractedly.

Brushing past Annie and Mary and Jennet, she strode straight along it to the kitchen where she knew there would be a fire. She was cold, so cold and wet, except for the small flame in the pit of her stomach that Josh Hayes had lit and which was the only thing keeping her from freezing to death. She wanted to get out of her wet things, perhaps have a hot bath in the tin tub before the kitchen fire, sip a soothing cup of tea and then go to bed where, she hoped to God, she might sleep. Tomorrow she would decide what she was to do. Creep back to the Grove Inn and beg forgiveness of the Ainsworths. Tell them she had been overcome, overpowered, overwrought, that she had not meant to go outside with . . . with the gentleman and if they would give her another chance she would work twice as hard and never, never look at any man. God almighty, what was she to do?

She had expected Josh Hayes to say goodnight to the others and, his duty performed, be on his way. He had done what he had said he meant to do, which was to see her to her front door, the perfect gentleman, despite what he had just done to her behind the inn, but when she turned with her back to the fire, her hands spread out behind her, there he was, tall and arrow-straight, lean and still angry by the look on his face which said he was far from finished.

"Mr Hayes, really." She could feel fresh rage welling up in her, ready to explode. Couldn't he see she was wet through, as he was, and needed to get out of her soaked clothing? What in hell's name did he want now? At his back she could see the same question in the faces of Annie, Mary and Jennet who crowded in the doorway.

"We must talk," he said abruptly. "I cannot leave until we have settled what is to be done."

"What is to be done?" She was astonished, her mouth hanging foolishly open, she knew. "About what?"

"You and me."

"*You and me?*"

"Really, Miss Brody, must you repeat everything I say? It is hard enough without you parroting—"

"Mr Hayes, you are the rudest man . . ."

"I've no doubt, but that is no excuse to avoid what has to be said."

"About what?" She had begun to shiver and at once he turned to the three women in the doorway.

"She needs to get out of these wet clothes or she will catch her death. Is there somewhere I can wait while she gets changed?"

Like three puppets whose strings are pulled by the same puppeteer the three women gestured as one towards the parlour, their faces a picture of slack-jawed consternation.

"Thank you. I'd be obliged if you would call me when she is decent."

"Now look here, Josh Hayes, I won't have my family ordered about as though they were your servants. When I am—"

"I'm sorry, ladies," bowing to the three spellbound women, "but the quicker she is changed the quicker I can get my business here done and be on my way. Now then, in here you say?"

They nodded. Then, when he had moved across the hall and into the parlour, which was unlit, they all three turned to stare in wonder at Nancy.

"Well, don't look at me like that," she snapped at them irritably. "I didn't bring him here, nor ask him in and what in God's name he wants I can't imagine."

"Can't yer, lass," Annie said enigmatically, before moving towards her and beginning to relieve her of her wet oilskin which was dripping all over her clean floor. "See, Mary, fetch some dry clothes. What? I don't know . . . that warm flannelette nightgown and her dressing-gown, the woollen one, and a pair of slippers. You, Jennet, run an' fetch two dry towels. Give one ter Mr Hayes an' then brew the tea, will yer, and set out two cups."

"Now see here, Annie Wilson, I will not be told what to do as though I were a child and if you think I'm going to sit down and calmly drink tea with that . . . that bully then you're sadly mistaken. He has just lost me my job."

"No doubt 'e 'as summat else in mind," Annie answered her mildly, stripping her of her wet skirt and bodice, rubbing her shoulders and bared breasts with the towel Jennet thrust into her hand. "Now off wi' them petticoats an' drawers."

"Annie!" Nancy was scandalised. "What if he should come in?"

"'E'll wait 'til 'e's called or 'e'll feel the flat of me 'and."

"And what did you mean, he's no doubt got something else in mind? He forces his way in here and orders everyone about as though he paid our wages and I won't have it, d'you hear?" Nancy was incensed and the funny thing was, she didn't really know why. It was nothing to do with losing her job, which was reason enough, but something else entirely; and when she was left alone to think about it she would organise it neatly in her mind as she did all her thoughts, but in the meanwhile she wished they would all leave her alone when, without losing another moment, she would see Joshua Hayes off the premises.

She was sitting in the armchair sipping her tea, her warm wrapper tied about her, her bare feet on the fender before the kitchen range fire when he was called back from the parlour by the glitter-eyed Mary who was beside herself with excitement. Annie had towelled her wet hair and it stood about her head in a cloud of damp curls, a halo of fire-bronzed loveliness. He stopped for a moment or two in the doorway, frozen to stillness by the ripe gloss of her, the radiance of her skin which Annie had rubbed with little regard for its fineness, by the gleaming amber of her eyes which slanted over her mug at him, by the slender grace of her ankles and feet, by the petal whiteness of her throat and the glimpse of the hollow below it.

"There's a cuppa tea for yer, sir," Annie told him, preparing to usher herself and the others out of the room, leaving him and Nancy to settle whatever it was he wished to settle, but he would have none of it, tearing his eyes away from Nancy to speak to her.

"No, please, Mrs . . ."

"Wilson."

"Mrs Wilson, I want you to stay, all three of you. Pour yourselves a cup of tea by all means" – just as though he were in his own drawing-room, Annie was thinking – "and then listen to what I have to say to Miss Brody. I need witnesses, you see, people who will help Miss Brody to see reason."

"Reason!" Nancy sat up indignantly then subsided hastily as her wrapper parted to reveal more of her leg than was decent. "Well, I like that. How am I to be reasonable when I have just lost my job? *You* have just lost me my job and I am staring starvation in the face. I have my family, my child . . ."

"I know that, Miss Brody." He was doing his best to be patient, a state he was not used to. "And if you will be quiet for a moment . . ."

"This is my house and I—"

"God's teeth, woman, can you not let up for a moment. Allow me to speak and then, when I have finished, it will be your turn. We will both say exactly what is in . . . what needs to be said and then, if we cannot agree I will leave and you need have nothing more to do with me."

Nothing more to do with him! She couldn't bear the thought, really she couldn't, but she was not about to let him see it. Though she had not admitted it to herself the high point of her dull and work-ridden life was the day she went to his warehouse with the secret, never-dying hope that she might see him. That somehow she might catch a glimpse of his tall, lean figure, his stern face, the way he turned his head to listen as she had seen him do in the past. The lift of his shoulders in a shrug, the movement of his hands as he made a point. God in heaven but she loved him and if he was about to say . . . what was he about to say? What was all this song and dance about? Why was he doing this – whatever it was he was doing – and why did he want the others here to see him do it?

She turned her head slowly to look into his slanted, silver grey eyes and the expression there made her heart trip and move even faster than it already was. His long, compassionate mouth curled in a small smile. He was sitting in the opposite chair, his elbows on his spread knees, his mug of tea cupped in his hands. The others were scattered about the kitchen in the shadows, on stools and the wooden bench, dark shapes that sat quietly and waited, as she did, for Josh Hayes to speak.

"Miss Brody . . . Dammit, Nancy. I may call you Nancy, mayn't I? After all this time . . ."

"Mr Hayes, I would be—"

"Call me Josh, Nancy. Say my name."

"What on earth . . ."

"Say my name."

The warmth, the feeling of exaltation, the *knowing* began

to spread through her but she could not accept it, for it went against all she had promised herself and her dead mam many years ago. But she had not bargained for Josh Hayes and the love she bore him. She was dazzled with what she could see in his face, in those grey eyes which had softened from silver to velvet.

"Josh." It was the first time she had ever spoken his christian name out loud. She chanced a small smile.

"Thank you. Now, where to begin. I suppose I had better tell you what I mean to propose. Having lost you your job I feel I must offer you some alternative."

"Alternative?"

"Yes, I have three from which you must choose and let me say that whichever one it is I will abide by your choice."

The three women who listened hardly dared stir and when the dog, who had fallen asleep at Nancy's feet, growled in a dream, they all three looked accusingly at her as though any sound might disturb the unfolding drama.

"Are you listening, Nancy?" His voice was like water flowing smoothly over a pebbled river bed, hypnotising, musical almost, soothing, getting inside her head, slipping through her veins like wine, a sweetness she wanted to sip at and yet was afraid to in case it all ran away into the cold ground.

"Yes." Her voice was so low the others barely heard it.

"Very well, here are your options. I can give you a job in my warehouse. You have a good business head and though the other clerks in the office – men, of course – might not like it you would not find it hard to manage them. You have done so all your working life from what I can see. I have watched you, from that very first time we saw each other in the mill yard when you told me in no uncertain terms exactly what you thought of me and mine. At the Arts Treasures Exhibition you were . . . I don't know . . . you stood out among the other women like a bright lamp in a roomful of cheap candles. Other times, at the ruined castle at the back of my house when I sensed your sadness over something but even then you were not about to ask for, or take if it was offered, sympathy from anyone. In fact everywhere I have looked I seem to have found you there, full of your own importance, proud of what you have achieved, meeting adversity head on and telling the rest of the world to sod off in no uncertain terms. You are a remarkable woman and I would have no qualms in putting you in charge of any business of mine. So, as I cannot do that and if you care to take it, I am offering you a clerk's job at the warehouse."

"Thank you." Her voice was coolly polite.

"You are not impressed?"

"It is better, certainly, than scrubbing floors."

"Then let me tell you of my next proposition which might be harder to accomplish but might suit your perceptions of yourself."

"Yes?"

"I will try and guarantee you a certain amount of cotton cloth every week. Enough to keep a couple of machinists busy and ensure you a small income until the crisis is over. It is not much, I'm afraid, for it will depend on my being able to obtain the raw cotton. I would also make you a loan which would get you going again and which can be paid back, with interest, of course, when things get back to normal."

She could feel her heart moving in slow but gigantic beats, conscious of the pulse of it at her wrists and neck. Her mouth was dry with some inner emotion. She sipped what was left of her tea and stared into the fire, not daring to look up at him for fear of what she might see, or not see, in his face. She loved him. She loved him and . . .

"Nancy," he said in a low voice, "I have felt you pull at me ever since that first day in the yard and on every other occasion we have met since. I know nothing about you except that you come from poor beginnings and have, by your own efforts, arrived at a decent way of life. But I have watched you, and admired you, though I would not admit it, not really, until last year when . . . when my mare ran into you in Market Street. You have never been out of my mind. I want to help you, make your way easier, more comfortable. Please let me. I cannot bear to think of you on your knees scrubbing floors, but if that is your choice then you have only to say so."

The silence in the room was unearthly. The three women in the shadows knew they were witnessing something tremendous in their Nancy's life, but not just tremendous, something moving, inspiring, touching. This man was offering her, and therefore all of them, make no mistake about that, peace and safety, warmth and a life free of worries. But more than that, though he had not said so, he was offering freely, truthfully, without reserve, even though he might be fearful of being refused, the love all women dream of from a man.

"I am willing to let you choose, Nancy. You may struggle on until good times come again. You may keep your independence which I know is dear to you and I will let you go. I promise you."

Again she was still and silent, looking into the glowing embers of the fire which Annie was about to let die out. They had to be so careful with coal. The fires of recent years when times had been good and getting better were a thing of the past. Her brain seemed to have atrophied so that she could not think, could not get past Josh Hayes's face which was imprinted, burned like a brand into her mind's eye, but he was asking a question of her and she must answer.

"And the third proposal?" Still she would not look at him.

"Is of marriage."

There was a sort of sighing, almost like a moan which eddied about the room so that even the dozing dog heard it and raised her head enquiringly, looking at the three women who had made it.

Nancy had not seen his answer coming and she gasped with the shock of it. She knew he wanted her and she wanted him. Their encounter behind the inn had shown them that, but she had thought . . . believed . . . expected . . . assumed that he was asking her, if she did not want to work for him, or take up his offer of a loan, to become his mistress. That's what gentlemen like him expected of women like her. A little house somewhere with herself installed in it, set up in style, naturally, a secret house where she would sit and wait for his visits which he would fit in whenever his business commitments allowed. A place where her natural inclination towards making things better, more worth while, which she had nourished all her life, would be stifled.

"Marriage!" Her voice was no more than a whisper and the three women leaned forward, straining to hear what was being said.

"Of course. What did you think I meant?"

"I thought . . . I . . ."

He smiled, leaning forward to lift her chin so that she was forced to look into his eyes.

"You thought I meant to take you as my mistress, didn't you? Dear God, Nancy Brody, don't you think I know you better than that? You'd go out scrubbing the flags of Piccadilly rather than be any man's mistress. You're the most stubborn, argumentative woman I have ever met and I'm sure I shall have a great deal of trouble with you, but it seems . . . it seems, Nancy, that I love you and I know you love me."

"You know no such thing," tossing her head to remove his hand from her chin.

"See what I mean." He leaned forward, grinning delightedly, and cupped her face with his hands, then bent his head and kissed her gently on the lips. "Will you marry me, Nancy Brody? Say yes, for despite what I have just said to you about giving you a choice I have no intention of letting you get away from me. And before you start pestering me on the subject of keeping your business ventures I mean to let you continue or I would never hear the end of it."

"*Let me!* I'm not sure I like the sound of that, Josh Hayes, and you've obviously thought it all out, even before this evening. I've a good mind to say no—" but his mouth came down on hers again and it was not until someone cleared their throat at the back of the kitchen that they remembered they were not alone. He stood up and drew her up with him, keeping a possessive arm about her and this time she allowed herself to lean against him, fitting her body to the shape of his, looking up into his smiling face, luxuriating in this moment of equality, for they would be equal, she knew that; of agreement, for she also knew, despite their love, there would be many times in the future when they would probably be at each other's throats, not with nuzzling kisses as now, but with hard hands and teeth. She had been too long in charge of her own destiny to bow her head to any man, even one as beloved as this. They were both strong-willed, ambitious, cunning in their determination to have what they wanted from life, at least in the world of business. She would not give up her dreams, even as Josh's wife.

They surged foward with wailing cries of joy, even the dog leaping to her feet in a frenzy of barking. They took her out of his arms and elbowed him aside as though he were the man come to sweep the chimney, he complained, but he stood it equably enough, letting them weep and kiss one another as women did at times like this.

"You approve then?" he asked Annie and was surprised when she swept him into her embrace and planted a smacking kiss on his cheek.

"Eeh, lad, if yer only knew 'ow long I've waited fer this day.

She's 'ad some bloody awful things done to 'er an' she deserves better."

"I'm sure, Mrs Wilson—"

"Annie, lad."

"Annie, and one day in the not too distant future you and I will sit down and—"

"Nay, 'tis not fer me ter tell yer what's what, Mr Hayes." Her face, for a moment, showed her disapproval, not of Nancy but of him for speaking of it, then she beamed. "But I'll say this. Yer'll do no better 'en 'er, Mr Hayes, not if yer search the 'ole o' Lancashire."

23

"I'll call for you at ten thirty. The train leaves—"

"What train?" Her tone was sharp and she pulled away from the circle of his arms. They were standing in the dimly lit hallway at Grove Place and the murmur of voices from the kitchen came to them through the half-open doorway where Annie, Mary and Jennet were clearing away the remains of the meal they had all eaten together. A shaft of suffused candlelight from the parlour, restored now that the sewing-machine had been taken away, formed a halo at the back of Nancy's head and lit her tumble of curls with soft golden streaks and Josh put his hands in it, drawing her close again. He was smiling, a narrow-eyed speculative smile she had grown to know well in the last few weeks, and it told her that he was dreaming of the day, or rather night, she supposed, when he would make her truly his wife. It made her shiver with delight, for it was something she longed for as much as he did but this was not the moment to be considering it.

"What train?" he murmured, smoothing his hands through the tangled mass of her hair. "The train to Lytham, my darling. I told you that I wanted to take you to meet my parents and—"

"But I meant to—"

At once he took his hands from her hair, putting her from him firmly, but still gripping her forearms as he gazed into her face.

"No, Nancy, no!"

"No what?"

"Hell's teeth, this conversation is becoming somewhat out of hand. Don't do this to me, Nancy."

"Do what?"

"There you go again and I know what you're going to say.

You're going to tell me you've got this or that to do. Matters concerning the shop that can't be postponed but it won't do. We are to be married in four weeks' time as soon as the banns have been called and I would like my family to be present. At the ceremony, I mean, as you would like yours. I don't fancy the idea of introducing you to them at the altar so . . ."

"Oh, Josh."

"What does that mean?"

"Well, I had hoped that . . ."

"What?" His voice became soft. "Now don't tell me Nancy Brody is afraid."

She drew away from him, slapping his hands from her arms, tossing her head imperiously, for was there anything more laughable than that Nancy Brody should be afraid of meeting Josh's parents, but . . . it was the truth, wasn't it? It was not exactly that she was afraid, but that she felt they might not exactly approve of their son's choice, especially after they had been told where she came from, which they would, of course. She had bettered herself and with her own efforts was as well educated, probably better educated, than Josh's sister who had had a governess. Thanks to Jennet she spoke in their well-modulated tones. Through her reading and the visits she and Mary and Jennet had made to the art galleries and museums in the city she had a fair degree of knowledge of art and literature and could converse about such things without shaming herself or Josh. She knew she could pass as a woman of their own class, mix perfectly well at any social function, for had not Jennet taught her all a well-bred young woman needed to know, like which knife and fork to use, the rather – she thought – odd customs and conduct that the gentry applied to their way of life, the behaviour that would be expected of her as Josh's wife. None of it had frightened her. Strewth, anyone who had ridden the runaway steeplechaser of the Brody girls' lives, suffered tragedy, poverty, indescribable hardship, brutality and the utter hopelessness – which she had throttled at birth – that was the heritage of most of Angel Meadow dwellers could cope with a little thing like becoming part of a family who had known none of these things. Besides, Josh was not landed gentry, nor was his father, or his father before him. They were manufacturers. Not of the aristocracy but of the *millocracy*, having made their fortune, not in land and the inherited wealth of their forebears but in hard work and shrewd business deals.

Still, it was a bit of a daunting task but one she knew she could not avoid. Not that she would, of course. After all, though she had an illegitimate child, so had Josh, so if his family had accepted Freddy, as it appeared they had, could they not be persuaded to accept Kitty? Not that it made any difference if they didn't. She and Josh had spent hours talking about things that had happened in their pasts. It had taken all her powers of persuasion to stop Josh from dashing from the house, leaping on his mare and riding hell for leather for Angel Meadow to pick up the trail of the man long gone now, when she had revealed how Mick O'Rourke had forced Kitty on her. He had raged for a long time, pacing the room and refusing to be tempted into her arms, not because he blamed her, as she knew many would, but because he was a man whose woman had been forced, held down like a bitch by the scruff of her neck, taken as a dog takes a bitch.

Then he had become very quiet, so quiet she had been alarmed, saying no more about it, kissing her gently at the door and riding off into the night, going, not towards Broughton but in the direction of town. He refused adamantly to say where he had gone and she had been forced to say no more.

He told her about Evie Edward whom he admitted he had seduced and who had died giving birth to their son. He still felt guilt about that, she could sense it, just as she felt guilt that she had allowed Mick to get close enough to her so that the Irishman felt justified in taking what she would not have given.

But that was all behind them. They were to start again, both of them, their love a joy and wonder to them both who had never expected to know it. They were to be a family with Josh's son and her daughter; and that was another thing: her lack of closeness to her daughter, but she would face that when it came. One hurdle at a time, Nancy Brody, and this with Josh's parents was to be the first.

"I'm not afraid, of course I'm not but I just . . ."

"Just what? We really do have to do it, sweetheart. My father's a bit of a tyrant but my mother is a very kind woman. It was she who persuaded my father to accept Freddy. Particularly after I adopted him legally which, by the way, might be a good idea with Kitty. That way we will all have the same surname."

Her heart skipped a beat then flooded with her love for this man. He was strong and often stubborn but there was a streak of sweetness in him, a tendency to be kind which he kept well hidden but it made her want to weep at times. She laid her forehead on his shoulder and his hand went to the nape of her neck under her heavy hair. He caressed it gently, putting his mouth to her ear.

"Have you the faintest idea how much I want you, Nancy Brody. All this hanging about in hallways stealing a hurried kiss while Annie's not looking is not doing my . . . er . . . manhood any good. Why don't we . . ."

"No, Josh." Her voice was muffled against his chest but her arms slipped round his back and her hands clung together in a vice-like grip. She could feel his body tremble a little and her own responded but, for some reason, probably to do with the way things had happened in their pasts, they had both agreed they would wait until they were married until . . . well, until they . . . but, Jesus God, it was hard. She knew that if the women weren't in the kitchen she would take him up to her room right this minute, no matter what they had agreed, and strip him and herself down to their nakedness, the smooth-skinned warmth, the feel of male flesh against female and give in to the scalding need that bedevilled them both. Ever since that night behind the inn when his hands had cupped her breasts she had wanted it again and again and, sometimes, when they lost their self-control, both of them together, it had almost happened and she had been alarmed by the fierceness of her passion. She had believed with all her heart that she had no . . . sensuality – was that the word? – after what Mick had done to her; that no man would ever arouse her body from its slumber but, by God, Josh Hayes had done it and if it was not satisfied soon she would go mad with it.

"Darling . . . my darling," he mumbled into her hair. "If you don't leave me alone I swear I'll throw you to the ground, lift your very pretty skirt and have my wicked way with you."

"And at this moment I'd let you."

He groaned and at the kitchen door Annie coughed dramatically to let them know she was coming through. They leaped apart, their faces flushed, their breathing hard, both of them fiddling with this and that as they straightened their clothing.

"T'sooner you two're wed the better," she said disapprovingly.

"You never spoke a truer word, Annie. So, tomorrow we are to visit my mother and father in Lytham and introduce them to the bride."

* * *

The journey took them an hour and a half to Preston and then on to Kirkham where they changed on to the branch line which took them to Wrea Green and Moss Side and then to the imposing railway station at Lytham. The first-class fare cost them nine shillings. Lytham, besides being a fishing village, was what was now called a sea-bathing resort and as they strolled arm-in-arm, it being a fine and sunny day, along the seafront in the direction of the house that Mr and Mrs Hayes had rented, there were bathing huts, drawn there by sturdy horses, taking bathers down to the gliding, blue-grey waters of the estuary. The sun caught the ripples formed by passing sailing ships going up to the docks, gilding them to a dazzling silver and gold. Ladies sat in deckchairs, trussed up in their elaborate gowns and bonnets, protected from the sunshine by dainty parasols. Gentlemen strolled about, dressed just as formally, taking their midday exercise, and little girls ran and swooped and bowled hoops despite the confines of their wide, flounced skirts, frilled pantaloons and large-brimmed bonnets. The boys fared better, for it was the fashion to copy the sailor suits and sailor hats worn by the Queen's sons which were less formal and therefore more adaptable for the games dear to the heart of a boy. Kites sailed the sky, dragging long coloured tails, borne on the salt breeze that came off the estuary. It was a charming scene, blue and white and gold where the sky and the sun and the sands merged into a warm summer haze and though she was increasingly tense – not nervous, oh, never nervous – Nancy breathed deep of the air, the like of which she had never known before. She had lived beneath grey-brown smoke spewed forth from a hundred mill chimneys, drawn its noxious fumes, unnoticed, into her lungs so that this was like drinking pure, spring water after a daily diet of the stagnant stuff that gathered in the alleyways of Angel Meadow and the like. It had a tang of sea-spray in it which was headier, she thought, than wine, and she had become more used to that in the last few weeks.

The house was set in its own gardens, surrounded by walls built of pebbles and well-grown wych elm trees planted when the house was built, moving now towards their full burnished autumn leaf. They had walked from the station, since it was not far and the weather was clement, and as Josh opened the gate for her, a small wrought-iron gate set beside the wide one which was closed expect when the carriage passed through, Nancy caught a glimpse of the house through the trees. It was not big, not by the standards of Riverside House which Nancy had glimpsed from the water meadow behind it, but it was sturdy, well built from the dark red brick which was predominant in the area, the walls decorated in pleasing patterns with the pebblestones that formed the surrounding walls. A "holiday cottage" Josh had described it as, which was probably how people like the Hayes thought of it, she supposed wonderingly, being accustomed to the grandeur of their home in Higher Broughton. There was a terrace with steps leading down to a wide lawn bordered with ribbons of bright flowers, and in basket chairs on the grass an elderly lady and gentleman were drinking from delicate china cups, waited on by a pretty, white-aproned and be-capped maidservant. In a third chair sat a young woman who was obviously Josh's sister. She had his colouring, his eyes and mouth, but what in Josh was attractive was too heavy for female features. She had his high forehead, his dark brows shadowing eyes that were heavy-lidded, narrow and a pearly grey, a strong chin that was markedly cleft and even the beginning of lines at each side of her mouth. The way she held her head was proud, stiff-necked, again like Josh, but there was a lack of humour in her which was so marked in Josh.

Nancy knew she looked her best. She wore an elegant day dress of cinnamon-coloured silk with full white undersleeves, the colours repeated in her "chip" bonnet which was lined under its brim with white ruched muslin and decorated with a flowing knot of ribbons of cinnamon-coloured velvet. The skirt of the gown, which measured a full six yards round the hem, was held out by her crinoline. Her cream kid boots, new and the first she had ever had that were not a sensible black, peeped from beneath it as Josh led her across the lawn.

"Josh, dearest, at last," the elderly lady called out. "We did not know what time to expect you so we have had lunch. Could you not have said which train you were to take? Really, dear, we are not mind-readers, though I suppose I should expect nothing else from you. I know you mean well but you are so—"

"Never mind that, Emma." The elderly gentleman interrupted her gentle rebuking flow of words. "He is here now and I suppose we should be glad of that." The shadowed sunlight that fell through the leaves of the tree beneath which the party sat was not kind to him. Not very long ago Edmund Hayes had been a rotund gentleman with a high colour. Now his face had slipped away into folds of slack, putty-coloured flesh, his eyes, which were heavy-lidded like Josh's, were underscored with shadow and even his grey moustache drooped sadly about his thin-lipped mouth.

"Yes, I'm sorry if you were expecting us for lunch but the first-class train did not run until eleven fifteen so . . . But please, let me introduce Miss Brody to you. Mother, this is Miss Nancy Brody. Nancy, my mother and father and sister, Millicent."

"Mrs Hayes, Mr Hayes, Miss Hayes." She smiled just as Jennet had said she should. No more. There was a polite bend of the head from both Mrs Hayes and Millicent, though Mr Hayes continued to stare suspiciously, or so Nancy thought, up into her face.

"Miss Brody, do sit down and perhaps you might care for a cup of tea. You must be thirsty after your journey." Just as though they had come from some far-flung corner of the world. "See, Primrose, get Madge to help you fetch out some more chairs and bring fresh tea. Or might you prefer coffee, Miss Brody?"

"Tea would be lovely, thank you, Mrs Hayes." She sat down in the basket chair the maid placed for her beside Mrs Hayes, smiling to herself as the girl, Primrose, sketched a polite curtsey, thinking to herself the maid was possibly a shade better bred than she was herself.

"This is a lovely house, Mrs Hayes," she ventured, after sipping her tea for a moment. "The garden and the proximity of the sea and sands, and I must admit to finding the air quite wonderful after what we are forced to breathe in Manchester."

"Indeed, Miss Brody. Your home is in Manchester then?"

"Oh, yes, I was born and bred there."

"Mother, before you begin to grill Nancy . . . Miss Brody, there is something you should know, all of you." Josh looked round the faces of his family, his mother's enquiring, his father's narrow-eyed and watchful, his sister's openly hostile for some reason. He leaned forward and took Nancy's hands between his own and Nancy knew that really, after that gesture, there was no need for him to say another word. He was looking into her eyes with that look of loving tenderness and desire that no one could mistake. The way a man looks at the woman who is the centre of his world, the core of his heart, his strength and saviour. She knew, for she recognised it in herself. Love was something that must grow slowly and sweetly, so it was said, and so it was with Josh and herself. All the years between their meeting in the mill yard and that moment behind the Grove Inn it had been growing, barely recognised, some gentle force that had drawn them together against all the forces of their different backgrounds and their circumstances which, though dissimilar, were strangely alike.

"I . . . we, that is, have come to tell you that we – Miss Brody and I – are to be married in four weeks' time. I meant to let you get to know her a bit before I said anything but . . . well, I find I cannot keep it to myself." His boyish enthusiasm was disarming, but it seemed they were not disarmed; at least Mr Hayes and Miss Hayes weren't, though Mrs Hayes was ready to smile and lift a wisp of lace handkerchief to her eyes if her husband would allow it.

"Oh dear," she said tearfully.

"Well, this is a pretty kettle of fish," Mr Hayes said stonily.

"This is rather sudden," Miss Hayes said suspiciously.

"No, it isn't, Milly. Nancy and I have known each other a long time, years, but it was only recently that we—"

"A long time? Where did you meet? We have never heard of Miss Brody, or any Brodys, have we, Mother?"

"No, dear, I don't think so. Brody? Do you know the Brodys, dear?" turning to her husband.

"You would not know my family, Mrs Hayes," Nancy began, lifting her head a little higher and straightening the aristocratic curve of her back and beside her Josh sighed and, though he still held her hand, for he meant her to know he would support her in anything she wanted to say, he leaned back in his chair with an air of resignation.

"Our circle of friends is very wide, isn't it, dear, but I can't remember any by the name of Brody." Emma Hayes did her best to fill the hostile quiet that had come about and that even she sensed but her voice tapered off gently into a whisper and she put her handkerchief to her mouth.

"No, Mrs Hayes, I don't suppose you will have." Nancy's voice was gentle. She was no longer nervous, if she ever had been. She wanted more than anything for Josh's family to accept her, not for her own sake but for his. She did not care one way or the other if his mother's friends did not care to drink tea with her, an activity she had heard they favoured on most afternoons, having nothing better to do, she supposed. She would not have time for it, anyway, since her new venture would take up all her time, but her heart was heavy at the thought that there might be a split between Josh and his family because of her. Josh was hoping that after they were married an apartment at Riverside House might be made available to them, a prospect that dismayed her, but as the house would be his when his father died he seemed to see no reason why they should not live in it at once. It was certainly big enough from what he had told her, with bedrooms by the score, parlours and drawing-rooms, studies and libraries, breakfast-rooms and dining-rooms and a whole floor of nurseries, with more than a dozen indoor servants and half a dozen outside to look after three people, four if you counted Freddy. His brother Arthur, who was on a walking tour with some school friends in Europe, was to take up his duties at Monarch Mill as soon as he returned and would live at home, which seemed to Nancy to be more than a houseful, especially with two small children.

"Perhaps you would care to tell us something about your people, Miss Brody," Millicent Hayes declared coolly, already sensing that Nancy's "people" would not be their sort of people, getting ready to enjoy Nancy's embarrassment. Nancy smiled.

"Of course, Miss Hayes."

"Darling . . ." Josh warned, but she turned to smile at him.

"I can only speak the truth, Josh. Would you have me lie?"

He relaxed and smiled lovingly at her and his mother, who was watching closely, smiled too, letting out her breath on a small sigh. Her son loved this woman, whoever she was, and that was enough for her.

"Go on, Miss Brody," Edmund Hayes told her, his voice stern, but there was something in his eyes that reminded Nancy of Josh and it gave her courage.

"I was born in Angel Meadow, Mr Hayes. You will have heard of it, I'm sure."

Though he winced, Edmund Hayes's gaze was steady.

"I have, lass."

"My mother left us when I was about nine years old."

"Us?"

"I have two sisters younger than me."

"And your father?"

"I knew of no father, sir."

"Oh, dear," Mrs Hayes whispered, feeling for her handkerchief.

"So, what did you do, Miss Brody?" Millicent Hayes's voice had a sneer in it, for what else could three young children do but apply to the workhouse.

"I found us work, Miss Hayes. In your father's mill. I was put on a spinning frame with no experience of how the thing worked but I learned, oh, I soon learned, Miss Hayes. My sisters were taken on as a scavenger and a piecer and between us we managed to pay our rent and feed and clothe ourselves, though it was damned hard . . . begging your pardon, Mrs Hayes."

She felt Josh's hands grip hers, warm and strong and comforting. He had heard it all on the night he had asked her to marry him, for she would not agree until he knew everything about her. His grip told her she was amazing, that he loved her and that he was proud of her and whatever his parents decided he and she would be married in four weeks' time. She turned and her eyes were a pure gold, deep and filled with her love, so that none of the three watching could doubt her feelings.

She turned back to them. "I took my sisters to Sunday school where we learned to read and write. We spent any spare time we had at the Manchester Free Library at Campfield, reading the newspapers and periodicals and became members of the library so that we might bring books home with us. We became different people and because of it we were scorned by our neighbours. I swore that I would get us out of Church Court, that I would make my family decent and respectable. I was determined to . . . to *be* somebody. Oh, not famous but worthy of the regard and respect of any man or woman in Manchester. And I have," she finished simply.

"How, lass?" Mr Hayes wanted to know.

"I began my own business. We saved hard and did without, my sisters and me. We learned machine sewing and when we were able we hired sewing-machines and began to make garments, baby clothes, shirts, things like that. I had a stall on the market and sold to decent shops in Market Street and Deansgate. We did well. We expanded. We moved out of Angel Meadow and rented a house on Bury New Road on the corner of Broughton Lane. Then . . . then the American civil war began and we . . . Mr Hayes, you will know what happened to our supply of cotton."

"Aye, I do that, so what . . ."

"Josh let us have as much as he could." Again she turned to Josh, giving him her dazzling, loving smile. "We were . . . we were not really acquainted then," meaning they were not in the state they were now, "but he did his best to keep my one remaining machine working. I could not have managed without him."

"No, I can see that," Millicent Hayes drawled nastily and at once Nancy turned on her, cementing the first brick in the wall that was always to stand between them.

"I had no more cloth than any other manufacturer, Miss Hayes, and certainly not enough to keep four women and a child."

"A child?"

"Yes, I have a daughter. I was forced to take work as a scrubber of floors to support her, while my sister and the lady who befriended us, my partner, in fact, worked to keep food on the table. Then Josh and I—"

"And your husband? The child's father? Where is he? Dead, I presume or . . ." Millicent broke in, determined to extract every nasty and debased exploit she was sure the woman who hoped to marry her brother had got up to.

"I have no husband, as I am sure my use of the title 'Miss' tells you."

"Then . . ."

"My daughter has no father. He – the man – left me."

"And did he give you that scar you carry on your cheek?"

Josh exploded with such force from his chair even Nancy, who had been expecting it, almost jumped out of her skin. Mrs Hayes squeaked in alarm and Mr Hayes sighed loudly.

"Now then, lad."

"No, Father, I will not sit idly by while my sister insults the woman I am to marry. You might as well know that whatever comes of this visit, whether you accept her or not, I shall marry Nancy Brody. She is the bravest, most courageous woman I have ever met and I love her *and* may I say I consider myself lucky that she loves me. The banns are being called at St John's Church and I have sent invitations to every person of our – what was the phrase you used, Mother? – our wide circle of friends. This is to be no hole-in-the-corner affair, believe me. I want the world to see the woman I am to marry."

"Josh, darling, it's all right, really. There is no need to give us all the rounds of the kitchen," Nancy declared mildly.

"Oh, yes there is. They must be made to see how much you mean to me."

"I think they might by now."

"Good, then that's settled then." He glared about him, his lean face hawk-like in his rage. "And you might as well know that when we are married Nancy is to start up again in a business of her own. She is not the sort of woman to sit at home and twiddle her bloody thumbs."

"Joshua, that is enough, my lad. I will have no language of that sort spoken in front of your mother."

"I'm sorry, Mother, but I really—"

"We know, lad. I think we've got the picture. Now, shall we ask Primrose to bring us another tray of tea? *No*, you sit down and button your lip, Millicent Hayes," to his daughter who, it seemed, had more she wished to say. "I want to ask this young lady a few more questions."

Though his face was set in a mould of stern, unbending resolution, there was a gleam in Edmund Hayes's sunken eyes that appeared to say he might just take a fancy to this woman who was to be his daughter-in-law. She had spunk and Edmund Hayes was an admirer of spunk.

24

She wasn't a fanciful woman. Life had knocked that out of her years ago. Even as a child in her mam's careless charge she had been practical, seeing things as they were and not as she fancied they could be, facing up to whatever the world chucked at her, and it was usually something nasty, something that would have knocked a fully grown woman to the ground, let alone a child. And if it knocked her down then she bit her lip, rubbed her bruised knees and the scraped palms of her hands, and got up again. She had suffered and survived, but now she had come through, and brought her family through with her, she could not truly believe that such happiness, such luck, such a haven of refuge she had found with Josh could really be hers. Could it be real, could it last, this great good fortune, this knowing that she was totally and limitlessly loved by this good man?

She had had great reservations that he would be able to persuade his family to accept her but it appeared that he had done so, even if they had agreed only reluctantly. His mother was so sweet-natured, so protected from life's calamities she believed nothing but good could come of the love her son had found, despite the small irregularity of his bride-to-be's past. His father, surprisingly, seemed to have seen something to admire in a woman who had achieved what Nancy had achieved, recognising, perhaps, a likeness to his own family's beginnings decades ago. Josh had told her that his grandfather had been a simple handloom weaver who had had the vision and intelligence to know what the new power looms would mean and his foresight was to start the upward spiral of the Hayes family fortune.

Nancy was only too well aware that Millicent Hayes would not be so accommodating! She had made it plain right from the start that she was not ready to make Nancy's life as wife to her brother an easy one. If she could cause trouble, she would, Nancy knew and though in those few weeks before the wedding she did nothing, as far as Nancy knew, to put a spoke in the wheel, which was running smoothly, she did not fool herself that this would continue.

In the weeks before the wedding Mrs Hayes, having taken to her son's future bride, wished to introduce her and her family to her own dear friends who she was certain would feel the same way about her, but Nancy, being far too busy, she told Josh privately, with her new business, persuaded him to convince his mother to wait until they were married. She and Josh's father, accompanied by an enthusiastic Millicent who could not wait to see her brother's intended wife snubbed by all and sundry, had come home from Lytham and settled back at Riverside House. Mrs Hayes had wanted to send out invitations to those of her friends she wished to meet Nancy, those who were already bewildered by Josh's wedding invitation, for who was this "Miss Nancy Brody" he was to marry? Like Mrs Hayes before them they had enquired of one another the history of a family called Brody, which sounded Irish to them, so was she some heiress from across the Irish Sea and, if so, where had Josh Hayes met her? It was a mystery, an exciting enigma and one which none of them would dream of missing and not one had refused his invitation to the wedding. Ever since Josh Hayes had adopted his own illegitimate son, and not only that but appeared to be exceedingly fond of him, they had wondered what kind of young lady would accept not only the boy, but a father with such strange ideas!

Dinner parties were therefore to be arranged to take place after they were married and for the first time since they had met four and half years ago Jennet and Nancy quarrelled.

"Well, I suppose we'd best get down to the dressmaker and order our dinner gowns," she told Mary and Jennet. "Though I don't suppose I shall need more than one in Lytham" – where she and Josh were to spend a few days after their wedding – "I shall, from all that Josh tells me, have to have several for later and so will you and Mary."

This was the most wonderful opportunity for her sister and one she had always hoped for, not visualising anything quite so grand, perhaps, but where Mary might meet a man, a gentleman, who would measure up to the sweet-natured and well-educated young woman Nancy had made of her. She deserved a chance and though Mary was terrified of it she was also excited at the idea of moving in the society from which Josh came. But if his family was as kind to her as he was then she knew she had nothing to fear. She was shy, but then Nancy had told her that shyness was considered to be a charming attribute among young ladies and she would do very well. Mary was seventeen or thereabouts, as far as Nancy could remember, and ready for marriage by the standards of those with whom she would mix. It was very unlikely that she would talk about their past and by the time the wedding was over everyone would know anyway, for Nancy had no intention of hiding where her roots were, nor how she had torn them up and transplanted them in sweeter soil. When she moved to Riverside House she would do all in her power to find a suitable husband for her sister, someone who would look after her, protect her, care for her as, she sadly admitted, had not been the case with Rosie.

She often thought of Rosie in those days before her wedding, brooding on where she could have got to. It was over two years since that appalling day when she had found her sister in the arms of the man who had brought Nancy down and by now, she was certain, Rosie would have a couple of children at her skirts, perhaps another growing in her body, for women like her had no choice in the matter. Was she still with Mick O'Rourke or, as seemed more likely, had he deserted her, for a man on his own can go much further than one with a woman and children at his back? Though she had told no one except Annie, who had found a woman who was willing to help her, a woman who would cause no curiosity in Angel Meadow, she had had enquiries made of the folk in Church Court on the whereabouts of Mick O'Rourke's "woman". Annie's friend had met with blank stares, shrugs of the shoulders and a shaking of the head, even a mouthful of abuse from Eileen O'Rourke, who missed her son and blamed the bloody Brody girls, she hissed venomously, for his disappearance. Nancy had no idea what she would have done if she had found Rosie, for her sister had made it plain she wanted nothing to do with her, but surely she could have made Rosie's life a bit easier, for there was no doubt in Nancy's mind that it would be very, very hard indeed with no one but Mick O'Rourke to support her.

The quarrel with Jennet began, as quarrels do, over a chance remark of Nancy's.

"Now, Jennet, my love, there is one of us who will have no need to feel out of place in the charmed circle of the Hayes acquaintances, for you are as well bred as any of them." She put her arms about Jennet's shoulders and gave her an affectionate hug.

"There will be no need of anything, Nancy, not even a new gown, for I'm not to come."

Jennet was seated before the parlour fire sewing a little dress for Kitty, a pretty thing of fine muslin, tucked and ruched and embroidered, white on white with a pale pink satin sash, which she was to wear on Sunday when she was to be taken to Riverside House for afternoon tea in the nursery with Freddy. Nancy was to inspect the rooms she and Josh were to occupy, which Josh had told her consisted of a large bedroom with adjoining bathroom, a sitting room that she could, if she wished, decorate to her own taste, and a small room that was to be turned into a dining-room where they might, as a newly married couple, dine *à deux* when they wished. All the rooms were on the first floor overlooking the gardens at the back of the house, the water meadows and the river, and where they might be completely private.

Now, as Jennet spoke, Nancy, who had been just about to leave the room, whirled round in astonishment.

"I beg your pardon?"

"I'm not to come to Mrs Hayes's dinner parties, darling. You might as well know now, I suppose, but if you had any intention of introducing me to Josh's family and friends then I must ask you to forget it. I would be out of place in such a society and—"

"You? Out of place! What bloody nonsense! I never heard anything so daft in all my life. Why, you *come* from their class. You, of all people, should feel at home in it. And besides, I need you."

"Why?"

"To guide me through it. To show me the way."

"Fiddlesticks! When did Nancy Brody ever need anyone to show her the way? You'll sail through it. Even if they turn their noses up at you, which they might at first, you will only stick yours higher and tell them to go to the devil. You love a challenge, Nancy. A fight! But I don't. I am content in this little house and with the work we do. I shall be only too happy to help you with the shop when it opens, but the rest of your life, with Josh, is . . . should not include me. I know you are hoping to further Mary's chances, find her a good husband and that is as it should be. She is your sister, but I'm not and I don't want a husband. I find the life I have here suits me admirably."

"Well, Jennet Williams, I never thought to see you so ungrateful. After all we have done together as well."

"What has that to do with anything? We shall continue to be together in our professional life. I shall come and take tea with the new Mrs Josh Hayes at Riverside and hope she will visit me in Grove Place but, as for the rest, I'm sorry, Nancy, I can't."

"You have disappointed me, Jennet. I imagined us sharing . . . well, not my married life, obviously, but the social side of it. I would have been glad of your support."

"You will have your husband's support and I shall always be here, with Annie and . . . and Mary, I suppose. When you are married you do not intend taking her to Riverside House, I presume."

"No, of course not, but I intend including her in . . . in whatever they do there. I want her to mix with young people: Josh's brother and his friends."

"Exactly."

"What does that mean?"

"I am not a girl, Nancy. I shall be twenty-four next birthday and have long since given up any idea of a husband and children, that's if I ever had any, which I don't believe I did. I am a spinster, one of life's natural spinsters. I do not care for . . . for parties and such and though I shall be quite happy remaining your friend, indeed it would break my heart if . . . if we lost one another, I shall stay here."

They had argued for an hour, silencing Annie and Mary in the kitchen to an appalled stillness, and even Kitty, sensing trouble, crept fearfully on to Annie's comfortable lap, her refuge when she was upset.

But nothing Nancy could say to her would change Jennet's mind and she had to be satisfied with it. This had taken place on the day Josh had informed her that his mother was eager to introduce her to her dear friends, adding that she was not to be nervous, for his mother had quite taken to her and his father approved of her, not, she suspected, as a wife for his son but because she had refused to let life grind her down.

"I am not nervous, Josh," she had interrupted him quietly, "and though I don't wish to upset you or your family I'll tell you why."

"Yes?"

"Though I'm sure your mother and I, and your father, I think, will get on, I don't really care about anyone else. Your mother's friends will not be a part of my life, *our* life, d'you see, and so whether they approve or not means nothing to me."

The expression of tender concern on Josh's face turned to one of frowning disapproval and she knew she had offended him. It meant more than she knew to Josh Hayes that the woman he loved should be accepted, that she should become a part of his world, his mother's world and though he had assured her, and believed he meant it, that she should continue with her career, in his male mind and heart and perception of what a woman of his mother's, and therefore his wife's life should be, he fondly visualised afternoon calls, carriage drives, functions at which Nancy would shine as brilliantly as the moon on a cloudless navy blue sky, and lastly, children, which would lead her irrevocably to a life in her own home, his home. Jennet and Mary would be there to run her business, or *businesses*, as she insisted it would be in a few years' time. He still hoped for this but if she was not to do her best to please his mother's friends then the changeover would be that much more difficult.

He was wise enough not to pursue the conversation, believing, as men do, that when they were man and wife she would change her mind.

They were married on a cool, clear day in September. Nancy felt an almost enchanted need to start this day with as little haste as possible, to gaze about her, to take in deep breaths of the sweet, scented air that drifted from the nursery gardens at the back of Grove Place. She watched with delight as long-tailed swallows moved in sweeping flight across the pale sky and listened almost painfully as a blackbird sang its heart out from the cover of Mrs Denby's sweet chestnut tree. She smiled serenely, knowing a great tranquillity of heart as Jennet helped her into the Hayes' carriage.

Mrs Denby next door and her John had been invited, as good friends and neighbours of Annie's, not only to the wedding but to the reception at Riverside House, much to Mrs Denby's gratification and had already departed, but the rest of Grove

Place was out in force to wave her off, their wide-smiling faces avid with curiosity. The eyes of the women drank in every detail of her gown which, she was well aware, they would be whispering to one another had cost a fortune, but then, they would tell one another, she was marrying a wealthy man to whom a few guineas meant nothing. They didn't begrudge her, not a bit of it, they would say, but when you remembered where she had come from, since they all knew by now, it was like a miracle, wasn't it?

Jennet, neatly and faultlessly dressed in her new gown, which she had reluctantly allowed Nancy's husband-to-be to give her as a gift, sat beside her in the carriage. It was as though this special day had given Nancy a clear-sighted vision, not just of the specialness of the day but of everything on which her gaze fell. She was acutely aware of the hedges lining Bury New Road which were full of berries, hips and haws, elderberries and blackberries, all scattered among the bright crimson of bittersweet. Of the horse chestnut trees and the mighty oaks under which the carriage passed and which bore a plentiful crop of chestnuts and acorns. The neatly enclosed fields beyond the hedges dazzled her eye, still carpeted with the brilliant yellow of corn marigolds mixed with the deep scarlet of poppy. It was as though some benign being had laid a hand on this, her wedding day, making it almost unbearably beautiful, a setting in which her love for Josh Hayes, to be consecrated and consummated this day, was in its proper place at last.

St John the Evangelist Church stood at the rear of a row of houses on Bury New Road, reached by a narrow lane beside the parsonage. The lane was lined with sightseers, those who can't resist a wedding, come to get a glimpse of the bride-to-be, standing shoulder to shoulder in the shade of the very old yew trees which are commonplace in country churchyards, no doubt due to their handiness when the yew foliage was cut as "palm" for Palm Sunday.

She knew she looked well. She had chosen not to wear a heavy satin or silk, which was the fashion, but had decided on a diaphanous, foaming tulle, a waterfall of flounces, each one laid delicately over the one beneath, the skirt held out by a crinoline so wide she wondered if she would get it through the church door. Each flounce was edged with narrow white satin ribbon. The bodice was plain with a high, ruffled neckline, on which her chin rested, the sleeves close-fitted. Everything white, no colour except in her bouquet. Defiantly virginal, she supposed was how she thought of herself though she was no virgin. Could the victim of rape, one who had borne a child from that rape, be considered innocent? she had agonised to Jennet, who, knowing there was not a more innocent, untouched woman in Manchester, a better and more honest woman, had told her stoutly that she could. Every woman deserved her wedding day and if this was what Nancy wanted, then begger the rest, she added.

On her abundant hair, coiled low on her neck, was a small crown of orange blossom. Her misted veil fell to her breast at the front but floated to her heels at the back. She carried pale, apricot carnations and white rosebuds. Her white satin slippers had a heel so high that when she reached her bridegroom at the altar, having walked entirely alone up the aisle, to the amazement of the congregation, for surely every girl has some male relative to give her away, she was no more than an inch or two shorter than he was. She thought of herself as looking her best. She was not to know that she looked quite exquisite, breakable and yet, at the same time, strong and durable, a worthy mate for any lusty man, or so many a lusty man in the congregation believed! Josh had turned to watch her come up the aisle, waiting for her, holding out his hands for her in his loving eagerness to have her at his side. He was ready to kiss her, then and there, his manner saying to hell with the convention, but she shook her head a little, watching as his shoulders rose in a rueful shrug. They continued to smile at one another, much to the consternation of the parson, who liked his brides to be shy with downcast eyes and his grooms to be nervous, her flowers discarded on the steps of the altar. The ceremony begun, there was a ripple of consternation – for was it legal? – when, looking round him in bewilderment, the parson asked the question, "Who giveth this woman?" and the bride spoke up with words none of them would ever forget.

"I do. I give myself right gladly!" which Nancy had thought appropriate and Josh an incredible act of bravery.

His mother wept out loud into her handkerchief and several women on *her* side of the church were seen to wipe away sentimental tears. They were ordinary women, plainly and decently dressed but working-class women, the ladies on *his* side were inclined to think, so where had they come from and why? They knew as little about the bride as they had done when they received their astonishing invitations, so who were they and where was her family?

They themselves were fashionably, even extravagantly dressed, for this was the wedding day of the son of one of the wealthiest and influential of Manchester Men, whose wife was their dear friend. Despite the peculiarities of Joshua Hayes's domestic arrangements, which was how they referred to the small boy in the nursery at Riverside House, many of the ladies had nurtured hopes that one of their daughters might catch his eye, for Josh Hayes was an exceedingly eligible bachelor. They had been disappointed!

They stole glances at the other side of the aisle where the pews' occupants in turn stole glances at them, overawed, dumbstruck, eyes out on sticks, mouths agape. Just three were suitably dressed for what might be termed a "society" wedding, one of whom was obviously the sister of the bride. She wore a misted shade of ivory, a simple and beautifully cut gown of plain silk with a wide sash in the palest duck-egg blue, eminently suitable for a girl of her age and for the occasion. Her ivory, wide-brimmed hat, which was tipped forward over her brow, had a low crown and broad ribbons tied under the chin to match her sash. She looked charming, with downcast, dewy eyes in a face as lovely as a flower. Beside her stood a small, plain young lady, dressed soberly in dove grey and white, perhaps her governess, they surmised. Next to her was an elderly woman dressed in good quality black who could only be the Miss Brodys' childhood nanny, and on her other side a stately, handsome, well-dressed lady of mature years. Was she Miss Brody's mother, though there was no resemblance, or perhaps an aunt? She was evidently not without money, so it seemed to them that Miss Brody must have come from a well-endowed family.

They had it all worked out to their own satisfaction before they had even left the church!

Nancy remembered the day in fragments. Snatches put together in her memory that did not form a whole, like a jigsaw puzzle that has pieces missing. Through it all Josh's lean, attractive face remained constant, her hand in his, his arm about her, protecting her, never straying from her side in his determination that none of these passionately curious guests of his parents might say or do something to upset her.

There was the splendour of the dining-room at Riverside

which she had scarcely noticed on her whirlwind tour of inspection when she had been shown her new home. Now it was decorated with massed flowers, apricot carnations and white rosebuds to match her bouquet, all come from the gardens and hothouses of Riverside, picked only that morning and arranged by a clever florist of her new mother-in-law's acquaintance, with the dew still fresh on them.

There was Annie, caring nought for the grand folk who drank Edmund Hayes's champagne from fluted crystal glasses, asking the frozen-faced butler if he could find her a drop of porter.

There was Jennet entirely at her ease among these people who were slightly less well bred than she was, for she was the daughter of a gentleman. Her father had had a cousin who was a baronet though she did not brag about it and even Nancy did not know of it.

There was Mary, keeping close to Hetty Underwood's side like a chick clinging beneath the wing of its mother hen. By the simple expedient of keeping her eyes lowered shyly and speaking only when spoken to, prompted by Hetty, and then in a soft murmur, she managed to charm every man in the room. Even the ladies who were more insistent with their questions, though they had to admit they could not get past the handsome Mrs Underwood who turned out to be a family friend, could not fault her.

There was her mother-in-law who had decided right from the start that this new daughter-in-law of hers was just the sort of kind-hearted, easy-going, brave young woman she would have picked for her son and she let every guest know it. She herself had been cushioned and cossetted and over-protected all her life, first by her father then by her husband and her admiration for this beautiful creature her son had married, who treated her with what seemed to her to be growing affection, was profound. She was determined to overlook her unpromising beginnings, for who, looking at her now, would ever guess that she had any. She could hold her own with anyone, she had told Edmund in the privacy of their own room, fully believing that Nancy was as eager to hide her past as Emma Hayes was. How she was to explain Kitty had not seemed to occur to her.

There was Arthur, who attached himself firmly to Mary, hardly daring to believe his luck that his new sister-in-law, whom he had met for the first time two days ago, had a sister who was just as beautiful as she was. He was engaging, still a schoolboy really, like a puppy who would be happy with a pat on the head, but good-natured and eager to please.

And then there was Millicent! Nancy could not help but be aware that she would have trouble with Millicent and though she knew Josh was very keen that they should reside at Riverside House, which, after all, he said, was big enough for a family twice the size to live in comfortably together, there might come a time when Millicent would make it impossible for them to do so. She said nothing to Josh about it, of course.

They took the same train, though later in the day, to Preston and then on to Lytham where her mother-in-law's housemaids had with the utmost delicacy and unobtrusive tact prepared the house on the seafront into a haven of peace and perfect solitude for the newly married couple. Their wide-bayed bedroom window looked over the golden sands down to the gently lapping waters of the estuary, a sound that sang to them as they lay in one another's arms in the lavender-scented bed. They talked hardly at all, just a sighing endearment, a soft laugh as he struggled with tapes and buttons then laid her naked on the bed. He brought over a lamp and with his hands and eyes touched and caressed her from the curve of her eyebrows to the rich swell of her breasts, to the softness behind her knees, to the hollows of her ankles and the high arch of her foot. His fingers were feather-light, rippling her skin to delight and, in turn, she laid her hand on his body, loving the feel of him, the smell of his fine-textured flesh, the taste of him, so it was more than an hour later before he finally penetrated her.

They sank into one another's arms and slept, perhaps for no more than two hours when she was kissed to a dreamy half-waking, taking his body into hers with a slow, slumbrous delight that enchanted them both, then drifting back to sleep in the certain knowledge that he would be there the next day and every next day of her life. His body had totally expunged any lingering memory hers might have of Mick O'Rourke's, for now her body was loved and knowing it was loved was clean and fresh and . . . yes, innocent of another man's touch.

Every day they walked the long strand of the beach, pausing every few yards to place a kiss on a chin or an eyebrow, oblivious of the stares of other walkers and at night slept and loved in the softly draped feather bed.

"I love you, Nancy," he told her a dozen time a day. "I need you."

"You have me, Josh." And so he had, for she knew she was entirely and irrevocably his.

25

Freddy Hayes and Kitty Brody were just over three years old when they were thrust into one another's company in the nursery at Riverside House.

Nancy had agonised for hours on end in the weeks preceding her marriage to Josh on what would be, in the long run, best for her daughter. Her daughter who loved Annie, Jennet, Mary and Scrap, in that order, before her own mother. Not that she could blame Kitty for that. From the moment Nancy had known she was pregnant she had bitterly resented her, not just because her own goal to become the best *something*, she hadn't been sure what exactly at the time, in all of Manchester, had been seriously disrupted, but because of the way the child had been forced on her. When a seed is planted as violently as Kitty had been, surely it was forgivable when the womb that received it found it intolerable? Of course there were women, hundreds of them in Angel Meadow alone, who were impregnated against their will every nine months and it was known, for she had witnessed it herself, that these same women, dragged down and weary from childbearing, sick and tired of being constantly pregnant, doted on the infant from the moment it was born and, should it die, which frequently happened, were heartbroken.

Kitty's birth had been as violent as her conception, hours, more than thirty-six of them, as Nancy struggled to rid her body of the terrible burden Mick O'Rourke had forcibly injected into her, and when it had finally arrived, that burden, her daughter, she had wanted nothing to do with her. She had done her duty by the child, naturally, for when had Nancy Brody ever shirked that, but nothing more, for by then she was hurrying from here to there and back again as though she had a pack of hounds at her heels, which was what it felt like: the journey to Oldham to buy her sewing-machines; setting them up in Church Court and then her move to Grove Place; her new workroom; the search for cotton at the Hayes warehouse; a hundred and one things that needed her urgent attention and which left no time for motherhood. Kitty would not feel the lack, Nancy had consoled herself, since the child had three doting women to pick her up whenever she cried, to pet her and hug her when she fell down, to soothe her to sleep, to watch her first steps, to listen, marvelling, to her first baby words. In fact to be her mother in Nancy's stead.

So, should she take her to Riverside House where she would be brought up as a little lady among little gentlemen or should she leave her in the decent, there was no doubt of that, comfortable, none about that either, but working-class environment of Grove Place? The residents and their children were a cut – several cuts – above those of Church Court. The fathers were in steady work with good wages coming in. The mothers were hardworking and thrifty, homemakers, respectable, most able to read and write, since their parents had been responsible and forward-looking and had made sure that they had at least a bit of education.

But they were very far from the society in which Nancy Brody, Nancy Hayes, would move; could she deny her daughter her chance to be included in that society and better herself even further? To mix, hopefully, for the test was still to come, with the children of the millocracy, or even higher, since many hard-up young men of the gentry class, the squire class, the landed gentlemen, were looking for well-dowered brides who might provide the wherewithal to keep and maintain that land, and where better to look but among the newly rich merchants and manufacturers of Lancashire. With this in mind a girl-child was taught from the nursery to be a lady and Nancy dearly wanted her daughter to be one of those. There would be nannies, tutors, governesses, a pony, the privileged life of the daughter of a well-to-do industrialist and could Nancy deprive her of that? She was well aware that the child might fret for Annie, Jennet and Mary and they would be bereft without her, since they all doted on her. Only Mary had said so, being more open with her affections, and also less aware of the advantages Josh's family could give her niece, but it was true nevertheless.

Almost up to the day of the wedding Nancy had still been

torn in two by the dilemma. Kitty would adapt, children of her age did, and, of course, she had taken instantly to Freddy. Even as young babies on the first day they met they had been drawn to one another like a couple of babbling magnets and been vociferously indignant when they were parted. To reintroduce them Kitty had been taken in the Hayes carriage with Nancy, an exciting diversion in itself, to play with Freddy in his nursery on the top floor of Riverside House.

Kitty was a bold child with great charm when she cared to display it, confident in her belief that, naturally, she would be the centre of attention as she was at home. She had marched into the plain, unadorned nursery which had been the same since Josh was a child, since it was believed that children needed nothing more than safety and warmth, gazing around her with great interest at the plain pine table, the four pine chairs that stood about it, the big cupboard from which toys spilled, the books lining the low shelves, the drab curtains, the bit of drab drugget on the floor. There was a blackleaded fireplace in which no fire burned but which was guarded by an oppressively polished firescreen and seated on Nanny's knee in front of it having a story read to him was Freddy Hayes.

At once, sure of her welcome, Kitty was across the room, leaning both elbows on the arm of the chair, her chin in her hands, her eyes on the story book.

"Say it to me, too," she ordered Nanny loftily, absolute in her belief that Nanny Dee, as Josh had told Nancy the nursemaid was called, would instantly do as she was told, just like everyone else did in Kitty's life, with perhaps the exception of her mother.

"I beg your pardon," Nanny Dee said mildly, while Freddy stared with great interest at this rude little girl who had the nerve to give orders to his nanny.

"Say it to me as well."

"*Read* it to me . . . what do you say?"

"Please."

"That's better, but now you are here" – for Kitty's visit had been expected – "I think you and Master Freddy might . . ."

"But I want to hear the story and Freddy does too, don't you, Freddy?" turning blue and brilliantly imploring eyes on Freddy.

"Yes, Nanny, please," Freddy affirmed obediently, reacting for the first time, as he was to do so often in his future life, to Kitty Brody's blandishments.

"Very well, but . . ."

"I want to sit on your knee. I always sit on Aunty Jennet's knee when we read a story."

"Well, I'm not sure there's room for two."

"Yes, there is, see." Kitty gave Freddy a shove and another gleaming smile, almost unseating him and obligingly he moved over to make room on Nanny Dee's lap, which luckily was capacious. The hapless nursemaid cast an appealing look at this challenging child's mother who still hovered in the doorway, wishing she would leave since she was readily aware that if she didn't gain the upper hand immediately with the little girl there would be trouble, and she could hardly begin at once to administer correction with the future Mrs Hayes smiling from the doorway, could she?

But she had not reckoned on the future Mrs Hayes's lack of the usual doting fondness mothers normally have for their offspring.

"Don't stand any nonsense, Nanny," Nancy told her cheerfully. "She'll twist you round her little finger given half the chance. Start as you mean to go on."

"Thank you . . . er . . . ma'am, I will, but for now perhaps . . ." Nanny Dee shrugged, indicating that she was prepared to give her new charge some small leeway, while in her mind was the determination that the first thing she would tackle was that almost black mop of tumbled curls which fell halfway down her new charge's back. A decent plait seemed to be the answer!

Nancy left Kitty comfortably ensconced on Nanny Dee's knee, leaning against Nanny Dee's deep bosom, shoulder to shoulder with Freddy at whom, from time to time, she smiled triumphantly. Nancy and Josh had taken the opportunity thoroughly to inspect the luxurious rooms they were to occupy when they were married, spending more time than was proper on their own, in Millicent Hayes's opinion, coming downstairs to the drawing-room for afternoon tea looking somewhat more flushed than Millicent liked, her sister-in-law-to-be with her hair leaping in escaping ringlets about her rosy cheeks. Millicent's hair never sprang about her cheeks, or even her forehead. It was too closely confined for that and really, those glances her brother and his future wife exchanged were quite disgusting! It made her go hot under the prim front of her bodice, really it did.

It had been decided on that day, as she seemed well disposed to settle with Freddy, that Kitty should accompany her mother to Riverside House, which was really only right and proper, Annie told Nancy stoically, for a child should be with its mother, doing her best to be cheerful about it. Nancy had promised her that she would bring Kitty to visit Grove Place, perhaps on a Sunday morning and she'd just have to make the best of it, she told herself, but it was hard when she'd practically brought the child up single-handed. Spoiled her, too, Nancy might have added if she could have read Annie's mind, though Jennet and Mary had a hand in it as well. It seemed to Nancy that Nanny Dee – whose surname was Dallington, a name Freddy could not get his baby tongue round however he tried – would soon have the measure of Kitty Brody. She was a kindly woman, fair, cheerful and unflappable but with a strict belief in discipline and, though Nancy suspected there would be tantrums in the nursery for a while, Kitty would soon settle down to it. She had Freddy after all.

From the very first Kitty Brody loved Freddy Hayes with a strength and passion that was amazing in a three-year-old child and quite unsuitable in one so young, so Nanny Dee believed, but then, what could she do about it. She was too kind-hearted *and* conscientious to try to separate them or turn them against one another, even if she could, and then they were neither of them what you might call ordinary children. Born out of wedlock, at least Master Freddy was, so the story went, and if the new Mrs Hayes had had a husband none of the servants had heard of it. Not that Nanny indulged in gossip, but the others did when Mrs Harvey the housekeeper wasn't about and she could hardly help but overhear it when she went down to the kitchen. Come from a poor part of Manchester, Mrs Hayes had, called Angel Meadow, but as Nanny Dee had been born on a farm up near the Trough of Bowland, she did not know the area. The others seemed to think it was appalling, but then it seemed to her all the more to the new Mrs Hayes's credit that she should have come so far, and brought her sister with her, too. Nanny Dee had a lot of time for fighters. She had had to fight to escape the drudgery of her father's farm and had it not been for her mother's brave intervention on her behalf would never have managed it.

All the same she became very concerned when she discovered that, after she had put the two children to bed in the night nursery and returned to the day nursery to get on with the mending, Miss Kitty left her bed and hopped lightly across the linoleum, joining Master Freddy under the bedclothes in his. She found the pair of them, faces rosy with the sleep of the innocent, twined together like two puppies in a basket. She had disentangled them and lifted the sleeping girl, putting her back gently in her own bed; but two hours later, checking on her charges on the way to her own bed, she found Miss Kitty was back with Master Freddy, this time with her arm firmly about him as though defying Nanny to prise them apart.

"Leave them, Nanny," Mrs Hayes told her, quite casually Nanny Dee thought, not at all concerned. She knew that in the sort of household Mrs Hayes came from, or so she had heard, children, whatever their sex, slept five or six or seven to a bed and indeed she herself had shared with four of her sisters but her brothers, five of them, had their own strictly male quarters in the barn. The sexes just did not mix and it was Nanny's belief that if this wasn't stopped while the children were no more than babies who knew where it might lead?

But Nancy Hayes was too enchanted with her new life to show a great deal of concern over what to her was no more than a childish whim. Kitty was still strange in her new environment, she told Nanny Dee, so what was more natural than that she should seek warmth and comfort in Freddy's bed, Freddy who was to be her brother, after all. When Nanny knocked peremptorily on their sitting-room door to inform her of this tricky situation, she and Josh had been lounging on the sofa before the fire, just about to embark on one of their lingering, languorous, totally satisfying journeys of shared passion and like young lovers fumbling behind the kitchen door had hastily leaped apart, patting themselves back to decency, struggling with buttons and tapes and belts, with cravats and collars, doing their best to hold in the almost hysterical laughter her stern appearance had caused. They had not been long married and it seemed that the moment they were alone they were in one another's arms as though it were months since they had made love instead of that very morning. Nancy had discovered, to her own delight and amazement, after what had been done to her by Mick O'Rourke, that not only was she in love with Josh but with the act of love itself. She adored what they did together in their bed. She adored his nakedness, and her own, the wonder of unconfined limbs, the sensation of his bare skin against her own. She could not get over the marvel of his male body, the smooth and rough textures of it, the coarseness of the scattering of dark hairs on his chest and belly, the odour of his masculinity, the satin-like width of his shoulders, the leanness of his waist and hips and long legs. His emotion and desire filled her with joy and she was convinced there was nothing so wonderful as the sudden flood of his release into her own body which responded so eagerly, so intensely, so blissfully to his.

Nanny Dee's sudden entrance, though she had knocked, startled them.

"We'd best lock the door in future, my darling," Josh whispered into her tumbled hair after Nanny had left, his eyes a pure silvery grey with mischief. "We might have been . . . er . . . further along and poor Nanny would have been mortified to find me in a compromising position with a woman even if she was my own wife. Now, where were we? Here, I think, or shall we start from the beginning again?"

So Kitty Brody and Freddy Hayes were allowed to continue their growing attachment to one another and Nancy was gratified with the way her child had settled into the nursery at Riverside. She gave no deep thought, beyond a vague surprise at how easy it had been, to her daughter's careless relinquishment of those who had loved and cared for her during the first three years of her life, only thankful for Freddy and Nanny Dee who had made it possible. Nancy had not yet realised the full potential of her daughter's strength of character. She was a baby still, but what nobody understood, least of all her mother, was that from a very early age Kitty Brody had learned to manipulate those about her and that her child, Mick O'Rourke's child, was well able to recognise even from infancy what would be to her best advantage.

Nancy was busy from dawn, when she rose from the bed she shared with Josh, stretching with the suppleness of a cat, flushed and satiated with love, until dusk, and even beyond sometimes. She lived in a constant whirl of activity, busy with the fitting out of the smart new premises Josh's money had enabled her to lease in St Ann's Square. The square was the smartest, most noteworthy shopping area in Manchester where the upper middle-class ladies of Higher Broughton and Cheetham, the exclusiveness of residential estates such as Victoria Park, and even from as far as Alderley Edge and Wilmslow came to purchase their hats and gowns and every other luxury garment ladies such as themselves required.

These were the customers Nancy was after. It had been Hetty Underwood who had given her the idea.

"With your head for business and your obvious flair for fashion, with Jennet's cleverness with a needle and, may I add, that certain air you both have of being *ladies*—"

"I'm no lady, Hetty. You should know that."

"So you are fond of saying but that does not matter, since you give the impression you are which is all that matters. And that being so I don't know why you don't open a good-class dressmaker's. And I mean really good class. Somewhere a lady can, with others of her sort, shop for an outfit exclusively designed for her. Are you able to sketch a design?"

"Hetty!" Nancy was so taken aback she was speechless. She had been planning to find a decent-sized workshop, hire or even buy half a dozen sewing-machines, employ half a dozen young machinists and take up again the manufacture of shirts and baby clothes, waistcoats and trousers to be sold on her market stall at Smithfield, in Hetty's drapery on Market Street and in any of the small shops along Deansgate, King Street or Exchange Street who had once bought her goods. With a husband well able to supply her with cotton cloth, when it was available, of course, for the war still raged in America, she was optimistic she could regain all she had lost. Expand even, when the war ended and cotton once again came flooding back into Manchester. Though she herself was secure now as Josh's wife it would be a means of support for Mary, Annie and Jennet. But a dress shop! A dressmaker's and milliner's! Designing and making the gowns, evening gowns, wedding gowns, perhaps, for the élite of Manchester and its surrounds. Employing clever seamstresses, perhaps a designer, a good shop in a good position with well-lit rooms at the top where . . . where . . .

"I can see you're taken with the idea," Hetty said with a ghost of a smile.

"But I'm not a—"

"A dressmaker? You could employ those who are."

"I know nothing about the business of—"

"You could learn. You knew nothing about spinning frames or sewing-machines a few years ago, but you learned."

"But, Hetty . . ."

"Nancy dear, do close your mouth. There are flies about. And let me add that there is no need for you to give up the idea of a workshop producing . . . well, for the lower end of the market.

Mary has become a competent young woman quite capable of running it, under your guidance. It is always wise to share out your eggs into more than one basket. You have a ready market. Your stall could be run by a reliable young woman. Heavens, there are enough of them about with so many out of work because of the cotton famine. I myself would be glad of good-quality baby garments. With your husband's backing and your mother-in-law's position in society, for where she leads her friends will follow, I would imagine a dress shop, providing the merchandise was what they wanted, could not fail. Just look at you. You're like a fashion plate and what woman would not sell her soul to look like you? To be as elegant and well dressed as you. Oh, I realise there are other dressmakers in Manchester, you go to one yourself, as I do, but with your brains, your talent, your determination never to be beaten you could be the smartest of the lot. You know you could."

Nancy stared into Hetty's eyes, hypnotised by the bewitchment of it, her mind scurrying from one brilliant possibility to another, then back to the first, turning over this idea and that, discarding this notion and scrutinising another, poring over the wonder of it, her thoughts like a flock of swooping starlings at dusk, unable to settle into anything that might be described as coherency.

Hetty watched her for several long minutes then laughed, breaking the spell.

"It really is a delight to watch your brain ticking away like an overwound clock, my dear. It could not be more plain if your head were made of glass and, of course, you must be aware that I would not have put forward the idea if, first, you were to be in direct competition to myself since I am a businesswoman too, and, second, if I had not heard of the very premises in St Ann's Square that would be perfect for you. The lease on—"

"Good God, Hetty, let me draw breath."

"Certainly not. You have no time for such a thing. Come with me right now and we will inspect the place. Miss Jenkins can take charge of the shop," and with a nod to Miss Jenkins she had handed Nancy her bonnet, put on her own and led her imperiously into Market Street, telling Miss Jenkins that they would be back "presently".

The shop was not large and the previous occupier had left it in a state of some disrepair. It had a single frontage, three floors, the top one having direct daylight from the tall windows at the back and the front and from skylights set in the roof. It was perfect.

A small army of women – women being readily available to perform even the most servile of tasks in this era of desperate unemployment – had scrubbed it from its deep cellars to its lofty attics. As they moved out, a small army of painters moved in, transforming the drab, bottle green walls, in what had once been a bootmaker's, to a pale peach picked out on the mouldings and cornices in white. In the main showroom, on the stairs and in the rooms where her ladies were to be fitted into their gowns, a pale carpet the colour of the sand at Lytham was laid. Pretty gilt chairs upholstered in velvet of the same colour were scattered about on which her clients might sit and drink a cup of her best orange pekoe tea, her finest Blue Mountain Jamaican coffee, her sweet sherry or even a glass of chilled white wine should they care for it. There were small, glass-topped gilt-legged tables on which she casually, but tastefully, displayed exotic fans of lace and ivory, plaster heads on which the bonnets made by her clever milliner were set out. There were embroidered gloves, lace caps and collars, parasols and exquisitely draped shawls, ermine muffs – for winter was coming – sashes of velvet sewn with pearls, gold hairnets, Spanish mantillas and dashing military caps with gold tassels. Not all at the same time, naturally, but with such taste it would be a strong-willed lady who could resist them. They came once to see what was on show, and then a second and a third time when it was discovered her displays were changed every single day. The same with her window, for in it she displayed a "ready to wear" gown of cream silk with a high-crowned straw hat to match or a plain, pastel-tinted afternoon gown contrasting exotically with a richly patterned crimson shawl, all tastefully put on show by the young woman, introduced to her by Hetty, whose sole job it was to show Miss Brody's goods so irresistibly not one lady could resist them.

And on the top floor in her workroom she introduced high tables so as to avoid the twisting of her seamstresses' spines, a condition that was endured, so Hetty told her, in every other workroom in Manchester. She provided footstools to give additional comfort to her embroideresses. Her ironing-room was set behind a partition, thus isolating the heat and steam of goffering and pressing which was the cause of the many headaches suffered.

She had pale peach hatboxes on which the name "Miss Brody, dressmaker and milliner" was printed in gold letters, since she was aware that her father-in-law would not care to have his illustrious name connected with an establishment such as hers, respectable as it was.

Eventually they began to come. First Mrs Edmund Hayes – though not her daughter – accompanied by her dearest friend, Mrs Jonathan Lambert, the latter only because dear Emma had begged her to, for society's views on the new Mrs Hayes, the Miss Nancy Brody in question, were still somewhat ambiguous. They had stepped across Nancy's threshold as nervously as two elderly tabby cats expecting heaven knows what debauchery, peering about them at the display Josh's wife had thought fit to set out to tempt them, knowing they were to come. They were both the wives of wealthy mill owners but they had neither of them ever had a female relative in "trade". Agnes Lambert's grandmother had "minded" a pair of spinning frames decades ago and Emma Hayes's grandfather had made his fortune in Yorkshire in the woollen trade, but both considered themselves to be ladies and had never mixed with the lower orders. Not that the new Mrs Hayes looked or acted other than a lady, her background completely erased by her ladylike manner, the way she spoke and dressed and, as Agnes Lambert said to her Jonathan, if Emma was prepared to accept her, how could she, Agnes, whose own antecedents were nothing to write home about, object? Give the girl a chance, despite that unexplained child in the Riverside nurseries.

In the weeks that followed, Mrs William Rivers, another friend of Emma Hayes, was prevailed upon to visit the "salon" owned by Emma's daughter-in-law, having been quite enchanted with the exquisite lace cap and elegant cashmere shawl Emma had purchased there. Mrs Algernon Pickup and her twin daughters, Sophie and Lottie, their horse-drawn carriage almost blocking St Ann's Square, came and bought generously. Sophie, who was to be married the following spring, begged her mama to allow "Miss Brody" to design and make her wedding gown and trousseau. Well, had Mama ever seen anything so lovely, so stylish as that walking dress of coffee-coloured – what was it, Miss Brody? – ah, yes, foulard des Indes, trimmed with black velvet. She simply must have it for the winter season. Her mama, quite horrified at the notion of her daughter wearing a *ready-made* dress, had been mollified by Nancy's calm assurance that the dress, should it not fit the perfect measurements of her daughter could soon be made to do so, had been quickly persuaded. And yes, Lottie might have that sweet little beaded reticule and the lace-edged Spanish parasol, totally ignoring, as she drank a glass of Miss Brody's excellent Madeira, her coachman's imploring face at the window.

They seemed to find no incongruity in the strangeness of frequenting Miss Brody's little dress shop during the afternoon and at night sitting down to dine with Mrs Joshua Hayes, or if they did they hid it for dear Emma's sake. They acted as though Miss Brody and Mrs Hayes were two entirely different women. They were all so fond of Emma who was the sweetest, most kind-hearted and generous woman they knew, perhaps easily led, or taken in, by a stronger character than her own. Not that Josh's wife had attempted to mislead her, indeed seemed to hold her in great affection, treating her with respect and good humour. And Emma responded like a flower turning its head to the sun, since her own daughter was a cold-hearted creature with none of her new sister-in-law's warmth. Edmund, being a man, was more reserved with what he allowed his wife's friends to see of his feelings but even he seemed to find his daughter-in-law acceptable. Her brother-in-law, Arthur, was obviously bewitched by her charm and beauty, it seemed, now that he was at home and working full time under Josh's supervision and was therefore no longer a schoolboy. She treated him with cheerful consideration, inclined to tease him as one would a brother, and he revelled in it. Sometimes her own sister was a guest, her demure shyness causing Josh's brother a good deal of torment, since it seemed he was torn between her innocent loveliness and Mrs Josh Hayes's more mature beauty.

As for her husband, Josh, his eyes followed her whenever he allowed her to stray from his side and, it was said, since servants will gossip to other servants, that he carried her off to their bedroom the moment dinner was over. In fact Longman, who was the Hayes' gardener, had told the Lambert gardener with whom he drank a glass of ale on a Friday night that he had come across the pair of them in the arbour beyond the rose garden one moonlit night – he having gone to check that he'd closed the vegetable-garden gate – in what he considered to be an indecent state of undress and oblivious to all but each other. The Higher Broughton Brass Band could have marched through and they'd not have noticed, he'd told the Lambert gardener, who'd passed it on, naturally. One of the footmen in the Lamberts' servants hall had unwisely remarked that he personally didn't blame Mr Josh Hayes and just give him half a chance and had almost been fired on the spot!

Mary had settled down, after a nervous start, to running the workshop where six machinists turned out baby clothes, shirts and working men's trousers of varying quality, the better stuff to go to Hetty Underwood and several drapers in Deansgate and King Street, the poorer, cheaper variety, which was all they could afford, to working-class women on the market stall where a sensible girl of Nancy's choosing stood for four days a week.

Jennet supervised the sewing-room in St Ann's Square, working over the girls she herself had employed, seeing to the fine embroidery. And in the little house in Grove Place Annie sat for hours on end complaining she'd "nowt" to do and wondering how that little mite was getting on without her up at the big house. But, true to her word, Nancy brought her over on a Sunday morning, and the lad Freddy, from whom Kitty would not be parted, but it was not the same. The child made more fuss of the damned dog than she did of Annie, begging her mother to be allowed to take the thing "home" with her, which she did in the end. She and the lad raced round the house with the two animals, for he had brought his an' all and it was bloody pandemonium when all Annie had wanted was to sit for an hour with the blessed child on her knee. And it wasn't the lad's fault, neither. Kitty was always the leader, always the motivator, the instigator in any wild game, a tomboy, a hoyden, despite the pretty flounced dresses that their nanny put her in. And when they had gone the house was like a bloody tomb, she said out loud morosely. Annie Wilson, though she wished her no harm for she was fond of the lass, rued the day Nancy Brody had caught the eye of Joshua Hayes!

26

Before she could catch her breath, or so it seemed to Nancy in her busy life, she had been married for almost three years and in April 1865, the war between the northern and southern states of America was over. Deprived for over four years of the main supply, manufacturers in Lancashire such as Josh Hayes had scoured the world for raw cotton. They had found a good new supply in Egypt where the long-stapled cotton had compared favourably with the American "Sea-Island" and with this, and the return of cotton from across the Atlantic, all the mills and weaving sheds of Lanchashire, those that had survived what was known as the "cotton famine", were in full production again.

To Josh's teeth-gritting annoyance, his father, who seemed to have recovered his health with the coming of the fine weather, began once again to accompany his two sons to the mill.

"He can't quite bring himself to believe that Arthur and I are capable of running the business without him. As if we haven't been doing it for years now. At least I have and Arthur is shaping up well. Father goes tramping round the spinning-rooms, peering under the frames, frightening the piecers to death. 'I can do that,' he tells them, to their astonishment, which he can, and which I know he has done when he was a lad, as I have, as Arthur has, for Father believed that if the spinner or the weaver was aware that his master was as capable as he, or she, no attempt would be made to 'cod' him. He *will* interfere, countermanding orders I myself have given and sending Arthur running from here to there as though he were an errand boy. For God's sake, Arthur's a man of twenty-one and I'm not far short of thirty so why can't he trust us? Business has never been so good. Why does he keep coming to the mill at his age and in his state of health, which I know has improved but is still poor. One morning my door opens, or I walk into a shed, or the counting house and there he is, going through the ledgers, checking up on me. God, I hate to say this but things were a damn sight better when he was confined to his bed."

"Sweetheart, he needs to feel useful, as we all do."

"I know that and I appreciate how he must feel, but it is bloody annoying just the same."

"Be patient, my love, and don't pout like that. You look just like Freddy when Nanny Dee has forbidden him something he has set his heart on."

"Pout! Me pout? I'll have you know, woman, I haven't a pout in me. Now come here and kiss your husband. You've been home at least five minutes and that peck on the cheek you gave me will just not do. In fact, I'm after more than a kiss so come upstairs and let me show you what it is."

"Can I take my hat off first?"

"I can't wait that long, Mrs Hayes."

"Oh, yes, you can, Mr Hayes, and look at you, you're wet through. Why do you insist on riding that animal in the rain when you could come with me in the carriage? Now let's have you out of those wet things before you catch cold."

"Do it for me, darling. I've always fancied having a slave girl."

"You're a wicked man."

"Be a wicked woman for me, my pet."

So even before they dined with the rest of the family, which they did most evenings, they spent a satisfying half-hour in their deep-scented feather bed to the pink-cheeked embarrassment of young Maddy, the chambermaid who had the job of making it all over again.

It was a week later. She was observing with the meticulous attention she gave to all her customers as her head seamstress skilfully pinned Mrs Dolly Baker, wife of the banker, Mr Alfred Baker, into a dark blue silk dinner gown when Summers, the Hayes' coachman, flung open the door of the shop, his face crimson and quivering with what was obviously not good news.

They were all greatly startled, the ladies who sat about her salon, which had become not only the place where Miss Brody dressed them but where they liked to congregate and indulge in gossip. The shop had been considerably extended last year when Nancy had purchased the lease on the shop next door as it fell empty. Her establishment had, at one stroke, been doubled, with two shop windows at the front, lined with midnight blue velvet, in each of which, with great simplicity, she displayed one gown or outfit, accompanied by suitable matching accessories: a stunning hat; shoes dyed to tone exactly with the colour of the garment; a parasol and gloves, a reticule, a choker of pearls, and there wasn't a passer-by who did not stop to admire it. On the windows was her name, MISS NANCY BRODY, nothing more. Nothing more was needed, for she was known by now as the most stylish and clever dressmaker in Manchester. She did not, of course, put a single stitch in any garment herself, since she had a dozen clever young seamstresses to do that for her. With the help of her unobtrusive and efficient staff she could create the perfect outfit for any lady, for any occasion, turning them out in not only the very best quality, the height of fashion, but in what exactly and perfectly suited them and they trusted her implicitly. She was more than a dressmaker, or a milliner but an "outfitter" and had heard herself described by Mrs Freda Pickup, both of whose daughters had had their complete wedding trousseaux designed and made by her, as her *couturière*. It had made her smile!

The ladies reared back in alarm as the coachman almost fell across the threshold, for though they all knew Summers and the smart carriage he drove for the Hayes family, his sudden male appearance where a male never ventured, or at least not very often and then accompanied by a wife, filled them with trepidation.

"Summers! My goodness, what *is* the matter?" Nancy moved hurriedly towards the man in the doorway, at the same time managing to contrive an air of calm imperturbability though even as she did so she knew something dire must have happened. Not Josh; please, not Josh, her frantic mind jabbered. I couldn't bear it if anything were to happen to . . . there are always accidents at the mill. God, she had seen enough herself when she had minded a spinning frame. Perhaps . . . perhaps his horse had stumbled . . . bolted, dragged him along behind it, his face, his beloved face, torn and bleeding, the jaunty elegance, the hard, arrow-straight lines of him that she loved so much smashed and broken . . . Not Josh . . . please, not Josh.

And all this in the time it took her to walk across her salon.

"Mrs Hayes, you're to come at once, ma'am. The mistress is

in a real taking and Miss Millicent's no bloody good— Eeh, I beg your pardon, ma'am, ladies," his blunt, North Country countenance turning aghast to face her customers, begging forgiveness for his lapse.

"What . . . what is it, Summers? Not my . . . my husband?"

"Please, ma'am, he says to come at once."

"Who . . . ?" She began to lose her control and her voice rose wildly and only Jennet's hand on her arm brought her back to the circle of shocked and curious faces, teacups and sherry glasses in well-manicured hands, who were watching her.

"What is it, Summers? Has someone been hurt?" Jennet asked crisply, her hand like a vice under Nancy's elbow, since it seemed to her that if anything had befallen Josh Hayes, who was the sun and moon of Nancy's world, it would be needed to stop her falling into the darkness.

"It's the old gentleman, miss. He's been took bad. He collapsed in the yard. We got him home, me and Mr Josh and Mr Arthur, and the doctor came but . . . oh, ma'am, they do say he's dying."

And poor helpless, frightened Emma Hayes would have fallen apart, Nancy was certain. The mother-in-law she had come to love would not be able to deal with this crisis and would need Nancy to get her through, since her own daughter, with her unfeeling lack of sympathy and abundant self-interest, would be no comfort to her at all. Emma would need someone, another woman, a woman who would understand what she was suffering as Nancy would understand, for had they not both loved a man.

For an hour she sat with Emma Hayes, holding her hand, not exactly begging her to believe that there was nothing to worry about but conveying to her the certainty that whatever happened Emma would be strong enough to survive it. That Nancy would hold her upright where necessary, that she would come through it bravely. She only left her when the draught the doctor had given Emma to "steady her nerves" took effect and she relaxed by her fireside with Ellen, who was head parlourmaid and could be trusted to be sympathetic, beside her.

Edmund Hayes was propped up in the centre of the vast canopied bed he and Emma had shared for nearly forty years. The familiar, scraping sound of air struggling to enter his diseased lungs filled the room, and Nancy, even without the strained expressions on the faces of Josh and Arthur, who hung over him, and the doctor, who hovered at the foot of the bed, knew there could be no doubt he was dying. The engine fumes, the factory smoke, the polluted air of the city was finally to kill him, as it had killed so many of his operatives, and for a moment Nancy knew an overwhelming terror, for was this how Josh would finish his days? Josh who breathed the same stinking air that his father did.

She stood by the door and waited. Edmund Hayes's eyes were closed, those piercing, far-seeing eyes that had seemed to see something in herself, despite her background, that suited him. Then they flew open and, beckoning to his sons to come closer, his hoarse voice whispered into their ears as they bent over him.

"Look after your mother . . . she'll not know what to do . . . you know what I mean," she heard him say and was overcome with a gush of tears which flooded her eyes and coursed down her cheeks.

"Of course, Father, you know we will." Josh's voice, though he spoke quietly, seemed loud and intrusive after his father's whisper.

"And . . . your sister. She's . . . watch her . . ." And for reasons best known to himself his blurring eyes strayed to where Nancy stood waiting her turn to say goodbye. "She can be tricky . . ."

"Now, Father, don't tire yourself."

"Don't be daft, son. What difference does it make now?" A faint smile curled the old man's grey lips, then once more he managed to lift a weak hand, indicating that Nancy was to come forward.

She knelt by the bed, disregarding the doctor who was not at all sure his patient should be subjected to so many people at the same time. She took her father-in-law's hand and held the back of it to her wet cheek.

"Nay, lass, don't waste your tears on me. I've had my time and bloody good it's been. See, come closer."

Nancy leaned over him until his lips were almost against her ear and his feeble breath fanned her cheek.

"That lad of mine . . . you've done him a power of good. He was beginning to shape but you've . . . made a man of him . . . made him what he is. I'm proud of him, and of you. You're a lovely woman . . ."

"Father-in-law . . ."

"Watch out for . . . Milly. She'll do you a . . . mischief . . . if she can."

"No, you're wrong. In three years she's—"

"Biding her time, my lass, so think on."

Before she could reassure him or even barely stand up and get out of the way, the door opened and the subject of his words burst into the room, wide-eyed and dramatically tearful, seriously offending the doctor who liked his patients to die in peace. Nancy wondered where she had been.

"Father," Millicent cried, throwing herself across her father's body before Josh could prevent her and over her shoulder Edmund Hayes's eyes looked into Nancy's and one of his eyebrows lifted wryly as though to ask did she see what he'd been getting at!

He died as the doctor had wanted him to, peacefully and with his hand in that of his wife whose own was held firmly in Nancy's. Emma's doze had relaxed her, as had Nancy's words and she was able to meet his passing with acceptance and quiet tears. She clung to Nancy as she was led from the room, totally disregarding her daughter who was ready bravely to receive her. As she was to cling to Nancy through the next painful days and during the funeral which was attended by many grand gentlemen of Manchester, including the mayor himself. Nancy stood beside her, always there just a hand away, which surprised the mourners since it seemed to them that her own daughter would have been the one the widow would naturally have turned to. Millicent Hayes was there, of course, tall in her black mourning gown and fine veil, her face beneath it quite expressionless, the look in her slate grey eyes hidden by her lowered eyelids. She stood beside her brothers at the graveside, making no move to comfort her mother, those who were there noticed, and it was left to Emma's daughter-in-law, who wore no veil and whose face was soft with sadness, to put an arm about her. They were close, Emma's sons and her daughter-in-law, ready to bind together in a circle of support which did not include Millicent, not because they withheld it but because she did not want it. At the house, where the mourners came to drink a glass of sherry and eat a slice of the rich fruit cake Mrs Cameron had made, she smiled icily at those who offered their condolences and took their gloved hands between reluctant fingers but again made no move to join the quiet groups who spoke kindly to Emma, to Josh and

Arthur, and to Nancy who, despite her humble background and strange fixation with business, had proved her worth. They paid little attention to the strange situation in the nursery, if they thought of it at all, for by now it was accepted as some awkward eccentricity in the Hayes household, like a fancy to hobnob with one's own servants, the whim some had to talk to a horse, or a favourite dog. The children were rarely seen, just now and again two small figures racing across a lawn with a couple of small dogs at their heels, or perhaps the high peal of childish laughter floating down from the nursery floor. It had all been handled very discreetly, in their opinion, though what was to happen as they grew was a matter of much speculation.

That night Josh, in the comfort of his wife's loving arms, wept silent tears, the first she had ever seen him shed. At first she had been surprised and alarmed, though it was no shame to cry for a loved one who has gone.

"Darling, oh my darling, I know you were fond of your father . . ."

"Dammit, Nancy, I'm ashamed to tell you my tears are more for myself than the old man."

"But why? Why should you . . . ?" She tried to look down into his anguished face but he hid it against her breast, straining her to him with desperate arms.

"Oh, I know it will pass, but don't you see I feel so bloody guilty."

"Guilty! Why should you?"

"Because of what I said, and felt, that it was easier for me when he was confined to his bed. I complained that he wouldn't stay out of the mill and now . . . now he bloody well will because he's dead!"

"Josh, sweetheart, that didn't mean you *wanted* him dead."

"Didn't it?"

She was shocked. "Of course it didn't. I won't have this; it's nonsense to talk like that. And not like you, for you are a man of common sense and rational thought."

"I believed I was, Nancy, but this is hard." He rolled away from her, shuddering, putting an arm across his eyes as though to hide his shame but she leaned over him, pushing it away, kissing his damp cheeks and tear-dewed eyes, murmuring endearments and small sounds of loving comfort until his body began to respond as she meant it to, as she mended him in the only way she could.

"Dear God, should we, today of all days?" he murmured, lying back and arching his throat.

"Your father would tell you to go ahead, my love. He was not a killjoy. I think it might even have amused him," she whispered.

"Sweet Jesus, I want you, Nancy."

"I know . . . hush . . ." and she slid down him, her body like silk against his, gathering him to her, giving herself and taking him, their bodies joining, fusing together as they had learned over the years so that no part of *her*, or of *him*, was entirely hers or his, no part of them where his body ended and hers began.

Breathing heavily, she sank back into the pillows and he turned, laying his arm across her, his face between her breasts, as breathless as she but beginning to laugh weakly.

"Good God above," he said.

"Yes," she gasped, and with their arms tightly about one another they fell together into a vast and healing sleep.

A week later it was as though the scene where Summers had burst into her shop to fetch her to Edmund Hayes's deathbed was being played again, though this time it was not the coachman who flung himself through the shop doorway, but Annie Wilson.

Again her customers were taken aback, for one did not expect to see a woman of the caller's class enter a shop of the quality of Miss Brody's. She was decently dressed, neat and clean, her boots as well polished as her rounded apple cheeks, her hair smoothly drawn back beneath her old-fashioned bonnet. They waited, eyes alive with curiosity, for what was to happen next, their avid expressions asked.

Nancy was transfixed for the space of five seconds and again Jennet was there beside her, her hand steady on Nancy's arm, but on her own face was a look of astonishment. She had left Annie no more than three hours ago, sitting placidly before her kitchen fire, a cup of the strong, sweet tea which she could not get enough of, having been denied it in earlier years, in her gnarled hand, murmuring that she was looking forward to Sunday and a sight of her little mite!

Though Annie had appeared to be relaxed her old eyes were as sharp as needles as she watched the girl she had employed, with Jennet's approval, to help her with the heavy work. A good girl of thirteen, strong and healthy, despite where she came from, silent and obedient and who did her best to please her mistress, which was how she thought of Mrs Wilson since she gave the orders. Mrs Wilson was a tartar who missed neither a speck of dust on the mantelshelf or a smear on a window, but the girl, whose name was Bridget, or Bridie, knew that as long as she did her best to live up to the standards Mrs Wilson expected of her, her life would be smooth, warm, well fed and vastly better than the cramped, terraced cottage in Old Mount Street where she had lived with thirteen other members of her family. She was the eldest girl and had been at the beck and call of her mam and, indeed, being simple and good-natured, every one of her brothers and sisters so that Grove Place was like heaven to her. Her pa, an evil-tempered old bugger, spent most of his time and his wages at the Bull on the corner of Angel Street, but it was not until he began to pay marked attention to her when she was eleven, slipping his hand up her tattered skirt and frightening her to death, that her mam sent her to Mrs Wilson who they all knew had bettered herself and might have an answer for her mam's dilemma. Bridie had never gone home again and for two years had striven to please Mrs Wilson whom she looked on as her saviour.

But Bridie was an uneducated, inarticulate girl and could not be trusted, though she would do her anguished best, to deliver a message, which was why Annie had come herself. In a hansom cab no less, for the urgency of the situation had seemed to warrant it, which still stood outside the shop as she had told the driver to do.

"Yer've ter come at once, lass," she said without preamble, paying no attention to the open-mouthed group who sat about the salon. "Cab's waitin' so best get yer 'at, an' look sharp."

Nancy felt her mind freeze in shock and a great many fundamental things inside her became suspended from their usual function, like the power to draw breath, or even blink in surprise, for just as on the day when Summers came to fetch her to Riverside House, she knew this was to be bad. Annie did not panic. Annie was calm, resourceful, well able to deal with any small emergency at Grove Place, which seemed to tell Nancy that this did not concern Grove Place, where, in any case, there was only Annie and Bridie and Annie was here and in full health. She would not have come on Bridie's behalf so what crisis had arisen that had dragged her across town in a hansom cab?

"Annie," she pleaded, longing for Annie to say there was nothing to be worried about.

"Come on, lass, don't 'ang about. I'll tell yer in't cab, an' fer God's sake 'urry up or it'll be too late."

"Oh, Jesus, Annie." The ladies gasped, shocked to the core. "Please, you're frightening me: too late for what?"

Pushing Jennet to one side and doing the same with the offended person of Mrs Agnes Lambert who had come to try on her new bonnet which was being created for her, she gripped Annie's arm, twisting it cruelly, since her instincts told her this was something that would hurt her, that she might not be able to withstand.

"Listen, chuck, yer don't want these ladies ter know all yer business, do yer?" Annie cast a disparaging glance about the circle of ladies, all of whom, in her opinion, did not know the meaning of a day's work and filled their idle days drinking tea, gossiping and spending their husbands' money.

"Annie, you must . . ."

Annie turned in exasperation to Jennet who, having no immediate family of her own over whom she might panic, could be counted on to be steady.

"Get 'er 'at, will yer, love. Not that she needs a bloody 'at where she's goin', an' I'll put 'er in't cab."

"Annie . . ."

"Give over, our Nancy. Just come wi' me."

"Where are we going? Annie, I swear I'll hit you if you don't tell me what's wrong. Is it Josh?"

Her clients could hear her voice through the open shop doorway, beseeching Annie, whoever she was, to tell her again and again what had happened and where they were going, and it was not until the cab drew away into the traffic, driving off at a speed that threatened to kill the poor, broken-winded hack that pulled it, that the ladies let out their breath which they had been unaware that they were holding. Miss Williams returned from the pavement where she had been watching Miss Brody's departure, smiling falsely. She snapped her fingers at the flustered milliner who had been about to place Mrs Lambert's new bonnet on her head.

"Now then, Mrs Lambert, shall we see how your bonnet looks? I'm sure you're going to love it."

The cabbie refused to enter, never mind wait for them in Angel

Meadow, saying it would be more than his life or the safety of his horse and cab were worth. Didn't the ladies know that the only person who did not live in the area who could safely enter was the midwife, or the police and then in twos or threes. There were some very shady characters hanging about, he warned them, all of them eyeing the two women with astonishment, as he had done himself when he saw where they intended to go. The eastern side of Manchester was well known for having the poorest housing and the worse slums to the square mile and Angel Meadow was the worst of the lot. The largest police force and the highest crime rate to go with it, so he'd be obliged if the ladies would give him his fare and let him get off. When they were ready to return he was sure they would find a cab on St George's Road.

It looked exactly as it had done when she had left it almost five years ago, even to the women who leaned idly against their sagging door frames or sprawled, legs apart, on their unscrubbed, broken-down doorsteps. Rotting brickwork, crumbling woodwork, broken windows, festering garbage against every wall, and children, unwashed, unshod, barely clothed, splashing in the foetid stream that eddied in the gutter running down the middle of the street and in which things unrecognisable, unmentionable, but known to be stinking, floated.

The mouths of the women fell open, for it was a long time since someone like her – in fact it *was* her – had walked their slimy, cobbled setts, and for several seconds, though they recognised her, they were speechless. But not for long!

"Well, will yer look 'oo's come ter call, ladies? If it ain't Miss bloody Brody 'erself payin' us a visit an' me in me old frock. Go an' put kettle on, Teresa, an' we'll 'ave us a nice chat over a cup o' tea." It was Kate Murphy who spoke, or rather cackled toothlessly, looking nearer fifty than the thirty-two she actually was.

"Bugger me if yer not right," chortled Teresa Finnigan, slapping her thigh with huge delight. "An' ter what do we owe the 'onour o' this visit, Miss Brody? Come ter see that there sister o' yours, 'ave yer? The one what's got 'erself in't same pickle as yerself an' wi't same chap, so I 'eard. Another bastard in't family. I dunno, you Brody girls'll lift yer skirts fer owt in trousers."

Ignoring them all, if she was conscious of them which

seemed unlikely, and though still deep in the shock into which Annie's news had thrust her, she still had the presence of mind to hold up her skirt and the white frills of her petticoats to avoid contact with the filth underfoot. Her fine kid boots, black to match her gown, for she was in mourning for Edmund Hayes, had no such attention and in the recesses of her mind Nancy told herself absently that they'd need to be discarded.

As they approached the door to what had once been the O'Rourke home, and still was apparently, it was flung violently open and on the step which bore the same filth it had known when Nancy was a girl stood Eileen O'Rourke. She was still the same slattern, the same foul-mouthed virago she had always been but this time her venom was directed at her neighbours.

"You shurrup, Teresa Finnigan. Yer know nowt about owt an' if yer was ter cast yer mind back to when yer got that poor sod of a 'usband o' thine ter wed yer 'appen yer'll remember yer were eight months gone at 't time. 'E only took yer because yer old man medd 'im."

Before Nancy or Annie could recover from this acrimony, Eileen had grabbed them both by the arm and dragged them inside, banging the door to behind them with such force the frame moved at least an inch. The parlour, if it could be given such a grand name, was dim, the accumulated dirt of years that coated the window effectively blocking out the light, and it stank of urine, unwashed bodies and cats, or so Nancy thought dazedly, almost overcome by it. The furniture, what there was of it, was stained, broken, ready to disintegrate at a touch, but held together by an assortment of what looked like string and cardboard. In the middle of the room was an ancient deal table on which the cluttered remains of a meal stood. Two cats, presumably one of the causes of the appalling, eye-watering stench, sat in the centre of it daintily licking their paws after, Nancy supposed with a shudder, cleaning the chipped and greasy plates. Sharing the table space was a cardboard box into which one of the animals peered with feline interest and was about to jump into, prevented only by Eileen O'Rourke's shriek and lunging backhand. It fled with a howl.

Eileen crossed grimy arms over her sagging bosom. "Right, Nancy Brody," she said truculently. "I sent our Angelina ter fetch yer – one o't women at mill knew where Annie Wilson'd flitted to – ter tekk away this 'ere," pointing at the box, " 'cos it's no use ter me. I reckon I done me bit so I'd be obliged if yer'd remove it. An' 'er upstairs an' all. I done me best but it were no use. She . . . well, she . . ."

For a brief moment Eileen O'Rourke's face lost the grim look of endurance which forty years of hardship, hunger, struggle and adversity had put there and she looked as once she might have done as a girl who had believed, with the optimism of youth, that her life would be different from that of her parents. There was a relaxing of her thin lips and what might have been pity in her eyes.

"It's your Rose."

"Angelina told Annie . . ."

"Aye, but yer too late," Eileen said briskly, the moment of sympathy gone. She'd no time for it. Life had taught her it got you nowhere so, along with all the other finer emotions which, after all, were only so much baggage to drag you down, she had jettisoned them many years ago. "I couldn't afford midwife so me an' Angelina did us best. She lives in your old 'ouse wi' 'er six kids an' we neither of us can manage no more. Anyroad we done what we could fer 'er but she were skinny as a bloody bootlace wi' no fight in 'er so yer can see why . . ."

"Rosie is dead?" Nancy's voice was so calm she might have been enquiring about the weather, though inside her a storm of such proportions raged she felt she might just get lifted up and blown away with it.

"Aye, that's wharr I'm sayin', an' bairn's none too clever."

Beside her Annie made a small sound in the back of her throat, somewhere between a sigh and a moan, for who could forget the bonny, spirited lass who had been Nancy Brody's little sister. Healthy and bright-eyed with the rounded cheeks and firm limbs of the well-fed. A head of curly hair that seemed to take life from the sun or any stray beam from a candle, crackling and shining as she tossed it defiantly at her sisters. Not plump, but strong-shouldered, deep-bosomed, like Nancy. The Brody girls, known for their teeth-gritting endurance and their determination to take life by the throat and twist it to their own liking and now one of them was gone. What the devil had Eileen O'Rourke's son done to her in the five years since they had fled the city? Where had she been, and where was the bugger who had reduced her to "a bloody bootlace"?

She moved slowly towards the table, leaning over to peer sadly into the unnatural silence of the cardboard box and Nancy was surprised to see her eyes come to life and glow warmly, even in the dimness.

She herself was rooted to the spot on Eileen O'Rourke's mucky, broken floorboards where she had come to rest as the door thundered to behind her. She had been told that Rosie was in labour, was in great trouble and she was to go at once to Mrs O'Rourke's, but nothing had prepared her for this. She had been busy in her mind as the cab flew along High Street and Shude Hill on its flight to Church Court with thoughts of removing Rose and the child, finding them decent lodgings, a woman to look after them until more permanent arrangements were made, but now, within the space of five minutes, life had twisted her about again, shattering her, leaving her, she was well aware, with no decision at all to make really. This was Rosie's child, and presumably her own . . . what? niece, nephew; half-brother or -sister to her daughter. Dear God in heaven . . . but whatever its sex or relationship to herself and Kitty she could not abandon it to the life Eileen O'Rourke would give it, that's if Eileen wanted it, which it appeared she didn't, having enough children and grandchildren to last her a lifetime.

Annie picked up what looked like a bundle of old rags which apparently contained Rosie's child, none of them as clean as the ones with which Bridie wiped over the back yard step and Nancy's face whitened even further, for she must have the answer from Eileen's own lips to the question she dreaded asking.

Painfully she cleared her throat. "The father . . . ?"

Eileen looked surprised. "Our Mick, 'oo else? She'd bin wi' 'im all this time, the bastard. She lost two others, she told me, but when 'e scarpered an' she come knockin' on my door I took 'er in. But that's an end to it, Nancy Brody. I can't keep no bairn."

"No, thank you, Mrs O'Rourke, and you will be suitably recompensed, believe me, for your kindness. Now, if I may see my sister."

"Well, it's a bit of a mess up there."

"Nevertheless . . ."

Eileen sighed. "Right, lass, up 'ere. Oh, an't by't way," turning back to Nancy for a moment, "she wants it calling Ciara. Don't ask me why."

27

Rose Brody was laid to rest in the churchyard of St John the Evangelist Church where Nancy and Josh were married and where, only two weeks ago, Edmund Hayes had been interred. There was no one there but Nancy and Josh, Mary, Jennet and Annie and, surprisingly, Arthur. The parson, who had reverently conducted the same office for Josh's father, rattled through the service as though he had a train to catch, Annie was to say later, but they were all in too much of a shocked muddle to complain, which you couldn't anyway, could you? Poor Rosie, that lovely, lively young woman who Annie had prophesied would come to a bad end, not meaning it, of course, or at least not this. To be shovelled away like some shameful reminder of the past, though Nancy had done her best. Flowers, you never saw so many flowers, white roses and lily of the valley heaped on the coffin which lay behind the polished glass and silver of the hearse, drawn by four magnificent black horses with silver accoutrements and black plumes on their nodding heads. In very poor taste, those of the Hayes circle who saw it go by were inclined to think, since the girl was a nobody, the criticism led by Millicent Hayes who had been not only at home but passing through the hallway when the hansom cab which brought Nancy, Josh and Rose Brody's daughter arrived at Riverside House.

It was nearly five o'clock on an overcast spring day when they drew up at the front door, for it had taken Nancy the best part of the day to complete the arrangements. She was forced to walk from Eileen O'Rourke's house to the nearest funeral undertaker's, which happened to be in Bridge Street, handily placed for the workhouse, she noticed, and arrange for a coffin, plain and unvarnished, at least for now, and a suitable vehicle, since she'd not have her sister carried on a handcart, she insisted. It was to come to Church Court . . . No, she did not care to be told that since the street was too narrow it would be impossible, nor that they did not do business in Angel Meadow, they were to do it, and at once. Did they understand? She was Mrs Joshua Hayes. They had heard of her husband, had they not, and just in case they were in any doubt he owned the largest mill and warehouse in the city. She herself would walk back to Church Court and she expected them to be no more than half an hour behind her and they were to bring clean . . . well, did they call them shrouds, or was it winding sheets? She was not sure, she told them, but she wanted her sister wrapped decently after she had been laid out and prepared for burial. Did they understand?

It seemed they did, her husband's name, her white, frozen beauty, her unnatural calm silencing them to total obedience to her orders.

She and Annie sat silently for ten minutes beside the appalling bed on which the tossed and bloody figure of Rose Brody lay, then Nancy sprang up, her face working with anguish, her eyes, normally such a lovely golden amber, turned to a thick, muddy brown.

"I can't stand this, Annie. I must get her clean. Look at her." For beside the detritus of birth which stained the bed and Rosie herself, she was coated with the grey grime that was usual in Church Court.

"Lass, I know, but where yer gonner get water?"

"From the standpipe, where else?"

"Dressed like that?" Annie, despite her compassion, was shocked, for Nancy's black but very elegant day dress was made of silk with a full, lace-trimmed black skirt over her crinoline.

"It's only a dress, Annie. This is my sister and I will not have her coated with filth for a moment longer than necessary. I am taking her to Grove Place where she'll . . . where she'll stay until . . ."

"Right, chuck, I'll 'elp yer. You go an' fetch water, though where yer'll find a decent cloth . . ."

"My petticoat will do."

"Eeh, lass."

"Annie, I can't bear strangers to see her."

"I know, lass, I know. Come on then, let's mekk 'er nice."

The whole street turned out to watch Nancy Brody lug bucket after bucket of water from the standpipe to Eileen O'Rourke's front door but now there was no jeering, no catcalls, no abuse. Her speechless, white-faced determination, and not just today, to bring decency to her family against overwhelming odds had finally silenced them and they watched her quietly, respectful, not just of her, but for the death of the girl they had watched grow from a skinny, neglected child into the young beauty Mick O'Rourke had destroyed.

They had stripped Rose, she and Annie, both of them weeping quietly, taking from her the tattered remnants in which she had given birth, in which she had died, washing her, even her hair which crawled with vermin, using the soap some woman in the street had silently handed in at Eileen's front door. They wrapped her stick-like body with its folds of flabby flesh into the snow white, immaculate sheets the undertaker's man passed up the stairs before he brought up the plain wooden coffin in which, temporarily, Rosie was to lie. She had to be carried from Eileen's house along Church Court to the corner of Angel Street for, as the undertaker had told her, the plain hearse, the smallest one they had, would not fit down the narrow alleyway. It was almost like the funeral to come, with four men carrying the coffin on their shoulders, Nancy, head high, behind, followed by Annie with the infant who had also been bathed and put in the remains of Nancy's petticoat. And in a respectful procession behind Annie came the inhabitants of Church Court, silent, the men with their caps removed, the women, some of them, crying quietly into their filthy pinnies. Even the noisy children were hushed, awed by the solemnity of the occasion, though they were not sure what it was all about.

Bridie had turned out to be a tower of strength in that first frantic hour after they reached Grove Place, brewing endless cups of tea, letting in the neighbours who offered to help, though none, at first, knew who lay in the coffin. She held the baby, who had begun to squawk indignantly over her lack of sustenance, jigging her up and down and even getting her to suck on a scrap of clean cloth soaked in sugared milk. Later, she was to hold Mary in her comforting arms, letting her weep all over her one good dress since it was Mary's sister who was dead, saying nothing, but there wherever and whenever she was needed. Annie was to say a dozen times what a find they had in the girl.

The plain hearse containing the coffin had drawn up outside the house after its journey along Bury New Road where, down its length, to Nancy's surprise, men stopped and stood with bared heads and women bent theirs reverently at the sight of the entourage. Strangely, their small mark of respect was a comfort to her in her pain, for it was as though their Rosie was finally receiving a small measure of the compassionate consideration she had not known for five years.

A message was sent to Jennet and another to Mary, a third to Josh and within minutes of receiving them, they were all there. Nancy walked blindly into Josh's open arms, glad suddenly of his strength, for hers, after so long, was gone.

But, of course, there was worse to come.

The hansom cab in which Nancy, with Rose Brody's baby in her arms, and Josh, who held them both silently but protectively within the shelter of his, drove up the neatly raked gravel driveway to the porch of Riverside House. Lamps had been lit in many of the rooms, the curtains not yet drawn and squares of golden light lay across the beds of spring flowers and the smooth lawn which had been mown that day. The smell of cut grass lingered pleasingly in the air. It was all so welcoming, a haven of refuge as a smiling Dulcie opened the door to them but even so Nancy's heart quailed, for she knew what would happen the moment she crossed the threshold.

Millicent was just about to enter the drawing-room, her hand on the doorknob as she turned to them.

"What's this then?" she asked suspiciously, bustling across the hallway, brushing aside the parlourmaid and peering in the darkening porch at the bundle in Nancy's arms.

"What does it look like, Millicent?" Nancy asked, doing her best to stay calm in the face of Millicent's obvious hostility. Her sister-in-law did not as yet know what was in Nancy's arms but already she was willing to disapprove of it, whatever it was. As though to give her a clue the baby grunted and awoke from the sleep into which the movement of the hansom cab had lulled her, and began to wail.

Millicent stepped back as though a cobra had emerged from the wrappings.

"Dear God in heaven, not another one," she shrieked, her voice so piercing it brought Emma Hayes to the drawing-room door.

"What is it, dear?" she asked anxiously.

"Mother, you can't possibly allow this," Millicent thundered. "I don't care whose . . . whose whelp it is you cannot allow it."

"Milly, be quiet."

"No, Josh, I will not be quiet. I have been quiet for three years now while those two bastards upstairs have spoiled any chance I had of a decent marriage."

"What bloody rubbish," Josh snapped. None knew better than he that it was his sister's acid tongue, her disagreeable attitude, her old-maidish appearance, her icy belief that she was cut from better cloth than her contemporaries, her insistence on airing her contemptuous views on every subject from the education of the lower orders, which she believed to be ill-advised, to Her Majesty's insistence in remaining in her widow's grieving, which was surely unwholesome, that kept any suitable gentleman from courting her.

Millicent Hayes was twenty-five years old and, without a doubt, would remain a spinster until the end of her days. She made no secret of her scorn for all men who, in her opinion, were hardly worth the air they breathed, but she wanted a husband. She wanted the status of a married woman, a household of her own to order, and servants to do her bidding. She did not like her role of "daughter at home" and its prolonged playing made her increasingly bitter, and it pleased her to believe that it was the bizarre situation in the Riverside nursery that was to blame for it. Two illegitimate children, one belonging to her brother, which she could just about accept since men were known for their depraved lust and could be forgiven for it, and the second to her brother's wife, who could not. Now, it appeared a third squalling infant was to be foisted on them, God knew from where, and she was not having it. She knew her mother would dither and weep and be overruled by any stronger will than her own, and Josh, poor infatuated fool, would do anything to please the trollop he had married, so it was up to her to put a stop to it.

"Whose brat is that and what is it doing here?" she hissed, doing her best to remain steady in the face of what she sensed would be a battle. She could see it on her sister-in-law's grim, white face and in her eyes, which were as hard as a topaz.

"This is my sister's child, my niece, and she is to join the children in the—"

"Oh, no, madam, she is not. I don't know why your sister cannot care for the child herself but let me—"

"She is dead. She died today giving birth."

"Oh, darling." The black-clad figure of Emma Hayes hurried from the entrance to the drawing-room, her arms lifting to comfort her daughter-in-law, who was such a comfort to her. Her face was soft with compassion, but as she made to pass the icy figure of her daughter, Millicent grabbed her arm, preventing her from doing so, while at the back of the hall, where she still remained, herself frozen in shock, the parlourmaid, Dulcie, put her hand to her mouth as though to hold in a wail of sympathy.

"Millicent, dear, please." Emma struggled to get free of her daughter's restraining hand and Josh took a step towards her.

"No, Mother, *no*. Leave it," Millicent went on furiously. "God knows where it has been. Probably in some lice-infested slag heap in Angel Meadow where its *aunt* came from. Heaven knows what disease might be on its breath. We cannot have it here and that is the end of it."

Emma, who had the softest heart in the world, was willing to accept any poor waif or stray, any beggar who knocked on her kitchen door for a hand-out, but at the mention of disease she blanched and sidled to a safer spot behind her daughter's strong shoulder.

Nancy's voice was weary but resolute as, for the first time, she made claim to what was rightfully hers.

"The child has been bathed and is perfectly clean and healthy. She is wrapped in my own petticoat which was laundered, with yours, only yesterday. And may I remind you, Millicent, that I am the mistress of this house. My husband, with the death of his father" – chancing a small smile of apology at her mother-in-law – "is master, and as his wife it is his word, and mine, that will be listened to, and obeyed. Now, if you will allow me to pass, the child needs—"

"Oh, no, you don't," Millicent panted, crouched now, arms held in the manner of a wrestler about to "take hold", hands curved into claws. "My mother is mistress of Riverside House and she will decide."

"Really, Milly, what Nancy says is correct," Emma faltered.

"No, I won't have it."

"For Christ's sake, Milly, get out of the way. This is no time for such histrionics. The baby needs attention."

"Not in this house, it doesn't, Joshua Hayes."

"Milly, can't you see you are upsetting Mother."

"*I* am upsetting Mother! God in heaven, first you fetch home this . . . this slut . . ."

"That's enough, Milly." Josh's voice was like the crack of a whip and his eyes, like his sister's, became flat grey pools of ice, but Millicent would not be silenced.

". . . and her bastard to live with decent people and now we are expected to take in, not only *her* illegitimate child but her sister's and I simply won't have it. D'you hear?"

The animosity of the past three years which had festered and grown inside Millicent Hayes was free at last. She had shown her dislike, her bitterness, her resentment in many ways since Josh and Nancy were married. Indeed it would be no lie to say that she had addressed barely a word, civil or otherwise, to her sister-in-law during that time and had done her best to turn everyone, friends, acquaintances, relatives, even the servants, against the young Mrs Hayes. But during those three years she had known that, amazingly, at least to her, her father had taken a liking for his son's new wife, had admired her strength, her resolution to succeed, her shrewd business sense, rare in a woman. And of course, despite the scar to her cheek didn't all men appreciate her beauty. She herself, though she and her brothers were so alike, had no claim to good looks as they did and her sullen detestation for her sister-in-law had corroded within her.

Josh sighed, then moved back to Nancy's side. He placed his hands on her upper arms, holding her steady, smiling into her weary, grief-stricken face, then bent his head to place a gentle kiss on the corner of her mouth. His whole attitude spoke of his own weariness with his sister, of his love and support for his wife in the face of what anyone might say, and his determination to ignore the former and stand by the latter.

"You go up, sweetheart, and you'd better take Dulcie with you," smiling over his sister's shoulder at the maid. "Nanny Dee will need some help until another nursemaid can be found. You don't mind for a few days, do you, Dulcie?"

Although Dulcie wanted nothing more than to get back to the kitchen to impart the astonishing news to the other servants, she smiled tentatively, bobbed a curtsey and turned obediently towards the staircase.

"Shall I take it, ma'am?" she asked Nancy. God forbid that one of the family should carry anything when there was a servant about, but Nancy smiled and shook her head, looking down into the red, angry face of Rosie's baby. It was as though she were looking at Rose herself.

"Just a minute, girl," Millicent shrieked, making them all flinch. Mrs Hayes edged away from her towards the safety of the drawing-room and Dulcie turned, ready to run for the kitchen, for Miss Millicent seemed to have lost her mind.

"Millicent, will you—" Josh began.

"If that child goes up those stairs, Joshua, I shall follow to pack my bags. I will not live another hour under the same roof as three bastards, probably four since I would imagine your wife does not know her own father." Her face creased in a sneer. "I presume you will continue with my allowance so that I may rent a place of my own somewhere?"

"Just as you like, Millicent." Josh shrugged as though it were a matter of complete indifference to him whether she stayed or went, but through his mind swept the thought that it would be a damn sight easier on them all if she went. "Now then, Dulcie, accompany your mistress to the nursery while I see to Mother," for Emma Hayes was in a state of collapse on the threshold of the drawing-room.

Millicent drew herself up, her face suddenly old, plain, grey with shock, for she had genuinely believed she had called her brother's bluff. She had no intention of leaving her comfortable home, not for anyone, least of all a wretched brat related to her detested sister-in-law, but still she fought on, using her last weapon with a smile of triumph.

"If that is your last word, Joshua."

"It is, Millicent," Joshua replied, beginning to lead his wife tenderly towards the clucking sympathy of the waiting parlourmaid, before attending to his mother.

"Very well, I'll have Mother's bags packed with my own, since I cannot leave her alone in this den of iniquity."

If he had not been so confounded Josh Hayes might have smiled. Three innocent children who, according to his sister, had turned her home into a place of sin and licentiousness, and now, because of it, Millicent was prepared to remove herself and his mother to some other place where they would not be tainted with it.

But he had not counted on Emma Hayes, nor her horror at the thought of being torn away from everything and everyone she loved – particularly her grandson – and living alone with her cold-hearted and unbending daughter. She placed a hand on his arm as he reached her quickly, convinced she was about to fall, but from somewhere Emma scooped up her courage and the words to amaze them all, especially Millicent.

"Oh, no," she said in a strong, determined voice. "No, Milly, I cannot go with you. This is my home. Nancy is mistress here now, but it is my home and I would prefer to stay here with her, and the children, if you don't mind," she finished politely.

"*Mother!*"

"Leave her alone, Millicent." Josh's voice was dangerous. "One more word and I personally will pack your things, call a cab and escort you off the premises. Now then, Dulcie, go with Mrs Hayes and the baby. Mother, come and sit by the fire and ring for Ellen to bring some tea and perhaps we'd best send for one of the other maids to see to the nursery's needs. See, Mother, take my arm."

Within five seconds the hall was empty but for the still, frozen-faced figure of Millicent Hayes who remained where she was even as Ellen brushed past her with a polite, "Excuse me, Miss Millicent." The bewildered figure of Tilly ran up the stairs in obedience to the request that she was to go at once to the nursery, and her brother, having seen his mother settled, dashed across the hall and up the stairs to his wife.

She didn't know how long she stood there and *hated*. She was conscious of the servants hurrying here and there, and their curious glances, but it meant nothing to her. She hated. That was the sum and substance of her in those few minutes. Hatred, jealousy, bitter and corrosive, venom, a biting thirst for vengeance, implacable and relentless. It was like her own blood pumping through her, her hatred of Nancy Brody, strengthening her, keeping her alive, urging her on to do what she became increasingly aware was to hurt her brother's wife. To get her own back, as she and her brothers used to say when they were children; and somewhere there was an answer, a step to take, a plan to be made, and she would find it, make it, and survive!

The front door burst open suddenly but she still remained frozen to the spot where her family had rooted her with their disloyalty to her and their support for the intruder. Her younger brother clattered across the black and white tiled floor of the porch, banging the door to behind him, coming to a halt when he saw her, startled, for he had not dreamed the death of Nancy's sister – whose existence he had not known of – could affect Milly so. She looked as though she'd been delivered of a mortal blow, eyes wild, jaw clenched, her hands curled into murderous fists.

"Hello, old thing," he said awkwardly. "I came as soon as the mill closed. How's Nancy, and Mother?" For as yet he knew nothing of the addition to the nursery. "Bad do, isn't it? Poor Nancy."

"Damn poor Nancy to hell," she spat between rigidly clenched teeth. "May she rot there for all eternity and all her family with her."

"Aye, steady on, old girl, she's just lost her sister," Arthur protested, wondering what the hell was up with Milly. He knew she did not care for Nancy, she had made that clear enough, nor for the bonny little girl in the nursery who was Nancy's daughter, but surely she could not blame her for the death of her own sister.

"Oh, yes, Arthur Hayes, lost a sister and gained a niece who is to be – yes, you've guessed it – fobbed off on to the rest of us. Three little bastards in the nursery now."

"Christ, Milly, you can't mean it!" Not that Arthur cared a jot or tittle. In fact he quite enjoyed the liveliness of the nursery, the sound of the laughter and merriment that echoed from the nursery floor and often went up there to enjoy – and add to – the fun and games. The house was alive with children's voices, with kittens mewing and dogs barking and the sight of Nanny Dee chasing Freddy and Kitty round the garden made them all smile.

"Oh, can't I? Well just go up there and see for yourself. I threatened to leave and take Mother with me but Josh wouldn't hear of it," revealing only half the truth.

"I should think not." Arthur was clearly horrified.

"But they've not heard the last of it, believe me."

"What d'you mean by that, old girl?"

"She'll not cross me for much longer, that floozy Josh married."

"Aye, steady on, Milly," Arthur protested again.

"I'll find something, see if I don't, and when I do she'll rue the day, she'll rue the day . . ."

"What d'you mean?"

"Wait and see, Arthur Hayes."

With that she turned and ran up the stairs, her footstep light, her back like a ramrod.

* * *

They sat together at dinner that night, Nancy and Josh, Emma, Millicent and Arthur, the ladies in the deepest black of mourning, though it must be admitted Emma and Millicent wore it not for Rose Brody but for Edmund Hayes. So did Nancy, in respect and affection not just for her father-in-law, but for Emma, and now it was for her sister. The gentlemen were in tight black trousers and frock coats, single-breasted with a narrow collar and fastened with only one button. Their silk neckties and waistcoats were also black, the ties fastened in a small bow. They were all keenly aware of the storm that had swept through the house that afternoon but it seemed Millicent had decided to let bygones be bygones and indeed went out of her way to be pleasant to her mother and brothers, though she acted as though her sister-in-law did not exist.

Nancy had not wanted to come downstairs, begging Josh to ring for a tray, perhaps some soup and one of Mrs Cameron's excellent soufflés, for she had no appetite.

Josh had knelt at her feet, leaning forward to look tenderly into her pale, weary face. They had just come down from the nursery after settling Rose Brody's daughter among its astonished occupants, none more so than Nanny Dee. Dulcie, herself one of a large family, had scooted up to the attic for the crib and the box that contained Master Freddy's and Miss Kitty's baby clothes and the "little mite" as she was called, since as yet they had not got their tongues round her name, had been bathed – the second time that day – smoothed all over with violet powder and dressed in the over-large petticoat and dress that Freddy, who had been a big, healthy newborn, not like this wisp, had once worn. Both Freddy and Kitty had been mesmerised by the whole procedure, hanging over the large bowl in which the tiny scrap of humanity was lowered while Nanny Dee soaped and sluiced, and the baby, who seemed to find the experience to her liking, gazed unblinkingly about her. They were fascinated by the newcomer's hopeful sucking motion with her baby lips which Nanny had rectified for the moment with a little oatmeal gruel, thin and smooth, and were amazed when the baby had fallen asleep on Nanny's lap. Kitty had begged to play with the infant, not to hold her like one did with a dolly, since she was scornful of such things, but to toss about and tickle as one might a playful kitten and had been seriously displeased when she was refused.

"But who is she, that's what I'd like to know?"

"Me too," Freddy echoed.

"And where did she come from?"

"Yes, where?"

"Papa and I will explain it all to you in the morning, Kitty. I'm very tired but I can tell you her name is Ciara. Ciara Rose."

"I don't like it," Kitty proclaimed loftily.

"Neither do I," her echo said.

And neither did Nanny Dee, who was used to plain, easily identified names for *her* children. No doubt when madam was rested she would reveal the identity of the tiny infant, but when Dulcie, who had been in the hall when the revelation came, whispered to her over the heads of the fascinated children that Mrs Josh's sister had died that day, the mystery was solved.

Josh had persuaded Nancy to dine with the family, convinced that Millicent, who had been in such a tear earlier, would not put in an appearance.

"Only for an hour, sweetheart. Mother would like it, you know. She loves you, Nancy, and will be genuinely grieved by Rose's death."

"Josh, I just cannot stand another scene with your sister, really I can't."

"I know, my love. I don't think she will dine with us but if she does I promise you the moment she starts, if she starts, we'll both come back upstairs."

Nancy sighed. "You promise?"

"Yes, my darling."

Millicent was there, keeping up a constant flow of bright conversation, gossipy, inconsequential conversation, as though to say the death of Nancy's sister was no concern for melancholy. Brittle conversation about the comings and goings and doings of their friends and the social functions that were planned for the coming summer. There was to be an engagement party at the Colemans, had Josh heard? Oh, yes, Della, who was the same age as Millicent and had long expected to remain a spinster – though Millicent did not voice this last – had finally got Andrew Mortimore to propose and there would be a wedding in the autumn. Della, who was very fashionable, very particular about her appearance, was to have her trousseau made for her by that stunningly clever young dressmaker who worked at Kendal Milne and Faulkners. Simply everyone was asking for her. She thought she might try her herself since she was exceedingly popular.

Emma gazed with anguish at Nancy, distressed by Millicent's lack of feeling, ready to chide Milly for her callousness, but Nancy placed her hand on her own, giving her a small smile and slight shake of the head, begging her to say nothing, for what did it matter? Josh fidgeted and at one point, as Millicent extolled the virtues of the young seamstress, seemed ready to speak out but again Nancy shook her head. What did it matter? Millicent Hayes did not matter. Her heart was too heavy with sadness for her sister to be damaged in any way by her sister-in-law's venom.

Millicent tinkled on. Had Josh heard that Johnny Arkwright was back from New Zealand where his regiment, the West Yorkshires, had helped to put down those fierce savages in the Maori Wars? He'd been wounded, only slightly, but enough to get him sent home and his mother, who had taken tea with them only yesterday, said he would call on them shortly. She did hope that Joshua and Arthur could arrange to be at home when he did, for it would be nice if the whole family could be there to greet him.

Arthur looked at Josh as though for guidance in this astonishing performance. He'd never seen his sister so vivacious and though none of the others seemed about to remonstrate with her, he thought it was really bad form for Milly to carry on like this on the very day Nancy's sister had died.

Josh watched Millicent, his face grim. It was as though the violent exchange between her and Nancy – violent at least on Millicent's part – had not taken place at all. Only at the end of the meal, as Nancy placed her napkin on the table and stood up, followed by Josh, was there a reminder of it and for a split second it looked as though it might explode again.

"I'll say goodnight, Mother-in-law," Nancy murmured quietly, bending to kiss Emma's cheek and patting the hand Emma placed on her arm.

"Goodnight, my dear. I hope you sleep a little."

"Thank you, but first I must go and check on Ciara Rose."

Emma looked mystified. "Ciara Rose?" she echoed.

"Yes, my niece. I must see that she has settled in the nursery."

"Oh, of course dear."

Though she had meant to say not one more word on the

matter, at least not until the time was ripe, Millicent almost choked on the coffee she was drinking.

"*Ciara Rose!* Dear God in heaven, isn't it typical of an illiterate Irish woman of the lower orders to call her child by such an outlandish name. But then, what can you expect?" She began to laugh and, at the sideboard, Ellen and Tilly, who had served the meal, exchanged glances. "I presume it *is* Irish."

"Yes, Ciara is, I believe, and Rose was my sister's name." Nancy felt herself sway. She really felt very frail and quite unable to fight Millicent as she would normally. It had been an appalling day. Her sense of desolation over Rosie, her Rosie, who had once been her little sister until Mick O'Rourke got his hands on her, had taken, for the moment, her spirit, her vigorous will and even her courage, as Mick had taken Rosie's, and all she wanted to do was escape Millicent's vituperative tongue. She held out her hand for Josh, who was at her side at once and on his face was an expression of deep sadness for her. It had been a mistake to persuade her to dine downstairs, he realised that now, even for his mother's sake. Nancy was still raw with pain and shock and Millicent was delighted to have the chance to rub fresh salt into that open wound.

"Ciara! What can it mean, d'you think?" Millicent chortled in great glee. "Do you think the man who fathered the brat chose it?"

"*Millicent!* That is enough. Really, your behaviour is totally unacceptable and I insist you apologise to Nancy," her mother said, but all Nancy could hear as Josh almost carried her up the stairs was Millicent's laughter.

28

The tall woman nodded disdainfully at the clerk behind the high desk in the lawyer's outer office, frowning, until, with the swift deference she seemed to demand, the clerk leaped to his feet.

"Good morning, ma'am," he said courteously.

"Good morning. I have an appointment with Mr Bellchamber at ten thirty. Be so good as to inform him that I am here."

"Certainly, miss. May I tell him who—?"

"He knows who I am," the woman interrupted coldly.

"Of course. Might I offer you a seat while—?"

"I'll stand, thank you. And kindly tell Mr Bellchamber that I do not like to be kept waiting."

The woman, or *lady*, the bowing clerk supposed he should call her, was dressed in the complete mourning of a recent bereavement. She was not elegant, or even fashionable as some ladies can be, even in the deepest black, but her gown and wide-brimmed bonnet were of the finest quality. She had a taut, unbending figure, straight up and down, but with good, well-defined breasts. Her lips were tightly compressed, her chin set at an imperious angle and her eyes were a pale, suspicious grey as though she suspected him of something unlawful. She could not be called handsome by any degree since her features were too strong, too masculine. She was too tall for a woman, he decided, and too narrow of build for her height. Her hair was completely hidden by her capacious bonnet and the only word the clerk could think of to describe her was *soldierly*!

Mr Bellchamber rose to his feet as she entered the room, bowing over her hand as he murmured her name, then indicating that she should be seated in the chair before his desk.

"May I offer you coffee, Miss—" but before he could finish his sentence she had refused.

"No, thank you, Mr Bellchamber. I am in somewhat of a hurry to get this business under way."

"Of course, ma'am."

"And before we begin may I say . . . nay *insist*, that no word of this visit reach my family. You are my brother's lawyer and it might seem strange to you that I am here without him." For what *real* lady conducts business with a gentleman when she has a male relative to do it for her, she seemed to be telling him.

"Not at all, Miss—" he began politely but again she cut him off. She had no time for the niceties, her manner implied. After all, their relationship was a purely professional one, similar to that of mistress and servant, and one did not fraternise with a servant. She was to pay this man for his services and he was in no way entitled to treat her as an equal.

"When our business is brought to a satisfactory conclusion I would be obliged if you would send your bill personally to me, Mr Bellchamber. To no one else, you understand?" she added sharply.

"Of course. And what is it you wish me to do for you?" The lawyer who, like his clerk, believed he had never met a more unfeminine female in all his long career, sat back in his chair, his elbows on its arms, his fingers forming a steeple which just touched his lips.

"Mr Bellchamber, I don't quite know what duties a lawyer can perform on his client's behalf. That is why I am here. To find out."

Mr Bellchamber raised his eyebrows in surprise, his mind for a moment grappling with what kind of duties this dried-up, unyielding woman might require of him. She could not be the victim of some man's broken pledge, a breach of promise case, for surely no man, no hot-blooded man which, despite his age, he was, could have proposed to her in the first place. She came from a wealthy family, a well-known Manchester family, which might attract a certain type of man but he was of the opinion that once this woman had brought a man to heel he would never be allowed to escape.

"Tell me what you have in mind, ma'am, and I will do my best to carry out your wishes."

Bending her head she opened the plain black reticule she carried. She fumbled for a moment inside it then lifted out an envelope. It was sealed. She placed it on his desk but before he could reach to take it she put up her hand.

"Just one moment, Mr Bellchamber. Before you open this envelope I want to ask you something."

Mr Bellchamber leaned back in his chair again. "Of course."

"If I were to ask you to find someone, is it . . . would it be in your power to do so? I mean have you in your employ a man . . . a certain kind of man who is experienced in this kind of thing? I am not familiar with the work a lawyer does." She wrinkled her nose distastefully as though she had no wish to; as though Mr Bellchamber conducted some low task such as clearing ash-pits or delivering coal.

Mr Bellchamber hesitated. He felt a distinct inclination to tell this arrogant woman to take her envelope and her business elsewhere, but her brother was a valued client and Mr Bellchamber could not afford to offend him.

"It would depend on what you meant to do with this person," he answered, indicating the envelope on his desk.

"Do with him! Surely that is my business, not yours?" His client was deeply offended and the lawyer could see the tussle she was having with herself. She would dearly love to snatch up her envelope and tell him to go to the devil, but if she was serious, which it appeared she was, then she would have to find another lawyer, one who did not work for her brother and might not be so easily persuaded.

"I mean this person no harm," she said coldly, swallowing her ire. "In fact, just the opposite."

"Very well, I'll take your word for it."

She clearly wanted to smack him in the face, but she controlled herself as he reached for and slit open the envelope. He read the name on the sheet of paper inside, then looked up at her.

"Have you any idea where this man might be?"

"None."

"That will make it more difficult and more expensive. My . . . chappie is an expert. He has done work for me before but he is not cheap. He will expect a certain remuneration each day, plus his expenses. Then there is my fee."

"Your fee!"

"I don't work for nothing, Miss—"

"But what are you to do besides put that note in his hand?"

"Ma'am, I do believe that unless you trust me with this I cannot help you." Mr Bellchamber stood up, his face cold and his client subsided, beaten but not liking it.

"Very well," she said icily. "I agree."

"Thank you. Now if you could tell me where this person was last seen it would help."

"In an area known as Angel Meadow."

It had not been difficult to get the man's name out of Mary Brody.

It was a month since Rose Brody's death and both Mary and Nancy had recovered somewhat from the appalling shock of it. Ciara Rose had settled well in the nursery where a young nursemaid by the name of Minnie had been employed to help Nanny Dee with the three children. The baby was thriving. A pear-shaped pewter feeding bottle with a hole in the side through which the milk was poured had been found in the same box in which the baby garments had been stored. It was old-fashioned but would suffice until Nanny could get to the chemist in Higher Broughton for a more up-to-date glass one with the necessary india-rubber teats, Nanny said practically. The pewter bottle had once been used to feed the infant Arthur, Emma had whispered fondly to Nancy, since she herself had no milk when he was born and what a pretty baby Ciara – was that how you pronounced her name, as though there were an H after the C? – was turning out to be. She put a gentle finger to the baby's cheek, deciding for the hundredth time that it had been a good day when Josh had married this lovely woman who had brought such joy into Emma's life, despite the irregularity of it. She loved babies, particularly her grandson, and was often to be found in the nursery with one or other of the children on her lap.

Of course Millicent Hayes was not privy to these delightful domestic arrangements. She never went near the nursery floor and should she meet either of the two older children it had not gone unnoticed that both of them, even the bold and outspoken Kitty, drew back fearfully behind Nanny Dee's wide grey cotton skirt.

"Is she a witch?" Freddy whispered, cowering at the back of Kitty but Aunt Millicent, who was Father's sister, they had been told, had sailed past them without a glance and they were truly thankful for it!

The news that a third baby had been added to the Hayes' unique nursery exploded like a bombshell within the circle of their friends, causing no end of anxiety. Should they continue to ignore Mr and Mrs Joshua Hayes's scandalous behaviour, they asked one another, since, having accepted two children with dubious beginnings, could they jib at a third! The trouble was they were all so fond of dear Emma and by casting the Hayes family from the social fold, so to speak, would it be fair on her who had no part in the matter? Joshua was the master of Riverside House now and unless dear Emma moved out, which would be vastly upsetting since it was her home, what could be done about it?

They decided, for the moment, to do nothing, since Emma was still in mourning anyway, which gave them a breathing space.

The kitchen also had been in an uproar on the day of the infant's arrival. Tilly, sent first up to the nursery then down to the kitchen for the warm milk and oatmeal that were required, had told them whose child was upstairs, having had it from Dulcie who had overheard the whole thing in the hallway, so it was true, Tilly told the circle of disbelieving faces. Mrs Harvey and Mrs Cameron, neither of whom cared for gossip, were for several minutes so stunned they allowed the servants to twitter round the kitchen table like a swirling multitude of noisy starlings.

"Her *sister's* baby. Dear Lord."

"What next, I ask you?"

"But will the mistress allow it again?"

"Don't be so soft, she is mistress."

"I meant the old mistress."

"It's nowt ter do wi' her, not now."

"Me mam'd 'ave a fit if she knew."

"What's it ter do wi' your mam?"

"She's a churchgoer and against . . . well, bastards."

"Eeh, two were enough, but three . . ."

"Well, I suppose wi't babby's mam dead, poor thing, an' Mrs Josh bein' 'er auntie . . ."

"Eeh, I know; in't it sad?"

After several minutes of pandemonium Mrs Cameron and Mrs Harvey came to their senses and at once collected up their minions and sent them about their allotted tasks, since there was still an evening meal to prepare whatever happened.

During the next week, when the baby carriage was got out and Nanny Dee, her older charges racing about with Scrap and Freddy's dog Button, took the infant for an airing, the servants found some opportunity to take a peep at it and admitted to one another it would be hard to turn away from such a dear little thing. Like a little rosebud in her nest of white blankets and the dead spit of Miss Kitty, who was her cousin. Within a couple of weeks it had been totally forgotten that the "little mite" had not been born in the very nursery where it seemed she was to remain.

It also seemed that fate, the gods, destiny, chance, by whatever name you liked to call it, was determined to shine on Millicent Hayes.

"Mother," her elder son said to Emma Hayes later that month, "I know we are still in mourning for Father, but would it distress you too much if I were to invite a business acquaintance of mine to dine with us? I spoke of him last week, if you remember. If you and Millicent don't feel up to it, then Arthur and I, with Nancy, will manage alone but he's a nice chap and would behave with great circumspection. He's from Liverpool. He's in cotton and will be doing business in Manchester for several days. He's staying at the Albion on Piccadilly which has one of the best cuisines in Europe, so they tell me, but nevertheless I felt it would be pleasant for him to dine with the family. Not to mention it would do me and the firm no harm to put him in our debt."

"Oh, dear, Josh . . ." At once Emma was in a dither, for would it be improper, as the widow of a man in his grave only a few short weeks, to begin entertaining so soon? The irony of her dilemma completely escaped her. Upstairs in the nursery were three children whose natural parents were not married to one another and yet she was afraid of offending society by asking to dine, in her own discreet dining-room, a business acquaintance of her son.

Help came from an unexpected quarter.

"Why, Mother, it could do no harm at all and I'm sure your friends would understand. So many cotton businesses collapsed during the American civil war that surely it is only our duty to support Josh, as he prospers again, in any way we can."

For an astounded moment they all, including Ellen and Dulcie who were serving, turned to stare, open-mouthed, at Millicent, and at once, into Josh and Nancy's minds at least, came the same wondering thought of what she was up to. Millicent Hayes did nothing that was not of benefit to herself but, having no conception of the hatred, the thirst for revenge, the vicious plans that seethed in her unsound mind, both jumped to the wrong conclusion. They exchanged a secret smile. Philip Meadows, of Meadows and Beswick, Cotton Importers, was a bachelor of about the same age as Josh, attractive in a homely sort of a way, and wealthy, a fact that had been mentioned when Josh had spoken of him a few days ago.

Nancy was looking better now. After her sister's death the shock and grief of it seemed to melt the lovely firm flesh of her face, making her cheekbones stand out prominently. The one that had been smashed by Mick O'Rourke had become very noticeable, the broken bone and the concavity of it clearly visible. She had lost her colour, her skin like marble, even her wide mouth, so full and soft, becoming pale, inclined to tremble. Before they came down to dinner they had made love, not slowly and languorously as they would have later, but in swift need, an urgent desire to be as close as two bodies can be without actually fusing into one. It had put a flush of rose in her cheeks and her eyes were as deep and golden as a cat's.

"Well, I don't know, dear," Emma faltered, turning to look round the table, even glancing at Ellen and Dulcie in her need for reassurance.

"Mother, really, where is the harm?" Millicent encouraged.

"I agree, Mother," Arthur added, smiling at Dulcie as she placed a dish of exotically coloured and flavoured ice-creams in front of him. There was an almond soufflé waiting to be served but Mr Arthur, just as though he were no older than the children in the nursery, did love his ice-cream and Mrs Cameron indulged him, as she did them.

"Well, I suppose if it were to help Joshua and the mill there could be nothing wrong in entertaining just one gentleman, could there?" Emma asked somewhat anxiously. "Particularly if he's as pleasant a young man as you say he is, Josh. He knows we are still in mourning and will respect that."

Josh laughed. "Mother, he is not likely to do a song and dance, you know. In fact, he's a quiet sort of a chap. You'll like him."

His mother sat back in her chair and let out a sigh of relief, then turned to Ellen to indicate that she was to serve the soufflé. She smiled round the table, picked up her spoon and for several minutes there was silence as they did justice to Mrs Cameron's mouthwatering desert.

"I was just thinking, Mother," Millicent began artfully. She spooned the last of the soufflé into her mouth, swallowed, since it needed no chewing, returned her spoon to the exact centre of her plate and wiped her lips delicately on her napkin.

"Yes, dear?" Emma turned to her enquiringly, as did the rest.

"Would it be in order to invite another lady, do you think? Just to balance the numbers. I know it is not exactly to be a dinner party but surely another member of the family would be in keeping?"

"Another member of. . . ?" Emma began doubtfully, her mind going to distant cousins, none of whom lived locally.

"Yes. I was thinking of Mary. She is in mourning for her sister, as Nancy is and so would not expect frivolities."

There was a moment or two of absolute silence in which, barring Emma, every person in the room, even Ellen and Dulcie, grappled with the question of what the devil Millicent Hayes was up to now. Nancy's sister, Mary, who, during the past three years whenever she had been included in a family function, had been icily ignored, Millicent making it very plain that while she was forced to put up with her brother's wife, she was in no way committed to her brother's sister-in-law. She was bog Irish, of working-class background, as Nancy was, even if she did put on the airs of a lady, and Millicent had wanted nothing to do with her. Now, here she was suggesting she come to dinner where an eligible young man was to be a guest to make up the number! What mischief was she planning?

"Well . . ." Josh looked from his sister's innocent face to his mother and then to Nancy, his own a picture of incomprehension. His eyes signalled to his wife that if she knew what Milly was up to he certainly didn't.

"I'm sure Mary would be happy to come," Nancy began hesitantly, "that's if Mother-in-law agrees."

"Of course she would be happy to come and Mother would be glad to see her, wouldn't you, Mother?" Arthur added enthusiastically, for though, so far, he had not made much headway with Nancy's shy and pretty sister, he was always delighted when an opportunity arose to try. Since his father died and all social activities had ceased he had apart from her sister's funeral, not been in her company once but now, thanks, amazingly, to his overbearing sister, it looked as though his wish might be granted.

"Well, I'm sure, that's if you all agree, that Mary would be a delightful addition to the evening." Like most of the older generation Emma found Nancy's sister to be the personification of young, well-bred womanhood, even if she hadn't been born to it. Shy, self-effacing, polite and always ready to listen to Emma's rambling reminiscences, which was not something that could be said about many young people today. Her own daughter, though Emma was sad to admit it and then only to herself, was impatient, brusque, inclined to cut in when Emma spoke, which was very hurtful, so it would be doubly pleasant to have Nancy's gentle sister at the dinner table.

It was evident from the moment she entered the drawing-room, her arm through Nancy's in that diffident way she had, that Philip Meadows thought so too. Millicent, who had not met him before, had him cornered on the sofa to the side of the intricately ornamented marble fireplace. The fireplace was the heart of the room, set off by a gleaming grate and fender. It was to here that the family gravitated, for though the fire roared ferociously up the chimney, it being a chilly and damp evening, the greater part of the room remained unheated.

The room was furnished – over-furnished – in the ornate and costly style of the day. Easy chairs and sofas of rich, honey-coloured velvet, plump and comfortable, some without arms to allow the huge skirts of the ladies to spill over their sides. It was an obstacle course of small occasional tables, scattered with ornaments which made moving about, especially in a crinoline, extremely hazardous. A multi-tiered whatnot, a cross between a bookcase and a table, stood against the wall, helping to take the overflow of books, newspapers and stray knick-knacks. There was a piano, which Millicent played, a massive grand, its heavy legs and broad sides lavishly carved. The curtains were of heavy red velvet, decorated with balls and tassels. The carpets, of bold colours of red and gold, were rich and deep and the wallpaper was of a thick flock. And in the midst of all this splendour, an elegant clutter of porcelain figurines, Chinese vases, potted palms, ornamental boxes and exotic paperweights jostled with one another for an inch of space.

On the mantelpiece were a dozen silver framed portraits in miniature of the three Hayes children when they were young and it was one of these that a simpering Millicent was displaying to their guest. She looked formidable in her black velvet evening gown, her fine bosom showing at its best. She had been at once surprised and pleased when her brother's business acquaintance had turned out to be such an admirable young man. About Josh's age, which was not young exactly, but evidently a gentleman, courteous and though not exactly well versed in the art of conversation, she was not put off, since the sound of her own voice gave her a great deal of pleasure. He was tall and well built. He had a pleasant and singularly sweet smile and warm brown eyes, an unexceptional face, she supposed, but he was known to be wealthy, or so Josh said, and came from a decent family, so his looks did not signify. The evening promised to be a great success. Not only would it afford her the opportunity to persuade the Irish baggage to confide any information she might have on the name and whereabouts – if she knew it – of the brat's father, but seemed to hold out an assurance of something that might be the beginning of a new friendship, and perhaps more, with this eligible gentleman.

"My mother wanted to have mementoes of us as children," she was saying as she handed him a silver-framed watercolour of a small boy on a pony, a very ordinary boy and a very ordinary painting. Mr Meadows smiled and murmured the appropriate remarks while Emma looked on encouragingly, since any suitable gentleman who took an interest in her daughter was welcome indeed.

Nancy and Josh sat side by side, Nancy's hand in his in the folds of her black silk skirt, her head drooping slightly towards his shoulder, for she was very tired. It had been a particularly busy day at the shop with, or so it seemed, every lady in Manchester planning her summer wardrobe and each and every one expecting her personal and individual help in doing so. Behind them at the window Arthur hovered on the lookout for the carriage that had been sent for Mary.

"And this is me, Mr Meadows. Not on a pony, as you can see. I was not fond of horses so Father did not insist. He was the kindest of men."

"Indeed, Miss Hayes, I'm sure he was," Mr Meadows replied, as Millicent lifted a dainty square of lace to her eyes. "I found him most congenial to deal with in our business transactions."

"Did you, Mr Meadows? But of course you did. He is sadly missed."

Seeing that his mother was beginning to look somewhat distressed at this turn in the conversation and wanting to steer the talk away from his father's death, over which Millicent loved to make a great drama, Josh stood up, gently returning Nancy's hand to her lap. Millicent turned and saw the gesture and at once her brows sketched a disapproving frown, for she was of the opinion that any show of affection, especially in public, smacked of ill-breeding. But then what could you expect from a girl dragged up in the slums of Manchester, her sniff said.

"Another sherry, Meadows, and perhaps a drop more Madeira, Mother?" Josh asked, reaching for his mother's glass. He looked very distinguished in the stark black and white of his evening clothes, and darkly handsome too, his maturity giving him something he had not had as a youth. His face was still moulded in the tender look he had just bestowed on his wife. They had not made love before dinner as they often did, since Nancy seemed unusually frail tonight. She had been inclined to tiredness over the last few weeks, which was not surpising in the circumstances. Her sister's death had hit her badly and she seemed to blame herself in some way. She had made herself responsible for both her sisters from an early age and her inability to put Rose on the course she and Mary had followed had been a bitter blow to her. She was drooping now among the cushions, her face pale, but in a strange way calm and glowing from within and he wondered what it was as she smiled up at him.

Millicent had returned to her self-imposed task of showing off the family portraits to their guest, who was beginning to look somewhat strained, even glassy-eyed, Josh thought. He really must try to get the poor chap away from her, he told himself, when Arthur whirled about, his boyish face flushed.

"She's here," he exclaimed in great excitement, so that Philip Meadows might have been forgiven for thinking royalty had arrived. Arthur was hot on Nancy's heels as she went into the hall to greet her sister and bring her in, and when she did so both men, Josh and Philip Meadows, were on their feet. Philip still had a portrait of an awkward group of children in his hand, Millicent and her two brothers, he had been told, but as his hostess led in the pink-cheeked, bright-eyed, shyly smiling and beautifully gowned vision of young womanhood who was her sister, it was dropped unceremoniously into Millicent's lap with barely a smile or a murmur.

Another nail was hammered into the coffin that was Millicent Hayes's hatred of the Brody sisters. She watched, unbelievingly, her eyes narrowed to slits of pure venom as naïve little Mary Brody, who had no conversation to speak of, no breeding, no proper education as far as Millicent could make out, swept the man whom Millicent had earmarked for herself off his well-shod feet. Though he had barely had a word for the cat before she arrived, letting Millicent do all the talking, she could not fail to notice that the Irish trollop and her brother's guest had a great deal to say to one another during dinner. It was quite disgusting the way she monopolised him, the hussy, and Millicent would have a word or two to say to Josh about it later. Of course the man was probably being no more than polite, but the smiles, even the laughter that swirled gently about the table were surely out of place with her father dead in his grave no more than a few weeks.

Neverthless, by the end of the evening Millicent Hayes had the name of the man who had fathered not only her sister Rose's baby but Nancy's as well, and Philip Meadows had Mary's promise that, with her sister and brother-in-law, she would dine with him at his home in Prescot.

And in the privacy of their bedroom Nancy revealed to her husband that, at last, after almost three years of marriage, she was pregnant with his child.

29

Mick O'Rourke's face was a picture of suspicious amazement. It was as though he couldn't quite believe the cheek of the bloody man. He pulled his arm from his grasp, backing away with his pint of ale held defensively before him, edging along the bar until he was back to back with another chap as burly as himself. There were a group of them, all dock labourers, all big men, truculent, ready to fly off the handle at the slightest provocation, for it was pay-day and they had been in the ale-house drinking steadily since their shift had ended two hours previously.

"Bejabers an' what's your game? Ye'll be takin' yer 'and off me arm, so yer will, yer spalpeen, unless yer want me fist in yer face," Mick roared, thrusting his pugnacious chin forward.

"There's no call fer that, lad," the man said mildly, a big chap who gave the impression he knew how to handle himself, which was why Mick had flinched away from him. Mick O'Rourke was no longer the bright-eyed, vigorous youth he had been years ago. Then he had strutted like the cock o' the north he had believed himself to be. Big, powerful, strong as an ox, well-muscled, at the peak of his young manhood, a fighter, coarsely handsome and believing it would last for ever. It hadn't, of course. Drink had done for him. Every purse he won had been poured down his throat until he could no longer dance round the prize-fighting ring on feathered feet. No longer land the vicious punches, nor avoid those aimed at him until, at last, he was told by fight promoters in no uncertain terms to "bugger off out of it". He was twenty-five, a powerful figure still, but gross. His muscles, once so hard a man could break a hand on them, were gone soft and flabby, his face even coarser and bewhiskered, his eyes sunk in his fleshy features. Strangely, he had kept his teeth, which were straight and strong, and his hair, which was thick and dark and curling though hanging in greasy draggles. During the years since he had left Manchester he had continued to wander from place to place looking for fights and, finding none, had taken up work as a casual labourer at Liverpool docks.

He was an Irishman among Irishmen, most of them, like him, who had never seen the green of the old country but who nevertheless spoke with the lilting brogue of those born there. He lived rough, dossing down in the straw of any cellar where space could be found for a copper or two a night, earning just enough to keep him in pipe tobacco and ale and the diet of potatoes he mainly ate, since they were cheap and filling. If he remembered Nancy Brody, or even Rose, who had trailed at his back wherever he went, since there had been so many like them in his earlier days, he would have had a hard job bringing either face to his drink-sozzled mind. It was months, almost a year since he had walked out on Rose, not knowing, nor even caring, that she was carrying his child for the fifth or sixth time and as he had been in some stage of drunkenness since, his brain and liver pickled and barely functioning, he would have looked blank had her name been mentioned.

"I'll say what's called for, mate," he told the man who had accosted him belligerently, making sure, nevertheless, that his fellow Irishmen were right behind him, since the man, though older than himself, had a face like a block of cement.

"Let me get ya' a drink," the man said genially, turning to nod at the barmaid whose mouth fell open, for Mick O'Rourke was well known in the Jack Tar and was not the sort of chap other chaps bought drinks for.

Mick was bewildered, evidently much the same thought creeping into his fuddled brain but looking a gift horse in the mouth was not one of his characteristics.

"Right," he muttered, then swigged down what was in his pot in readiness for the next one.

"Can we go an' sit down?" the man asked him politely, nodding at an empty table by the window.

"Wha' for?"

"So we can talk uninterrupted."

"Sure an' why would we want ter be doin' that?" Mick blustered. There were men about who had no time for women, dirty beasts whose preference was for other men, but Jesus,

Mary and Joseph, this big chap couldn't be one of them and if he was, would he choose Mick O'Rourke?

"Because I've somethin' ter tell yer."

"Summat ter tell me? About wha'? I don't know you from one o' the little people, so I don't, an' . . ."

"Is yer name Mick O'Rourke?"

Mick looked flabbergasted, then nervous, for he and his mates had several little fiddles going at the docks and if this chap was a scuffer . . .

"I'm not the law, Mick. I've bin lookin' for yer for weeks."

"Oh, 'ave yer, an' why's that?" Mick managed to splutter.

"Come an' sit down an' I'll tell yer."

It was the first week in September and in the nursery at Riverside House four-month-old Ciara Rose Hayes, as she had been christened, thrived and grew plump, doted on by all the servants from Mrs Harvey, the housekeeper, right down to Alfie, the boot boy. She was the prettiest baby she had ever seen, Nanny Dee was fond of saying, though not when Miss Kitty was about. Miss Kitty took some beating where looks were concerned, with eyes like the bluest sapphire, and as transparent, surrounded by lashes so long and so thick it was a wonder she could see through them. Kitty Hayes was six years old now, growing tall, but with the sweet plumpness of the young child still about her. She was bright and self-assertive, shouting with all her father's arrogance and bluster to be the first, to be noticed, to be the leader, to be the most important girl in the nursery. She thought the new girl who had appeared so suddenly and so surprisingly to be "nowt a pound", an expression she had picked up from one of the servants. She was seriously put out that she and Freddy should have this intruder thrust upon them and said so frequently in the beginning. Then, as time passed and the baby did nothing to interfere with the possessive love she had for Freddy, indeed merely lay in her crib and watched the dancing shadows on the ceiling thrown by the nursery fire, Kitty forgot she was there. She and Freddy, who shared a birthday, did everything together, though her mother, whom she viewed with a certain antipathy, had put a stop to her sharing Freddy's bed.

Though they had Josh Hayes as a father, one naturally, the other by law, Kitty and Freddy could not have been more different in their nature and their looks. Where Kitty had a tumble of glossy curls that rioted abundantly over her skull and halfway down her back, and the bluest of blue eyes, Freddy's hair was a mixture of brown and gold, fine and silky and his eyes, big and framed by long brown lashes, were a pale velvety grey striped with darker lines. Kitty was rebellious, sometimes lovable, always exasperating, childishly defiant of any authority, good-humoured if not crossed, with a total lack of fear, which terrified all those who had her in their care. Where she decreed they should go, Freddy followed, trusting her with his life. They each had a pony, Punch and Judy, and, should the groom who accompanied them on the rides within their childish capabilities look away for a moment, the pair of them would be off, Kitty in the lead, of course, galloping across the water meadow at the back of the house towards the narrow bridge that crossed the river and the open fields beyond. A little madam, she was, the groom gasped, white-faced with terror when he caught up with them, Miss Kitty laughing and flushed, Master Freddy pale and big-eyed but defiant in support of his sister.

"We only wanted to see what was at the top of the hill, Charlie, that's all," the little madam told him huffily.

"What hill?" He had almost said "what *bloody* hill" he was so frightened.

"Kersall Hill. Father mentioned it and I—"

"Never mind that, miss. You could have broken your neck, or the pony's legs, gallopin' 'er like that. She's not meant fer jumpin' nor fer goin' like a bat outer 'ell."

"Judy can go anywhere, can't she, Freddy? And so can Punch and I shall tell my father . . ."

"If you don't, I certainly will, miss, if yer don't be'ave yersen. Poor Master Freddy looks right peaked."

"He's not peaked, are you, Freddy?"

Freddy shook his head, unable to speak.

"Anyway, what does peaked mean?"

"Never you mind. Now gi' me those reins an' we'll ride back proper like."

The episode was only one of many. Almost every day the pair of them, to Nanny Dee's despair, were up to something that Miss Kitty, with her fertile imagination, her fearlessness, her careless indifference to anyone's feelings but hers and Freddy's, dreamed up. They had a governess now, Miss Croston, who had been chosen by Nancy for her dedication to discipline as well as her qualifications as a teacher. Miss Croston had impressed Nancy with her no-nonsense approach to the training of young ladies and gentlemen and her honesty in expressing it. Should it lose her the position, Miss Croston would not hide her belief that children needed a stronger will than their own to guide them, perhaps not a trait many indulgent parents, especially of girls, might value, but exactly what was needed in the case of young Miss Kitty Hayes. Now Freddy, without Kitty to encourage him to mischief, would have lived his days placidly, equably, sweet-natured as his mother had been, wanting to please, content with the slow, dreaming days of his happy and protected childhood. Perhaps Miss Croston might be a little severe for his gentle nature, but by God she was needed to tame the hellion Nancy's own child could turn into at the first hint of restraint. Where did she get it, this streak of wildness that flamed her eyes to gleaming blue pools of molten lividity? Nancy often anguished. Her father had been hot-tempered and lawless, self-willed and strong-minded, and she herself had a strength and resolution that had carried her through many a crisis, but Kitty's wilful determination to have her own way and to take Freddy with her was quite frightening at times.

But still, they were only six years old. Babies really, and Miss Croston's firm hand on the tiller might be all that was needed to steer them into the calm waters of the well-behaved and treasured childhood Nancy envisaged, not only for Kitty and Freddy, but for her sister's child.

Ciara Rose! What a treasure she was, everybody said. An amiable baby, no trouble to anyone, Nanny Dee remarked fondly, with a black look in Miss Kitty's direction. She resembled Kitty, which was not unusual since they were cousins, Nanny said to Minnie, but in Ciara, even at four months, there was a brightness, a sweetness that was heartwarming, drawing the members of the household to her like pins to a magnet. There was always one or other of them hanging over her crib or her baby carriage for a sight of her delighted smile. She smiled at everything that moved, enchanted with them all, her small, pouting rosebud mouth stretching over her shining toothless gums, her small tongue quivering, her hands reaching to clutch at a strand of hair or a playful finger. She had an endless gift of enjoyment, sharing it with them all, the gardener Mr Longman as dear to her as Nanny Dee and Minnie. Her hair was a fluff of black curls on the top of her shapely skull, her cheeks were round and pink and her eyes a deep, almost purple blue and there was no doubt whose favourite she was at Riverside House. Certainly not Kitty's, who was only concerned with Freddy in any case.

And at Christmas, not only to the ecstatic delight of the father-to-be who, though he had said nothing to his beloved wife, had begun to give up hope, but to the prospective grandmother, there was to be a fourth child in the nursery. Emma could not have been more enraptured if the good Queen herself had sent messages of congratulations. At last, a legitimate child in the house. A baby whose father was Emma's son and a mother who was Emma's daughter-in-law. A baby conceived and to be born in holy wedlock and though she adored her grandson, Freddy, she had never been able to bring herself to boast about him to her friends who were also grandparents. To brag about his skill in reading even though he was only six, his graceful horseman's seat, the way he grew out of his clothes, his sweet nature, in fact all the things so dear to a grandmother's heart.

Her daughter, who, lately, had gone about looking like the cat who has swallowed the cream, was less enthusiastic. It was not that the children in the nursery ever crossed her path and if they did it was doubtful she would have recognised them, but she resented their very presence in her genteel life. *Three* illegitimate children, that's what they were even if her besotted brother had legally adopted them and given them his name. The last brat with the outlandish christian name was child to neither Josh nor his wife, the bastard daughter of Nancy's own sister, and – she had to admit it – that roughly attractive man she had met in Mr Bellchamber's office.

That had been a month ago, though he had been found in June, or so Mr Bellchamber had told her.

"He . . . well, to be honest, Miss Hayes, he was not fit to be in a lady's company when my man found him, and to be blunt I am astonished and dismayed, and not a little bewildered, as to why you should want him found. He is a common man, Miss Hayes, a labouring man and—"

"What he is, or is not, is no concern of yours, Mr Bellchamber. I have a particular interest in this man and—"

Mr Bellchamber interrupted her coldly.

"You would have had no interest in him when he was found, Miss Hayes, believe me. He was a lout, a guzzler of beer and gin when he could afford it. Yes, you might well wrinkle your nose in distaste, for the smell of him was enough."

"Mr Bellchamber, really. Is there any need to be so brutal?"

"You are dealing with a brute, Miss Hayes, and I must say I find myself somewhat alarmed for your safety. I beg you never to remain alone with him, if you value your . . . your . . ."

Mr Bellchamber evidently did not know how to phrase his fears for Miss Hayes's person, though he did admit to himself that it would be a brave man who took on this grim-faced woman. It had taken many weeks of hard and demanding work to bring Michael O'Rourke into anything resembling a male human being, the whole process paid for out of Miss Hayes's pocket. She wanted him presentable, she said, halfway fit for decent company, his drinking stopped, or at least cut down, his body, as best it could, returned to the health of a man in his mid-twenties, and today, after weeks of fighting with the man who had found him and in whose care he had been put, O'Rourke was at last deemed fit to meet Miss Hayes. He hadn't been told why, only that there was something in it for him.

Mr Bellchamber sighed. "Very well, Miss Hayes, though I do wish you would consider letting your brother—"

"No!"

"Well, don't say I didn't warn you. My chap will bring him in but don't be surprised to find him uncouth and he can be foul-mouthed."

"That is of no consequence, Mr Bellchamber."

Mr Bellchamber shook his head in mystification. Whatever this woman was up to boded ill for someone and he wondered, not for the first time, whether he should have insisted upon having a word with Josh Hayes. But there was the question of client confidentiality which could not be ignored.

The man who came into the room, cat-like, but not nervous, was tall, his dark head on which gleaming curls sprang almost brushing the top of the door frame. He was big, some of the weight on him still fat but a great deal more prepossessing than when Mr Bellchamber had last seen him. Since then he had been working out daily in the local boxing gymnasium and his muscles had become firmer under the smooth cut of his decent jacket. His face, though it would always be coarse, rough, had regained some of his old bright-eyed charm and when he smiled at her, his sensual mouth curling appealingly, his instincts guiding him to the one who could do him the most good, his teeth were white and even in his brown face.

"Aah, O'Rourke, there you are. Come in, man, come in."

For some reason Mr Bellchamber felt a quiver of discomfort ripple across his flesh. Was it something to do with the way Michael O'Rourke and Miss Hayes were studying one another or had the room become suddenly cold? Was he imagining the strange, atavistic gleam in O'Rourke's eyes, an unforgotten memory that reminded the man of how he had once had women falling on his neck, or at his feet, or into his arms? Could he believe his own eyes? Richard Bellchamber asked himself as he watched, quite mesmerised, the rush of colour that flooded Millicent Hayes's sallow face, or the hand she lifted as though to a gentleman, putting it into the enormous fist Michael O'Rourke held out to her. They might have been alone, so little notice did they take of him and into his heart trickled a slither of icy fear.

He cleared his throat hastily, blinking at the foolishness of his own thoughts, for the man was an uneducated Irish labourer and the woman a withered spinster from one of the wealthiest families in Manchester. A lady who would not condescend to wipe her well-bred feet on the man.

"Mr O'Rourke," he heard her say.

"Aye, ma'am, 'tis 'imself. An' who do I 'ave the 'onour of addressin' on this foine mornin'?" He grinned with all his old charm and again Mr Bellchamber was pole-axed by the expression on Miss Hayes's face.

"My name is Millicent Hayes, Mr O'Rourke."

Dear sweet Christ, would you look at the pair of them? A bog Irish prize fighter and a tight-buttocked, poker-backed, strait-laced virgin. He'd bet his life on the last, since he was certain she'd known the touch of no man.

"Miss Hayes." O'Rourke bowed his head impishly over Millicent Hayes's hand. Clever, thought Mr Bellchamber. Polite, not pushy, though any man could read what was in Millicent Hayes's eyes.

She was slightly breathless when he let go of her hand which she put to her throat as he looked enquiringly down at her.

She drew a deep breath, her hand still to her throat, her voice still breathless and Mr Bellchamber saw the ghost of a smile twitch at the corner of O'Rourke's mouth.

"I have a job for you, Mr O'Rourke, but . . ."

Abruptly she stood up, her silver grey eyes, which a moment ago had the texture of velvet, turning to the lawyer.

"We can't talk here, Mr O'Rourke," nodding in the direction of Mr Bellchamber. "I wonder if you would care to take me to lunch?" And though he hadn't a brass farthing in his pocket Michael O'Rourke professed himself delighted.

Mr Bellchamber was horrified. He had seated himself as O'Rourke came into the office and now he stood up again, putting out a hand as though physically to restrain his client but she gave him a look of frozen disdain before turning to beam at O'Rourke.

"Send me your bill, Mr Bellchamber, if you please," she said over her shoulder. "I have no further use for you."

They sailed from the room, the spinster and the Irish labourer, passing the open-mouthed clerks and the chap who had returned the Irishman to his – somewhat diminished – former self, with the casual aplomb of gentry ignoring peasants.

"Great God alive," Mr Bellchamber whispered. "What in hell's name have I done?"

For the first time in her life Millicent Hayes had fallen under the spell of a man. She had been bitterly disappointed in her brother's business friend, Philip Meadows, who, since the evening of the dinner party had been ardently pursuing Nancy's simpering, empty-headed hussy of a sister and to whom, if what Nancy hinted at, he was about to announce his engagement! But now, though she did not consciously think of it that way, she had a man of her own. He was not a suitable man, of course, not a gentleman, but as she revealed to him what she had planned for him, that did not matter, for when it was over, she assured herself, she would never see him again. It wasn't as though he were about to be introduced to her friends or family. She and Michael needed to meet, naturally, to discuss and plan what she had in mind and the best way to go about it, and they had done so frequently since she had met him in the lawyer's office. She found him charming!

In the beginning she found it disconcerting to oblige him with cash, quite a lot of cash, so that he might pay for their lunches, tip the waiter, hail cabs and even, since he had to put up somewhere, settle his hotel bills which were quite astounding. She had never stayed in a hotel so she was not competent to judge prices and values, but even so his bills seemed exorbitant. She paid, knowing it would be worth it in the end. It was necessary to her plans to have him in Manchester. He had chosen the hotel himself, the best in Manchester, the Albion, where Mr Meadows stayed when he was in the city on business and she admitted to herself it was very pleasant lunching there.

Michael O'Rourke, who had never had more than two farthings to rub together in his whole life, discovered the power and pleasure of money, lots of it, and liking it, was unwilling to give it up, even when Millicent Hayes told him what she required of him.

She only wanted him to kidnap his own bloody kids, the daft bitch! She would give him money to take them away, she told him, she didn't care where as long as they were out of her home. After all, they were as much his as anybody's, she added. He had a right to them, she proclaimed, since he was the father of both of them, a revelation that had sent her reeling when the ignorant slut who was Nancy's sister had revealed it to her. He hadn't even known about the second one, nor would he have cared if he had, though he didn't say as much to this soft-headed cow. She only wanted him to keep them both until they were old enough to fend for themselves, she pleaded beseechingly; find some woman to see to them until then. She didn't expect him to bring them up alone, of course, but she'd make it worth his while if he quietly removed them from Riverside House. Anything to get them out of her father's house where they did not belong. Children of trollops and hussies, the two of them and better they had been drowned at birth like unwanted kittens. Even her brother's son was unwelcome, though he at least had Hayes blood in his veins, as would the new brat when it arrived. But the other two were interlopers and must go and who better and more natural to take them than their own father?

Michael O'Rourke listened patiently, nodding with the gravity of a priest in the pulpit, his face composed into the lines of how he imagined a responsible father would look. Milly darlin', as he now called her, to her secret delight, had not the vaguest notion of what his life had been before he met her. The viciousness, brutality, depravity, sheer bloody hunger as money meant for food was spent on drink in his downward spiral into the world he knew before Mr Bellchamber's bully boy found him.

No, Michael O'Rourke had other plans. Plans of his own and they did not include the offspring of the Brody sisters, even if he had fathered them.

"Milly darlin'," he said tenderly, deliberately softening his Irish brogue as he took her hand and brought it to his wide, curving mouth. He pressed his lips to her knuckles, smiling to himself to see the colour flood beneath her skin and the shiver of delight that rippled her angular frame. They were lunching yet again at his hotel as she made her last-minute plans known to him, drinking the champagne he had ordered and Milly was ever so slightly tipsy, whether by his nearness or the sparkling, expensive glasses of golden, fizzing liquid he had encouraged her to drink.

"Ye look as bonny as a star in the heavens wi' that sparkle in yer eyes, so yer do," he murmured, his blue eyes narrowing in what even Millicent recognised as . . . as a lovely but wicked expression. No, not wicked, mischievous, for they were so beautiful, such a deep and brilliant blue, a blue she had seen in another face but could not for the life of her remember where. His eyes were smiling, the thick black lashes surrounding them almost meshing together, hypnotising her, so that the coarseness of his features, the lumpy, broken nose, the veins in his cheeks, the slight stubble on his chin, since he needed to shave twice a day, went unnoticed. His elbows were on the table, as were hers, their faces no more than twelve inches apart and more than one diner wondered at the incongruous sight of what seemed to be a pair of lovers, *mismatched* lovers, with their feelings so boldly, so improperly on view.

"Michael, please . . . there are people watching," she tittered, her heart thumping delightfully in her breast.

"To be sure I find I don't care, me darlin'."

"*Michael!*"

"No, sure an' it has ter be said, an' I'm after sayin' it, Milly. We've only known one another a wee while but . . . well . . ." He ducked his head in a pretence of shyness but actually to hide the expression in his eyes and to avoid the one in hers.

"'Aven't I come ter think the world o' ye. No, don't speak, mavourneen. Don't I know yer worth a dozen o' me but can I 'elp me feelin's, fer aren't I a man an' you a bonny woman."

"Michael, please, you must not . . ." Millicent Hayes was so flustered, so enchanted, so overwhelmed by this man's declaration of his feelings for her, which, in her ignorance of men, she saw as genuine, she completely lost the good, hard-headed sense she had been born with. She was not attractive to men, she had recognised that before she was twenty and had hoped for no more than a suitable marriage with a suitable man, not love, of course, but a solid relationship on which to build her life. Now, almost overnight, she was being swept along on a tide of something she had never before experienced. Her body seemed to be all of a tingle, from her neatly coiffed head to her sensibly shod feet, and there was the strangest feeling in the pit of her stomach which excited her. This man thought she was bonny and when she was with him she was! She felt womanly and now she felt desired and the feeling went to her spinning head so that when he stood up and held out his hand to her, she stood up with him and took it.

He led her out of the restaurant and across the foyer which was packed with guests coming and going and so they were not noticed. Still leading her by the hand, smiling inwardly at the pixilated look on her face, he took her up the wide staircase and along the luxuriously carpeted hallway to his room. Inside he locked the door behind them.

She began to take alarm then, for though she was, for the first time in her life, sexually awakened to a man she was not ready for this.

"Michael, I think we should go downstairs again," she trembled. "This is not right. Only married couples should be alone together in—"

"Sure an' won't that be remedied as soon as may be, me darlin'," revealing at last the preposterous plan he had formulated, "but while we're waitin' let's you an' me get a taste of it."

"Michael, you can't . . ."

"Now then, Milly, never did I tekk yer for a prick-teaser."

She had no idea what he meant as she began to back away, coming with a thump up against the wardrobe, doing her best to regain that superior, better-than-thou demeanour with which she treated those she considered beneath her, which this man was, despite her fascination with him.

"I don't know what that means, Michael, but this has gone far enough and I'd be obliged if you would unlock that door."

"Would yer now." He smiled and took off his jacket, throwing it on the bed, then before her horrifed gaze, since she had never before seen a man unclothed, he stripped himself naked and took hold of some dreadful thing that hung between his thighs and began to fondle it. She was not to know that it was the only way Mick O'Rourke could prepare himself to make love to a woman he didn't fancy.

"Now ye, me darlin'," he pronounced, his voice like silk, and when she refused he did it for her, fighting her over every garment, which *did* excite him until she cringed against the wardrobe door, doing her best to cover her nakedness with her two hands. On her face was a livid handprint where he had been forced to hit her.

"On the bed, me darlin'. Sure an' we might as well do the ting in style."

Ignoring her moans, he threw her on the bed, admiring her full breasts which took him by surprise, pried apart her legs with his knee and raped her with the same unconcern he had shown Nancy Brody.

30

"Whatever's the matter with Milly this morning?" Arthur asked his brother and sister-in-law as he strolled into the breakfast-room. "She's just run past me towards her room as though she were on fire and her face was as white as that tablecloth. Has she been here?"

Josh and Nancy looked up, surprised. Nancy was buttering toast and Josh had just passed her the marmalade, but they both stopped what they were doing to look enquiringly at each other.

"Yes, she was having breakfast but she did leave the table rather hurriedly," Josh answered.

"She ate her porridge and—"

"No, she didn't, ma'am," Ellen interrupted. "She left half of it," holding out the dish to prove it.

"Oh dear! Can she be sickening for something? I'd better go and see if . . ." Nancy pushed back her chair in readiness to rise but she was seven months pregnant, heavy and clumsy and before she could get to her feet Ellen was beside her.

"No, Mrs Josh, you stay there, lass, I'll go." They were all of them very fond of Mrs Josh and most solicitous of her condition. Josh, who had been about to stand up too, subsided, smiling.

"Thank you, Ellen," they said in unison.

It was Sunday, a day of rest and relaxation in the Hayes household, or as restful as a house can be with three healthy, lively children in it. It was nine thirty of a beautiful autumn morning and since it had rained persistently for the past fortnight, drowning the garden and the meadows at the rear of the house, the bright and sunny day was doubly welcome.

Though it held the servants back, this late rising, since they didn't know where they were with various members of the family drifting down to breakfast as they pleased, they were becoming accustomed to the less restrictive practices that the young Mrs Hayes had introduced since the master died. The old mistress always breakfasted in her room, usually around eight every day of the week. On weekdays, as Mr Josh and Mr Arthur were off to the mill or the warehouse by six thirty, breakfast was served at six o'clock. Once Mrs Josh had always joined them, saying that although her salon did not open until nine thirty there was always something to catch up on, and her carriage was waiting on the drive by seven. Now, with the joyous wonder of the coming child, due at Christmas, Mr Josh had prevailed upon her to stay in her bed until a decent hour since Miss Jennet was perfectly capable of seeing to anything that might need to be done in St Ann's Square, which was only sensible.

The servants were all made up with the expected happy event. A baby, another child on the way, and though they had plenty of those in the nursery already, this would be a special child, a legitimate child of the master and mistress. Not that Mr Josh would cut out Master Freddy, who was his son, after all, his birthright tied up legally by his adoption, but a properly born child of the house would be a blessing. The old mistress thought so, they could see that, for she'd been a different woman since the news was broken to her. She had not cast off her widow's weeds, of course, but she'd cast off the heavy burden of her melancholy, tripping round the house, the nursery, the gardens where she even pushed the baby carriage as though getting in practice, much to Nanny Dee's chagrin. She seemed fond of the little girls, though they weren't her own blood, and they made much of her, that Miss Ciara Rose holding out her little arms to be picked up, shouting a lusty welcome when she saw her. Aye, there was no doubt about it, Mrs Josh had brought a lot of love and laughter and happiness into this house, even if she was the most unconventional woman they'd ever known.

The sun lay in rich, golden shafts across the breakfast-room carpet. Ellen had opened the window a crack and the mindless, repetitive crooning of a wood pigeon carried on the mild air from the trees surrounding the house. The green of the foliage was turning now, to flame and scarlet and gold, its beauty a pain to the heart and yet a joy to the eye and the soul. The horse chestnut trees had been a glory in the spring and summer with their thickly clustered brilliant cascades of pinky white flowers, and still were in autumn, though now they were clothed in yellow and deep gold. Conkers were beginning to fall, collected by the children and threaded on a string as Alfie had shown them, since he was an expert at the energetic conker duels fought at this time of the year.

Mr Longman and his thirteen-year-old twin sons, Thomas and Joseph, could be seen raking the fallen leaves, a trial, since they were so wet with the recent rain, Mr Longman glancing up into the branches irritably as more fell on his head and shoulders. He couldn't keep up with the dratted things, he was heard to say and would Joseph stop larking about like a fool and fetch the wheelbarrow. Chrysanthemums of every colour, from coppery red, yellow, bright orange and white, stood tall on their stiff stems in the flowerbeds, nodding companionably beside lavender and white asters, all as neat and perfect as Mr Longman – who was a perfectionist himself – could make them. He knew old Mrs Hayes liked a few cut flowers from the garden and "mums" were splendid at this time of the year.

It all seemed so safe, so unchangeable, so secure, so immune to the dangers of the outside world, that when the cab drove in at the gate and up the drive to the house they none of them had any premonition of what was to come. Though the breakfast-room was at the side of the house the drive curved in a wide sweep from the gate, past the breakfast-room window and beyond to the front door where it was lost from view.

"Who the devil can be calling at this time of the day, and on a Sunday, too?" Josh exclaimed irritably. After Nancy and he had taken a careful turn round the garden in the mellow morning sunshine they had been looking forward to a visit to the nursery and, though Josh had not said as much to Nancy, or to anyone, to seeing the sweet, enchanting face of the child who was Nancy's niece. He loved his son, because he was his son, though sometimes it was disconcerting to see Evie Edward's pretty face looking back at him and to discover her gentle ways in the boy. He often thought that if it had not been for the volatile and darting restlessness of Nancy's daughter, his son would play as happily with Ciara Rose's dolls and teddy bears, with his games and books and the two placid dogs, Scrap and Button who crept up to the nursery each day to doze before the fire, instead of the wild "adventures" as Kitty called them, which often left the boy white-faced and sick with fright. Only yesterday they had eluded Miss Croston and finding a rotten piece of piling on the river's edge, the water of which was dangerously high, had been about to go "sailing". Had it not been for the quick thinking of Charlie and Jack who had, from the stable yard, seen the pair of them go past, and alone, they might have been drowned. He often wondered what they were to do with Nancy's daughter who, at six years old, and after a careful upbringing, was as wild as a young colt.

But the little one who was not only her cousin but her half-sister was an absolute joy, sunny-natured and affectionate, with no sign of the alarming tantrums with which Kitty rocked the nursery. She was beginning to crawl about the floor, her delight in her own mobility pasting a wide grin on her rosy face and exposing the two pearly teeth of which Nanny Dee, as though she herself were alone responsible, was so proud. She usually made a beeline for Freddy who greeted her as rapturously as she did him, after looking about furtively to make sure Kitty was not watching, which, he already knew, would cause a jealous fuss.

The sound of the door bell pealing rang through the house. After a moment there was a murmur of voices outside the breakfast-room door, which Ellen had closed behind her, then silence as the parlourmaid showed the caller into the drawing-room and went away, apparently to tell his mother, Josh thought, or . . . or . . . who the devil could it be? No one with any understanding of the social niceties which prevailed among their friends would dream of calling at this hour so . . . so was it an emergency, some crisis, but then surely the master of the house, himself in fact, would have been summoned?

He and Arthur exchanged glances, their eyebrows lifted, then turned to Nancy as though for enlightenment.

"Don't look at me, my darling. I haven't the faintest idea. Oh, unless it's Annie or Mary . . . perhaps Jennet has . . . but then Tilly would have fetched me and . . ." Her voice bcame anxious and she struggled to get to her feet.

"Exactly. Now stop where you are, sweetheart while I go and find out what the hell's going on. Tilly must have gone upstairs for Mother or Milly but I'll just take a look."

Arthur pushed back his chair and stood up. "I'll come with you."

Nancy got laboriously to her feet and began to follow.

They had reached the door and opened it, the two men almost colliding with one another in their sudden haste, as though the strangeness of the call had awakened a small shred of anxiety in both of them, when the sound of feet running down the stairs brought them both to a halt just beyond the door. It was Millicent, her face still like wax but in her eyes glittered what seemed to be excitement and even as they stared at her in surprise, a hectic spot of red sprang to each cheek.

"Oh, there you are, Josh. I was just going to send for you. There is someone I want you to meet." She put out a hand to the drawing-room door which was half open and an expression Josh could only describe as "arch", lightened her face.

"Oh, yes," he answered suspiciously. What in God's name was up with Milly? She had been acting a bit peculiar for weeks now, fidgeting about the place, going out a lot, he recalled, first almost bubbling over with some inner feeling of what seemed to be rejoicing and then quiet and cast down as though that lovely bubble she had inside her had burst.

"Yes, do come into the drawing-room. You too, Arthur, and of course," peeping triumphantly over Josh's shoulder, "we must not forget Nancy."

"Who is it, and what time does she call this, for God's sake?" Josh spluttered, some animal instinct warning him that Milly was up to something and whatever it was he was not going to like it.

"Oh, it's not a she, Josh." And her eyes glittered with a dreadful animosity, directed not at him but over his shoulder at his wife. Nancy stood like stone, her hands crossed protectively over her distended belly, for unlike her first child this one was loved and wanted. Like Josh she had no idea what Milly was so pleased about, nor who the man might be – it seemed he was a man – in the drawing-room, but she was mortally afraid. The hatred in Millicent's face raged almost out of control, swamping her brilliant eyes to the murky depths of an old, neglected pond and Nancy could feel her senses begin to reel at the impact of it. She put a faltering hand on Josh's back and at once he turned and drew her protectively – her and her child – into his safe arms.

"Do come in, all of you," Milly said, her voice high with hysterical excitement. "Oh, and Tilly," for the parlourmaid still hung about, goggle-eyed, at the foot of the stairs, "fetch the mistress, will you?" Her gaze passed contemptuously over her brother's wife, who would never be mistress in this house, not in her eyes at least.

"Yes, miss." Tilly sketched a curtsey and, turning, began to climb the stairs but the whiplash of Josh's voice stopped her on the third tread.

"Hold on, Tilly."

"Yes, sir?"

"Let us just find out what you're up to, Milly, before we drag Mother from her bed. I don't want her upset."

"Very well, you can go, Tilly. We will tell Mother later. Now then . . ."

With a dramatic flourish she flung open the door to reveal the burly figure of a man whose face at once split into a broad grin. He had evidently been having a look about him, for there was a dainty porcelain figure of a shepherdess in his hand and on his face an expression that said plainly that he was well satisfied with what he had seen. His free hand was in the pocket of his trousers and across his belly rested a gold watch chain which, with strangling horror, Josh recognised as his father's. He wore a bowler hat on the back of his head from under which a riot of black curls fell.

"Top o' the mornin' ter yer." He grinned, showing his good teeth, his only redeeming feature, for already the good living of the past weeks had put the gross weight back on him.

Nancy made a deep, inhuman sound in her throat and Josh felt her sway against him. Had he not had a firm hold of her she would have fallen.

"Oh, God . . . oh, Jesus God," she whispered, every vestige of colour draining from her face, even her lips, as she froze in a thunderclap of recognition. Josh felt his own face become cold as the blood left it, for he too was almost brought to his knees with the knowledge of who the man was. He had only seen him once before at the Arts Treasures Exhibition many years ago and he had been no more than a youth then, but his description exactly fitted with what Nancy had told him of the man who had violated her. And if this wasn't enough, the eyes of Kitty and Ciara Rose shone blue and glittering from his brutal face.

They stood in the open doorway, the three of them, Arthur with a comical expression of bewilderment on his face, Josh and Nancy clinging to one another as though they were buffeted by the waves of a stormy sea and Millicent Hayes smiled in jubilation.

"Aah, I see you remember Michael, Nancy," she gloated. "I thought you might since both his children, to whom I am about to introduce him, bear a strong resemblance to him. The same lovely blue eyes."

"Now then, darlin', don't yer be flatterin' me," Michael O'Rourke drawled, his eyes running nastily over Nancy's swollen figure.

"Oh, I don't think I could do that . . . sweetheart," Millicent answered, amazingly, and Arthur gasped, shocked to the core, while both Nancy and Josh appeared to be struck dumb and paralysed.

At last Josh found his voice though when it came from him it was no more than a croak.

"What . . . the devil's . . . going on?" he managed to say, still holding on fiercely to Nancy.

"I'll tell you what's going on, brother dear, shall I? This gentleman," with a smirk at the man beside her, "is Michael O'Rourke who I think your wife recognises, as he is the father of her child, and also of her niece, which is why I've brought him here. He has a right to see his daughters, wouldn't you say, having been kept from them all this time."

"Kept from them!"

"In a manner of speaking. Now, you can't deny they are his children and so I am taking him up to the nursery."

Nancy came suddenly to life. "Over my dead body," she shrieked, tearing herself from the support and protection of Josh's arms. Her teeth were chattering so vigorously she was forced to clench them together; nevertheless she still managed to demonstrate her virulent outrage. "This is the man who raped me on a grave in a cemetery making me pregnant. This is the man who dragged my young sister from one hell-hole to another before he killed her. He did this to me," pointing to her scarred cheek, "smashing his pugilist's fists into the face of a defenceless woman."

She didn't look defenceless now and Mick stepped back apprehensively as Josh caught her arm.

"His own mother disowned him and yet you have the bloody nerve to bring him here, you bitch. You planned this in your own twisted, jealous mind, didn't you? But, believe me, you have made a grave mistake." It appeared that the full blast of Nancy's fury was aimed not at Mick, but at Millicent Hayes. She swayed forward like a leopard on the attack, throwing off Josh's hand, her belly, in which the child twisted and rolled, swaying dangerously, her cheeks gone from white to blazing red fury.

"You foul hell-hag, I'll kill you for this. Bringing this . . . this monster to my home."

"*Your* home, madam. Since when has Riverside—" but Millicent got no further, as Nancy reached for her hair, dragged her forward and deftly butted her in the face as she had seen men do in her childhood.

"Michael . . . Josh," Millicent shrieked as blood flowered from her nose and it was only then that Josh regained his stunned senses, his mind clearing of the bestial images of this brutish, smiling intruder with his hands on the soft, white flesh of Josh's wife.

He strode forward and, though it was like trying to wrestle a tiger defending her cubs, managed to get a grip on Nancy's shoulders, dragging her backwards, tearing her hands from Millicent's hair, clumps of which came with them.

"Arthur, for Christ's sake, ring for Ellen. Nancy, hush . . . hush, darling. Now stop this and sit down. The child . . ."

Nancy jerked convulsively, her mouth working, tears of shock and fury streaming across her face.

"No, by God, I won't sit down. I won't rest until this beast and . . . and this woman have gone from my home and you can tell Ellen I have no need of her."

She never took her slitted, golden cat-like eyes from the couple who stood before her, her gaze slithering from one to the other, her shoulders twitching as Josh's hands did their best to soothe her. She would not be soothed. She panted and the front of her gown heaved with the child's movements.

There was silence for a moment or two, broken only by the sound of Milly sniffling and snuffling, then Josh, with a calmness he did not feel, let go of his wife, took his cigar case from his inside pocket, extracted a cigar, lit it, drew deeply on it, then blew its fragrant smoke into the air above his head.

"I wouldn't mind one o' them, Squire," Mick O'Rourke was unwise enough to say.

"You can go to hell and quick as you like," Josh snarled. "I don't know what the bloody hell you're doing in my house and I don't want to know but, the sooner you leave it the better it will be for you since I intend sending for the police."

"I ain't done nothin' wrong."

"I'm sure I can find something. For God's sake, Milly, stop blubbering and do something about that face."

"Joshua Hayes, are you going to stand by and let her get

away with it after what that guttersnipe you married has done to me?" Milly whimpered. At least that was what they thought she said, for she spoke as though she had a heavy cold. She held a blood-soaked scrap of lace and cambric to her nose but it was far too insubstantial to staunch the deluge.

"Here," Josh said wearily, passing his own clean and folded handkerchief to her. "If you won't go and have your face attended to, then use this."

Nancy stood like a statue, tall and dignified now, frozen in this horror that had come about. Her insides were twisting with hate and loathing and disgust and yet burning with a need to do something, whatever that something might be. She longed to go on shrieking as the women in Church Court shrieked without restraint when something got their dander up, but she must consider her baby, Josh's baby. She must stand back and let Josh and Arthur, and perhaps the men in the stable yard, see to Mick O'Rourke, though it was hard to remain calm.

"I don't know how you can be so calm, Joshua really I don't," Millicent began.

"Believe me, Millicent, it's not easy. There is nothing I want more than to take off my coat and give this . . . this piece of filth the thrashing of his life, but this is my home. My children are upstairs."

"*Your* children, Squire?" Mick sniggered.

"Yes, *my* children. My wife's children, not to mention my mother who, Millicent, as her daughter, I believe you might consider. She is frail after—"

"Well, I'm sorry for that."

Josh ignored her, staring with unblinking eyes into those of the man who stood with all the aplomb of an invited guest in the centre of his mother's drawing-room. Josh's face was expressionless save for whatever burned at the back of his ice grey eyes and the Irishman fell back another step, some of the impudent, confident boldness slipping from his face. He was not a timid man, but he was not sure he liked the eerie calm of the man who faced him. Still, he had every right to be here, as Milly was about to tell them, and the sooner it was done, the better. Earlier he'd noticed the decanter of whisky on the side table with several cut-crystal whisky glasses beside it. In fact, he'd just been about to help himself to a nip when they had come into the room. A bit of Dutch courage would not have gone amiss. A glass of whisky, or maybe two, and one of those fine cigars Milly's brother was smoking would be very welcome, then they could all sit down and get about their business.

He moved across the carpet, his bowler hat still on the back of his head. He placed the ornament, which he had forgotten he was holding, on the table and put his arm about Milly's waist.

Josh's mouth tightened and beside him Arthur swallowed painfully as though something broken had been forced down his throat. Nancy made a small, nauseated sound.

"Milly, for pity's sake," Arthur rasped. "Are you to let this . . . this bruiser put his hands on you? Dear God, what is happening here? Who is this man? Really, Josh, why don't I call a couple of the men to throw him out, or, better yet, let's you and I do it. The impertinence of—"

"Hush, Arthur, there's a good lad."

"Aye, Arthur, do as yer brother tells yer. Ter be sure me an' Milly 'ave a thing or two ter tell yer, ain't that right, darlin', so best let's get it over. An' that face o' yours needs seein' to, mavourneen. Shall yer tell one o' yer maids ter fetch water?" On his face was clearly written how very pleasant it must be to have the ordering about of servants, which he hoped to do very soon.

With sudden violence Josh threw his cigar into the fire, his smouldering rage, his distaste at seeing his sister handled so carelessly, and her acceptance of it, his overwhelming need to smash in the face of the man who was presumptuous enough to do it and his terrible need to get his wife upstairs and away from all this, giving him the appearance of a man tormented beyond endurance.

"Get out of my house, you bastard," he roared and his voice was heard in every corner of the house.

"Now then, Squire, 'ad yer not better be 'earin' what me an' Milly . . . ?"

"Yes, Josh, please be quiet. Michael has something to say and you will do him the courtesy of listening to it," Milly mumbled from behind her rapidly darkening handkerchief. "I need medical attention," throwing a malevolent look at Nancy, "so if you'd ring the bell, Arthur, and ask for one of the men to go for the doctor—"

"*Will . . . you . . . be . . . quiet!*" Josh yelled. "I've had about as much as I can take of this . . . this . . ."

"Ye'll 'ave ter know sometime, Josh, so ye will."

"How dare you use my name."

"What else would I be callin' me brother-in-law?"

Josh's face changed colour, the flame of violent temper turning to the ash grey of shock and beside him a whisper, "Sweet Jesus, oh sweet Jesus," from Arthur. Nancy carefully felt for the arm of the chair and when she had found it lowered herself in to it.

"Aye so, we're gettin' wed, me an' Milly, so we are, an' 'oo should be't first ter know but 'er family." He gave Milly's waist a squeeze and grinned down into her eyes which, even as he looked were turning the colour of ripe plums. He didn't think he'd ever seen a more unappetising sight in his life but it would be worth it all to live in a bloody big house like this one. He had no intention of moving to some small and poky villa, which Milly had babbled on about, and living on her allowance which, after what he had been used to, seemed phenomenal, but why make do with a jug of milk a day when you could have the whole sodding cow? It didn't matter to him that he'd be living side by side with Nancy Brody, or them bairns of his. The former rather titillated him, since she was a fine piece and as for the kids, they need not bother him. No, he thought, in the depths of the irrational, senseless, downright moronic bit of matter he called a brain, all he wanted was to live grand as these folk did, as Nancy did, and if she could do it, who came from the same street as he did, why not him?

Amazingly, Josh smiled and his stiff, defensive, tight-fisted posture relaxed.

"God's teeth, I've never heard anything so bloody preposterous in my life." He began to chuckle and then to laugh out loud. Mick O'Rourke didn't know what "preposterous" meant, nor did he care to be laughed at. His short Irish temper flared and his fists clenched.

"Now, Michael," Milly snuffled, putting a hand on his arm. "Joshua didn't mean it."

"Oh, but I did, Milly. It is quite ridiculous and you know it. Apart from his . . . connection with this family, you could not live with a bully boy like this. He comes from the dregs."

"Like your wife, you mean," Milly hissed.

Again a wave of maddened colour washed over Josh's face and Nancy struggled to get to her feet in her need to restrain him. "It's not the same thing at all," he spat out. "Nancy is educated. She has . . . *is* a lady."

"Rubbish, she's a shameless hussy who trapped you into—"

"Be careful what you say, Millicent, for you are to live in this house beside Nancy, who is its mistress."

"I don't think so, Josh. You heard Michael. He and I are to be married."

Josh whirled away, reaching for his wife's hand in a desperate attempt to control himself, breathing hard as though to hold in the explosion that was about to burst out of him.

"Bloody hell, Milly," he said over his shoulder, "will you come to your senses."

"No, we are to be married."

"That's right, darlin', ye tell 'im."

Josh turned back, composed again. From beyond the window came the sound of Mr Longman's deep voice mingling with the lighter tones of his sons as they trundled the wheelbarrow round the corner to the front lawn. With a part of his mind not seared by what was happening in this madness, Josh had time to wonder at the way the day moved on, time moved on and everything was just as it always was at Riverside House, except that it wasn't.

He sighed. "Let's just get something straight, shall we? I know I can do nothing to stop you marrying this oaf, since you are of age, but I beg you, Milly, to give it more thought. He is not of your class."

"Neither is your wife."

"Goddammit, leave Nancy out of this. She has adapted, is accepted in our circle, even if she was not born to it, but can you see this lowdown scum . . ."

"'Ere, 'oo are ye callin' scum."

". . . sitting down to dine with the likes of the Lamberts? Think, Milly. There is someone better waiting for you than this," waving a contemptuous hand in Mick O'Rourke's direction. "And then . . ."

"Listen 'ere, Squire, we're ter be wed, so we are, an' nothin' yer say'll stop us, ay, Milly?"

"No, that's right."

"Very well, as I said I can't stop you but let me just draw the contents of Father's will to your attention. He left you nothing, since he knew I would always take care of you. Give you a decent dowry when you married, that sort of thing. So, everything you have is in my hands. I can reduce your allowance. I can make it more generous. I can also stop it completely, so perhaps you and this man would care to discuss that before he drags you up the aisle to the altar. Can he support you, I wonder, or—"

"You bastard!" Both Millicent Hayes and Michael O'Rourke spoke the same words together. Mick's jaw had dropped and he looked ready to swing his fists at someone in his frustrated rage: Millicent, her brother, the goggle-eyed speechless youth at his side, Nancy Brody, or any of the priceless ornaments in the room, anything would do. Then his face cleared and a sneer lifted the corners of his loose mouth.

"Well, an' might yer not feel different, Squire, if we was ter tell yer there's a nipper on't way. Aye, I thought that might mekk yer sit up an' tekk notice. Shurrup, Milly, we 'ad ter tell 'im an' now's as good a time as any!"

31

The house was quiet, the servants tiptoeing about the place as though any loud noise might awaken another explosion of violence; but in the drawing-room, though no one spoke, the silence was loud.

Nancy sat in her chair, straight-backed, head high, eyes bright as a golden-eyed eagle, wishing her heart would stop thundering against the squirming, obviously distressed child in her womb. She knew this was not good for her, or the baby, so she must, *must* keep calm, though all she could think of was leaping from her chair and smashing the smiling faces of Millicent Hayes and Mick O'Rourke to pulp. She would revel in it. She would like to dabble her fingers in their blood like some ancient warrior of old but, God, let her be calm . . . please, dear Lord, if You are there, let me be calm.

Josh and Arthur stood side by side, their backs to the closed door, Arthur keeping his shoulder pressed against Josh's to let him know that if this ruffian made a move neither of them liked his brother could count on him. They had both heard what the man had said, of course, unbelievable as it was, and one glance at Milly's shamefaced look of guilt and embarrassment was enough to confirm it, but even so, surely it could not be possible? Not Milly, his battle-axe of a sister who, from childhood, had been able to cowe him with a glance. Not Milly, who, it seemed to him, had been sewn into her corsets each morning and probably wore two pairs of drawers to keep her precious chastity safe. How could it have happened? The man was a plug-ugly bruiser, a low fellow of the common classes, the sort Milly had professed to despise, who could not speak the Queen's English with any degree of correctness. He was inarticulate, crude, and not even very clean for God's sake, and it was evident that he had not shaved this morning. He still had his arm about Milly and Arthur could feel his gorge rise, for though he had little love for his sister, she *was* his sister, a lady, and the way she nestled up to the man was disgusting. She looked like some ruffian's moll herself with her hair all over the place, her gown every which way, a bloody handkerchief clutched to her face and what was not hidden beneath it was bruised and swollen.

"Well, I think it's about time we sat down and talked this over," Milly said at last, smiling up at the Irishman, then moving to sit down on the sofa at the side of the fire.

"Good idea, darlin'," the man agreed, flushed and triumphant, since he had just dealt his trump card and had a winning hand. He moved to sit beside her on the honey-coloured velvet sofa but Josh's icy voice brought him to an abrupt stop.

"Sit down on my mother's sofa and I'll knock you to the floor." His voice was dangerous. "I'll not have you contaminate it, d'you hear. There is nothing to discuss. I presume you are speaking the truth since my sister is not denying it but how in hell's name she allowed herself to be . . . handled by someone like you is beyond me." His voice was filled with disgust

"Is that right, boyo? Well, let me tell yer she did, an' enjoyed it, didn't yer, darlin'. I've a way wi't ladies, so I 'ave. Ask yer wife if yer don't believe me."

Josh hissed in the back of his throat. His eyes became suffused with the red of his rage, the blood of it leaking into the white. At once Nancy was out of her chair as though the burden she carried was featherlight. With a defensive movement, like a mother protecting her child, she placed herself before him, her arms outstretched.

"No, Josh. No, I say."

"Don't you foul my wife's name with your filthy tongue," he bellowed over her shoulder, longing to brush her aside to get to O'Rourke but some instinct of protectiveness, not only for Nancy but for his child, prevented him, as she had known it would. All over the house those who were still wondering what the master was shouting about in the first place, cringed and looked fearfully at one another

"Oh, what is going on, Ellen?" Emma asked tearfully. "What on earth can Josh be so cross about?" She clutched Ellen's arm, lifting a trembling hand to her mouth, her eyes round with terror.

"I couldn't say, Mrs Hayes, but there's nothing for you to be concerned about. Mr Arthur is with Mr Josh and if there's any trouble, which there won't be," she added hastily as Emma moaned pitifully, "the men are handy."

"But who has called and what is all the shouting about?"

"Now then, ma'am, I'm sure it's nothing. Probably some problem at the mill."

"Yes, I suppose so," Emma said doubtfully. "I think I'll just go and have a word with Mrs Josh," who could always be relied upon to comfort Emma's fears. But Ellen, knowing the young mistress's whereabouts, which must not be divulged to this one, shook her head.

"I believe she's sleeping, madam," she lied.

"Sleeping! At this time of day?"

"Well, ladies in her condition and so far along easily get tired, ma'am," Ellen added soothingly.

"Of course." Emma relaxed. "I was just the same."

Ellen noticed and was not surprised by it that her mistress did not ask for her own daughter.

Downstairs it was clear that Mick O'Rourke was longing to defy this bastard, this gentleman, this member of the loathed upper classes who had kept Mick ground down all his life, which was how he saw it. For two pins he'd knock him into the middle of next week, *and* his snot-nosed brother an' all. The trouble was he was not quite so nifty on his feet as once he had been, nor so handy with his fists, and besides which it would not do to get on the wrong side of the man who held the purse strings, would it, the man who was to be his brother-in-law.

He smiled ingratiatingly and remained standing, though he kept his hand in a proprietorial way on Milly's shoulder.

"Look, Squire, you an'—"

"If you call me that again I'll hit you."

"Oh, yeah, I'd like ter see yer try, so I would."

"Come outside then and when I have done so I shall throw you into the street."

"Josh, for goodness' sake," Milly cut in. "There's no need for this. There is absolutely nothing to be done about the . . . circumstances." She looked down, dabbing at a spot of blood on her skirt, then lifted her head in what seemed to be pride. "I am with child."

"I heard him, God help us."

"There is no need for this language. Michael is the father of my child."

"How many more does he mean to foist on this family?" Again Nancy made a small distressed sound in the back of her throat, then, urged by Josh's gentle hand, resumed her seat, though it was evident by the way her eyes never left his face that she was ready for any sudden outburst on his part. Hers was over. His, it appeared, was still to come.

"Believe me, this is . . . different. We love each other. The child must have a father and I must have a husband. There is nothing more to be said."

From the lawn beyond the partially open French windows where Mr Longman and his sons still vigorously brushed up leaves, some small altercation over the wheelbarrow arose, then died down. No one in the room noticed.

Josh studied this sister of his who, up until an hour ago, he thought he knew well. Fastidious to the point of obsession, stubborn, self-willed, self-absorbed, a woman who did her best to dominate and now it seemed it was she who was being dominated, mesmerised in some way by this appalling man and it seemed to be purely physical. She was blind to what he was, or so it seemed; how in hell's name had it come about? Where had she found him? Who had led her to him and what game, for God's sake, did she think she was playing? The man was dangerous. He no more wanted to get to know his daughters than he wished to make friends with a couple of pretty kittens. Somehow he had – he could hardly bring himself to contemplate it – he had persuaded Milly to . . . to drop her drawers, the picture sickening him and . . . God in heaven, the images were . . .

He pulled himself together, shutting out the dreadful pictures of Milly and this man.

"You believe there is nothing more to be said, Milly, but there is. You may marry this man since, as you tell us, you need a father for your child and a husband to support you. You shall have it. There he is, take him. Pack your bags and go with him. I never want to see him in my home again."

"Very well." Millicent sprang to her feet and reached for Mick's arm. "So be it. I will let you have my address when we are settled so that my allowance can be—"

"What allowance is that, Milly?" Josh's voice was as hard and cold and solid as packed snow.

"Oh, come now, Josh, you would not turn me out without a penny."

"No, Millicent, while you remain unmarried to this lout you shall have a home here, you and your child, but I will not support him, nor entertain him in my house a moment longer than necessary."

"Now then, me lad, we'll be 'avin' none o' this. Begorra, this is yer sister," Mick blustered.

"Who carries your child which you must support. I won't see her or her child starve but you can rot in hell for all I care. In fact, it is my hope that you do."

"Well, bugger me. What a way ter speak ter the man 'oo's ter be a member o't family."

"Not this family. Now I swear to God if you're not off my property in five minutes, you *and* my sister if she wishes it, I'll have you thrown off and if you come back I'll see you in the New Bailey."

"Josh . . . please, Josh," Milly began to wail, blood and snot dripping down her chin. "Let me keep my allowance. How shall we manage?" For even she knew her lover's limitations.

"That is no longer my concern."

"Not even for the child?"

"Only if you remain at Riverside with your family."

Millicent's face hardened, her moment of weakness over. Her eyes narrowed to slits of pure loathing. She gripped Michael O'Rourke's arm with the obvious intention of leading him from the room, and from the soft life he had envisaged for himself.

"Come, Michael," she said, her head high, her expression contemptuous.

"Just 'old on a minute." He plucked her hand from his sleeve. "Let's ge' this straight."

"By all means," Josh said frostily. "Which part don't you understand?"

"Are yer sayin' there's nowt? Not fer 'er or't bairn."

"You seem to have the general idea."

"Even if I wed 'er she's ter get nowt?"

"Especially if you wed her she gets . . . nowt!"

Mick O'Rourke lowered his head and swung it from side to side as though he were a bull tormented by a swarm of midges. He shook it so vigorously his bowler hat fell off and rolled away beneath a table. He shuddered violently, then with a huge sigh of what seemed to be a resigned "well, what the hell," went to retrieve it.

"Right then, darlin'," he proclaimed to Milly, "I'm off. Back to bloody Liverpool an' when I look at sight o' yer I'm buggered if I'm not beginnin' ter believe I'm well out of it, so I am." He planted his hat squarely on the back of his head and grinned. "Well, it were worth a try, Squire, even if I 'ad ter tekk on this dried owd stick. A bag o' bones she were to be sure, except for them titties which I enjoyed, though not a patch on't Brody girls. Now there were juicy tits, so they were, especially yours, mavourneen," turning to smirk at Nancy and this time she was too late.

With a howl of rage Josh hurtled across the room, knocking the Irishman to the floor, going with him and taking several small tables as well. He was not a brawler but his fists were loaded with his blood-red male hatred of the man who had known Nancy before he had. It did not matter that it was without her consent, he wanted to kill him, wipe out the pictures so that it would be as if it had never happened

"Josh!" Nancy screamed, dragging Arthur with her in a desperate attempt to separate the two men, but they were like snarling dogs fighting over the same bitch, oblivious to everything but their need to kill each other, teeth snapping, eyes glaring and up in her room Emma cowered in Ellen's arms.

"Josh! God in heaven, Josh," Arthur was shouting, not quite knowing which part of his brother to get hold of.

"Michael . . . don't hurt him please . . . please, Josh," Millicent shrieked. It was not clear who she meant, her brother or her lover.

The door burst open and into the mêlée tumbled Charlie and Jack, summoned by the good sense of Mrs Harvey, and in a moment the two men were dragged apart. Both had blood streaming across their faces from wounds which were not yet discernible and with a foul gesture Mick O'Rourke spat a bloody tooth on to the carpet.

"Sir . . . ?" Charlie asked his master enquiringly, ready to give the visitor another going-over if required, but Josh, his madness dissipating, turned away and reached for Nancy.

"It's all right, darling," she murmured, her arms going about him.

"Jesus, I wanted to kill him. Just get him out of my sight, Charlie."

"Don't be after worryin', I'm off," Mick mumbled. "Keep the owd cow an' 'er money an' may the lot o'yez rot in 'ell."

"Michael?" Milly stammered, not awfully sure she'd heard aright. "Michael, where are you going? I don't understand. Liverpool? What are we to do there?"

"Not *we*, mavourneen. *Me*. Yer don't think I want an owd maid like yerself, do yer, not ter mention a bloody kid 'angin' on ter me coat tails."

"*Michael!*" Millicent's wail of terror was heartbreaking and Josh felt pity for her surge through him. For a moment he was tempted to relent, but then the thought of what this man had done to her, had done to them all, stopped him. What sort of a life would she have with him, even if she had her allowance? He'd rob her of it and probably leave her anyway. Dear God, what trouble the bastard had brought on this family.

"Show him the door, Charlie, but before he goes I'll have my father's watch and chain."

" 'Ere, that's mine," Mick blustered.

"Take it off him, Charlie."

"Pleasure, sir." And only Jack – and Mick – saw the slight nod Charlie gave the other groom.

With a quick turn, reminiscent of his days in the ring, Mick twisted from Charlie's grasp, pushing past Millicent, almost knocking her from her feet as he made for the open French window. In his fear and confusion he whirled, not to the front of the house and safety, but towards the back.

"Michael!" Milly's penetrating shriek raised the hairs on the forearms and neck of everyone, not only in the room, but in the house.

Mr Longman and his lads stood rooted to the sodden grass where their boots squelched and sucked in the mire, their mouths open in amazement as the man whose face was covered in blood erupted through the French windows, closely followed by Miss Millicent whose own face was a sight to see. Instinctively, as though knowing their place even now, the two grooms had stood aside to let her pass them.

Mr Longman and his boys stared in amazement. Had there been a fight? Surely not! Surely not between the man and the stern, old-maidish daughter of the house. Before the three of them could disentangle their thoughts Miss Millicent was followed by Charlie and Jack.

"Michael!" Miss Millicent was screaming, there was no other

word for it, making Mr Longman's hair stand on end. "Wait for me, Michael, please. I'm coming with you." But the man ran on as though the devil himself was at his heels, disappearing round the back of the house.

"Eeh . . ." said Mr Longman and without another word began to follow in the direction the man, Miss Millicent and the two grooms had taken. White-faced with excitement, Thomas and Joseph were hot on their father's heels.

"In the name of God, get after her, Arthur," Josh rasped through his swollen throat and split lips. "Go on, lad, run like hell. I'm right behind you. God knows what she's likely to do. Hell and damnation," turning to Nancy who was lumbering after him. "You can't come, sweetheart, have a bit of sense."

"Go to hell, Josh Hayes, just try and stop me. I hope they catch him and I hope they kill him and I want to be there to see it."

"Nancy, please. The baby . . ."

"The baby's fine. Now let go of my arm."

The maidservants, alerted by the shouts and the general commotion, crowded, eyes out on stalks, at the back kitchen door, their faces as white as their aprons as the visitor, whoever he was, followed by Miss Millicent, the stable lads, Mr Longman, his sons, Mr Arthur, Mr Josh and, a long way behind and losing ground steadily, Mrs Josh, streamed like a pack of hounds across the stable yard, down the side of the vegetable garden and along the fences of the paddock where the horses whinnied and began to race about in alarm.

With a jump as sprightly as a hare, the man cleared the back wall, landing in the squelching grass of what was aptly named the water meadow. His boots, as he landed, sank up to his ankles in the thick, undrained mud and oozing grass of the field, and were dragged from his feet with a plopping sound. Discarding them with a panic-stricken look over his shoulder at the two burly grooms who were thirty yards behind him, he ran on in his stockinged feet, the saturated ground, which held two weeks' rain, slowing him down. He knew he had not misinterpreted the look the two men had exchanged in the house and the greater the distance he put between himself and them the better. The heavy going was slowing them down as well.

"Michael. Stop, Michael, wait for me, please. We can manage, you and me. I love you. Don't leave me, please, Michael," Millicent sobbed behind the grooms who had overtaken her, her breath gasping in her throat. The grooms exchanged amazed glances but blundered on. Catching up with them were Mr Josh and Mr Arthur who seemed to be more concerned with Miss Millicent then the fleeing man, and who could blame them.

"Milly . . . please, Milly, come on home," Mr Josh was yelling, his face a mask of drying blood. The two boys, wild with excitement, for not much ever came their way to break up their tedious days, and being young and fleet of foot, overtook their master and even the grooms, flying over the ground in pursuit of the bloody-faced stranger, they didn't know why. They only knew it was much more fun than raking leaves.

The water meadow was no more than two hundred yards wide and then there was the river!

When he reached it Mick O'Rourke turned, like a fox cornered by the hounds, a fearful look of terror on his face, which was a vivid scarlet with his exertions but scraped raw to reveal white patches in his mortal fear. His eyes strained from their sockets and his breath sobbed in his throat. The two boys, big boys but unsure what to do now they had reached him, hung back and, clutching at his chance Mick darted to the right, his eyes flashing along the backs of the splendid houses that stood adjacent to Riverside House across the meadow through which he had just run. If he could reach one, get over a fence or a wall he might escape through a handy garden to the road at the front where there were bound to be passers-by, carriages, cabs, the safety of the avenue that led to busy Bury New Road. But as though they sensed his plan the two grinning grooms separated, one to the left, one to the right, effectively blocking his escape, ready to beat him to a pulp to get at the old man's watch which Milly had given him. He could hear her shrieking his name as she fell across the waterlogged field, dragging herself up again and again and behind her were her brothers. He didn't know why, really, he was running. He had panicked, that was all. He hadn't stolen the bloody watch. He hadn't broken the law in any way, though that sod of a brother of hers would probably trump up some charge against him. But, surely, with their master plainly in view the grooms wouldn't touch him, would they? He was giving up all claim to the bugger's sister and to the bastard she carried so he could see no reason to run any more. He'd just retrieve his boots and be on his way, he'd say to Milly's brother and there was nothing they could do to stop him.

He grinned brazenly. They had all come to a halt in a semicircle about him, except for Nancy Brody who was still floundering across the wet grass and mud of the meadow. The men and the two boys watched him warily and some old chap – where the hell had he come from? – bent down and put his hands on his knees in an effort to get his breath back.

Josh and Arthur, now that they had caught up, were beginning to wonder why the hell they were chasing him, apart from their father's watch. Of course, they weren't chasing him really. It was Milly they were concerned about. He could take himself off for all they cared and the watch with him, never to be seen again, they hoped, though what was to become of Milly, who was weeping with the heartbroken intensity of a whipped child, was another matter.

Mick was standing on the extreme edge of the fast-flowing river. It was at least two feet higher than normal, its waters lapping at the slippery grasses and when Milly, with a final shriek of despair, launched herself against him, desperately seeking his arms, since she still could not believe what was happening, she caught him off balance.

"Mind what yer doin', yer soft bitch," he snarled, the last words he was ever to speak. They both went, seemingly in one another's arms though in actual fact he was doing his best to disentangle hers from about his neck. As they entered the river a high arc of spray shot up into the air and a wash of littered water erupted up the bank, lapping at the feet of the horrified watchers. They all leaped back instinctively and when they looked again at the place where Michael O'Rourke and Millicent Hayes had fallen there was nothing there but a widening circle of ripples and a frothy foam of bubbles. The swollen water surged past them with the force of a mill race. The banks were awash with litter, debris carried along and deposited here and there in rotting heaps, brought down for miles during the past fortnight of rain.

"Jesus wept," Charlie muttered, his face quite ghastly in the golden glow of the morning sunshine.

"Holy Mother of God." Jack, who was a Catholic, crossed himself and was about to turn away, for what could anybody do in the headlong torrent that swept along beside them, when a movement to his right caught his eye. It was his master whipping off his jacket and preparing to jump into the swollen waters.

"No, sir . . . no," he shrieked, leaping in an effort to get a good grip on Mr Josh to prevent him going in. "Charlie, for God's sake, gi' me a hand."

Mrs Josh, still only halfway across the field, was screaming her bloody head off while old Longman and his sons, white-faced but no longer excited, stared in silent horror at the spot where Miss Milly and the bloody-faced chap had hit the water.

"Let me go, you fools," Josh was yelling as he struggled with the grooms.

"No, sir, it's no use . . . they've gone."

"That's my sister in there."

"Aye, sir, we know, but yer can't go in after 'er, sir. See, 'ere's Mrs Josh. Oh, ma'am, please don't let 'im go in; e'll drown."

Josh sank to his knees in the mud, his face desolate and contorted with agony, tears mingling with the blood and Nancy, clumsy in her pregnancy, sank down before him. She put her arms about his heaving shoulders and drew his head down, watching as the men, Charlie and Jack, Mr Longman and his wide-eyed, silent sons, ran up and down the bank staring into the swiftly moving waters for a sight of Miss Milly and the stranger.

They were all so fixed on their purpose none of them saw Arthur, who had stood petrified to stone by the horror of it, suddenly come to life. With a cry of, "There she is, I see her," pointing excitedly to a rotting plank of wood, "I'll get her," he flung himself into the turbulence and, like the other two, vanished from sight.

Other men were running from the direction of the house, Billy the stable lad, Summers the coachman, even young Alfie who had been peacefully polishing Mr Arthur's best boots, and it took all of them to hold on to the master who was screaming blue murder and to the mistress who clung to him like a terrier to a rat.

For an hour they ran and cried out Miss Milly's and Mr Arthur's name – not the other chap's for they did not know it – before Mrs Josh, her face ashen, gently turned her husband, who had slipped into a merciful state of shock, and began to lead him, stumbling, towards home.

Alfie, who was only a little lad, wept in Mrs Cameron's comforting arms, broken-hearted by the knowledge that Mr Arthur would no longer be needing the boots Alfie had been polishing.

* * *

Milly's body was never recovered, though Mick O'Rourke and Arthur were found several days later some miles downriver, lodged companionably together against a small tree-trunk which had caught on the bank. The police inspector, since a family of such high standing in the community and who had suffered such a terrible loss commanded a high rank, promised to keep searching for . . . for Miss Hayes, he told their grieving brother, who held on to his wife's hand as though he were afraid of drowning himself. He was not to know that Joshua Hayes blamed himself for the accident, which in itself was a bit of a mystery. The man, one Michael O'Rourke, was said to be a friend of the family, though what they were all doing larking about beside the swollen river, especially with Mrs Hayes in her condition, was never revealed. The servants were as unforthcoming as the family, blank-eyed, uncommunicative as clams and as stricken with grief as the family they served.

The man had no one, Mrs Hayes told him quietly, the only one still to have her senses about her, it seemed, except his elderly mother and if the inspector didn't mind, she herself would go and see her and break the sad news. She lived . . . close by. It was somewhat irregular but the inspector, unable to stand against Mrs Hayes's pale-faced sorrowing beauty, agreed.

The Brody girls! Had there ever been three children like them, those who were there that afternoon asked one another as they observed the eldest of them descend from her spendid carriage at the end of Church Court and move slowly up the street with a burly chap in attendance. Three children who had grown into three bonny, clever women and all achieved by the resolute strength and bloody-minded determination of this one who was, amazingly, hugging filthy old Eileen O'Rourke as though she were her own mother. Her mother who had been Kitty Brody, God bless her, who must have had something in her that she'd passed on to this one.

They shook their heads in wonderment as they watched intently, somehow uplifted as they had always been by the colour, the entertainment, the lift to their own drab lives the Brody girls had always afforded them. Nancy was all in black and ready to drop a bairn any day by the look of her and what she said to Eileen inside Eileen's crumbling parlour was a mystery to them and they could hardly wait to get over there to find out.

They sighed, the women of Angel Meadow, every eye following her as Nancy Brody, which was how they would always think of her, heaved herself up the street on the arm of the big chap in a uniform to where the carriage waited at the end.